02/19

Praise for Susan Mallery

"Susan Mallery never disappoints and with *Daughters of the Bride* she is at her storytelling best."
—Debbie Macomber, #1 *New York Times* bestselling author

"Heartfelt, funny, and utterly charming all the way through!"
—Susan Elizabeth Phillips, *New York Times* bestselling author, on *Daughters of the Bride*

"An emotional and humorous look at the bonds between the women in an endearingly flawed family."
—*Kirkus Reviews* on *Sisters Like Us*

"Mallery is the master of blending emotionally believable characters in realistic situations. Her engaging and comically touching Mischief Bay series continues to satisfy lovers of women's fiction."
—*Library Journal* on *A Million Little Things*

"Bestselling romance author Mallery presents a heartwarming stand-alone novel about a family brought together under unusual circumstances.... A compelling contemporary fairy tale that culminates in a satisfyingly happy ending. Readers will snap up this escapist summer read."
—*Booklist* on *When We Found Home*

"The characters will have you crying, laughing, and falling in love.... Another brilliantly well-written story."
—*San Francisco Book Review* on *The Friends We Keep*, 5 stars

"It's not just a tale of how true friendship can lift you up, but also how change is an integral part of life.... Fans of Jodi Picoult, Debbie Macomber, and Elin Hilderbrand will assuredly fall for *The Girls of Mischief Bay*."
—*Bookreporter*

"Mallery blends the friend-and-family relationships and self-actualization focus common to women's fiction with the racy love scenes and happy ending of a contemporary romance, making this an excellent summer read for fans of both genres."
—*Booklist* on *Secrets of the Tulip Sisters*

California Girls

SUSAN MALLERY

mira

mira

Recycling programs
for this product may
not exist in your area.

ISBN-13: 978-0-7783-6896-0

California Girls

Copyright © 2019 by Susan Mallery, Inc.

For questions and comments about the quality of this book, please contact us at
CustomerService@Harlequin.com.

BookClubbish.com

Printed in U.S.A.

Also by Susan Mallery

When We Found Home
Secrets of the Tulip Sisters
Daughters of the Bride

Happily Inc

Not Quite Over You
Why Not Tonight
Second Chance Girl
You Say It First

Mischief Bay

Sisters Like Us
A Million Little Things
The Friends We Keep
The Girls of Mischief Bay

Fool's Gold

Best of My Love
Marry Me at Christmas
Thrill Me
Kiss Me
Hold Me
Until We Touch
Before We Kiss
When We Met
Christmas on 4th Street
Three Little Words
Two of a Kind
Just One Kiss
A Fool's Gold Christmas
All Summer Long
Summer Nights
Summer Days
Only His
Only Yours
Only Mine
Finding Perfect
Almost Perfect
Chasing Perfect

For a complete list of titles available from Susan Mallery,
please visit SusanMallery.com.

California Girls

Chapter One

"They're frying bacon!"

Finola Corrado tried not to smile at the panic in her assistant's eyes. "The cooking segment is potato salad five ways. Bacon is the cost of doing business."

Rochelle's horror morphed into indignation. "Yes, and right before that is the 'What's New in Sundresses' segment. I'm very familiar with the schedule." She set down her tablet, put her hands on her narrow hips and leaned forward, as if stressing the importance of her point. Her long, dark braids moved with her. "Finola, we have *models* in the building. Tall, skinny, *hungry* models. They're starting to look feral and turn on each other. I'm convinced it's the smell of bacon. Can't they cook it somewhere else?"

And people assumed television was glamorous, Finola thought, still trying not to laugh.

"Move the models to the backup greenroom and tell them

we have a humidity problem on set so they need to use extra hair spray. They won't be able to smell the bacon after that. Tell the food prep person to clean up when the bacon is finished so there won't be any more odor."

"Oh, that will work." Rochelle, a smart, ambitious communications graduate, relaxed. "I should have thought of that myself."

"You will soon enough."

Her dark-haired, dark-eyed twenty-five-year-old assistant would soon be capable of running the show, Finola thought as Rochelle left. In a few months, Rochelle would move on, taking a job that would give her more responsibility, and Finola would hire a new assistant, to begin the process again.

Getting your foot in the door in the TV business wasn't easy. There were plenty of crap jobs, but not all of them gave the right kind of experience. Finola prided herself on hiring the best and the brightest. She was very clear with her demands—she expected a killer work ethic, absolute loyalty and 100 percent of their focus. In return, she would teach them about the business, introduce them to the right people and throw them a big party when they moved on to greener pastures.

Finola's dressing room door opened again. One of the production assistants stuck her head in and whispered, "She's here! *She's here*. I can't believe it. I'm so excited. Aren't you excited?"

Before Finola could answer, the assistant was gone, no doubt to spread the joy to others.

Finola wanted to be cynical, but even she had to admit she was looking forward to meeting Treasure. *AM SoCal* was a successful show in a crowded media market. Being based in Los Angeles meant more access to celebrities than most shows like theirs, but even they didn't expect to land a massive country-pop star like Treasure.

At twenty-three, Treasure was a music phenom. Her last single had a million downloads in the first six hours after release and her YouTube videos all had over a billion views. She was appearing on the show this morning for a ten-minute interview followed by a live performance of her new single "That Way." The hungry models' fashion show and the potato salad segments would follow.

Except for Treasure being such a big star, today's rundown was pretty typical. Finola greeted her audience—both live and on television—with a bit of chitchat and a few jokes, then she invited her first guest onto the set. By eleven, the show was over and by noon, everyone on staff would be focused on doing it all again for the next show. Everyone but her, she thought with a smile. She was off next week.

"Hawaii, here we come," she murmured to herself.

She and her husband needed the time away. They'd both been so busy lately, caught up in their respective careers. The week would give them time to focus on each other and their marriage. And maybe something just a little bit more.

She was ready, finally ready, to get pregnant. Nigel had been eager for them to start their family for a couple of years now. She'd been the one dragging her feet. But turning thirty-four, listening to her mother complain about having three grown daughters and no grandchild, not to mention the realization that there would never be a perfect time, had convinced her they should go for it now. In honor of the decision, she'd packed a present for Nigel to open when they checked into their suite in Maui. She had a feeling the gift of sex toys and baby booties would get the message across very clearly. Nigel was nothing if not a man of action—they were going to have fun.

She heard a knock on her door, followed by a loud, "Thirty minutes."

Thirty minutes until showtime, she thought, settling into her makeup chair and closing her eyes.

She was already dressed and made-up, she knew her topics, had listened to enough of Treasure's music to qualify for fan club membership, and she'd skipped carbs at breakfast so she could taste-test potato salad to her heart's content.

"Good show," she whispered to herself as she slowed her breathing for her preshow relaxation ritual.

She had fifteen minutes of quiet. Fifteen minutes when no one would knock on her door or burst into her room. She would collect herself and then head to the set where she would be miked and given a final dusting of powder before starting her show.

She inhaled to the count of four, held her breath for a count of eight, then exhaled—

She heard her door open, followed by, "Finola, we have to talk."

Her eyes popped open. Nigel was standing in front of her. He grabbed her chair by the arms and stared at her intently.

"Nigel, what are you doing here? I go live in less than thirty minutes. What's going on?"

Nigel, a Beverly Hills plastic surgeon, didn't see patients on Fridays and they were leaving on their trip in the morning. What was so important that it couldn't wait until after the show?

He looked at her. "I'm sorry."

It wasn't the words that got her attention so much as the tone, and maybe the stricken expression on his face. Her stomach clenched.

"What happened?"

Visions of her sisters or her mother lying prone on the road filled her mind. Or maybe there had been a fire. Or a—

"I don't know how to say it," he began, only to stop.

Bile rose in her throat. Her heartbeat jumped a thousandfold and there was a ringing in her ears. Someone was dead—she knew it.

"I'm having an affair."

As he spoke, Nigel released the chair and paced the length of the room. He was still talking—she could see his lips moving—

but for the life of her she couldn't hear anything. The roaring, rushing sound was too great.

The words repeated over and over in her head until their meaning sunk in. Years ago, she'd fallen off a tall porch onto the grass below. She'd landed on her side and all the air had been forced out of her lungs. This felt like that. She couldn't inhale, couldn't stop the surge of panic that swept through her as her body began to tremble. The lack of breath was followed by a sharp gut-wrenching pain in her heart.

How could he? When? With who? Why? They were *married*. They loved each other. He was her best friend. She was going to get pregnant on their trip to Hawaii.

No, there had to be a mistake. He couldn't have. Only as she watched him watch her, she knew he wasn't lying and that he really had, with four simple words, shattered her and their marriage.

"You have to understand," he said, his voice low. "I'm sorry to have to tell you now. I know the timing is less than optimal."

"Less than optimal?" she shrieked, then had to consciously lower her voice. "*Less than optimal?* I'm about to go on live television. It's not enough to dump this on me, but you had to do it right this second, to screw with me even more?"

"I've tried to tell you so many times over the past few weeks, but you're too busy to listen. There's always another show."

She felt a flicker of rage and reached for it with both hands. At least anger would provide temporary strength.

"You're blaming this on me?" she demanded. "You waltz in here and announce you're having an affair and it's *my* fault you waited until just this second to tell me?"

"It's not like that."

"Oh, really?" She brushed away tears. "What's it like?"

He turned away. "I thought you needed to know."

Before she could figure out if she was shaking too hard to stand, he walked out. Just like that. She was alone with the nausea, the aches, the broken life and a ticking clock that warned her she had eighteen minutes and twelve seconds until she was live.

None of this is real, she told herself frantically. It couldn't be. It wasn't happening and Nigel hadn't just told her about an affair. He couldn't have. Not her Nigel. Not the wonderful, warm, loving husband who was always there for her. She knew *him,* not the cold stranger who had just left.

If only her ears would stop ringing, she thought desperately. If only she could breathe or cry or scream or run. An affair. Another woman had been in his life, his heart and his bed. *Their* bed. No. No! He'd slept with someone else, had whispered to someone else, had touched someone else, had orgasmed with someone else.

Her mind refused to believe even as her heart began to bleed. Betrayal and sadness and disbelief churned together until she choked. She had to get out of here. She had to go home and—

Her gaze settled on the clock. No, she told herself. She couldn't leave. She had a live show in fifteen minutes. She had to go on the air and act as if nothing was wrong, as if she were fine and the world hadn't just fallen off its axis and into a black hole from which it would never escape.

She sucked in air, being careful not to hyperventilate, then hurried to the mirror. After flipping on the harsh, unforgiving lights, she studied herself for a second before reaching for a tissue, then concealer. She looked wide-eyed and shell-shocked. As if she'd just seen something horrific. Or maybe just experienced it. Dear God, she couldn't do this.

"Finola?" Rochelle knocked once before entering. "They need you on set."

Finola nodded without speaking. She added a little more powder, then took one more breath before forcing a smile. "I'm ready."

Her assistant frowned. "What happened?"

"Nothing. I'm fine."

"It's something and it's not fine."

Finola faked another smile and hurried past her. "I have no idea what you're talking about."

She made her way along the corridor toward the studio. She wove her way around false walls, backdrops and cables. The show's producer smiled at her.

"Have you met Treasure yet? She's gorgeous. I only saw her from a distance, but wow."

Finola didn't bother to say she had yet to meet the star. She'd been too busy watching her marriage collapse around her. Not that Treasure had asked for an intro—her request had been that they meet in front of the live audience so the experience "was more spontaneous." As far as superstar demands went, it was easy and doable, and it beat one singer's request for "six snow-white kittens to play with before I sing."

Gary, the sound guy, handed her a small microphone. She clipped it on her jacket's lapel while he snaked the thin cord over her shoulder. He clipped the battery pack to the waistband of her skirt.

Usually she joked about him touching her. Their friendly banter was a regular part of her "get ready" ritual. But today she couldn't think of a single thing to say. And in eight minutes, that was going to be a big problem.

Breathe, she told herself. She would breathe and trust herself to know what she was doing. She'd done this show for nearly four years. She was good at it. She loved her work and she would be fine. If only she didn't hear the echo of the screams she didn't dare give in to.

Gary smoothed her jacket into place, winked at her and smiled. "You're good to go, Finola."

"Thank you." She cleared her throat. "Testing, testing."

The mike would have already been checked, but she always confirmed it was working.

Gary gave her a thumbs-up before handing over the earpiece

that would connect her with the control room. Theirs wasn't a news show, so she wasn't getting breaking information, but she still needed to be linked to the control room in case a major story broke. Then she would be able to smoothly transition her viewers to the fact that New York was going to interrupt the show.

She adjusted the earpiece then heard the soft voice of Melody, the director. "Finola, good morning. We're at five minutes. Good show."

"Good show," she said automatically. She turned off her microphone to give herself one moment to be truly alone just as someone touched her on the shoulder.

She turned and came face-to-face with Treasure. The country-pop star was about Finola's height, with long, dark red hair worn in cascading ringlets. Her eyes were deep green and even with heavy TV makeup, her skin was amazing.

Finola blinked in surprise.

"Hello. I thought you didn't want to meet before the interview." She managed a smile and held out a hand. "It's lovely to meet you, Treasure. I'm a big fan."

The twenty-three-year-old smiled at her. "No, you're not," she said softly. "Or if you are now, you won't be."

She ignored Finola's outstretched hand. "You're older than I thought. Thirty-four, right? You couldn't be my mom, but you wouldn't be an older sister, either. Maybe an aunt."

Finola had no idea what she was talking about. "Okay," she said slowly. "I need to go out and greet the audience. Everyone is so excited to see you and watch you perform."

Before she could turn away, Treasure grabbed her upper arm. Her fingers dug in just enough to be uncomfortable.

"It's me," she whispered, leaning close. "I'm the one he's sleeping with. I'm the one who's done things with him you can't even imagine. It's not just the sex, you know. It's all of it." She rolled her eyes. "He didn't want to tell you about us, like he could hide me, but I had my manager book me on your show so he didn't have a choice."

Treasure's smile turned cruel. "And now you know."

Finola could only stare at her, even as her mind rejected the words. *This isn't happening,* she thought desperately. *It can't be.* Nothing the other woman was telling her could be true. Before she could react in any way, Treasure released her and walked away. Finola pressed a hand to her stomach, hoping to slow the bleeding just enough to not die that very moment.

She had to run, she told herself. She had to get out of here. She had to—

"Finola?"

Melody's voice competed with the very loud buzzing in her head.

"Finola, you need to get on set now."

The show. She had to do the show. It was live, so there was no second chance. She had to walk out there and face the two hundred people in the audience, not to mention the million or so in their homes. *AM SoCal* was hugely popular. She was well liked in the community and today they had on a massive star. Ratings would be huge.

"Finola?"

"I'm here."

She drew in a breath and dug as deep as she could for every ounce of professionalism, not to mention self-preservation, she'd managed to accumulate in her life. She had to survive sixty minutes. Just sixty minutes and then she would be able to collapse. Just the next hour. That was all.

She walked out to face her audience. They immediately burst into applause. She waved and smiled at them, focusing only on the people in the first few rows. Near the center aisle were what looked like three generations—grandmother, daughter and granddaughter, all clapping happily. There were a few of her regulars—those who always came to tapings, but the rest of the audience was filled with teenagers.

The Treasure fans, she thought grimly. How was she going to survive? She glanced at the teleprompter and breathed a sigh of relief. Thank God.

Good morning, everyone, and welcome to the show. We have something very special in store for you today, although based on the demographics of my audience, word has already spread—Pause for laughter.

She stepped into place and waited for the countdown to live. Normally she would have chatted with the audience a little, but not only wasn't there time, she couldn't have done it. Not today.

"Five, four, three." She watched the fingers indicate the silent "Two, one," then thought of puppies and kittens playing and how drunk she was going to get later. When the red light on the camera illuminated, she was fairly confident her smile was something close to genuine.

"Good morning, everyone, and welcome to the show."

Finola worked the introduction. She never fully felt like herself, but the shock and pain faded just enough that she could inhale. She consciously relaxed her body and focused on what she had to get through.

"Here she is, and I'll confess I'm a little starstruck myself. Treasure!"

Finola turned to where the singer would enter. Treasure sauntered across the set, her familiar coltish walk and easy smile bringing the audience to their feet. There were plenty of screams and whistles. Treasure waved at everyone, then looked at Finola. For a second something dark and evil seemed to turn her face into a sinister mask, but then it was gone, leaving Finola to wonder if she was imagining things or if, in fact, the superstar was about to discuss her affair on television.

They sat angled toward each other. Finola was grateful her overly efficient team had loaded questions into the teleprompter. She didn't have to think, she reminded herself. She simply had to look engaged and ask the prewritten questions.

"Your new album is doing incredibly well," she began. "Congratulations."

"Thanks. I'm really happy with the way my fans are responding. Especially to the first single." She flashed the audience a smile. "'That Way.'"

"It's a provocative song."

Treasure leaned toward her and lowered her voice. "It's about sex."

The audience laughed.

Finola couldn't tell if she was blushing or if she'd gone totally white. She was light-headed and hoped she wasn't swaying in her seat. The potential for disaster was massive and if Treasure said anything...

Treasure sighed. "You know, there are men who just get how to please a woman. The way they touch you and kiss you—it's magic."

There was more laughter. Finola did her best to join in.

"You've always played with unexpected topics in your songs. This album continues that tradition."

"I know." Treasure winked. "I'm not a sweet person. I'm not mean, but when I want to talk about something, or have something, I make it happen. So what was your favorite sexual experience, Finola?"

The question hit her like a slap. Finola managed to hang on to her composure enough to chuckle and say, "Treasure, I'm old enough to be your aunt. No one wants to hear about that from me. You're going on tour in a couple of months. What does it take to get ready for a show as big as yours?"

"I need to be rested and happy. You know what that's like. To be with the right person. It's such a good place to be."

Tell us about the man in your life.

Finola stared at the teleprompter and knew God had moved on to helping someone else. She couldn't do it, she thought grimly. She couldn't keep talking, couldn't keep it together. She was going to fall apart on live television and then the whole world would know everything. She would be a laughingstock, she would be pitied, she would go viral in the worst way possible and at the end of the day, her husband would still have cheated on her with Treasure.

"All this talk about your album makes me want to hear you sing," she said, not caring she was two minutes early for the transition.

"Finola?"

Melody's voice was questioning in her ear, but Finola only motioned to the other side of the set where they'd set up a microphone in front of a screen. Treasure's music video would play behind the singer.

"Okay," Melody murmured. "We'll go early."

The spotlight came on and the music cued.

Treasure hesitated just long enough for Finola's stomach to cramp. *Go,* she thought desperately. *Just go sing your damn song and get out of here.*

Treasure stood and walked toward the microphone. Finola knew she had four minutes for the song, then two minutes more for the commercial break. Six minutes to figure out how on earth she was going to get through the rest of the show.

She waited until Treasure started to sing before standing up and quietly slipping off the set. Rochelle met her in the corridor.

"Are you all right?" her assistant asked, looking worried.

Finola pressed both hands to her cheeks, trying to physically hold herself together.

"I think I have food poisoning," she lied. "My stomach is

writhing." It was the only explanation she could think of and had the added benefit of explaining why she was off.

"Is that what's going on?" Melody asked in her ear. "I wondered. Honey, I'm so sorry. Can we get you anything?"

"Just some cold water," she said. "I'll hang on through the show and then I'll be fine."

Another lie. The bigger of the two but at this point, honestly, who cared?

Rochelle looked sympathetic. "I'll go get it right now. And some ginger ale. I think we have it in one of the vending machines. Let me check. I hope you feel better soon. You and Nigel are flying to Hawaii tomorrow. You wouldn't want to miss your flight."

Finola lowered her hands to her sides without saying anything. Fortunately Rochelle didn't seem to expect her to answer. Instead she hurried off to get ice water and ginger ale. Not that either would help, Finola thought, doing her best not to give in to tears. Nothing could help. Nigel had cheated and destroyed their marriage and possibly their lives.

She pressed her hands against her stomach as acid churned and she fought against the need to vomit. While that would make the food poisoning fib more believable, she would prefer to avoid it as long as possible. She had—she glanced at the countdown clock—forty-three minutes left. Just forty-three minutes. Then she would be alone and have the time to figure out when, exactly, she'd lost everything.

Chapter Two

Oh good, *you're still here*, were not words Zennie Schmitt wanted to hear eight minutes before the end of her shift. She'd been on her feet for ten hours already. The relatively light day had included two angioplasties that had gone surprisingly well, considering the age and physical condition of the patients. She'd been on her way to the locker room to grab her things when she'd heard herself being paged over the intercom.

Dr. Chen had expressed his relief that she was still in the hospital. "I have an emergency bypass surgery. Are you up for it?"

Zennie understood the question. She'd already put in a full day. She was tired and if she didn't think she had the stamina to assist Dr. Chen through a coronary artery bypass operation, then she was expected to tell him. She was more than a perioperative nurse—aka scrub nurse—she was part of an elite nursing team that worked in one of the country's most prestigious and busy cardiac care hospitals. They saw some of the sickest patients in the world and when someone was on their table, it was often a life-or-death situation. Giving less than 1000 percent wasn't permissible.

Zennie took a second to close her eyes and breathe. Yes, she was tired, but not exhausted. With luck they would only have to replace one artery, but odds were more were involved, stretching a three-to-four-hour surgery into something much longer. Still, she and Dr. Chen worked well together and she enjoyed being a team player.

"I'll swing by the café, then be right there," she said.

"Excellent."

Dr. Chen hung up without saying anything like *Hey, that's great* or the somewhat expected but rarely heard *thank you*. He was a gifted, brilliant surgeon who practically worked magic, reviving hearts others thought past saving, but when it came to his people skills…not so much with the glibness. As Zennie hurried to the café, she wondered if they'd ever had a single conversation that wasn't about a patient.

She bypassed the coffee and went straight to the espresso machine. She knew exactly how long a double shot would take to ramp up her alertness. She would crash toward the end of surgery, but by then adrenaline would be pumping, so she would be fine. Tomorrow she would be extra nurturing with her diet to make up for the abuse her body would take in the night.

Eight hours and forty minutes, not to mention one double bypass later, Zennie finally made it to her car. She was beyond tired and she ached all over. The bright lights of the parking garage were at odds with the quiet and darkness beyond. It was well after midnight, and the good news was she wouldn't have to worry about traffic on the drive home. In fact the normally twenty-five-minute trip took all of twelve minutes. She stumbled into her bedroom just after one.

She stripped off her scrubs, then washed her face and brushed her teeth. Before sinking into the welcome softness of her bed, she grabbed her phone and checked for messages.

She had a reminder for her 5:00 a.m. running date. No way that was happening, she thought with a yawn. Not that anyone would be surprised. She was always a firm *maybe* on Fridays, but a for-sure yes on the weekend, barring her being on call. She also had a ten-thirty appointment with her baby sister, Ali, to get fitted for her bridesmaid dress.

Zennie did her best not to groan as she thought about the upcoming nuptials. Not that she didn't love her sister, but weddings were a pain and to be honest, Zennie wasn't a huge Glen fan. He just didn't seem to ever look at Ali with undisguised love and affection. Nigel, her sister Finola's husband, was totally different. When he looked at his wife, you could feel the heat.

Speaking of heat… Zennie shoved her heating pad under her back. Her muscles were tight from hours spent in surgery.

There was a text from her dad showing his sailboat anchored in a gorgeous Caribbean bay. Wish you were here.

She smiled. Wish I was there, too. Miss you, Dad.

She knew she wouldn't hear from him for a few hours. Between the time difference and her father and stepmother living on "island time," texts could take a while to be answered. Still, the thought of a couple of weeks on a sailboat somewhere like the picture was nice.

Her last text was from her mother. Zennie held in a laugh at her mom's offer to set her up on a blind date with "a handsome young man that you will absolutely adore," before ending the text with, I'm not getting any younger and I expect grandchildren before I die.

Zennie was still chuckling when she fell asleep.

Morning came early, despite the lack of an alarm. Zennie showered, drank a protein-packed smoothie, then did about a half hour of stretching before heading off to meet Ali.

The bridal shop in Sherman Oaks was by appointment only and very elegant. Zennie thought maybe wearing yoga pants and a T-shirt had been a mistake, then told herself it didn't matter. She would be undressing anyway.

Ali was already there, practically dancing with excitement as Zennie entered the store.

"Hi. The dresses are here and they're so beautiful. You're going to look great. Probably better than me. Finola will, for sure. It's hard having beautiful sisters."

Zennie hugged her. "You're going to be the bride. The bride is always the prettiest one."

Ali rolled her eyes, even as she grinned. "Yeah, yeah, we'll see. I tried on my dress last week. It's good I didn't get the smaller size. I seem to be the only bride in history who didn't bother sticking to her diet."

Zennie didn't know what to say to that. When Ali had first gotten engaged, she'd come to Zennie and asked for a diet and exercise program. Zennie had done her best, but Ali had never been one for either. She'd carried an extra twenty pounds since puberty and claimed spending a day working in a warehouse was enough exercise for anyone. Zennie had tried to point out that being on her feet wasn't the same as *exercise*, but Ali would never be a believer. Still, she had a wholesome, girl-next-door kind of beauty, with brown hair and brown eyes. She was the shortest of the sisters, and the curviest. Finola was the tall blonde beauty who kept herself TV-thin by eating sparingly and avoiding carbs. Zennie had tried to convince her of the importance of variety in her diet, but Finola had refused to listen.

"Ready to see your dress?" Ali asked. "Finola had her fitting with me last week."

"I'm excited," Zennie lied, then chided herself for not being more with the program. The wedding was a big deal—she should be happy and a willing participant.

It was just the whole getting married thing, she thought as

Ali led the way into the dressing room. No, she amended. It was more than that. It was the two-by-two expectation. She'd grown up with the assumption that when she was an adult, she would pair up, just like the animals on Noah's Ark. Falling in love followed by marriage followed by family. Only it hadn't happened and to be perfectly honest, she wasn't sure she wanted it to.

"Ta-da," Ali sang as she pushed open the dressing room door.

A long navy dress hung from an ornate hook on the wall. The dress had cap sleeves and a sweetheart neckline, and was fitted to the waist before gently falling to the floor. Finola's dress was the same color but a different style. Ali had been determined to find styles they both liked, which was a lovely quality in a bride-to-be. One of Zennie's friends had gone full-on bridezilla, dressing her crew in hideous frilly, lime green concoctions.

Ali had requested they wear navy and had otherwise left the decision up to them.

"It's beautiful," Zennie murmured, thinking it was perfectly fine and actually nice for a bridesmaid dress.

"Did you bring your shoes?" Ali asked.

Zennie patted her tote bag. "Right here."

She was sure Finola would have picked a designer something with a four-inch heel. Zennie had gone with a simple ballet flat. No way she was wearing heels, even for her sister.

She toed out of her slip-on athletic shoes, then pulled off her yoga pants and T-shirt. She hadn't bothered with a bra, so didn't have to worry about straps showing. After unzipping the dress, she stepped into it and pulled it up. Ali moved behind her and took care of the zipper, then Zennie slipped on her shoes. They both stared at her reflection.

"Perfect," Ali breathed. "Come on. Let's look at you in the big mirror. The dress fits great. I doubt there'll be many alterations."

The sales associate met them in the main room. Zennie found herself stepping up onto a platform in front of a huge mirror that was more than a little intimidating. As she stared at herself she thought maybe she should have put on a little mascara or fluffed her hair or something.

Instead she looked as she always did. Fresh-faced, with short, spiky hair and not a lick of makeup. She pushed the guilt away, telling herself she put in the effort when she was on a date and wasn't that enough?

"Are you happy with the look?" the saleswoman asked Ali, as if Zennie's opinion didn't matter. "Is this what you imagined?"

"Sadly, yes." Ali laughed. "See, I told you both my sisters were fabulous. No one is even going to notice me."

"Nonsense. You'll be the bride." The woman climbed onto the platform and started pulling pins from the pincushion strapped around her wrist. "I'll do a little tucking to give you an idea of the look, then we'll get our seamstress out here to do the final pinning."

The two women discussed everything from lowering the neckline—Zennie said no to that—to the length of the dress.

"Are you sure you don't want to wear some kind of heel?" the salesperson asked.

"Very."

Ali sighed. "Zennie won't budge on that. Good thing her boyfriend isn't that much taller than her or they would look weird together."

Zennie looked at her sister in the mirror. "Boyfriend?"

"Duh. Clark."

Zennie stared blankly.

"*Clark*. You've been seeing him awhile now. He works with the zoo. He's a primate specialist or whatever it's called."

"Primatologist, and he's not my boyfriend. We've only gone out three times." She barely knew him and had no idea if she liked him or not. Boyfriend? As if. She hadn't even told her mother about Clark, which explained the evening text offering to set her up on yet another blind date.

"You said you were bringing him to the wedding."

"No. I said I *might* bring him to the wedding."

"Zennie! I planned on you and a plus-one. You have to bring a date."

Why? That was the question, Zennie thought as Ali was distracted by whether or not to shorten her sleeves. Why did she have to bring a date? Was she less socially acceptable without a date? Was her conversation less sparkly, her love less welcome? She had no idea why she'd even mentioned Clark, let alone discussed him as her plus-one at the wedding. She wouldn't want him there, regardless of the state of their nonrelationship. For one thing, people would ask too many questions. For another, her mother would go totally insane at the possibility of Zennie finally settling down with someone and giving her grandbabies. No one could survive that much pressure.

The pinning and tucking finished, Zennie stared at the dress. She would never admit it to her sister, but to her everything looked exactly the same. Of course she had the pins poking her to prove it wasn't.

"Can you finish up here without me?" Ali asked, glancing at her watch. "I have to stop by the florist before I need to race back to work for a meeting."

"I'm fine. I will stand here until they release me." Once again she thought about how Nigel looked at Finola and how Glen didn't look at Ali. "Shouldn't your hubby-to-be handle some of this?"

"I would never trust Glen with the flowers. He's a red roses kind of guy and that would be all wrong." Ali stepped up on the dais and kissed her cheek. "Thanks for doing this. Love you."

"Love you, too."

Ali raced to the door, then looked back. "Bring a date!"

"Bite me."

Ali was still laughing when she ducked out of the store.

Zennie looked at her reflection and tried not to think about the wedding. It was four, maybe five hours out of her life. Yes, they would be torturous hours, but they were for a good cause. In the name of sisterhood and all that.

As for a date, well, that might be a problem. Because Clark was a nonstarter for sure.

Finola gripped the steering wheel so hard, her fingers ached, but she didn't dare relax. Not until she was home. She drove slowly, careful to stay under the speed limit as she turned into her exclusive Encino neighborhood. As she approached the gate in front of their small community, she felt her control beginning to slip.

Almost there, she chanted silently. *Almost there, almost there, almost there.*

She made two rights, then a left before pulling into the driveway and pushing the button to open the garage door. As she eased forward, her hands slipped and the car veered a little to the right. She jammed on the brakes and started to back up, only to realize that she didn't have to. Who cared if she wasn't fully in her own section of the garage? It wasn't as if Nigel was going to be pulling in next to her anytime soon. Of that she was sure.

She turned off the engine and collected her tote bag and purse. Once she closed the garage door, she walked into the house.

She was greeted by silence. She and Nigel had never wanted a housekeeper. There was a cleaning service that came twice a week and a meal delivery service, but both had been put on hold because of the upcoming Hawaii trip. As of two hours ago, the plan had been for her to meet Nigel at home after the show so she could finish packing. They would leave for the airport first thing in the morning. Only none of that was going to happen now. Not the packing, not the trip, not them being together and making a baby.

She dropped her handbag and tote to the floor, then kicked out of her shoes. She needed a plan, she told herself. She had to figure out what to do first, then second, then third. Only with each step she took, the blessed shock faded, leaving behind pain and disbelief and humiliation. The tears came first, then the sobs. She stumbled before sinking to her knees where she covered her face with her hands as she screamed out the agony.

Finola cried until her chest hurt and her throat was raw. She cried until there was nothing left but emptiness and the knowledge she would never be whole again. She stretched out on the cold, hard tile and wished she could be anywhere but here. Anywhere that wasn't—

"No," she said aloud as she sat up and wiped her face. "Not anywhere." Not on television, she thought. Being here, alone and confused and sad and angry was better than staring at that stupid camera, waiting for everyone watching to figure out what was going on.

Nigel had done that to her, she thought as she scrambled to her feet. The bastard had come to *her* dressing room to tell her about his affair.

No, it was so much worse. He'd told her about the affair, aware his mistress was going to confront her seconds later. That was why he'd chosen today, right before the show. That was why he'd needed her to know. He'd softened her up, knowing Treasure was going to try to take her down. He'd cheated on her and then he'd thrown her to Treasure.

He could have told her who it was. He could have warned her, given her a second to catch her breath, but he left her to be blindsided. He hadn't just cheated, he hadn't had her back. He'd exposed her. There'd been no thought of her job or her career or what would happen on live television. What if she'd fallen apart? What if Treasure had said something to the audience?

Possibilities paraded in front of her like a nightmare. Thank God she was strong, she thought grimly. Strong enough to survive Nigel.

She fished her phone out of her purse. No text from her husband. Hardly a surprise, she thought, tears flowing again. What did she think, that he would apologize and beg to come back to her? Even she wasn't that much of a fool.

She walked barefoot through the quiet house before going upstairs. The master bedroom was large with French doors leading to a balcony. She ignored the beautiful space that she had, until this moment, loved. She ignored the big bed, the linens she and Nigel had picked out together. She fought the feeling of being exposed, she fought the pain and sense of betrayal. She had to keep breathing, keep moving. She had to figure out what on earth she was going to do now. Wait? Did she just wait to hear from him? Was he gone forever? Was this just a fling? How long had he been sleeping with Treasure? Were there other women? How long had he been lying, emotionally setting her on fire, while laughing with his mistress?

The tears returned. She ignored them and walked into Nigel's part of the his-and-hers closet. Entire sections of his closet were missing. Shirts and suits, jeans, T-shirts. She reached up, as if the clothes weren't really missing, they were just invisible to her.

Her fingers grasped nothing. There was only the space where her husband's clothes had once been. She closed her eyes and sank onto the small bench in his closet. Just last night they'd gone to dinner, she thought desperately. Just last night they'd been talking about Hawaii. They'd been at their favorite little bistro on Ventura Boulevard, at their favorite corner table. They'd talked about their previous trips and he'd made her laugh, as he always did. He'd made her feel loved and special, because that was who he was. Or who he had been.

She'd nearly told him her plan. She'd nearly mentioned that she'd gone off her birth control and was ready—no, eager—to start a family with him. But she'd waited because she'd wanted to surprise him.

It had all been a lie. Every gesture, every word, the way he'd held her. They hadn't made love, but he'd held her and told her he loved her. All the while he'd known what he was going to do to her today. He'd planned it.

She wrapped her arms around her midsection and rocked on

the small bench. She cried out, the keening sound echoing off the empty spaces. Why had he done it? Why had he hurt her? Why had he—

Her phone rang. The sound startled her, then she jumped to her feet, searching for the phone. She spotted it on a shelf and lunged for it, knowing it had to be Nigel. He'd realized his mistake and he was sorry.

"Hello?"

"You were off your game this morning. Are you all right?"

The familiar voice should have comforted her, but didn't. While Finola's mother had always been supportive, she wasn't exactly nurturing. Nor would she understand how her oldest daughter had managed to lose her husband to some country-pop star tramp. In the split second before she spoke, Finola considered blurting out the truth, then knew that wasn't going to happen.

"I've been, ah, fighting food poisoning," she lied, thinking it was easier to stick with what she'd already told Rochelle and Melody. "I just threw up."

"Oh, that explains it because you were really stiff with that Treasure person. I didn't like her song, by the way, but then I'm not her target audience, am I? Are you going to be well enough to fly to Hawaii tomorrow?"

"That's the plan." Finola did her best to keep her voice light even as tears poured down her cheeks. "Going to Hawaii with my husband."

"You should talk to him about getting pregnant. It's long past time, Finola. More important, I want grandchildren. All my friends have them. Most have several. A few of them have so many they complain about it. You're the only one who's married, so it's up to you."

The words were meant to induce guilt. Finola doubted even her mother would want to know how much pain they caused. She sank back on the bench and tried to stem the emotional bleeding.

"Ali's getting married."

Her mother made a dismissive sound in the back of her throat.

"Oh, please. She'll wait at least a year before getting pregnant. I want grandchildren now."

"Too bad you can't order them off Amazon. You're a Prime member. You could have one by Tuesday."

"Very funny. All right, I can see you're going to ignore me, as per usual. Regardless, I love you and I hope you and Nigel have a wonderful time. Once you're back from your vacation you can help me get the house ready to sell. There's a lot to go through and I expect you girls to do a lot of the work."

Not anything Finola could deal with at that moment. "Sure, Mom. I'll call you when I'm home. Bye."

She hung up before her mother could say anything else, then dropped the phone on the carpet.

Now what? She had no idea what to do or how to make the pain at least bearable. She wanted to crawl into a dark space and hide like a wounded animal. She wanted to go back in time so she could stop the affair from happening.

How could he have done this to her? He was supposed to love her forever. They were a team, a partnership.

Her phone buzzed as a text message flashed on the screen. She pushed the button to make it appear again. Her heart pounded when she saw it was from Nigel.

We need to talk. I'll be by Sunday around noon and we can figure out what happens next. There's the Hawaii trip. You have all the paperwork there. Can you cancel it?

A second text filled in below the first one.

I'm sorry.

"That's *it*?" she shrieked at the screen. "That's all you have to say? Just that? Where's my explanation? Why aren't you making this right?"

33

There was no answer, no sound, nothing but her phone screen slowly fading to black.

Finola stood. Nigel was gone and she didn't know if he was coming back. He'd always been there for her, loving her, making her feel amazing and now it was all gone. Just gone. Worse, she didn't know how much of their marriage had been a lie.

She walked into her own closet and changed into jeans and a sweatshirt. After she washed off her makeup, she went into her small study and booted her laptop. Thank God for the internet, she thought bitterly. It only took a few clicks and zero conversation to undo their trip. Once that was done, she went into the guest room and closed the blinds before crawling into bed and pulling the covers up over her head.

She curled up as tightly as she could and told herself to keep breathing. That was all she had to do. Everything else would take care of itself. Nigel wasn't an idiot—he would remember how much he loved her and how good they were together. Treasure was just a fling. He would get over her and come back where he belonged. They'd go into couples therapy where he would realize how much he'd hurt her and he would beg for forgiveness. She would refuse at first, but then he would win her over with his love and kindness. The break in their marriage would be healed and they would go on, slightly scarred, but wiser and more in love than ever. They would grow old together, just like she'd always imagined. It was going to be fine. It had to be.

Chapter Three

"I've got a guy who needs fog lights and brackets for his '67 Mustang. The computer says we have fog light kits but when I went back to get them, I couldn't figure out what was what."

Ali Schmitt waited as her printer spit out the end-of-week inventory control log. She looked at Kevin and raised her eyebrows.

"Really? What was unclear?"

The eighteen-year-old shifted uneasily from foot to foot. "You know. Ah, which ones he, ah, wants. Ray said to make sure I got it right because there's a difference between the '67 and '68 Mustang."

Kevin had been with the company all of six weeks. He'd hired in as a picker—the person who literally picked parts off shelves and took them over to the shipping department, where they were boxed up and sent out to customers. Ray, Kevin's boss and a man who lived to terrorize all the new hires, had given the kid a difficult job, probably for sport.

Ali looked at Kevin and knew she'd been just as confused when she'd been hired. She'd had the added disadvantage of not being that into cars, although in the past eight years, she'd certainly learned plenty. While she would never physically quiver at the thought of a fully restored 1958 Thunderbird, she could hold her own in most car-related conversations. She was also something of a motocross expert, at least when it came to parts. In truth, she'd never been on any bike with an engine and her skills on the kind you pedaled were average at best.

"What year?" she asked, putting her inventory sheets on her battered desk, then walking over to one of the computers used to check availability. "The Mustang. What year is it?"

"Um, a 1967?" His tone was more question than statement.

"You need to be sure," she said as she punched in a few keys, then arranged two pictures side by side on the screen.

She pointed. "The one on the left is a 1967. See the bar across the front grille? That bar runs behind the fog lights and holds them in place. No bracket required." She pointed to the picture on the right. "On the '68 Mustang, there's no bar, so the fog lights are held in by a bracket. If you're looking for a '67 with brackets, there's no such animal."

Kevin was nearly a foot taller than her, but as she spoke, he seemed to shrink.

"Okay." He drew the word out into three syllables. "So there's a problem with the order and I need to get it confirmed."

"Exactly." Ali smiled. "You need to talk to Ray."

Kevin went from confused to scared. "Do I have to?"

Ali sighed. "Yes. He's your boss." She hesitated, then gave in to the inevitable. Somehow she was always the one shepherding the new guys through their journey with the company. "He has a dog. Coco Chanel. There's a picture on his desk. Do not, under any circumstances, make fun of the picture. Simply notice it and tell him she's the cutest dog ever. Then ask him to help you confirm what the customer wants."

Kevin's expression of confusion returned as he considered her advice. Ali knew once he saw the picture of a five-pound Chihuahua dressed as a pirate all would be revealed.

"Thanks, Ali." Kevin started to walk away, then he spun back to her. "Didn't Ray already know there was a problem when he told me to go find the fog lights?"

"Probably. He wanted to see if you could figure it out on your own."

"Oh." Kevin's skinny shoulders slumped again. "But I couldn't."

"Not today, but with time. When in doubt, look up the car and confirm you have the right part."

"Good advice. Thanks."

Ah, to be that young again, Ali thought with a smile, then she picked up her inventory sheets before glancing at the clock on the wall. Not that she didn't love her job, but she had so much to get done this weekend. The wedding was only seven weeks away and her to-do list had quadrupled in the past few days. Tonight she wanted to check for RSVPs, pack another cupboard in her kitchen, then narrow the centerpiece options down to two. She'd already chosen the flowers and now had to pick the style of the centerpiece itself. The florist wanted a final answer by Monday morning and Ali was determined to settle on her favorite by then. If only her favorite didn't keep changing.

She left work right on time, a big win on a Friday, then headed for her local grocery store. She was on a strict low-carb diet—again—so bought salad and a rotisserie chicken. Despite the loving whispers from the tortilla chips and the macaroni salad, she kept to her list, paid in the self-checkout and reveled in a bit of self-congratulation. She'd accepted she wasn't going to be skinny for her wedding, but now that she'd had her final fitting, she couldn't put on any weight. Not that it was ever the plan, but there were days when the only thing standing between her and madness was a cookie.

She drove to her apartment and parked. She was halfway up the stairs to her place when she saw someone standing by her front door. A tall, male someone with dark hair.

She recognized the set of his broad shoulders and narrowness of his waist. When he turned, she saw the familiar three-day beard on his strong jaw. One thing she and Glen had in common was that neither of them was the most attractive sibling in the family. She had to contend with both Finola and Zennie being prettier than her while Glen had to deal with his younger brother, Daniel.

Although Daniel wasn't conventionally handsome, there was something about him. Something dark and just a little bit dangerous. A woman knew, just by looking at him, that she was taking a risk—while the sex would be amazing, there was at least a fifty-fifty chance he would steal her car afterward.

Metaphorically, of course. Because Daniel wasn't a thief—far from it. He was a successful businessman who owned a motocross track. He was, ironically, a really good customer of hers—all those bikes he rented needed maintenance and therefore parts, which was where she came in. In theory that connection should have made them friends, and they were. Kind of. There was just something about the way he looked at her. She couldn't tell what he was thinking, but in the back of her mind she was fairly sure he found her lacking. Or just plain uninteresting. None of which explained why he was standing at her apartment door.

He watched her approach. For a second his whole body stiffened. As if he didn't want to talk to her. As if he wanted to be anywhere but waiting for her. She stumbled to a stop, not sure what to do or say. She instantly felt defensive and resentful—both of which were a huge overreaction considering the man hadn't even spoken. Jeez. Daniel was Glen's brother. After the wedding, he would be her brother-in-law. She really had to figure out how to get along with him.

She forced a big smile. "Hey you. This is a surprise. I'm going to be picking out floral centerpieces later. Want to offer your opinion? You can represent all the men attending, and if any of them complain, I can say it's all your fault."

She waited for him to say something. Anything. Instead he simply stared at her. The defensiveness returned, accompanied by a big dose of insecurity. Why did he have to be a jerk?

"Ali, I need to talk to you."

There was something in the way he spoke—an urgency that got her heart beating faster. It suddenly occurred to her that this wasn't a social call at all. Something was really, really wrong.

"Is it Glen? Is he hurt? Was there a car accident?" Glen was away on a job. "Did his plane go down?"

"Nothing like that. Glen's fine. Can we go inside?"

Ali managed to open her front door. She shoved the groceries into the refrigerator, dropped her purse onto the counter, then turned to find Daniel standing in the middle of her small living room as if he had no idea what to do next. She ignored the rapid beating of her heart and the way her legs were shaking. Whatever it was, if Glen was fine, she would handle it. There might be screaming or crying or both, but she would get through it.

"Tell me," she whispered. "Just tell me."

He motioned to the sofa. "Sit down."

"I'd prefer to stand."

He took her hand and led her to the sofa. When she was seated, he sat down next to her and stared into her eyes.

His irises were dark brown with flecks of gold. She'd never noticed that before, but then she'd never been this close to him. Emotions flashed across his face. She would swear she saw real pain, which didn't make sense.

"Daniel, I have no idea what you're going to say but in about thirty seconds, I'm going to start shrieking, so just blurt it out. Is Glen really okay?"

"Yes. It's not—" He turned away and swore under his breath. "Ali, Glen isn't…" He looked at her. "Glen is breaking off the engagement. He's too much of an asshole to do it himself, so he told me to tell you. When I refused, he threatened to simply pretend everything was fine for the next few weeks, then not show up on your wedding day. I don't know if I believe him or not but I couldn't take the chance. I'm sorry. I wish you could know how sorry I am."

No. No! The words bounced around in her brain, repeating themselves, breaking apart, then reforming. What? No. Glen wasn't breaking off their engagement. He couldn't be.

"You're lying."

"I'm sorry."

She sprang to her feet and glared at him. "Why are you doing this? Do you think it's funny? I won't believe you. I can't."

She felt a tightness in her chest and suddenly found it impossible to breathe.

She hurried to the door, started to open it, then collapsed against it, tears burning in her eyes. No, she thought frantically. He couldn't leave her. They were about to get married. He *loved* her. She'd just mailed the invitations two days ago!

Only even as the pain gushed through her and she felt her heart cracking into tiny pieces that would never be whole, a faint voice whispered that she wasn't completely surprised. That somewhere deep inside she'd known something was wrong.

Before she could argue with that horribly cruel voice, strong arms captured her, spun her around and held her close. Daniel cupped the back of her head in one of his hands and pressed her cheek to his chest.

"Ali, I wish I could make this better. I keep saying I'm sorry, but I don't know what else to tell you. If it helps at all, I hit him. He's got a bloody nose and a black eye and he's the stupidest guy alive. One day he'll regret giving you up and he'll have to live with that for the rest of his life."

She heard the words, but they didn't mean anything. Nothing meant anything. She was going to crumble into dust and blow away. Before she could gather any strength, she simply plopped down on her butt on the floor.

Glen had ended things. No—he'd made sure the humiliation and horror was worse than just dumping her to her face. He'd sent his brother to do it. Only this wasn't a breakup. This was their *wedding*.

Daniel crouched next to her. She brushed the tears from her face. "Why? Did he say why? We're getting married. I have a dress and his ring and we're supposed to go on our honeymoon. How could he—" She had to swallow to keep talking. "He was supposed to love me. He said he loved me. He *saw* me."

The shaking started up again, claiming her body and making it impossible to talk. Daniel got up and disappeared from view. She half expected to hear the front door open then close, only instead of that, he returned with her phone in his hand.

"Who can I call? You need someone here. A friend? Your mom?"

"No," she managed. "Not my mother." Not only wouldn't she understand, she would make it all about herself. "Finola." Yes, her sister would— "Wait. She and Nigel are leaving for their vacation tomorrow. I don't want her to know."

Not when they got away so infrequently and Finola was going to surprise her husband with the happy news that she was ready to get pregnant. Telling Finola what had happened would ruin everything.

Ali sniffed and pointed to the phone. "Zennie. I just saw her. She's off today." There was more to say but she couldn't manage it. Not when the sobs returned and it was all she could do not to shriek at the unfairness and the pain. What had happened? Why would Glen do this to her? They were good together. Everything was so pleasant. Sure there wasn't a lot of passion, but a lot of people didn't want that. Passion could be exhausting.

The whispering, slithering voice returned, murmuring that Glen had been less attentive lately and that she'd wondered, more than once, if something was wrong. Only she hadn't asked because she hadn't wanted to know.

"You're wrong," she whispered out loud. "Glen loves me." Except his were not the actions of a man in love. His were the actions of a total jerk who had never really cared.

She looked up just as Daniel pushed a button on her phone.

"Zennie's on her way," he said, looking both sad and compassionate, which only added to her humiliation. "I'll stay until she gets here."

Instead of telling him he didn't have to, she scrambled to her feet and grabbed her phone. She quickly texted Glen.

Is it true?

She didn't have to wait very long. Less than twenty seconds later, a single word appeared.

Yes.

"Rat fink weasel lying shithead bastard!"

She threw her phone against the wall and watched it shatter into a thousand unfixable pieces. Obviously she would be replacing that in the morning, but so what? She automatically backed up everything every time she charged it and she had phone insurance. Besides, compared with a canceled wedding and losing the man, if not of her dreams, then at least the guy she'd planned to marry, did it really matter?

Seconds later, she realized the flaw in her plan. She turned to Daniel.

"I need to make a call."

She had to give the man credit. Despite what he'd just witnessed, he handed over his phone without so much as a blink.

She walked into her kitchen and pulled open a drawer. After

sorting through her takeout menus, she chose the pizza one and dialed.

She gave her name and address, then placed her order. "A large all meat with extra cheese and garlic bread. Two pints of Cherry Garcia. Oh, and the chocolate Bundt cake." She listened, then said, "Forty minutes is great. I'll be here with cash."

She handed Daniel back his phone, then pulled out two bottles from the pantry. She offered Daniel the corkscrew. While he took care of the red wine, she chugged a mouthful of tequila. Because if she was going to be heartsick, she might as well have a hangover, too.

She waited for the alcohol burn to start in her stomach and hoped it would be bigger than the pain in her chest. Every part of her hurt and she couldn't believe what was happening. Just like that it was over. Just like that, everything was different. She wasn't going to be Mrs. Glen Demiter. She was just going to be herself and didn't that suck.

"You don't have to stay," she said as she carefully screwed the top on the tequila bottle. "Zennie will be here soon and I'll be fine."

"I don't mind waiting." He nodded at the bottle. "You've got quite the party going."

"I wouldn't exactly say it's going to be a good time," she said as tears filled her eyes.

"I know. I'm sorry. I didn't mean—"

"I know what you meant." She brushed the moisture off her cheeks and tried to smile. "Daniel, you've been way more decent than I would have expected. Thank you for that, but to be honest, I just want a few minutes alone. Okay?"

He hesitated before nodding slowly. "I'll check on you tomorrow."

"You really don't have to."

"I want to." He surprised her by moving close and lightly

touching her face. "Try not to get too drunk or you'll have a really bad morning."

Her mouth twisted. "No offense, but I'm going to have a bad morning regardless."

She walked him to the door and waited while he walked to the end of the landing and headed down the stairs. When he was gone, she sank to the floor and leaned her head against the wall. Sobs overwhelmed her as she fought against the ugly reality that once again she was the one left behind.

Glen had promised to love her forever and he couldn't even get through an engagement. What was it about her that made her so easily abandoned? Why didn't anyone love her best?

A flash of light caught her attention and she glanced down only to realize she was still wearing her engagement ring. The modest but pretty diamond winked up at her, mocking her and her pain. She pulled off the ring and threw it in the direction of the phone. It bounced a couple of times before sliding to a stop in the electronic debris.

The bits and pieces lying there were the perfect tableau of what had been her life. Once whole, and now just a bunch of garbage.

Chapter Four

When Ali opened her eyes Saturday morning, her first concern was to question whether or not she had to throw up. Thanks to the wine and the tequila chaser, much of last night was a blur. Zennie had been sweet and supportive, but she'd never been more than a single glass of wine kind of girl, which meant the two empty bottles of wine were mostly Ali's doing.

She shifted on the sofa, assessing her situation. She felt awful—her head pounded, her stomach hurt and her heart was little more than a torn and damp tissue, but she didn't think she was going to vomit.

"Yay, me," she whispered before pushing herself into a sitting position.

She winced at the bright sunlight filling her living room. Her headache cranked up two levels. Why couldn't she live somewhere that it rained all the time, like Seattle? Rain would suit her mood better.

She leaned back against the sofa and tried to summon some small measure of energy. She needed to pee and she should probably brush her teeth. After that, a shower would be good. Once she'd done all the normal stuff, she was going to have to face where she was in her shattered life and deal with the detritus that was her broken engagement.

Glen was gone. That much she remembered from the previous night. Zennie had been sympathetic and caring but at no time had she tried to convince Ali that it was going to work out. Sending Daniel to do Glen's dirty work kind of said it all. Glen was past done with her. There was no going back, no turning this into a funny story to tell the grandkids.

"Not my first breakup," she reminded herself, speaking aloud, then winced at how loud she sounded. Or maybe that was just the hangover. No, not her first, but by far her worst, because she'd allowed herself to believe Glen really loved her.

She wouldn't think about that, she thought as she stood and waited for the room to stop spinning. Once again she assessed her need to throw up and found that, despite the thudding in her head, she wasn't feeling that awful. Maybe the pizza, ice cream, Bundt cake combo had mitigated the wine.

She took a couple of steps, only to trip over a half-open pizza box. Once she got her balance back, she looked around and saw there were dishes everywhere, along with a second pizza box and remnants of the cake. She vaguely recalled her sister wanting to clean up, but Ali had insisted she was going to party on, even after her sister left. Zennie had offered to stay, but Ali had been feeling drunk enough to think she would be just fine on her own.

At least she'd survived the first night, she told herself, then nearly fell over when someone knocked on the front door.

"Stop," she said, hurrying over and opening the door. "Just stop making that—" She blinked against the blazing sunlight, then blinked again because she had to be seeing things.

"What you doing here?"

"Checking up on you," Daniel said, stepping past her and into the apartment. "How was your night?"

"What?" She stared at him, trying to figure out why he was so much more in focus than everything else in the room.

He'd obviously showered. His clothes were different from the ones he'd worn the previous afternoon, but maybe not. He looked a lot fresher than she felt, but his beard was confusing. The three-day growth thing never changed, and how did that happen? And how was it so perfect all the time? Every hair exactly the right length. Did guys take a class on how to do that, or maybe use a special razor or clippers?

She felt herself smiling. Yeah, it had to be clippers, like those dog clippers that measured how long you wanted the cut to be. Not that she could imagine Daniel using dog clippers, but still, the thought was amusing.

"I might still have a little alcohol in my system," she murmured more to herself than him.

"I wouldn't be surprised." He handed her a large to-go cup. "I made this for you."

She took it but didn't drink. "What is it?"

"A smoothie. Coconut water, red ginseng, prickly pear and ginger. Do you need to throw up?"

"I might now." She wrinkled her nose. "I don't even know what prickly pear is."

"Everything in there will help with your hangover. Drink it and go take a shower. When you're done with that, we'll see if you want to eat." He held up a grocery bag. "I brought breakfast."

"You need to talk in shorter sentences," she told him before taking a sip. The smoothie wasn't half-bad. It mostly tasted of chocolate and maybe a little of coconut, which made sense because of the coconut water. Except coconut water didn't really taste like—

"What were we talking about?" she asked.

He smiled at her. Now *that* got her attention. She wasn't sure she'd seen Daniel smile before, at least not because of something she'd said or done. He was usually stern-faced and disapproving. As if she smelled bad, which she didn't, except possibly this morning and hey, that wasn't her fault.

"Do you like it?" he asked.

His smile? That seemed like a really personal question. Oh, wait. "The smoothie? It's good."

"Drink it down. You'll feel better." He glanced around. "So you and your sister did okay last night?"

"It was fine. I mean horrible because of Glen, but Zennie was very sweet. I cried and got drunk and called him names and she offered to take out his liver."

Daniel raised his eyebrows. "That's very specific."

"Zennie's an OR nurse. I'm not saying she'd do a great job, but it's not like we'd want him alive at the end of the surgery so hey." She drank more of her smoothie, only to remember Daniel was Glen's brother.

"You know I'm kidding about his liver, right?"

"Yes. And even if you weren't, under the circumstances, you get to be pissy."

"Damn straight. What a jerk. It's not fair. I loved him. I was going to marry him. Why can't he be more like Nigel? That's my sister Finola's husband. Nigel is wonderful. So handsome and successful. He's a plastic surgeon, not some stupid engineer who designs sewers. I hate him. Glen not Nigel."

"I got that." Daniel put his hands on her shoulders and turned her. "Shower, then breakfast. After that, we'll come up with a plan for the day."

"Okeydokey."

She drank a little more of the smoothie, then walked into the bathroom. She flipped on the light, closed the door, then turned and saw herself in the mirror. And then she screamed.

"Oh, my God!"

"You okay?" Daniel asked from the other side of the door.

"Mortified. Why didn't you say something?"

"About what?"

She heard the humor in his voice. "Go away."

"Going away."

The sound of his chuckles faded a little. She flipped on the fan so she couldn't hear them at all, then assessed the damage.

She had a serious case of bed head, with half her hair sticking up, all gross and matted. There were chocolate smudges on her cheeks, pizza stains on her shirt and her eyes were bloodshot and puffy.

Kill me now, she thought as she stripped out of her clothes and turned on the shower. Because getting dumped less than two months before the wedding wasn't hideous enough? She had to wake up looking like she'd barely survived a frat party?

Thirty minutes later, she was ready to face the world. Sort of. She was hoping Daniel had left, but didn't think her luck was that good. Still, she'd showered, washed and dried her hair. She'd both flossed and brushed her teeth and put on clean clothes. She'd also finished the smoothie, which had been surprisingly restorative. Except for a very slight headache, she didn't feel half-bad. Not counting the breakup, of course. There was always that.

She walked into her living room to find it transformed. Gone were the pizza boxes, the empty bottles of wine and the dishes. Her coffee table was wiped clean and the remnants of what had been her phone sat in a little plastic bag next to her engagement ring.

She flushed with embarrassment as she realized her apartment had looked just as bad as she had. Because, hey, there could never be enough humiliation for one person, right?

Daniel stood in the kitchen, slicing mushrooms. For such a macho guy, he looked perfectly at ease. There was a carton of eggs on the counter, along with a package of bacon. She smelled coffee and her whole being perked up.

"You didn't have to stay," she began as she headed for the coffee. "Seriously, you've done enough." She waved the empty drink container. "This worked great. Thank you, but I'm sure you have plans for the day."

And while they were on the subject, she wasn't totally sure how long she would be holding things together. She was fine now but at some point the pain was going to slap her upside the head again and then she would be sobbing and blubbering like a fool, all over a man who hadn't had the balls to dump her face-to-face.

"I do have plans," he said, putting down the knife. "First, I'm going to make you breakfast. Then we're going to get you a new phone."

She glanced at the little bag filled with phone bits. "Probably a necessary thing. Mine now has a Humpty Dumpty–like quality and I have no king's horses or men."

He flashed her a grin. "You're feeling better."

"It was the ginseng."

"Or the prickly pear."

She grimaced. "Let's not talk about that."

"Not a problem. After we get you a new phone I thought we'd come up with a game plan."

"For what?"

"Canceling the wedding."

Her mouth dropped open. Well, crap. She had to cancel the wedding. As in undo all that had been done. There were venues and food and…

"I just mailed out the invitations," she said.

"I got mine Thursday."

"We already have gifts from the save-the-date cards. I have to tell everyone. That's nice." She poured herself coffee. "Hey, world, Glen changed his mind and no longer wants to marry me. Sorry there won't be a party."

Daniel finished cracking the egg he held, then wiped his hands on a towel and walked over to stand next to her. He put his large, manly hands on her shoulders and stared into her eyes.

"My brother is a jerk and a fool. He's making a mistake, but I hope that by the time he figures that out, you are so over him, you can only laugh at his patheticness. You are sweet and pretty and funny and kind and he never deserved you."

She knew he was just being nice, but still. Wow. The words, the intense gaze, the closeness.

"You're really good at the whole consoling thing," she told him. "You should consider it as a part-time gig. You could make a fortune."

He smiled. "I'm happy with my current job, but I appreciate the compliment."

He went back to his egg cracking and she was left with the reality of having to cancel a wedding. Glen hadn't even bothered to dump her himself, no way he was going to help.

"Don't take this wrong, but I hate him."

"Right now I hate him, too." He looked at her. "I downloaded some articles on what to do in what order. I brought them over."

He pointed to a plain folder sitting by her handbag on the small table next to the front door.

She thought about all the work she'd done to get married and how much more work it was going to be to undo it all. She thought about how she'd been so happy before and how she wasn't happy now. Everything was different. No, she corrected herself. Everything was exactly the same. That was what had been lost. The promise of something better, with Glen. Now all she had was who and what she'd always been. Talk about sucky.

She looked at Daniel, then at the food. She thought of the

hope she'd had, how she'd wanted to be a part of something, to make a family. With Glen, of course. He'd been the center of her...

Her eyes began to burn and not from lack of sleep. "I can't do this," she whispered.

Daniel turned toward her. "Ali?"

"I can't do this. I can't be the perky post-breakup girl who has it all together and I don't know you well enough to have a meltdown in front of you. No offense."

He wiped his hands on a dish towel. "None taken."

"I just need to process this. I'll get a new phone and distract myself for a few hours. I want to just keep breathing." She nodded at the folder. "I really appreciate you bringing me information on how to cancel my wedding, but I'm going to put that off until tomorrow." She tried to smile and failed. "You're being really sweet and I appreciate it, but I—"

"You need some time alone. I get it."

He crossed to her, put his hands on her shoulders and lightly kissed her cheek. "Breakfast is on me. I'll check in with you tomorrow."

"You don't have to."

"I want to."

"It's guilt, right? You feel guilty because of what Glen did."

"Yes."

"I can live with that."

She walked him to the door. When he was gone, she closed her eyes and tried to come up with a plan. She needed a new phone. That was number one. After she'd gotten that, she would go to the movies. There had to be some kids' movie that would distract her. Or a nice horror flick that would terrify the sad out of her. Or maybe both. Later, she would sob her heart out and tomorrow she would get her act together. For today though, she was going to wallow. She'd survived the first night. Now there was only the rest of her life to get through.

★ ★ ★

Zennie spent Saturday doing the usual errand stuff that kept her life running smoothly, but even as she checked things off her list, she couldn't escape the feeling of a dark cloud hanging over her. She felt awful for her sister—no one deserved to be dumped like that, ever. Glen was a total jackass and Zennie hoped he came to a slow and painful end. Not that bad things happening to Glen would make Ali feel better. Only time would do that, but Zennie felt there had to be something to be done or said. Not that she had a clue. She wasn't exactly a touchy-feely kind of person and of the sisters, Ali and Finola were the ones who were the closest. They shared a bond that had never extended to Zennie. Maybe it was because there was a large age gap between the oldest and youngest—seven years. Finola had helped raise Ali while Zennie had been much closer to their father.

Zennie almost texted Finola a couple of times Saturday morning, then told herself Ali was right. Finola and Nigel needed their week away. Not to be overly insensitive, but Ali would still be brokenhearted in a week when Finola returned.

After her three o'clock hot yoga class, Zennie went back to her apartment and got in the shower. She had a date with Clark that night—her own fault. She should have canceled. It wasn't that he wasn't a nice guy—he absolutely was—but he wasn't anyone she saw herself with in the long term. Not that she ever did. She'd never been the girl who'd played with dolls and had done pretend weddings. She'd rarely played with dolls at all. She hadn't ever imagined what it would be like to grow up, fall in love and get married. She just wasn't wired that way. The whole two-by-two thing was great for other people but less interesting for herself.

She stood in front of her tiny closet and thought longingly of an evening spent home alone, binge-watching the new season of *The Crown*, but it would be rude to cancel this late, so she had to suck it up.

She pulled on her go-to black capris and a black tank top, then chose one of her three loose, flowy tops that worked in most social situations. She slid on flat sandals before returning to the bathroom where she suffered through the indignity of applying mascara and a little lip gloss. Honestly, men didn't put on makeup before they went out—why did she have to? It was barbaric. Like preparing herself to be sold at some concubine marketplace.

The overly dramatic image made her smile. Zennie pulled her small bag out of her tote and headed for the door. The restaurant Clark had suggested was close enough for her to walk. As she wasn't going to be driving, maybe an extra glass of wine would make the date more bearable.

Zennie arrived at the trendy Italian restaurant right on time. Clark was already there, speaking to the hostess. Zennie took a second to study him, to see if she could figure out why he wasn't working for her.

He was good-looking enough. She'd never been all that into appearances, but he was certainly in the "Yes, this is nice" category. He was about six feet tall, with curly dark hair and dark eyes. He wore glasses and always had a faintly earnest expression on his face. He was intelligent, dedicated to his work and a good listener. She should have been excited about their date instead of impatient for it to be over. Which meant what? If there was nothing wrong with Clark, then she had to be the problem, but then she'd always been the problem.

He turned and saw her. His eyes lit up as he smiled broadly. "Zennie, right on time. How are you?"

He took her hand in his and leaned in to kiss her. Despite telling herself not to, she turned her head at the last second and his lips grazed her cheek.

"I'm good," she said. "Thanks for the dinner invitation. I'm looking forward to it."

He straightened and she saw some of the light had faded from his eyes. As if her not kissing him on the mouth had hurt his feelings. She wanted to roll her eyes and scream. What was wrong with everyone? Why did everything have to be about love and sex and pair bonding? Now she had to make him feel better or the evening would be a disaster. Better to make things right and get it over with. Then she could go home and watch *The Crown*.

"Sorry," she said, linking her arm with his and leaning into him. "It's been a crazy day. Ali got dumped. She's devastated and I don't know how to help."

Clark's whole body changed. He relaxed as he reached over and hugged her.

"She was engaged, right?"

Before Zennie could answer, the hostess appeared to take them to their table.

Once they were seated in a quiet corner, Clark leaned toward her. "What happened?"

"Nothing good. Apparently Glen didn't even dump her face-to-face. He had his brother do it. They're seven weeks from getting married and he does this? What's wrong with him? Ali never had much confidence to begin with and now this happens. I'm not sure how she's going to recover."

She felt guilty using her sister's tragedy to get through her evening and told herself she would be extra nice all week to re-align her karma.

"She and Finola are so close. I wish she was here, but Ali didn't want to tell her right before Finola was supposed to leave on vacation."

"Finola is the one who's on TV?"

She nodded. "She and her husband don't get away very often, so Ali didn't want to mess with that. I just wish I knew what to say. Maybe I should take up boxing so I can beat him up."

Clark smiled. "You'd humiliate him on multiple levels. I respect that."

Their server arrived and took their drink orders. When he left, Clark asked, "Is it hard having a famous person in the family?"

"I don't ever think of Finola as famous. She's just on TV. But I suppose she gets recognized, at least locally. Sometimes, when we're out shopping or something, someone comes up and wants to talk to her, but not that often. I guess it could be because we're all together. Finola has said people approach her all the time."

"Would you like that?" he asked.

"God, no. It would make me insane."

"Me, too. I prefer small groups of people I know well, rather than large crowds of strangers."

"Same here, although family can be challenging. My mother has decided to downsize. She's still living in the house where we all grew up so it's been about thirty years since the last move. When my parents divorced nearly a decade ago, Dad took almost nothing. Partially, I'd guess, by design but mostly because he was going to be living on a boat." She smiled. "No room for power tools there."

"Barely room for a screwdriver," he joked.

"I know. So Mom plans to relocate to a much smaller place by the beach and she expects us to go through everything in the house and figure out what we want, what she should give away and what she should keep. It's going to be a nightmare."

Their server arrived with their drinks.

"Family's nice," Clark said. "Even when they're being a pain."

She realized she'd spent the past twenty minutes doing all the talking.

"You never talk about yours," she said, once again feeling guilty. Apparently it was the theme for the evening.

"I don't have any. None that's close." He shrugged. "I lost my parents when I was a kid. I was raised by distant relatives who did their best, but had never wanted children. They did the right thing, which I appreciate, but I knew I was in the way."

"That's terrible." No one should grow up feeling unwanted.

"It's okay. I got through it. In a way, what happened shaped who I am today. I wanted to get out of the house and we lived close to the Memphis zoo. I went there almost every day. It's where I got interested in primates. I started volunteering and knew I wanted to spend my life studying them."

He took a sip of his vodka and tonic. "Having direction helped. I never really fit in at school so the zoo became my refuge. After a couple of years, I knew that I wanted to save orangutans. When I went to college, I already had a leg up on everyone else, thanks to my work with the zoo. I went back every summer and volunteered. When I graduated, I already had some experience, which helped me get a job. And here we are."

Zennie had known that Clark worked at the LA Zoo, but she hadn't known his history. Probably because she'd never asked. She'd never even tried to get to know him, she realized. Which begged the question—why had she gone out with him in the first place?

"Zennie, this is our fourth date," he said suddenly.

Her stomach immediately tightened. What did that mean? What was magical about the fourth date? She so rarely got that far in a relationship that she didn't have a lot of experience past dates one and two.

"Okay," she said slowly. "You're right, it is."

He looked from her to his drink and back. "Don't take this wrong, but I get the impression you're just not that into me." His mouth curved up slightly. "Ignore the movie reference."

She honestly didn't know what to say. While he was nice and all, she wasn't the kind of person to get all giddy about a guy. But how to say that without making it sound like she was blowing him off?

"I like you a lot," he continued. "I think you're great. Smart and interesting and pretty. But this can't be one-sided." His dark gaze met hers. "Don't get mad, but is it possible you're a lesbian?"

She sagged back in her chair and glared at him. "No, I'm not.

Jeez, why do people ask me that? Is it the short hair? You know that's a cliché, right? I'm not gay."

"You sure?"

"Yes. The problem isn't men, it's me. I'm just not good at relationships. I don't get the appeal. I have a great life. I have friends and my family and my work. So why do I need more? Why do I need to be paired up? I just don't have that in me. As for the lesbian thing, I've thought about that a lot and I'm honestly not interested in women sexually. I went to college, I could have experimented and I didn't. It's not about wanting to be with a woman."

"I'd wondered."

"Now you know." She leaned forward. "Not everyone has to pair up every single second. I get there's a biological element to it, but that was established back when everyone died before they were thirty. I don't think it's necessary these days, but we still do it and maybe I don't want to. I don't think that means there's anything wrong with me."

"I don't either." His voice was annoyingly mild. "Have you had sex?"

She wanted to pound her head against the table. "Yes, I've had sex. With a man, before you ask. Really? You think a penis is going to make this better?"

"I just wondered."

"It was fine. Nice, but a lot of things are nice."

She waited for a smart-ass comment that the guy must have been doing it wrong and that he could save her or change her or convince her.

But instead he said, "It sounds like you've figured out exactly what you don't want and I'm on that list."

"What? Clark, no. That's not what I meant."

"Zennie, I started this by suggesting you're really not that into me, and nothing you've said has changed my mind. I think you're terrific and I wish this had worked out. I'm really sorry because I'm going to miss you, but I don't think you could say the same thing about me, could you?"

Instead of waiting for an answer, he put two twenties on the table. "To cover the bill," he said, before he stood. He hesitated only a second, then walked out of the restaurant.

Zennie sat there, not sure what had just happened. Obviously she wouldn't be hearing from Clark again. Normally she was the one ending things, but he'd beaten her to it. She was okay with that, she told herself. It wasn't as if she was in love with him. They barely knew each other. Now she could return to her regularly scheduled life.

As she got up and started for the door, she realized that in the space of twenty-four hours, both she and her sister had been dumped. Not that what had happened to her was anything when compared with what Ali was going through. Still, they were both now single. Their mother would be less than pleased, that was for sure. Her dream of grandchildren was fading by the second. Poor Finola—it was going to all be up to her. At least they could count on one of their relationships staying strong, no matter what.

Chapter Five

Sunday morning Ali started her day with yet another hangover, only this one was emotional rather than liquor-induced. After getting her new phone and going to two movies, she'd come home to face the reality of her broken engagement. She'd spent Saturday night looking at pictures of her and Glen, had played their favorite songs and sobbed until she was empty of tears. Then she'd slept on the sofa again, fighting dreams of standing in an unfamiliar church, surrounded by everyone she'd ever known, waiting on a man who never showed up. She woke up with a sore back and determination that she was going to be a grown-up, regardless of how much she didn't want to.

She fixed herself breakfast using the groceries Daniel had left. While her omelet was no one's idea of a thing of beauty, all the elements were there. She ate it, then filled her mug with coffee and opened the folder he'd dropped off the previous day.

There were a half dozen articles on what to do to cancel a

wedding. One even provided a checklist. She read a couple, then closed her eyes and told herself it was okay. She could get through it—only, the concept was daunting. Basically canceling a wedding was the same as planning one, but in reverse. She was going to have to print out all her contracts, read them for terms, then contact her vendors. Payments would be due for some, regardless. She was pretty sure everyone had required a cancellation clause. Given that the wedding was nearly seven weeks away, the payments might not be too horrible, but still.

Because he made so much more than her, Glen had been paying for most of the wedding. Her parents had both claimed poverty and had offered her a thousand dollars each. She'd used that money to pay for her dress. As Glen had been the one to walk away from their relationship, she doubted he would be very willing to cough up any cash to pay for what remained. Regardless, she was going to have to figure out a way to make him cover at least half of what they still owed. She'd signed all the contracts in good faith and...

She groaned. *She'd* signed all the contracts. Not her and Glen, just her. She'd been the one to find the various vendors. Glen was always so busy with travel. So if he didn't come through, she was going to totally be on her own. Not a happy thought.

She glanced at the to-do list and wished she hadn't already wasted her first-of-the-morning groan. Item number two, after informing vendors, was to tell the guests.

Humiliation flooded her. All the people she loved most in the world were going to know Glen had dumped her. All her friends and his friends and everyone she worked with. She was going to have to come clean.

She pulled out her new phone and started a text to him.

What the hell happened?

After a second, she deleted that and tried again. We have to talk. We have a wedding to unravel.

She started to put her phone down only to realize he was answering her right away. She waited a minute or so, then gasped when she read his message.

I never wanted to get married. This is on you.

"No!" Ali came to her feet, glaring at her phone. "No way, you jerk." She typed furiously.

This is not on me. You proposed. Until that moment, I hadn't said a word about marriage. You bought a ring and you proposed. This is on both of us. There's a lot to undo and you should help. I also expect you to pay for half of what's left.

The three dots appeared and she waited.

I'm not going to help but I'll send a check.

She supposed that was something. She hesitated for a second, then typed, Want to tell me why you ended things and why you couldn't tell me yourself?

More dots followed by, I don't want to be with you anymore and I didn't want to listen to you beg.

"What? Beg? In your dreams, you sick bastard."

She almost threw her phone again before coming to her senses in time. This was good, she thought. Better to suffer before the wedding than to have married him, popped out a couple of kids and then discovered he was a total asshole. Beg. As if.

Tears burned, but she blinked them away. Just send the check, she typed and tossed her phone on the sofa.

After pacing back and forth a few times, she managed to regulate both her breathing and her temper. There was lots of work to be done and she was the only one showing up. She would do the right thing and accept that she was building her character.

Once everything was taken care of, she would find someone to make a voodoo doll of Glen and then stab it over and over again with a very sharp, very large pin.

She got a pad of paper, used her all-in-one printer to make a couple of copies of the checklist, then sat down to figure out what to do when. Contracts, vendors, guests and a thousand things more, she thought.

Two hours later, Ali had a rough idea of all the work that had to be done. She'd read a couple of the contracts and had learned that she was on the line for cancellation fees for sure. The venue—a building and garden high up in the foothills at the north end of the valley—would bill her for the full amount unless they could book the space within two weeks. Ali hoped all their talk about a waiting list was true. The same with the bartenders and the caterer. She wouldn't be able to get anyone on the phone until Monday, so she was going to have to cross her fingers that it worked out.

The florist had a kinder, gentler contract. She could get back 75 percent of the total amount due for the flowers, which was about the amount of her deposit. Yay on that. She was stuck with the dress. It was bought, paid for and altered already. No way she could return that.

While there was more to deal with, the last issue Ali wanted to solve today was notifying all the guests. She didn't want to have to make a bunch of phone calls, which meant doing another mailing. She had the addresses in a file on her computer, so in theory all she had to do was get something printed and send it out.

She searched online for ideas about how to do it and settled on something simple. A couple of minutes on the Vistaprint website later, she had postcards ordered. She paid for rush delivery, then made a note to swing by the post office to pick up stamps.

With that completed, she was ready to be done, at least in the short term. A girl should only have to face so much wedding deconstruction in a day, she thought grimly. She would pick it back up tomorrow. It was a beautiful Sunday. She should go do something, although she had no idea what. Normally she and Glen would have had plans. Or she would have hung out with Finola. If she'd known she would have a free day, she would have made arrangements to spend time with one of her friends. Well, that and maybe back the car over Glen.

Before she could figure out if there were any movies she still wanted to see, someone knocked on her door. She opened it and tried not to look as surprised as she felt.

"Again?" she asked before she could stop herself.

Daniel flashed her a sexy grin. "I'm happy to see you, too."

He brushed past her as if he always dropped by on a daily basis and walked into her apartment.

"How's it going?" he asked when she'd closed the door and turned to stare at him.

"I haven't broken another phone, but only because I remembered in time. Glen is being a dick."

"Not a surprise. I take he won't help with undoing the wedding?"

She nodded. "I texted with him and he wasn't exactly cooperative. He said he wouldn't do any of the work but he did offer to send me a check."

"Where are you on things?"

"I've made a few lists. Basically it's planning a wedding in reverse. I've read the articles you brought. Thanks for that. They really helped. Now I get to plow through my contracts and figure out who gets what."

She felt awkward sharing this with him, but figured it was okay—they'd almost been family.

"I also have to let all the guests know the wedding is canceled." She wrinkled her nose. "Not exactly my idea of a good time."

"Are you calling everyone?"

"God, no! That would make things worse. I don't want to have to hear their pity or have anyone tell me they 'just knew' something was wrong." She used air quotes. "I ordered cards on Vistaprint and will mail them out when they get here. I still have the database for the mailing labels."

It occurred to her she should invite him to sit down, only that felt weird.

"Why are you here?" she blurted. "I mean that in a nice, curious way, but it is, you know, odd."

"I'm worried about you. What Glen did is unforgivable."

Which meant what? He was picking up the slack? Acting as a stand-in for her fiancé? Being the good brother?

"Daniel, you've been great. The smoothie from yesterday should put you firmly in line for sainthood, but I'm dealing. It's hard, I feel sad and stupid and angry all at the same time. Eventually the anger will fade and I'll start to miss him, although that hasn't kicked in yet."

"Still want him dead?"

"Not dead so much as mangled."

"I can respect that."

They looked at each other. She turned away first.

"So, um, did he happen to say why he didn't want to marry me anymore?" she asked, hoping she sounded curious rather than pathetic. "He wasn't exactly forthcoming in his texts."

Daniel shoved his hands into his jeans pockets. "I'm sorry, but he didn't say anything other than it was over for him. I wish I knew more."

"I know. And hey, you hit him, so that was nice. I'm sure when things calm down, he and I will talk and I'll get some answers. Or not."

"I'm sure you will. So, I want to help with undoing the wedding."

"Thanks, but not necessary."

"You shouldn't have to do it yourself. Give me something

easy, say the contract with the photographer. I'll call them tomorrow and work things out. If I do a good job, you'll promise to trust me with something more challenging." His dark gaze seemed sincere. "I mean it. You don't have to do this all alone."

Which sounded really nice, especially when he looked all three-day scruffy with his beard and Sunday-relaxed in jeans and an LA Dodgers T-shirt.

"Why are you doing this?" she asked. "Brother guilt?"

"That and because I want to."

"Why on earth would you want to help me unplan my wedding?"

He looked at her and smiled. "Because I like you." He held out his hand. "Give me that contract and no one will get hurt."

He liked her? He *liked* her? What did that mean? Nothing, of course, she told herself. He meant in an almost sister-in-law way. Daniel was sexy and dangerous with his motocross business and his tattoos and swagger. She was the kind of woman who attracted the sucky Glens of the world. Besides, no and no. He hadn't meant it any way other than to be nice. He liked her the way people liked cucumbers. They were acceptable and innocuous. She was like a cucumber.

Okay, that sounded strange, even for her. She sighed. The whole breakup had affected more than her heart, she thought sadly. She was starting to lose her mind.

"One photographer contract coming up," she said.

He glanced at his watch. "I'll get it later," he said. "We need to go."

"Go where?"

"The Dodger game. It starts in an hour so we have to hustle. Come on. Do you have a Dodger baseball hat? If you don't, it's okay. I have an extra one in the truck." His smile returned. "We're on the good side of the stadium—the third base line. The sun will be at our backs, so no squinting to see what's going on."

She stared at him. A Dodger game? She'd never been into baseball but it beat sitting home alone and moping.

"You're being really nice to me," she said, as she grabbed her purse.

"I know. I'm one of the good guys."

He spoke lightly, as if joking, but his words hit her in the heart and the gut. She'd assumed Glen was a good guy. She'd assumed it so much, she'd allowed herself to fall in love with him and plan a future together. Only he'd betrayed her. He'd abandoned her and their future without even bothering to speak to her directly, which made everything worse.

She tried to shake off the thoughts. No more Glen suffering—at least not today. She'd been offered an afternoon watching baseball, which was an unexpected distraction. She needed to throw herself into the moment.

As they walked to his truck, she hid her smile. "So baseball. That's the outdoor one with the bats, right?"

Daniel looked at her. "You're kidding, right? Please be kidding. You understand the concept of the game."

She smiled as she climbed into the passenger seat. "Of course I'm kidding. I know baseball is the one where they kick the ball."

"You're killing me, Ali."

"Then my work here is done."

Zennie arrived at the park a few minutes early. She used the time to warm up and stretch. She'd been a bit aggressive at yoga yesterday, stretching past her comfort zone, and was paying for it this morning.

She was also tired. She hadn't slept well, probably because she'd been thinking about her abbreviated date with Clark. It wasn't that she was going to miss him as much as the idea that there was something wrong with her. Which there wasn't.

Right on time, Bernie pulled up in her sensible sedan. Zennie walked over to meet her.

Zennie Schmitt and Bernadette Schmahl had been roommates their freshman year at UCLA. Bernie had known she was going to be a teacher while Zennie had been equally determined to become a nurse. They were about the same height and size, they loved to work out and they both thought the old Monty Python TV show was the funniest thing ever. It had been roommate love at first sight for both of them. The only difference between them was their looks. Zennie was a boring blue-eyed blonde while Bernie was "the pretty friend" with high cheekbones and dark tan skin.

They'd stayed close after college and Zennie had been Bernie's maid of honor at her wedding to Hayes. The two friends ran together every Sunday morning—sometimes just the two of them, sometimes in a group. The only time they'd had to take a break from running had been three years ago when Bernie had been diagnosed with uterine cancer. She'd endured surgery and chemo and had survived both. Now she was happy, healthy and moving on with her life.

"I appreciate you showing up," Bernie said with a grin as they started their run with a slow jog. Their route would take them along the Woodley Park/Lake Balboa loop. It was just over five miles long and relatively flat. Not exactly challenging, but today's run was about hanging out as much as it was about getting exercise.

The morning was still cool and the sky was clear. Later it would warm up but right now the low sixties felt really good.

"Why wouldn't I show up?" Zennie asked.

"I saw the surf report. You could be out on the waves right now."

"I'd rather be with you."

"Aw, that's so sweet. Thank you. How are things?"

"Complicated," Zennie admitted. "Glen dumped Ali."

"What? No. He couldn't. The wedding's in what, two months? Hayes and I already got our invitation."

"She found out on Friday."

Zennie filled her in on what had happened. As she spoke, they picked up the pace.

"Ali is devastated and with Finola out of town…" She grimaced. "I spent Friday night at her place. I should probably call her later, to make sure she's okay."

"I'm sure she'd appreciate that. I've never met Glen but now I have to hate him for sure."

"You and me, both. I just had the fitting for my bridesmaid's dress. It was a good one, too. Navy and a pretty style."

Bernie grinned. "No lime green ruffle extravaganza?"

"Nothing like that." Zennie grimaced. "It's so awful. I swear, if I didn't have Finola's marriage to Nigel and your marriage to Hayes to believe in, I'd say the whole concept of falling in love and being happy is a hoax."

"Uh-oh."

"What?"

Bernie shook her head. "You had a date last night. If you're talking about love being a hoax, then it didn't go well. What happened? I thought you liked Clark. I thought you two had a chance. He sounded adorable. Anyone who devotes his life to caring for animals has to be a nice guy, and you need a nice guy."

Zennie groaned. "It was only four dates. How can you be this upset?"

"I want you happy."

"I am happy. I love my life. Not everyone needs to be paired up. It's not the law."

"Fine. Be a freak. I'll still love you no matter what. So how did you end things? Please tell me you were gentle. I'd hate to think you hurt poor Clark's feelings."

The question was oddly unsettling, Zennie thought as they picked up the pace. They always ran the middle three miles faster and used the last mile as a slow cooldown.

"I didn't break up with him. He's the one who said it was

over. Actually what he said was that he could tell I wasn't that interested in him." She decided not to mention the lesbian thing. That was just too weird and embarrassing.

"No! Did you tell him he was wrong?" Bernie glared at her. "You didn't, did you? Zennie, come on. What didn't you like about him?"

"Nothing. I liked him. Just not that much. Look, can we talk about something else? How's your work? How's Hayes? Are you still thinking of getting a cat?"

Bernie laughed. "We were never thinking of getting a cat. I'm much more a dog person and we're still talking about it. As for work, things are great. This week our main focus is money."

"Isn't six a little young to enter our capitalistic society?"

Bernie taught kindergarten at a prestigious private school in Sherman Oaks. She was the most popular teacher at the school, and parents put their kids on the waiting list for her class within six months of their babies being born.

"We're learning about different types of money. That's part of our math studies. Next week I'm going to bring in currency from different countries and blow their minds."

Conversation continued through their run. When they got back to the parking lot, Bernie collected smoothies from a cooler in her back seat. They walked over to the picnic benches. After stretching they sat across from each other.

This was part of their ritual, as well. A protein-based smoothie and a half hour more of conversation before they returned to their busy lives.

Bernie picked up her drink, then set it down. "I had my two-year scan a couple of weeks ago."

Zennie's stomach instantly knotted as fear, worry and terror bathed in her cold sweat. "And?"

Bernie's smile was big and broad. "It was clear. It was perfect in every way. The doctors are convinced they got it all and while I still have to have scans, at least for the next couple of years, they told me to go live a happy life."

Relief was sweet and immediate. Zennie sagged a little. "You scared me. Next time lead with the good news."

"Sorry. I didn't mean for you to get upset. I'm fine. I feel great. Better than I ever have."

"Hayes should take you on a fancy trip to celebrate. You both deserve it."

"Funny you should say that. Hayes and I do want to celebrate, but in another way. We want to have a baby."

Zennie was both thrilled and sympathetic. Bernie's cancer treatment had included surgery that had taken her uterus and her ovaries. There was no way she could carry a child or even use her own egg. Because of her cancer diagnosis, some pregnant women looking at adoption might not want to consider her and Hayes.

"What's the plan for that?" Zennie asked, doing her best to sound upbeat. "Adoption?"

"Surrogacy. We'd use a donor egg and Hayes's sperm. We've been doing a lot of research and it's a relatively simple procedure."

Zennie smiled at her. "So basically artificial insemination. That would be easy enough. I think they use a turkey baster to insert the sperm."

Bertie rolled her eyes. "There's no turkey baster, but the process is similar. We find a surrogate, wait for her to ovulate and ta-da, pregnancy."

"That sounds a lot easier and faster than adoption. And it's legal, right? You wouldn't have to worry about the surrogate changing her mind?"

"It can always be a concern, but California is ahead of the curve when it comes to surrogacy." Bernie gripped her smoothie. "Zennie, I want to say something. Just listen and then speak from the heart. No matter what, you're my best friend and I'll always love you. Please, please feel free to say no."

Zennie stared at her friend. She half knew what Bernie was going to say, but was still surprised to hear, "Hayes and I would like you to consider being our surrogate and egg donor."

It made sense, Zennie thought. She was young, healthy and strong. She wasn't in a relationship, she had good insurance, and it wasn't as if she was using her girl parts for anything else. But carrying a baby was a big deal, wasn't it? Honestly, she didn't know much about pregnancy beyond her nursing school rotation in delivery and pediatrics.

"We'd cover all your expenses," Bernie went on. "Co-pays and your maternity clothes and any special food you needed. You would be entitled to maternity leave when you had the baby and we'd cover an extra month at home so you could fully recover."

She paused and shrugged. "I want to say more, but I'm going to stop now. If you need to say no, then do it. I'll totally understand."

Zennie reached across the picnic table and squeezed Bernie's hand. "Stop. I'm not going to say no this second. I'm surprised, but I also think I've totally been expecting this. I mean, I never thought about it, but who else? I'm your best friend, Bernie. I love you and Hayes and I want you to be happy. I know you'd be great mom. It's just big and I need to mull for a bit."

Bernie's eyes filled with tears. "Of course. Take as much mulling time as you'd like. Take a year. You have to be sure. You have to know what you're getting into."

"I will think and investigate and I won't take a year."

Bernie brushed away her tears. "Thanks for even considering this."

"Thank you for asking. It's an honor. Now we need to get going. You have to go home to your handsome husband and I need to do a little research."

They stood and hugged.

"I'll be in touch," Zennie promised.

"Thanks."

As she got in her car, Zennie knew she had a lot to consider and think about. While her first instinct was to immediately say of course she would be their surrogate, she understood that this was possibly the biggest decision of her life and not one to be made lightly. Still, it was Bernie and she had no idea if it would be possible for her to ever say no.

Chapter Six

Finola had a little trouble reading the digital clock on the nightstand. The numbers were big enough and even projected onto the ceiling. The problem wasn't the size of the display or the brightness—it was that they wouldn't stop moving.

Back and forth, they jumped like numerical fleas doing a dance that made her head spin. Dang numbers, she thought, wondering if the concept was funny enough to make her smile because nothing else had.

She was pretty sure she was still drunk. She'd been chugging vodka steadily since, oh, sometime Friday night, and now it was Sunday. She still hurt all over and she constantly felt sick and inside her chest, where her heart was supposed to be, was just a hole.

She looked back at the clock and saw it was maybe nine forty. At night, she told herself, looking out the window just to be sure.

Yup, it was dark, so nighttime. Nine forty on Sunday night. A day she'd spent entirely alone because, despite his promise, Nigel had never stopped by.

She'd known he wouldn't, she admitted, but only to herself. There was no way he would want to talk to her after what he'd done. Nigel loved pointing out her flaws but didn't like hearing about his own. There was no way to put this on her, no matter how he tried, so of course he was avoiding her. It was just a character flaw.

She'd been telling herself that for hours and hoping that, at some point, she would believe it. Only now, lying on their bed, in their bedroom, in their house, knowing he was probably fucking Treasure right this second, she was finding it harder and harder to believe that was all it was. Her spinning head and muddled mind weren't enough to distract her from a horrific truth. That Nigel hadn't failed to come by because he was ashamed or because he was busy having sex. He hadn't come by because he wasn't here anymore.

In LA, she clarified for herself. She wasn't thinking he was dead.

She reached for her tablet, put it down, then swore under her breath. After sitting up, she drank more vodka, grimacing when she realized the ice had melted, diluting her drink. Stupid laws of physics or whatever it was that controlled melting ice cubes. She didn't want watery vodka, she wanted *cold* vodka.

She opened the tablet and went directly to the TMZ home page. She didn't have to look hard to see the headline: Does Treasure Have a New Man?

Her vision blurred more as she started crying again. Finola angrily brushed away the ridiculous, useless tears and clicked on the link that took her to the page. There were more pictures than text, which was fine with her. The last thing she wanted to do was to give herself a headache from reading impossibly small and moving print.

Instead, she studied the photos, trying not to care about how young Treasure was and how incredible she looked in a very tiny bikini.

"Look at her ass!"

Finola thought about the hours she spent working out and how every year it was just a little bit harder to keep things high and tight and firm.

Life was many things, but fair wasn't one of them, she told herself.

There were more pictures, all of them of Treasure. Once Finola had accepted the other woman's incredible body, she started paying more attention to where the pictures had been taken. One word jumped out at her. "Bahamas." Her already shaky stomach sank.

"He's not there," she whispered, even though she knew he had to be. She scanned the pictures again, looking more closely at the people in the background. No Nigel, no Nigel, no…

She turned back to one of the pictures she'd already studied, peering at it more closely. There, in the background. The image was blurry, but she recognized the man. He was with her. Nigel had gone to the Bahamas with Treasure.

"Bastard!"

She reached for her drink, only to remember the watery contents, then bounded out of bed. That last thing was a mistake as the room spun and her stomach lurched. She hung on to the nightstand to steady herself. When she was pretty sure she wasn't going to fall over, she headed for the landing and, clinging to the railing, made her way downstairs to the kitchen.

There were two empty bottles of vodka on the counter. A third still had most of its contents. She dumped the tepid liquid from her glass into the sink, added ice, then poured in more vodka. After two big gulps, she set the glass on the counter and closed her eyes.

Nigel had gone away with his twenty-three-year-old mistress. Right now they were together, having sex or mocking her or something awful and hideous. He'd left her, just like that, with no warning. He'd left her on the weekend she'd wanted to tell him she was ready to get pregnant.

Sadness overwhelmed her. Sadness for what had been lost. For all her hope of him being sorry and them getting over this, she honest to God didn't know if that was possible. Even before she decided if she was willing to forgive him or not, Nigel had to come home and that sure wasn't happening now.

Tears returned, along with frustration and anger and hurt. She hated Nigel, *hated* him. She didn't want him dead, she wanted him punished and humiliated. She wanted him naked and in public with lines of people pointing and laughing at his dick. She wanted him tied up and left in a public square until he was forced to pee and shit on himself. She wanted his fingers broken so badly, they would never heal right and he would have to stop doing surgery. But mostly she wanted it to be last Thursday so she didn't know about the affair and she didn't have to hurt this much.

She went back to their bedroom and walked into his closet. Finola grabbed an armful of the clothes he hadn't taken. She carted them over to the French doors, then stepped out onto the balcony. She didn't hesitate at all—she simply flung the clothes off the balcony, onto the patio below. A few shirts fluttered into the pool.

She went back inside and repeated her actions until all his clothes were in the backyard. The last to go was his winter coat—a beautiful camel-colored cashmere that he wore when they went back East. She tossed it, hurling it as hard as she could so it would fall into the chlorinated water. When she was done, she went inside. She sank onto the bathroom floor and rested her head on her raised knees.

He was gone, she thought to herself. Just gone. He'd left her and their marriage as if he'd never loved her. The leaving was bad enough but to have chosen a public figure for his transgression was just as unforgivable. Because under the torment of having lost her husband and her marriage was an even more devastating truth.

Unlike most women going through this, her anguish would not be played out in private. Instead the whole world was going to know. Maybe not today, maybe not tomorrow, but at some point a photographer would put the pieces together. In her line of work, there were very few secrets. Until today, she hadn't cared about that. She wasn't a secret kind of person. But all that had changed and now it was just a matter of time until she was put on trial by a fickle public and a hungry, uncaring press. Losing Nigel had nearly killed her—what was going to be left when she lost herself?

Ali got through work on Monday with a minimum of fuss, mostly because she didn't tell anyone about Glen. Yes, it was probably the coward's way out, but she was fine with that. Eventually she would have to come clean, but not right this second.

She finished her quarterly inventory inspection by noon, then filled in when the quality guy had to leave early to go pick up his kid. She measured parts against the specs and declared them good to go, all the while thinking only positive thoughts. She spent her lunch break making phone calls from the privacy of her car, and canceled the wedding venue and the caterer. Daniel was taking care of the photographer she'd hired.

After finishing her calls, she stayed in her car until her break was officially over. She leaned back against the seat and marveled at life's sense of humor.

The brother she'd assumed was dependable and normal and honorable had turned out to be a total douchebag while the brother who was a little dangerous and put her on edge had turned out to be the world's nicest guy.

At the Dodger game, Daniel had been nothing but charming. He'd distracted her with funny stories from the world of motocross. He'd stuffed her with hot dogs, peanuts and beer and had reminded her to put on sunscreen. Before they'd left, he'd insisted on buying her an official Dodger T-shirt and baseball cap. She'd gone from wary to grateful. At this point, she didn't much care if she was his good deed project for the year. Daniel was a good man and he was determined to help her. Only a fool would say no to that.

Now if only she could figure out a way to ask him to tell her mother for her, things would really be looking up, but alas, no. That wouldn't be right. He'd been incredibly kind to her—she wouldn't repay that by making him face her mother. And if she *was* willing to be that awful, she would gain nothing. Her mother would still want to hear all the gory details from her regardless.

Ali finished her shift and like the dutiful daughter she mostly aspired to be, made her way from Van Nuys to Burbank, avoiding the insanely crowded freeway. She took Victory east, then cut across on North Buena Vista, heading to her mother's side of Burbank. Traffic was brutal, but she was in no hurry and didn't mind missing a few lights. Eventually, however, she arrived on the narrow residential street where she'd grown up. She parked in front of the house and braced herself for what was to come. In theory her mother should be totally on her side, but in this family, unless you were Finola, that was never a sure thing.

The house itself was typical for the neighborhood. A one-and-a-half-story ranch with a porch in front and a detached garage. Upstairs was a bonus room Ali's mother had used for crafts and storage. On the main floor there were four bedrooms, two bathrooms and a family room that had been added on when Ali had been five or six. The sisters hadn't shared a bedroom, but the three of them had shared a bathroom, which had turned out to be surprisingly easy. By the time Ali wanted to spend time on her hair and experiment with makeup, Finola had long since left for college and Zennie had never been one to primp.

Ali's mother had gotten the house in the divorce. Mary Jo always complained it was too big for her, but she'd been loath to move until a couple of months ago when she'd announced she was buying a friend's cottage near the ocean in Redondo Beach. Selling the family home first meant getting rid of thirty-plus years of memories and crap, something she expected her daughters to help with. Ali figured odds were at least even that the first, or possibly second thing her mother said when she found out about her broken engagement was that Ali would now have more time to help with the purge.

She pulled into the driveway next to her mother's silver Civic then braced herself for what was to come. In theory, her mother should be someone she could turn to in a time of need for comfort and advice. What was the old saying? Her mother should be a soft place to fall. But whoever had come up with that one had never had Mary Jo for a mother.

Ali got out. She'd texted her mother earlier, saying she wanted to stop by without saying why. Now, as she walked to the front door, she braced herself for whatever was to come.

She knocked once and opened the door. "Hey, Mom, it's me."

"I'm in the kitchen."

Ali made her way through the living room to the large eat-in kitchen where her mother sat at the table working on what she would guess was a script. In the past couple of years, Mary Jo had joined a local theater group. She mostly wrote plays and directed, which was kind of weird considering she'd been in retail her whole life, but if it made her happy, then sure.

Her mother looked up as she walked into the kitchen. She slid off her glasses and set them on the table. Mary Jo had always been a beauty. It wasn't anything Ali could relate to—she looked more like her father, which was okay, but also kind of a drag, truth be told. Growing up with a beautiful mother and stunning older sister hadn't been easy. Even Zennie was striking, while Ali was left being nothing other than almost average.

"What?" her mother demanded. "Something happened. I knew it the second I read your text."

"Maybe I just wanted to see you."

Her mother only stared at her. "Just tell me. Did you get fired?"

Ali told herself not to be surprised. Of course her mother would think the worst and assume it was all Ali's fault. Although considering her news, maybe her mother wasn't *totally* wrong.

She took a seat at the old round wooden table and set her bag on the floor. "I didn't get fired. Things are great at work. It's Glen. We, ah… He broke off the engagement."

"What? Are you kidding? You're getting married in six-plus weeks. The invitations have gone out. What happened? Why did he change his mind?"

"I have no idea. He won't talk to me. He sent his brother to tell me, and we haven't had a conversation since I got the news. All communication has been via text and it's been more about logistics than anything else."

Ali was pleased she got through her little speech without even tearing up. To be honest, she was much more concerned about her mother's reaction than her own pain.

"You must have done something," her mother muttered. "What did you say to him that made him so mad?"

Ali felt something odd inside and realized it was righteous indignation. She was so thrilled to feel something other than hurt or shame that she decided to indulge.

"Why do you always do that?" she asked, her voice firm. "Why do you have to assume I did anything wrong? Maybe Glen's a dick. He didn't even bother telling me himself. He sent someone else to do his dirty work. For what it's worth, he's refusing to help cancel the wedding. I'm on my own with that. So for once, could you possibly consider that maybe I didn't screw up?"

Her mother sighed. "I can see you're upset."

"Yeah, just a little. The guy I thought I was going to marry and love forever dumped me. *Upset* might be a good word."

Her mother turned over the script and rested her hands on the table. "I'm sorry. You're right. I'm sure you're not to blame. Anyone who would act like that isn't right in the head. Have you considered apologizing and asking if he'll take you back?"

"Mom!"

"What? It's a reasonable question."

"It assumes, once again, I did something wrong. Have you considered the possibility that Glen changed his mind and then was too much of a coward to deal with the consequences? This totally came out of the blue. Besides, even if it hadn't, after the way he's acted, I don't want him back. I could never trust him."

Ali had spoken from the heart and even she was surprised by those last words. Was it true? Did she really not want Glen back? And if so, when had she made that decision?

"It's just he was such a nice man and an engineer. He would always have a good job."

"Mo-om!"

"Fine. You're well rid of him." Mary Jo pressed her lips together. "I'd so been hoping for grandchildren. I'm not getting any younger."

"You're barely in your fifties."

"All my friends have grandchildren."

It was a familiar refrain and one Ali didn't want to hear today. "I'm sorry if the consequences of my broken engagement are getting in the way of your wants and needs."

"There's no need to say it like that."

"Mom, I'm suffering here and you're making it about you."

"I'm not. I'm sharing how I feel. Is that a crime, now? I'm sorry about the engagement. I really am. I had high hopes for you and Glen. If you're looking for a distraction, you can help me go through the house. There's plenty here that needs doing."

"While that sounds amazing, I still have the wedding to unwind. It's a lot of work and I can't count on Glen." Daniel was helping, but this didn't seem to be the time to mention that. Her mother would assume he was the reason for the breakup, which was so ridiculous as to be laughable. Ali had seen a couple of Daniel's girlfriends and they all had Victoria's Secret model potential. As if.

"Well, you can help me after you're done canceling the wedding," her mother said. "What are you going to do about your apartment? Isn't your lease up?"

Ali felt the room dip and sway. Not an earthquake, she thought grimly. Nothing that simple and predictable. Nope, her reaction was pure shock because until her mother had asked, she hadn't once even *thought* about her apartment.

"No," she breathed. "No, no, no."

"Ali, you simply have to be more responsible," her mother began.

"Not now," she said firmly, even as her mind struggled to figure out a plan and fast.

Foolishly, she'd assumed she would be moving in with Glen after they were married. He had a nice little condo in Pasadena, and while her commute would be longer, hey, she was getting married, so of course they would live together. To that end, she'd given notice on her apartment and had to be out a couple of weeks before what would have been her wedding date.

She and Glen had worked it all out—what furniture they would keep, what they would get rid of. Most of hers was to go, which had been fine because his was nicer and she didn't feel a deep sense of commitment to her secondhand dresser or coffee table.

"I'm going to have to talk to the building manager," she said.

"Hopefully they haven't rented the place out from under you," her mother said. "If they have, you're going to have to find somewhere else. Rents are going up."

"Mom, this isn't helping."

"I'm simply pointing out the reality of your situation."

"I'm clear on the reality of my situation."

"You don't seem to be." Her mother studied her for a second, then sighed. "I suppose you could move back here, with me. You could stay in your old room and help me pack up the house."

Or not, Ali thought, hoping the wave of horror washing through her didn't show on her face. Move back *here*? Um, no way, nohow. She might not be moving forward in her life, but that was no excuse for moving backward. Not to mention the hell of having to deal with her mother 24/7.

"That's very generous of you," she said evenly. "Thanks, Mom. Let me figure a few things out before I commit." Which was a very polite version of what she wanted to be saying. "I don't think they've rented out my place yet so I'll just keep that."

"If you say so."

Ali glanced at the rooster clock on the wall. "I should, ah, be going. I want to talk to my building manager before she leaves."

Her mother stood and hugged her. "I am sorry about Glen. You'll find someone else eventually, Ali. Goodness knows you work with men all day long. Aren't any of them dateable?"

"It's complicated, Mom." Mostly because dating someone at work would be dumb and for reasons she couldn't understand, she was more best friend than babe. No one ever asked her out or hit on her or even made lewd remarks. Not that she would encourage the latter, but was just once too much to ask?

On the way to the front door, Ali paused by the big grand-father clock in the living room. It was old and ornate and definitely not in style right now, but she had always loved it. Her bedroom had been the one closest to the living room, so she heard the chimes all night. When she'd been younger, she'd thought the clock chimed only for her.

"Mom, are you taking the clock with you when you move?"

"That monstrosity? No. It's old and ugly. Besides, the salt air would destroy it. Why?"

"I'd like it."

"Don't be ridiculous. You don't even have a place to live. What would you do with a grandfather clock?"

Ali ignored the sense of always being the afterthought kid. "Zennie isn't going to want anything to do with it and Finola doesn't care about it. Why can't I have it?"

"Do you really need to take this on right now? We'll talk later. Now go save your apartment."

Her mother hugged her and shooed her out the door. Ali told herself not to take any of it personally—it was just her mother's way. Only it was difficult not to feel slighted and dismissed—feelings she'd grown up with.

Finola was clearly her mother's favorite. Mary Jo had married young and then had tragically lost her husband in a car accident. Finola had been the result of their undying love. When Mary Jo had married Bill, everyone had known she was settling. It had taken her a good twenty-plus years to figure it out for herself.

Zennie was their firstborn and Bill could not have been more smitten with his daughter. Ali wasn't sure why they'd bothered having another kid. Maybe Bill had secretly hoped for a boy or maybe she'd been an accident. Either way, she was no one's special child. Everyone knew parents weren't supposed to show preference for one child over another, but in her house, the lines had been clearly drawn.

"Apartment first, mope later," she told herself as she got in her car and headed home.

She got to her apartment in North Hollywood a good thirty minutes before the offices closed. Elema, the building manager, was in her office when Ali knocked on the open door.

The fiftysomething woman smiled at her. "How are the wedding plans going? You're already getting packages delivered here. It's very exciting. Oh, Sally said someone dropped off an envelope for you earlier." Elema pulled it out of her desk and handed it over.

Ali glanced at the plain white envelope. She recognized Glen's handwriting and hoped a big fat check was inside. Or at least one for enough to cover half the expenses. She tucked it in her back pocket and took a bracing breath.

"Yes, well, that's what I want to talk to you about," she said, settling in the chair by the desk. "Glen and I have gone our separate ways."

Elema's smile faded. "Ali, no. What happened? He seemed like such a nice man. Oh, this makes me so sad. Are you all right?"

"I'm getting there. The thing is, I won't be moving and I was hoping to stay in my apartment."

Elema's mouth twisted. "I'm sorry, but we've already rented your place. You know how it is—the building is newer and on a quiet street. We usually have a waiting list. They're a nice young couple with excellent credit."

Ali had done a great job of holding it all together through her visit with her mother and on the drive home. Now she felt her fragile connection to anything close to calm fade away.

"Isn't there anything you can do?"

"We've signed a lease with them. We can't break it." Her expression was sympathetic. "I'm going to have a studio available in two months, if you'd be interested in that. It's smaller than what you have now, of course, and a hundred and sixty dollars more a month." One shoulder rose and lowered. "Rents are climbing. The new lease on your place is three hundred dollars more than what you're paying."

How was that possible? And if rents were more here, they would be higher everywhere else. Damn Glen—he'd screwed with her life in more ways than she would have thought possible. Why had she ever trusted him or believed in him? She'd been a fool and now there was no going back.

"I'm really sorry," Elema added. "If you want I can try to make some calls to other properties I know of to see what they have."

"That's sweet. Let me think about this for a while. If I need some help, I'll get back to you."

"I'll be here. And I'm really sorry about Glen. Hopefully you can work it out and still get married."

Rather than answer, Ali offered a fake smile. She made her way to her apartment before giving in to the urge to scream. After throwing herself on her sofa, she pressed her face against a throw pillow and let loose.

"Dammit all to hell, why is this happening to me?"

She kicked her feet for good measure, then rolled onto her back and sucked in a breath. Tears flowed down her temples and into her hair.

This was so not fair, she thought, hugging the pillow. First the wedding and now the apartment. Stupid, awful Glen. May he rot in hell.

She lay there for several minutes, alternately crying and yelling into the pillow, then sat up and wiped her face. She pulled the envelope from her back pocket. At least the pressure of paying off the wedding would be eased a little, she thought, opening the envelope and pulling out the check.

Five hundred dollars. He'd written her a check for five hundred dollars. Canceling the wedding would cost her at least five thousand. Maybe more. Plus there was her dress—that was money she would never see again. Now she had to worry about finding a place and first and last months' rent and moving her stuff *and* paying off the stupid wedding.

Hatred rose up inside of her, boiling into anger and disgust. "Wherever you are, rat bastard, I hope you get food poisoning and a rash and go bald. I hate you. Hate you!"

She threw the pillow against the wall. It was less satisfying than when she'd thrown her phone, but she couldn't afford another replacement. Then she curled up on the sofa and told herself she was going to feel sorry for herself for the whole night.

In the morning she would be strong, but for now there was just pity and maybe some brownies she'd stashed in the freezer. Because right now, her life totally and completely sucked.

Chapter Seven

Zennie did her best not to listen to the conversation happening in the office next to the locker room. Dr. Chen wasn't yelling or raising his voice in any way. Still, the words were clearly audible and his combination of frustration, anger and disappointment had Zennie cringing, and she hadn't done anything wrong.

Molly had screwed up. As the circulating nurse, her job was to keep things flowing smoothly through the surgery. She was to have equipment in place, have supplies at the ready and enough staff to manage the difficult and lengthy procedures that often occurred whenever a surgeon had to crack open a chest.

Today essential supplies had been missing and Zennie had had to scramble to help Dr. Chen make do. Carol, another of the nurses, had been forced to break the sterile field to get what they needed. Not an ideal situation under any circumstance but when they were performing open-heart surgery, it was unforgivable. Molly probably wouldn't lose her job over the mistake, but she would be off Dr. Chen's team. He was one of the best surgeons in the country and as such, he often had the most critical patients and the most difficult surgeries. Mistakes could literally mean the difference between life and death.

"It won't happen again," Molly said, her voice muffled by the wall and what Zennie would guess were her tears. "Please, Dr. Chen. Don't throw me off the team."

Zennie tugged on an oversize T-shirt and hurriedly shoved her dirty scrubs into her bag. She pulled on her athletic shoes and quickly tied them before hurrying out of the locker room.

Once in the hallway, she paused to take a breath. She wasn't meeting her girlfriends until five, so she had some time to kill. She headed to the cafeteria, not wanting to hear any more of the not-so-private conversation.

Monday night workouts were a standing date with her friends. They were meant to counteract whatever wildness happened over the weekend. In addition to sweating out carbs and alcohol, the women used the time to catch up, offering advice for the crisis du jour.

The gym was only a block away. The state-of-the-art facility offered everything from spin classes to rock climbing. The dues were insanely expensive, but hospital employees got a sizable discount and for Zennie, the price was worth it. She loved trying different classes and staying in shape. Given Dr. Chen's preference for predawn start times for his surgeries, she usually went after her shift was over rather than before.

The Monday night workouts were more social than challenging, but she figured taking it easy once a week wasn't going to kill her.

Once she reached the cafeteria, she settled at a back table. It was too early for most people to be eating dinner, and the floor nurses were right in the middle of shift change, so she practically had the place to herself. All the easier to think, she told herself, which was handy, as she had a lot on her mind.

Ignoring Molly's plight, about which she could do nothing, there was still her own life to deal with. Her friends would want an update on Clark, and they weren't going to like what she told them. Sadly, they would all be more upset than she was. For her part, she would be thinking about Bernie's request. She'd thought of little else in the past twenty-four hours.

Zennie had decided not to do any research—not right away. She wanted to let the idea sit for a few days, to see how it felt. Her instinct had been to call Bernie as soon as she got home and say of course she would be her surrogate, but she'd stopped herself. This was a big decision and she needed to be both prepared and informed.

She remembered how scared she'd been when her best friend had first been diagnosed with cancer. How she'd wanted to help and, despite her medical training, there'd been exactly nothing she could do. Driving Bernie to chemo, stocking the refrigerator and cleaning her house had been insignificant things. She couldn't cure her friend or stop the vomiting or give her hair or promise her a long, happy life. That sense of being useless had depressed her, although she'd done her best not to show it. Now there was a tangible act she could perform. Saying no didn't feel like an option.

Still, Zennie knew she had to make a thoughtful decision. Having a baby would change things for her. Being pregnant would impact her body and her life.

She grabbed her backpack and walked to the stairs. She went up to the sixth floor, past the nurses' station to the nursery.

Ten babies lay swaddled in pink or blue blankets, tiny heads covered with delicate caps. Several visitors stood together, pointing and talking, some laughing, others giving in to joyful tears.

Zennie had never been a baby person. Her mother's pleas to make her a grandmother fell on deaf ears. But now, staring at the newborns, she tried to imagine what it would be like to desperately want children and know you could never give birth to your own. It was an emptiness that would never go away, she thought sadly.

She closed her eyes and remembered how easily she and Bernie had become friends, how they'd gotten through college together. She remembered Bernie's mom dropping off food for them at the dorm and sunny afternoons she and Bernie had spent at the beach. She thought of the laughter and the cramming for tests and the nights they'd stayed up for hours talking about life after they graduated. She remembered meeting Hayes and knowing the second he smiled at Bernie that he was the one. She remembered their wedding, and the terror when Bernie had told her she had cancer.

She would do her research, Zennie promised herself. Because it was the right thing to do. But unless she discovered something totally awful, there was no way she could turn down her friend. She loved Bernie and she would do anything for her, especially if it gave her her heart's desire.

Vistaprint came through with flying colors, Ali thought as she opened the box delivered on time and in perfect condition. She'd had the wedding cancellation cards shipped to her work location so she could get started on spreading the not-so-joyful news.

She stared at the postcards. The font was nice, she thought, trying to find something to like in the simple graphic and carefully worded message. Nowhere did she call Glen an asshole or indicate his dick was inadequate. She'd taken the high road and one day she would be happy about that. One day she would be proud of herself for being mature and selfless. Until then, she was going to think about how much she hated him because that was easier than being humiliated every second of every day.

The hate was actually really interesting, she thought as she pulled out a stack of cards. It chased away all the good feelings she'd ever had about him. She knew she was still in shock but honestly she wasn't missing him as much as she would have thought. Of course having to cancel a wedding might have something to do with that. It was difficult to feel all warm and fuzzy when she was negotiating with an angry caterer.

Ali put the box of cards in her locker, other than the stack on her desk to distribute before she left for the day, then went to see her boss. Outside of family and Daniel, Paul would be the first to know. His reaction would give her an idea of what to expect.

Paul Battle was a grizzled old guy with curly hair and a perpetual frown. He was gruff, demanding and more than a little intimidating. Ali had been terrified of him for nearly a year until she'd suffered through a stint working at the customer service counter. The company did most of their business through internet orders but there were a handful of local customers who came in personally.

Ali had been on her second day of filling in for a guy on vacation and she'd been having trouble figuring out how to process a return. The customer had started screaming at her, calling her stupid and yelling for a manager.

Paul had intervened, glowering at them both. Before Ali could explain the situation, the customer had lit into them both, calling her names and demanding she be fired. Paul had looked at her, then at the customer before telling the guy that this was his fault. He was the moron who had ordered the wrong part to begin with. And if he didn't like being called names, he should stop doing it to other people. Ali was good at her job and filling in with little notice and minimal training. He'd said for the other guy to act like a human being or shop elsewhere.

Ali still remembered how stunned she'd been by Paul's complete defense. When she'd tried to thank him later, he'd brushed off her comment, muttering she did a good job and he wanted to see her advance in the company.

Now, as she approached his office, she tried to figure out what to say and how to say it. When she knocked on his half-open door, she was still clueless, so she walked in when invited and handed him the postcard.

"I wanted you to know," she said as he began to read.

Paul scanned the postcard, turned it over, then looked at her. "He ended things?" he asked.

The question was unexpected, but she nodded. "I don't know why. He won't talk to me."

"Let it go. He's not worth it. He was never going to make you happy."

"Why would you say that?"

Paul shrugged. "Just something about him. You okay?"

"I'm dealing." She stared at him. "You're not surprised, are you?"

"No, but I'm sorry. You should still take off the vacation week you had planned. You know, to get over him."

She had the time coming so why not? Wedding or not, she would be moving and could use the week to get settled.

"I will." She pointed to the card. "I'm going to slip one of those into all the lockers before I leave. I'll deal with the questions tomorrow."

"Good idea. I really am sorry, Ali. Glen's an idiot. You'll find the right guy someday."

She smiled and left his office. When she was back at her desk, she tried not to read too much into his use of the word *someday*. As if the prospect of her finding anyone was possible but unlikely.

The rest of the afternoon passed quickly. She got a text from her father saying he'd heard what had happened and was sorry. A text, she thought grimly. God forbid he should pick up the phone and call. She felt herself battling crabby and hurt in equal measures and knew it was just a matter of time until she snapped.

On the drive home she mentally went through the to-do list she had to plow through that evening. Daniel had told her he would be by to discuss how canceling the photographer had gone. Honestly, if he'd done a halfway decent job and was willing, she was going to give him more to do. Her workload had just increased, what with her having to find somewhere to live.

She pulled into her parking space. Before she could collect her bag and the box of postcards, Daniel was opening her car door.

"How's it going?" he asked, his voice both caring and upbeat.

At the sight of him, she relaxed. Whatever crap was going on, she knew she could count on him to help. He wasn't going to say anything stupid or hurt her feelings or tell her to get back together with Glen.

Unfortunately relaxing her body led to relaxing the tight control she'd been keeping on her emotions. Before she knew what was happening, she was out of her car, throwing herself into his arms and bursting into tears.

"Everything's a *mess*," she sobbed, clinging to him. "I can't believe it. My boss wasn't even surprised, my dad texted me to say he was sorry instead of calling, my mother wants me to use the free time I supposedly have to help her go through her house, I've lost my apartment and Glen sent me a check for *five hundred dollars*! Like that will do anything. I keep thinking I've hit bottom, but I haven't. It's only getting worse."

Daniel held on to her, rubbing her back as she gave in to those ugly choking sobs that always ended in hiccups. By the time she stepped back, she was pretty sure she looked just as bad as she felt—all blotchy and puffy and damp.

She sniffed and wiped her face with her hands, then reached for her handbag and the Vistaprint box.

"I'm not usually so emotional," she said, knowing she sounded defensive and embarrassed. "I want you to know I generally keep myself together."

"Ali, don't waste time explaining all that to me. I know you're a very capable, smart, caring person. Your only flaw was falling for my brother."

"You can't know that," she told him. "Before Glen dumped me, I barely ever saw you and when we were together at family functions, we didn't talk."

"I know."

He took the box from her, then put his arm around her as they walked to her apartment. Once they were inside, he pushed her toward the bathroom.

"Go wash your face or take a shower or whatever you'd like to feel better. I'm going to go grab some Chinese food for dinner. We'll eat and we'll plan and by the time we're done, we'll have it all figured out."

She doubted that, but appreciated his optimism.

"I know you're doing this out of guilt because of Glen, but I want you to know that I really appreciate you taking care of me," she told him. "You are the best guy ever. I mean ever. I couldn't have gotten this far without you."

He shoved his hands into his jeans' front pockets. "Yeah, I'm not feeling that much Glen guilt. I think he's an idiot, but that's his problem. I'm helping because I want to."

For a second, she would have sworn he was going to say more, but instead he flashed her that sexy smile of his.

"Anything I should steer clear of when I order the food?" he asked.

"I like all the usual stuff. Oh, lo mein instead of rice for me, please." She grinned. "It heats up better for lunch. The rice can dry out."

"A lady with a plan. I like it."

Twenty minutes later she had showered and put on her favorite cropped jeans and the Dodgers T-shirt Daniel had bought her. She hadn't bothered to blow out her hair, letting it dry curly. She'd always been so careful to do her hair because Glen liked it straight. Maybe this weekend, she would take a few minutes and put on makeup. She could use her favorite black eyeliner and do that little cat eye thing she'd always thought was cute and sexy. Glen had hated that, too.

While she was de-Glenning her life, she should get rid of all the button-down shirts she'd bought because he said they were more attractive than the T-shirts and sweaters she favored. Ali had always thought the button-down shirts looked awful on her body type. She was too busty and curvy and they always bunched on her. And the loafers, she thought, walking barefoot to the kitchen. She actually owned *loafers* because of a man. Just as soon as she got her financial house in order, she was going to go buy the funkiest sneakers she could find and wear them proudly.

She went into the kitchen and set the table. Once she'd put out plates and flatware, she got her tote bag and the files she carried with her. Planning the wedding required organization and scheduling. Unplanning was much the same, only in reverse. This weekend she wanted to make up a master spreadsheet so that nothing was missed.

Daniel returned with a bag of Chinese takeout in one hand and a six-pack of beer in the other. He held up the beer.

"I took a chance on this," he said. "If you'd prefer wine…"

"Beer is so what you drink with Chinese food," she said with a laugh. "Everyone knows that."

He set out two beers and put the rest in the refrigerator. She looked in the bag and then back at him.

"There's food for twenty in here."

"You said you'd take it for lunch. I wanted there to be enough."

How much did he think she ate in a day? Not that it mattered. She grinned. "I'll make up a lunch for you, too," she told him. "You'll see what I mean about the lo mein."

She started to set out cartons of food. He'd bought kung pao chicken, Mongolian beef, honey shrimp, combination lo mein and combination fried rice, crab wontons, BBQ spare ribs and crispy green beans. By the time the bag was empty, Ali was laughing.

"You went a little crazy."

"I wanted to make sure you had something you liked."

"I could eat all of it." She put the carton of lo mein in the refrigerator. "We can have this tomorrow and eat the rice tonight."

He sat across from her and they began opening cartons and dishing up food. "How did it go with the photographer?" she asked.

"You should have an emailed cancellation confirmation waiting for you. There's no cancellation fee and you'll be getting back half your deposit."

She felt her eyes widen. "Are you serious?"

"Very. The guy told me he had at least three other events that want him that night. It was no big deal."

It was to her. The deposit had been a thousand dollars. Getting half of that back doubled Glen's measly check.

"You're amazing."

Daniel winked. "Yeah, that never gets old. You have any other vendors I can call?"

"I do. The flowers for sure. Oh, and the limos and the DJ." She winced. "Is that too much?"

"No. I'll get the contact information before I leave tonight and take care of it first thing tomorrow. I also want you to give me the file with all the addresses. I'll get your postcards labeled and mailed."

"You can't possibly do all that."

"Yeah, well, I won't be doing the postcards myself. I have office staff who will put on the labels and the postage."

"I don't care if you're exploiting your employees, you're really saving me."

His gaze was steady as they spoke. He was nothing like she'd thought. For some reason every time she'd met Daniel before, she'd assumed he didn't like her or disapproved of her, but that wasn't him, at all. He was a kind, dependable guy who gave great hugs and overbought Chinese food. Talk about a miracle.

"Did Glen really send you five hundred dollars?" he asked.

Her good mood popped like a balloon. "He did. He's such a jerk. Why didn't I see that before? Did everyone know but me? Has he always been hideous or did I bring out the worst in him? I wish I could—"

She stopped talking and glanced at Daniel. "Sorry."

"What?"

"You're Glen's brother."

"Not an issue. To answer the question, he's always been a jerk, but this is the worst thing he's done. A close second was threatening to take me to court over our uncle's will."

"I don't know anything about that." She picked up her beer bottle. "Tell me."

"My dad's older brother John was a rebel. He raced motorcycles and disappeared for months at a time. No one knew where he went or what he did." He looked at her. "All this was before I was born. Apparently he was a legend in the family. So one time he came back with a lot of money. Like a couple hundred thousand dollars. In cash."

"Where did he get it?"

"No one knows. He bought some land in Sunland and put in a motocross track. The sport was just getting going then. By the time I was seven, he had added a couple more tracks and the concession stands."

"Your empire," she teased.

"I like it." He grabbed a rib. "My dad took Glen to try out the bikes when he was nine. I remember being really upset because my mom said I had to wait until I was his age to ride a bike. Glen went a couple of times and hated it. I begged and begged and my mom finally relented when I turned eight. My uncle set me on my bike and I was hooked."

"When Glen first told me who you were, I looked you up,"

she admitted. "You've won a lot of championships. You were a big deal."

His mouth turned up at the corner. "I like to think I still am."

She rolled her eyes. "You know what I mean."

"Yes, I do. I worked hard and I had some breaks."

More than that, she thought. The motocross circuit was grueling, with twelve races over four months. The racers crisscrossed the country with as little as a week between some races. Not much time for bodies to heal and equipment to be repaired.

In addition to being physically fit and skilled enough to compete, the riders had to have sponsors. The bikes and gear weren't cheap, nor were entry fees or transportation. Daniel had been on top for three years before walking away a winner.

"What made you give it up?" she asked.

"I knew the odds of something going wrong. I meant what I said—I was lucky. There were pileups that I avoided and even when I couldn't, I managed to walk away. But eventually everyone has a bad crash and I didn't want to stick around for mine. It's a young man's game."

She wanted to joke that he wasn't that old now, but she knew what he meant. Every professional athlete paid a physical price for being the best. Motocross was no different.

"Back to my uncle," he said. "I was in my last year of racing and talked to him about buying into the business. I had plans to expand what he was doing, and we were both excited about that." Daniel's expression sobered. "He had a massive stroke and died in his sleep. No one saw it coming and we were all devastated."

"You especially," she said quietly. "I'm sorry."

"Thanks. Me, too. I still miss him. He was a great guy. He believed in me from the first. Anyway, he left me pretty much everything. Glen got a hundred thousand dollars, but that was it. He was pissed because he thought we should have both been left half. He threatened to sue the estate."

"But he'd never had anything to do with the business. You'd been involved since you were eight."

"He didn't see it that way. He ended up not suing, though. I suspect a couple of lawyers told him he didn't have a case."

She groaned. "I can't believe I was so incredibly stupid as to think he was a decent human being." She scooped up more shrimp. "I know what it was—I felt like he saw me, which probably doesn't make sense to you. You've never been invisible, but trust me, it's not fun. Even with my parents. Finola is my mom's favorite and Zennie is so my dad's. That left me with exactly zero parents. I'm not trying to say poor me or anything like that, but when I met Glen, he seemed to be really interested in me. I guess I was wrong about that."

"Whatever happened in your relationship isn't your fault. It's all on him."

"While I'd like that to be true, we both know that in any relationship, both parties are to blame."

"That's pretty rational for less than a week into the breakup."

She sighed. "I know and in a way, it's really sad. I mean if I can think that clearly, doesn't it mean that I was a whole lot less in love with him than I thought? In some ways that's worse. I should still be crushed and hysterical, but I'm not."

He glanced at her quizzically. "I didn't know you had curly hair."

"Oh." She touched the now-dry curls. "I usually blow it out straight."

"Why? The curls look great on you."

"Thank you. Glen didn't like them."

Rather than comment on that, Daniel rose and walked to the refrigerator. "Another beer?"

"Yes, please." When he was seated, she said, "I appreciate you not judging me for being so stupid about your brother."

"I can't explain Glen, but I do know he's going to be sorry he lost you."

"I can only hope," she said lightly. "Now let's see... I've whined about my family, my ex-fiancé and pretty much everything else. I'm going to be done now. Let's talk about happy things."

"You mentioned you had to move. What's up with that?"

"Not a happy topic."

He waited.

"Fine," she grumbled and explained about the lease. "I'm looking for something now. It's just I need it so fast. No way I'm moving in with my mom. When Finola gets back from Hawaii I might ask if I can crash in her guest room for a few weeks while I get it all together. Don't worry, I'll figure it out, I swear."

Daniel studied her for a second, then nodded. "I know you will. Now about those happy topics, I bought us tickets to another Dodgers game."

"You did? Yay! I can't wait. I had such a good time."

"Me, too."

His gaze locked with hers and for a brief second, she would have sworn she felt something. Not heat, exactly, but something unexpected, like a pretingle.

Stop, she told herself sternly. *Just stop.* Daniel was being the world's nicest guy when he didn't have to do anything. He'd saved her. The last thing she was going to do was turn weird and get some kind of inappropriate crush on him. He would be embarrassed, she would be humiliated and it was a terrible way to thank him for all he'd done. No, she would be a good friend who didn't take advantage of him. As for the almost-tingles, well, no doubt they were the result of too much Chinese food. In the morning she would be completely fine.

Chapter Eight

Cheetos stains were difficult to remove. Finola had never had to learn that before, what with rarely eating carbs, but in the past few days she'd let go of alcohol and had moved on to Cheetos. Cheetos and potato chips with ranch dip and, embarrassingly enough, a box of instant mashed potatoes. She felt bloated and a little nauseous and worried when she realized there were orange fingerprints all through the downstairs.

After spray cleaner and a sponge had done little, she'd found one of those white eraser things and it had done an excellent job on everything but her laptop, where she'd spent hours looking at funny baby videos while sobbing for the child she and Nigel would never have, and eating Cheetos.

Under normal circumstances, she would have left the stains for the cleaning service that would start up again next week, only these circumstances weren't normal.

Nigel had texted to say he was back from the Bahamas and

wanted to come by. She'd read his words a dozen times, trying to find hidden meaning in the brief message. Was he coming by to pick up something? To talk to her? To beg her to reconcile? She had a feeling it wasn't the latter, but she couldn't help hoping for the best.

To that end, she showered and washed her hair, using a scented body wash Nigel liked. While she dried her hair, she applied a plumping eye mask under her eyes, then put on just enough makeup to look fresh.

What to wear required thought. She wanted to look fabulous without appearing to have actually tried. She pulled on jeans and a tank top, then a loose weave sweater that always fell off one shoulder. Flat sandals completed the outfit. She knew she looked good, at least for her. When compared with the twentysomething Treasure, she was less sure.

She went downstairs to wait for Nigel. Emotions chased each other through her stomach. She tried to hang on to righteous anger and indignation—they would give her strength. Unfortunately loneliness and hurt were right there beside their friends and threatened to take her down.

She tried to relax on the sofa, then got up and paced. She was just about to retreat to her office where she could at least pretend to be busy on her laptop when she heard Nigel at the front door. He turned the handle and walked into their living room.

Her heart jumped in her chest, a happy bounce filled with love and hope. He looked good. Nigel was tall and lean, with curly brown hair and hazel eyes. Normally he looked slightly harried and tired but today he was tan and relaxed. At least until he saw her.

"Oh, you're here."

Her happy heart deflated. "What do you mean? You said you wanted to talk."

"No, I said I wanted to come by." He looked away. "I'm sorry. I should have been more clear."

There was something in his tone, she thought in dismay. As if she were an unwelcome inconvenience. Not that an inconvenience was ever welcome, but how could he sound like that? She was his wife!

She half turned away, then forced herself to stare him down. He wore khakis and a Hawaiian shirt she'd never seen before. Despite his obvious discomfort, there was a contentment about him, no doubt brought on by sex with Treasure.

She squared her shoulders. "This is my house, Nigel. Where else would I be? Oh, wait, I know. Hawaii with my husband. Hmm, what happened there?"

Nigel had never handled guilt well. She waited for him to shift uneasily and then start talking. She found herself anticipating the apology and told herself no matter what, she would wait before she begged him to come back to her.

"Do we have to discuss this now?" he asked.

"Why yes, we do." She walked toward him. "I think our marriage is worth a few minutes of our time."

He was being a jerk on purpose, she told herself. Trying to rile her so she would lash out and he could play the victim. He wanted to distract her so he wasn't the bad guy. Well, he could try, but that wasn't going to happen. He'd betrayed her. Betrayed *them*. He'd let her face his mistress on her own, *on live television*. He'd never warned her, never even hinted about what was going to happen.

"I'm sorry about what happened," he said.

Before she could go off on a rant he more than deserved, he added, "But I really just wanted to get my ski stuff."

His statement was so at odds with what she was thinking that she had trouble processing the meaning.

"It's almost summer."

He sighed heavily. "Yes, Finola. It's summer here, in the northern hemisphere. In the southern hemisphere, it's nearly winter and there's good skiing. We're going to Valle Nevado in Tres Valles, Chile."

He glanced toward the garage, where his ski equipment was stored, then back at her.

"I suppose you're right. We should talk."

"Talk?" she asked, feeling anger burning inside of her. "No, Nigel, I don't want to talk. I want you drawn and quartered. I want you suffering in every way possible. How could you do this? It's one thing to have an affair. That's its own pool of slime, but what you did to me last Friday was inhuman."

"Don't you think that's a little dramatic?"

"No, I don't. You announced you were having an affair right before I was going on live television. As if that wasn't bad enough, you didn't have the balls to tell me your mistress was my first guest."

His eyes widened. "She told you?"

"Of course she told me. Why do you think she booked the show in the first place? It certainly wasn't for the exposure. She told me and left me hanging there, not knowing if she was about to announce it to the world on my show!"

He had the grace to look chagrined. "I didn't know that. I didn't think she would..."

"You suspected it, otherwise why tell me about the affair?"

His shoulders slumped a little, as if the guilt was starting to get to him.

"I can't believe you did this. I can't believe you abandoned our marriage. What were you thinking?"

He straightened and glared at her. "I was thinking that you walked out on us a long time ago. You're all about your career. Nothing else matters, certainly not me. You put off having kids for five years. Five. Every year we'd talk about it and you said it wasn't a good time. Well, I got tired of waiting."

"Poor you. Is Treasure going to give you children? I don't think so. This is just like you, blaming me for what you did.

You've always done that. I never cheated, I never moved out, but hey, sure, make me the bad guy."

"I had to do this, Finola. I didn't have a choice."

"There's always a choice."

His tone gentled. "No, there isn't. I wasn't looking for anyone. I've never done this before. I was doing consults and she came in with a girlfriend who had a botched nose job. The second I saw her, it was electric. I can't explain it, but one minute everything was ordinary and the next, it wasn't."

Each word stabbed her, going so deep she didn't know how she stayed standing. There was too much pain, too much of her love for him pouring out until she knew she would die. She had to—no one could survive this.

"So that's it?" she managed, pressing her hand to her midsection to physically hold herself intact. "We're through?"

"I don't know. I honest to God don't know." He looked at her. "I have to be with her. I'm sorry if that hurts you but that's where I am. I hope you can understand."

Understand his affair? Understand how magical it was? "I don't want to understand, you asshole. I don't care how great things are. You are destroying us. We are never going to be able to put the pieces back together. Don't you see that?"

"I see I've hurt you and that was never what I wanted. I wish…"

"What? Oh dear God, don't you dare say you wish you could have us both. Don't be that much of a jackass."

She wanted to scream at him. She wanted to stab him and beat him and most of all, worst of all, she wanted to beg him to not want Treasure anymore.

She hated him and loved him and hated herself for her weakness. She knew, no matter what, she couldn't give in to it. She couldn't say the words because if she begged, she would never be able to recover.

"Treasure has a reputation for using up her lovers and tossing them aside," she said instead. "Have you considered that?"

"I have, but it will be different this time."

For the first time since hearing the news, Finola's smile was genuine. "Is that what you think? That you're her one true love and you'll be together forever? She's what, fifteen years younger than you, and one of the most famous women in the world. She has a thing for married men. I'm sorry to break it to you, but you are just one of many."

"You don't know what it's like with her."

"Maybe not, but I'm familiar with Treasure's type. I have loved you for a long time, Nigel, but make no mistake, you're not going to win her heart. Not the way you think."

Her brief moment of humor and bravado faded, leaving her bleeding once again. She felt old and used and more tired than she'd ever been in her life. There was nothing to be done here, she thought grimly. Better to just have him gone.

"Take your ski trip and enjoy your pop singer. When things go bad just remember the price you've paid. When she's done with you and you want to come home, it's going to be too late. In the end, you will have lost everything and all for a piece of ass."

"Don't call her that."

His defense of Treasure was yet another slap. As the words hit her, Finola realized she had nothing left. No way to convince him, no actions to show him. It was as if all the years of their marriage had never been. Nigel was on a romance high and until he crashed, he wasn't the least bit interested in them or her or what they'd had together. Their joint life was nothing but something he had to escape.

She pointed to the garage. "Get your crap and get out."

He started to speak, only to shake his head and walk away. She went into her office where she looked up a locksmith online and called.

"Yes, I need to get all my locks changed. Today, if possible. Four o'clock is great. Yes, I'll be here."

She gave her address and hung up. It was a small gesture, but at least it was something. She felt shattered and vulnerable, but despite how much she hurt, she wasn't going to die. Not even if she wanted to, which meant she had to take one step, then another. She'd never given up on anything in her life. She sure as hell wasn't giving up on herself.

Zennie parked in front of the house and pulled out her phone. The text from her mother, sent to all three sisters, reminded them of the meeting they all had Friday afternoon to talk about how they were going to help her go through the house. Finola was still in Hawaii and was excused, but the rest of them were expected to be there, and on time.

"The rest of us?" Zennie asked out loud. "That would be Ali and me. You could actually use our names, Mom."

But that thought was for herself. She dutifully texted back that she would be there, then turned off her car and walked up to the house.

Bernie opened the door before she could knock. The two friends looked at each other before Bernie said, "I know this is awkward. I want to make it clear that whatever you've decided, you'll always be my best friend. If the answer's no, I'll never bring it up again and we'll go on as we were, I swear."

She stepped back. "Come on in. Hayes is in the living room."

The two-story house was typical for the neighborhood— twenty-eight hundred square feet, four bedrooms, with a formal dining room and a great room. About fifteen years before, an old shopping center had been torn down and houses put in its place. There were wide sidewalks, a playground and access to a desirable school system.

Bernie and Hayes had bought the house right before their wedding and had been so excited to move in. Over the past few years, they'd done some updating and had turned the tract home into their own.

Bernie led the way to the small formal living room. Hayes stood when they entered. He looked nervous, Zennie thought. They both did.

Zennie perched on one of the wingback chairs while Bernie and Hayes sat next to each other on the small sofa. The room was completely silent.

Zennie thought about the few minutes she'd spent online, looking up the basics of the procedure. She figured pregnant was pregnant and she would learn about that as she went. She was healthy, fit and she loved her friend. The decision had been an easy one.

Zennie smiled at them. "I want to do it. I want to be your surrogate."

Bernie reached for Hayes's hand. "But? Is there a but?"

"There's no but. I talked to a friend of mine who works for an ob/gyn and she said it's a relatively simple procedure. I already have an appointment with my gynecologist to check blood work and have a physical. Once we know everything is fine, we wait for me to ovulate. When that happens, Hayes, um, provides us with his sample, then it's inserted into me and we wait to find out if I'm pregnant."

She smiled. "I've contacted my HR department and they're sending over information on what's covered through my health insurance. My paid leave is six weeks, which should be plenty." She paused. "I think that's all I have now. So if you two still want to do this, I'm in."

Bernie and Hayes looked at each other, then Bernie ran over and pulled Zennie to her feet. "Thank you," she breathed as they hugged. "Thank you, thank you, thank you."

Zennie hugged her back, then looked from her friend to Hayes. "I'm happy to do it. I just need you to be clear on one thing."

Hayes and Bernie exchanged another look.

"What?" Hayes asked, sounding worried.

Zennie moved next to Hayes. They were both blondes. He had hazel eyes while hers were blue, but their coloring was the same.

Zennie shrugged. "You've got to be okay with getting a white baby. I want to say we could be hoping for a very pale olive skin tone, but it seems unlikely given what we're working with here."

Bernie burst out laughing and rushed over to hug them both. "I have a white husband and best friend. I can deal with a white baby."

Hayes pulled her close and kissed her. "Good to know. If we move to a nicer neighborhood, everyone will assume I'm sleeping with the nanny. It's kind of sexy."

Zennie was glad they were keeping things light, but she'd wanted to bring up the race thing. Bernie wasn't going to look like her child and that needed to be okay.

She and Bernie sat together on the sofa while Hayes ducked out.

"Are you sure?" Bernie asked.

Zennie grabbed her hand. "Look into my eyes as I say this. I want to be your surrogate. Nothing would make me happier. Once we start the process, you have to promise you'll never ask me that question again. Got it?"

"I swear."

Hayes returned with a folder. "We've drawn up a contract. You'll want to read it and have a lawyer go over it. Basically it says we'll pay every expense you have. Everything from deductibles to prenatal vitamins."

"Which you need to start taking," Bernie said with a smile.

"We'll cover your salary if you need more time after delivery," Hayes added. "We're also taking out an insurance policy on you so if something happens and you can't go back to work, you'll get two million dollars."

"That seems excessive," Zennie murmured, slightly overwhelmed by what was happening. She reminded herself that she'd only been thinking about this for a few days while they'd been planning it for months.

"It's just in case," he told her. "We've also made arrangements to have the baby given up for adoption, if we die while you're pregnant. We've researched different agencies and have found the one we think is best."

"We're not going to die," Bernie assured her. "But if the worst happens, you're covered."

Zennie hadn't considered the possibility that something could happen to them, leaving her with a baby.

"This is a lot," she admitted.

"It's overwhelming," Bernie told her. "That's why we wrote it all down and want you to read everything before you make your final decision. You can still back out. It's perfectly okay."

"I'm not backing out. I will look everything over, as you said, then we'll move forward with the pregnancy." Zennie had made up her mind—she was sure. The details were intimidating, but once they got through this initial part, everything would be easier.

"Then we're doing this?" Bernie asked.

"We are. Now let's go out to dinner and celebrate."

Hayes looked at his wife. "I made reservations at that great vegan place you like." He turned to Zennie. "The food is great and now that you're going to be eating for two, every bite counts."

Oh, goodie, Zennie thought as she smiled. *Vegan for dinner.* And based on the fact that she'd just agreed to get pregnant, there wasn't going to be any wine to wash it down.

Chapter Nine

By Friday Finola couldn't stand her own company anymore. The disastrous conversation with Nigel had meant a sleepless night. She was tired, heartsick, emotionally battered and mentally lost. She needed to be around people who cared about her. She needed sympathy and hugs.

Based on the text loop with her mother and her sisters, she knew everyone would be at her mom's house after work today to come up with a plan to go through the house, sorting years' worth of memories and junk so the place could be sold.

Finola didn't want to feel this awful, she thought as she drove from Sherman Oaks to Burbank. She didn't want to be in pain or face the humiliation. She wanted her old life back with her great husband and her plan to get pregnant. Why couldn't she have that?

"I can't have that because my jerk of a husband can't keep

his dick in his pants," she yelled while she waited at a stoplight. "Damn you, Nigel!"

She ranted the entire drive, then pulled up in front of the house where she'd spent much of her childhood. Zennie's and Ali's cars were already in the driveway. The whole gang was there.

Finola paused before getting out of her car. She had to be strong. She had to hold herself together. It was one thing to get some sympathy, it was another to scare her family with her overwhelming sadness and anger. She could lose it, but only if she stayed on this side of normal.

She let herself inside and listened to the sound of voices coming from the kitchen. No doubt they were having an organizational meeting before they got to work. After dropping her bag on the small table by the front door, she called out, "Hi, everyone. It's me."

"What?" Mary Jo cried. "Finola, darling, is that really you?"

All three of them hurried through the living room. Ali reached her first and hugged her.

"What are you doing here?" Ali asked. "I thought you were in Hawaii until tomorrow night. Did I have that wrong? I'm so happy to see you. Did you have an amazing time?"

Her mother pushed Ali aside and reached for Finola. "You're not tan at all. Good girl. You're using sunscreen. When did you get back?"

Zennie simply waved. "Hey."

"Hey, back."

Finola looked at the three members of her family. She knew she could trust them with her broken heart, that they would be there for her and take care of her. She let her grip on her self-control slip a little and tears instantly filled her eyes.

"Nigel left me."

"What? No!"

"That's impossible. He adores you."

"Are you okay? What happened?"

The questions flew around her. Finola covered her face with her hands and started to sob. She was led through the house to the kitchen where someone helped her into a chair. A box of tissues appeared in front of her. Mary Jo and Ali sat on either side of her while Zennie boiled water for tea. Her mother kept rubbing her back.

"Tell us what happened," she said, her voice gentle. "Once we know what's wrong, we can help you fix it."

"There's nothing to fix." Finola grabbed a handful of tissues. After wiping her face, she blew her nose. "You can't tell anyone. No one can know. I mean it. You can't tell anyone, no matter what. If this gets out, I'll be ruined."

It was going to get out, she thought grimly. It was just a matter of time.

"Of course we won't say anything," Ali assured her. "But, Finola, Nigel couldn't have left you. He loves you. We can all see it, every time he looks at you."

"I wish that were true, but it's not. He's having an affair."

"With who?" her mother asked. "What bitch did this? Was it someone at his office? It's always the young receptionist."

"Mom, don't," Zennie said from the stove.

"You don't know it wasn't her."

"You don't know it was."

Finola took Ali's hand and laced their fingers together. She and her sister had always been close. Ali would give her strength.

"He told me last Friday, right before the show."

"I knew it!" her mother crowed. "You said it was food poisoning but I knew you were off for another reason."

Finola told them what had happened. She started with Nigel's blunt declaration and ended with Nigel's visit the previous day.

"They've gone to Chile to ski," she said, still crying. "I don't think he's coming back. I think it's over."

"It's not over," Ali said soothingly. "I can't believe he would do this. Maybe he hit his head or something because we all know he loves you."

"I'm never getting grandchildren," Mary Jo complained.

"Mom!" Ali and Zennie said together.

"You're not helping," Zennie added, setting a mug of tea in front of Finola.

"I wish he'd hit his head, but he hasn't," she said, releasing Ali and taking the mug in both hands. "He says it's my fault he cheated."

"What? No." Zennie sat down across from her. "That's crazy. You're way too good to him. You spoil him."

"It's important to spoil a man," her mom said, looking point-edly at Zennie. "Something you would know if you ever stayed in a relationship more than fifteen minutes."

Finola sniffed. "What happened?"

"Nothing," Zennie said, glaring at their mother. "Clark and I broke up, but we were hardly dating. It's no big deal."

Mary Jo sighed. "What a horrible week. First Zennie, then Finola, then—" She jumped, as if someone had kicked her.

"Not now," Ali said quickly, glaring at her mother. "This is more important."

Finola knew there was something going on, but honestly, she just couldn't find it in herself to care about anything but her own pain.

"You don't deserve this," Ali continued, turning back to Finola. "You were always so careful. You knew you wanted a career, so you never played around with guys. You barely dated in college because you didn't want to be distracted. You chose Nigel. Doesn't he know what he has in you? You're perfect."

Finola basked in the warm praise even as she knew her sister wasn't right about any of it. At least not the perfect part. She *had* been careful in college, not wanting to get tied down. It was easier not to date than to risk falling in love. When she'd met Nigel, she'd known right away he was the one, and he'd felt the same way about her. Everything had been so easy with him, she thought, fighting new tears. So wonderful. They'd been good together.

She'd warned him her mother could be difficult, so the first time she'd brought Nigel to this house, he'd been charming and attentive to Mary Jo, winning her over when no other guy ever had. He'd been sweet to Ali and Zennie, remembering all the birthdays and helping her buy presents. How could he have changed so much?

"I just don't know what to do," she whispered. "It's going to come out. If he was dating a regular person, no one would really care, but this is Treasure. The press follows her every move. They know she has a thing for married men and they always go after the wife. Most people get to suffer through an affair in private, but not when Treasure's involved."

She thought about her show and her viewers and how they were all going to judge her. At some point she would have to tell her producers and Rochelle. She shuddered, thinking of the humiliation and how people would pity her.

"You can stay here if you want," her mother offered. "In your old room. It's all still there." Mary Jo put an arm around her. "No one will find you here. You'll be safe."

"Thanks, Mom. I might take you up on that."

Not this second, but if she had to, at least she had a refuge.

Ali started to say something, then stopped. She patted Finola's arm. "We're all here for you, no matter what. I even know someone who probably knows a guy who can beat him up."

Mary Jo glanced at her. "Who would you know?"

"Daniel, Glen's brother. I suspect he has some interesting friends. Or maybe he'd just do it himself."

While Finola wanted Nigel bleeding and in pain, she didn't think hiring someone was a smart move. At least not today. "Thanks. I'll think about it."

"I'm really sorry," Zennie said from the other side of the table. "He's such an asshole."

"Tell me about it."

"I know what will take our minds off everything," Mary Jo said cheerfully. "Let's start with the junk room. It's a big mess. We'll each take a side and be done in no time."

"Zennie and I will tackle the closet," Ali said. "Finola, do you feel up to it?"

"Of course. I could use a distraction." Anything was better than being home alone where she alternated between trying to figure out a plan to win Nigel back and wondering if she could find a few anthrax spores to send him in the mail.

They went upstairs to the bonus room. It was long and narrow, with a peaked roof and one small window at the far end. Shelves lined the two long walls, and there was a huge craft table under the window. Right by the stairs was a massive walk-in closet with more shelving.

Finola looked at all the boxes and bins, the stacks of fabric and grocery bags filled with who-knows-what and knew there was no way they could get through all this.

A distraction, she told herself. She was here for that and nothing more. Mindless sorting would help.

She and her mother started on the shelves, while Zennie and Ali tackled the closet. Finola reached for a couple of small bins and set them down. She opened the first one and stared inside.

"Fabric scraps?"

"From my quilting projects," Mary Jo said. "I just couldn't get inspired. Maybe if I'd had grandchildren."

"Mom!" Ali and Zennie said together.

"You're not helping," Zennie added.

"It's not my fault," Mary Jo complained. "At least one of you should have popped out a baby by now. Speaking of not being in a relationship and giving your mother the only thing she's ever wanted, Zennie, I'm setting you up on a blind date. I'll text you the details."

Finola turned toward the closet. "Won't you need time to get over your breakup?"

"We'd only gone out a few times. It's not a breakup."

"It is to me," her mother muttered. "Finola, be a dear and go into the garage and bring back a couple of boxes. We'll put what I'm giving away in one box and trash in the other. Things I'm taking with me can stay on the shelves."

Finola did as she was asked. By the time she was back with the boxes she saw that Zennie and Ali had found the family's Christmas village. The sight of it reminded her of many holidays, when each of the girls had been allowed to add to the village. There wasn't a master plan and they each liked different styles, so their village was a hodgepodge of Victorian and modern, ceramic and wood. There were three pet stores and at least five churches. Lots of trees and lampposts and a big carousel Finola had picked for her sixth Christmas.

She touched the beautiful carved horses, remembering how much she had loved it. The carousel could be wound so it moved and played music. Since the divorce, Mary Jo hadn't bothered decorating much for the holidays, but she'd also refused to give anything to her daughters. She was saving it all for when she had grandchildren, or so she'd claimed. Now she looked at the collection and shook her head.

"Take what you want. I won't have room for any of it in my new place. It's too small."

"Ali, isn't the Victorian church your favorite?" Zennie asked.

"You mean the one she broke?" Mary Jo sighed. "You might as well take that one, Ali. No one else will want it."

"We were all playing," Finola said sharply. "It wasn't her fault." She moved close to Ali and smiled. "Remember how we used to make streets out of cotton balls so it looked like snow?"

Ali smiled. "Yes, and then we'd sprinkle on glitter. We made a really big mess."

"Maybe, but it was beautiful. Which pieces do we all want?"

Zennie took one of the pet stores and a church. "I don't need anything else. Just these two. Okay, and the toy store if no one cares."

"Go for it," Ali said, touching the carousel. "You'll want this, Finola. It's always been your favorite."

Finola nodded because her throat was too tight for her to speak. She remembered sitting with the carousel for hours, winding it up over and over again, listening to the music and watching the horses move. She used to daydream about where she would go if they were real. Her destinations were always far away, where she would meet interesting people and learn things no one else knew. Years later, she'd imagined setting up the carousel in her own house.

Only she hadn't. She and Nigel had a professional service that came in and decorated their place at Christmas with carefully coordinated trees and garland. Their house had been a showpiece at the holidays—not a place the carousel belonged at all.

She admired it now, stroking one of the horses and wishing it would come to life and take her far, far away. So far that her heart wouldn't be broken anymore and she could think about what was going to happen without a growing sense of dread.

Saturday morning, after the nice young couple who had bought her bedroom set left, Ali dusted the baseboards and vacuumed the carpet. Once that was done, she carried in moving boxes that she would have to, at some point, fill. Maybe when she had a place to move to.

She couldn't shake a sense of impending doom and knew that it had nothing to do with her situation. She was still trying to take in what had happened with Finola. How could Nigel have cheated with Treasure? Ali was as much a fan of the country-pop star as the next person, but jeez, not when you were married, and certainly not when you were married to Finola.

She was still trying to figure it all out when Daniel arrived. She opened the front door and said, "You can't tell anyone. You have to totally promise not to say a word. Please, I need to talk about this and there's no one else I can trust and just say you won't repeat it or anything."

As she spoke, he dropped the backpack he carried onto the floor, then closed the door behind himself and pulled her into a hug.

"Ali, what's wrong? I won't say anything. I swear. Just tell me."

He felt so good, she thought, clinging to him, letting his warmth and strength seep into her. She didn't care if he thought she was needy or weird or if he felt he totally got why Glen had dumped her. Right now she needed him.

She took his hand and led him to the sofa. When they were both seated, she stared into his dark eyes and said, "Nigel left Finola for another woman. He's having an affair. I don't know if it's serious or he's just playing around, but he left her!"

Daniel's expression shifted from worried and confused to sympathetic. "I'm sorry to hear that. She's got to be upset."

"No, you don't understand. This is *Finola*. She and Nigel love each other. They have a great marriage. They belong together. You just had to be around them for a few minutes to know they were the ones who were going to be together forever. And he cheated on her. If Finola can't keep Nigel, then there's no hope for the rest of us."

"Slow down, Ali. You're extrapolating way too much from what happened. You're understandably upset. She's your sister and you love her. Plus, you're going through some crap of your own, so this is really hard. But the state of Finola's marriage doesn't affect anyone else's relationship."

His words probably made sense, but she wasn't in the mood to listen. "What is wrong with your gender? Halle Berry's husband cheated on her. And Beyoncé. Why would anyone cheat on Beyoncé? Men are stupid. I'm sorry to say it, but there it is."

Daniel surprised her by smiling. "We *are* stupid. I'm really sorry about Finola and I won't say anything to anyone. You have my word."

"It's because she's on TV. There could be press." There would be press when the whole Treasure thing came out, but while Ali was willing to spill some secrets, she couldn't share them all—not even with Daniel.

They were still holding hands. She wasn't sure how that had happened, but his hand was in hers or vice versa. He stroked his fingers against hers, as if offering comfort. At least she assumed that was what it was. Regardless, his touch was nice. Like him.

"You're being so good to me," she said softly. "Through all of this. I really appreciate it. I couldn't have done it without you."

"I'm sorry for the circumstances, but I'm happy to be here. I mean that, Ali."

She smiled. "I believe you, but it's so strange. Until Glen dumped me, you were always so stern and it seemed as if you didn't want to be in the same room as me. Remember the first time we met? We went to lunch."

"At The Cheesecake Factory at the Sherman Oaks Galleria. I remember. It was a Sunday, last November. A couple of weeks before Thanksgiving."

She stared at him. "That's either impressive or scary. How could you remember that? I knew it was last year, but that was about it." She laughed. "Next you'll be telling me I had on a blue dress."

"You wore jeans and a white sweater."

"Okay," she said slowly. "Now you're freaking me out."

He started to say something only to drop her hand and stand. "Ali, what's going on with your bedroom?"

She turned and followed his gaze. "What? The empty boxes? I have to get more serious about packing."

"Where is your furniture?"

"Oh, that." She drew in a breath. "I sold it." She held up a hand before he could speak. "I sold it a few weeks ago. The people who bought it agreed to wait until today. I kind of forgot until they texted me yesterday, confirming everything."

"Why did you let them take it?"

"They'd already rented a truck and they'd given me half the money. I didn't know how to tell them no."

She knew it was dumb, but honestly, the thought of telling one more person about the wedding being off was just too depressing. She'd already had to deal with sympathetic words at work and, from her perspective, far too many knowing glances, as if the entire world had suspected Glen wouldn't go through with the wedding.

"It was easier to let them take the bed. It's not like I've been sleeping there," she added. "I've been sleeping on the couch."

"Any other furniture disappearing in the next few days?"

"Um, there are a couple more things, but I've texted the people to let them know it's not for sale anymore." Well, not counting the lady who had bought her kitchen table and chairs. Ali didn't have a phone number for her, so maybe she wouldn't show up.

"Okay then." He got his backpack and returned to the sofa. When he was seated, he pulled out a couple of folders. "Here's where we are on the rest of the vendors."

He went over what he'd done. As expected, Daniel had gotten better terms than she would have. She was still going to have to cough up more money than she had, but at least it wasn't as horrible as it could have been.

"What are you doing about the ring?" he asked. "You could sell it."

"Aren't I supposed to return it?"

"Not after what he did. Every state has different laws, but in

California, if the breakup is mutual, the ring is returned. When the groom acts like a jackass, you get to keep the ring."

She grinned. "Good to know." Her humor faded. "I'm not ready to sell it, but I like knowing I can."

"I could go shake the money he owes you out of him."

"Daniel, no. We talked about this. I appreciate all you're doing for me. You have no idea. But please don't go beat up your brother. He's still family and that's important. I'm figuring it out. Once the dust settles, I can think about what I want to do. I've done some research on small claims court. I might go that route."

"Whatever you decide, I'm here for you."

"I know." She flopped back against the sofa and sighed. "You're so much better than he is. Why didn't we fall in love?"

Before he could react, she put her hand on his arm. "Kidding. Don't freak out."

"I'm not freaked. I guess it's just one of those things."

"It is. All right, I'm going to free you from your wedding canceling duties. I have laundry and then I'm going to depress myself by looking at apartments in my price range."

"Don't sign any leases until we talk," he said as he stood. "I'll want to check out the neighborhood first."

She supposed his attitude could have been annoying, but for her, it was heaven. She liked knowing he was around to take care of her. After all she'd been through, having a little caretaking was nice.

"I won't even put down a deposit," she promised. "When I find something promising, you'll be the first to know. I swear."

"Good." He pulled her close and kissed her cheek, his stubble tickling. "Call me if you need anything. I'll be at work and reachable."

"I will."

She walked him to the door. When he was gone, she again

had the thought that things would have gone a whole lot better for her if she'd fallen for Daniel instead of Glen. Fate was sure a bitch with a sense of humor.

Chapter Ten

Monday morning Finola got to the studio extra early. She had a meeting to review the upcoming shows and also needed time to get back into what had been her regular life. The week of her vacation, the station had rerun shows and now they would be live again.

She'd spent the weekend getting ready to fake her way through her life. She'd gotten a spray tan and had a facial. There'd been no more binge eating and Saturday she'd flushed her system with water and vegetable juice. Sunday she'd switched to a low-fat, high-protein diet that she would stay on until she was just shy of scary thin. Only then would she relax about her appearance. It was bad enough that she was a dozen years older than Treasure—Finola refused to be the frumpy wife, as well.

She parked in her usual spot, greeted the security guard and made her way to the studio. She'd worn her favorite jeans, a sloppy-chic T-shirt and big sunglasses, and her hair was pulled back. It was how she always dressed when she started her day. Her large dressing room was filled with her "TV clothes"—lots of dresses and separates that she mixed and matched, a season at a time. Her contract included a generous clothing budget, which Finola appreciated. She never wore her TV clothes outside of the station and when the season ended and new things were purchased, her assistant got to pick one of the outfits for herself. The remainder of her barely worn things were donated to Dress for Success and a local women's shelter.

"Welcome, Finola," one of the crew called. "You look great. Hawaii agrees with you."

She smiled and waved but kept moving. She didn't want to talk to anyone about her trip. Today was about work, nothing else. She was willing to lie, but she didn't want to have to sweat a lot of details. Not when the truth would come out eventually.

She reached her dressing room. Rochelle was already waiting for her, looking impossibly young and well dressed as she steamed the dress she'd picked out for Finola to wear that day.

"Good morning," her assistant said. "How was your vacation?"

"Busy, how was your trip back home?"

Rochelle had flown to North Carolina to be with family. Like Finola, she was one of three sisters. Her father was a minister, her mother an accountant. She was the first daughter in three generations not to go to Howard University, instead attending USC. Her conservative parents were equally unhappy that Rochelle had settled in Los Angeles, instead of returning home to find a good job and settle down.

Finola had met them shortly after she'd hired Rochelle. She'd done her best to allay their fears about their daughter's safety in the immoral wilderness that was the entertainment industry.

Rochelle sighed heavily. "I have nothing in common with anyone anymore. My sisters are both pregnant. Again. My mom lectured me daily on my relationship with God and my father just looked disappointed."

"That sounds awful."

"It was what it always is. Parents can be that way. I know they love me and they don't understand me. I'm doing what I want to do." She grinned. "When I win my first Emmy, they'll be thrilled for me."

Finola laughed. "Make sure I'm mentioned in your acceptance speech."

"You'll be the first one."

"I'm holding you to that." Finola enjoyed the moment of normalcy for another couple of seconds, then closed the door. "We have to talk."

Rochelle immediately turned off the steamer. "Tell me."

Finola motioned to the sofa. She took a chair. *And here we go,* she thought sadly. The telling had begun. There would be lies, an attempt to conceal, at least for as long as she could. This business being what it was, she knew she wouldn't take any flak for that when the truth came out. Everyone she worked with would understand. Those higher up the food chain would be unamused, but there was no way she was going to tell them what had happened. It would all hit the fan eventually and when it did, she would deal.

But Rochelle was different. Finola needed someone on her side, someone who could watch out for her and run interference if necessary.

"I didn't go to Hawaii," she said as calmly as she could. "Nigel is having an affair and he moved out."

Rochelle's eyes widened. "No. No! But…he was just here on Friday. I saw him. You were supposed to be on vacation." She dropped her voice. "You were going to get pregnant."

Finola ignored the wave of humiliation. "Change of plans," she murmured. "On all of it. As for why he was here, it was to tell me what was happening."

"I can't believe it. That's why you were so upset?" She started to stand, then sagged back in her seat. "Are you saying your husband showed up less than thirty minutes before you were on live TV to tell you he was having an affair?"

Finola nodded. Her assistant's indignation was heartening.

"There's more," she said, knowing she had to get it out quickly. "And it's bad."

She went on to explain that the woman in question was the world's most popular country-pop singer, and how Treasure had confronted her right before their interview.

Rochelle pressed her hand to her chest. "Finola, I'm so sorry. I can't believe how amazing you are. You were so professional. I would have bitch-slapped her, then set her on fire. You had to *interview* her! And all the time you knew what Nigel had done to you."

She stood and crossed to Finola and hugged her. "I'm sorry. I hate her. My daddy would say it's wrong to hate people, but I hate her."

The hug was comforting, as was the support. Finola leaned against her. "Thank you. It's been a really hard week."

Rochelle sat back in her seat. "What can I do to help?"

"What you've been doing. Please have my back around here and let me know if there are any rumors about what's happening. I want to keep it quiet as long as possible."

Rochelle winced. "Because when it comes out, it's gonna be bad. Have you talked to a lawyer?"

Finola didn't understand the question. Why would she—

"You mean about a divorce? We're not there." A divorce? No. Nigel was going to come back to her. He would be sorry and beg her forgiveness and never do it again. They were *married*. They had a life together. A good life that was important to both of them... At least it had been.

"You think I should?"

Rochelle held up both her hands. "That's not for me to say. You have to do what's right for you."

"What would you do?"

"After what he put you through? If he's not sorry and begging for forgiveness the second he was caught, then he should be tossed to the curb. He needs to respect you and right now there's no respect." She softened her tone. "I'm sure you know what you're doing, Finola. Don't listen to me."

"It's just all so sudden and confusing. I never thought he would do this to me. I thought we were happy."

She'd sure been wrong about that, she thought sadly. What else hadn't she known about her husband? What else had he kept from her?

She closed her eyes and wished it would all go away, but when she opened them, the world was just as it had been.

Her phone chirped. Rochelle handed it to her without glancing at the screen. Finola read the alert and flinched, then passed it over to her assistant.

"I signed up for alerts when Treasure Tweets," she explained. "Just so I know what's coming. So far there hasn't been anything about Nigel."

Rochelle read the Tweet out loud. "'It's sad when people get old and no one will love them.'"

"Not very subtle," Finola murmured.

"You think this is about you? It's not. You're not old."

"Compared to her, I'm ancient."

"You aren't and you are loved. She's just being a bitch. We're going to ignore her. Come on. People have stood in line for two hours just to see your show. It's time to get ready to dazzle them."

Finola didn't bother saying she wasn't really up to dazzling anyone. Not only because Rochelle wouldn't want to hear it but because in the end, how she felt didn't matter. She had a responsibility to the show, and maybe to herself. If she couldn't *be* strong, she could at least fake strong. For now that would be enough.

★ ★ ★

Ali got back to work from her lunch break with two minutes to spare. She walked into the warehouse, doing her best to, from the outside at least, seem strong and confident. In truth she'd just seen the ugliest apartment ever. Not only had the unit overlooked the trash dumpsters, it had been small, dark and desperately in need of paint and carpet. But the worst part had been the weird, musty smell—sort of a combination of mold and dampness.

She'd already looked at four places and had hated them all. If nothing else, she was going to have to up her budget by at least another hundred dollars a month. But with having to pay off the wedding and deal with the cost of moving, she just didn't see how that was possible. Yes, she could pay the more expensive rent and still eat and take care of her bills, but there wouldn't be anything left for savings. She'd always had an emergency fund. The wedding had taken care of that, leaving her in fairly desperate straits. At the rate she was going, she was going to have to choose between living with her mother and living out of her car.

She found Ray and Kevin waiting at her desk. Ray appeared to be his normal grumpy, bearlike self, while Kevin looked fairly frightened. She was about to ask what was wrong when she saw Ray holding the postcard she'd slipped into his locker.

He set it on her desk. "I'm sorry about Glen," he told her. "We're all sorry." He drew in a breath and seemed to brace himself. "Would you like to take Coco Chanel for the weekend?"

Her bad mood instantly vanished as she recognized the sweetness in his offer. There was no person or thing Ray loved more than his ridiculous little dog, and his offering her Coco Chanel was a genuine act of kindness.

She found herself fighting tears yet again, but these weren't about hurt or frustration, instead they were about finding support in very unexpected places.

She smiled at Ray. "That is the most amazing gift anyone has ever offered me. Thank you so much. I wish I could, but with canceling the wedding and all, I couldn't possibly accept. I'd worry I wasn't taking good care of her."

Ray visibly relaxed. "I understand. She's kind of a diva, so a lot of work, but just in case you need to spend some time with her, you can."

"Thank you."

Ray glared at Kevin, then walked away. The teen shook his head.

"Damn, he must really like you. I didn't think he'd trust his dog with anyone. I'm sorry about the wedding. I didn't know Glen but from what everyone is saying, he wasn't a great guy. They all think you were too good for him."

She hated knowing she'd been the subject of office gossip, but it was to be expected.

"Thanks. It's a lot to deal with."

"Ray said no one is really surprised. I don't know if that helps or not, but I thought you'd want to know."

She told herself that Kevin was a kid and wasn't being mean on purpose, then promised herself later, when she was home and by herself, she was making brownies and eating the entire pan.

"Okay, then," she murmured. "I need to get back to work and so do you."

Kevin nodded and left. She sank onto her chair and told herself eventually all this would pass. In a few weeks, she would barely remember that she'd ever been engaged. Glen who?

Her cell phone rang. She pulled it out of her jeans pocket and glanced at the screen. She didn't recognize the number and wondered if it was one of her vendors.

"Hello?"

"Ali? Hi, it's Selena. I just want to confirm we're still on for tonight."

Ali's mind was a total blank. "Tonight?"

"I'm picking up the table and chairs, remember. I'm so excited.

Our voucher came through so my daughters and I were able to move into our apartment over the weekend."

Selena's voice was full of emotion. "I know it's a silly thing, but we've been in and out of shelters for so long. Having a place of our own is a miracle. Your table and chairs are going in our kitchen. My girls will do their homework there, just like a regular family."

Ali knew in her head that there were dozens of free or almost free dining sets available online. That if she said hers wasn't for sale anymore, Selena could find another one in about five minutes. That was what her head told her. Her heart, however, melted.

"I'll be home at five," she said. "Does that work for you?"

"Yes. My boss is loaning me his truck for a couple of hours. I remember you said the table wasn't heavy, so he and I will be able to handle it ourselves. We'll see you then."

Ali tried not to feel stupid. She was doing a good thing, she told herself. For someone more in need than her. It wasn't as if she had an apartment for her furniture anyway. What did it matter?

The problem was she had a feeling her actions were a lot more about beating herself up than being altruistic. She was caught up in an emotional death spiral and she didn't know how to make it stop. Maybe she should spend a couple of days fussing over Coco Chanel.

Her phone rang again.

"Ali Schmitt?"

"Yes."

"It's Veronica at the bridal shop. Your dress is back from alterations and ready anytime you want to come get it."

Of course it was, Ali thought, resting her head on her desk. "Great. I'll be by in a couple of days to pick it up."

And then she would have to decide what to do with it. Perhaps some kind of sacrificial burning as a way to cleanse her spiritual life. Of course she would need sage for that, and possibly a permit.

She straightened. Brownies, she promised herself. Later there would be brownies. And wine. Then she would figure out what on earth she was going to do with the rest of her life.

Finola arrived a few minutes early for her dinner with Zennie. As she walked into the café-style restaurant, she tried to remember the last time the two of them had gotten together without Ali and honestly didn't think it had ever happened. Usually it was the three of them or just her and Ali.

She spotted her sister already at a table and made her way across the restaurant.

"Thanks for suggesting this," she said as she sat down. "I appreciate the support. Everything has been so awful lately. I keep waiting for word to get out."

She didn't get more specific—who knew who might be sitting nearby. She picked up her menu. "What's good here? I am so having a cocktail. What about you?"

"I'm going to pass on the alcohol, but you go ahead. As for the food, it's all good."

There was something in Zennie's tone. Finola studied her short hair and unlined face. Zennie had never been one for makeup or high style. She dressed for comfort, and her idea of a good time was a five-mile run or a 6:00 a.m. surf session. Finola didn't have the athletic gene but she worked out plenty—mostly to stay camera thin.

When their server arrived, she ordered vodka and soda, to stay on her low-carb program, then scanned the various entries. There was a nice grilled ahi she would get with a salad and a side of broccoli. She'd already calculated a second drink into her daily calorie plan and should be fine. She'd lost a bunch of water weight and had upped her strength training. In a week her clothes would be loose and in two, the weight loss would be noticeable. She couldn't wait for the compliments.

Zennie asked for herbal iced tea with extra lemon. When

their server had left, Finola leaned toward her. "You doing all right? You seem...different."

"What do you mean?"

"I'm not sure. You tell me. Everything okay at work?"

"It is."

"Good." Finola sighed. "I'm exhausted all the time. I know it's the stress, but still. I keep waiting to hear from, ah, you know who." She glanced around again, but none of the other diners seemed to be interested in them. "So far the shows have gone well. We've had good guests and no surprises." She wanted to say the house felt empty, but once again was aware of who might be listening. Damn. She should have suggested they get takeout at her place or something.

Zennie looked at her. "Finola, I didn't ask you here to talk about you. I wanted to tell you what's going on with Ali. I've been waiting for her to say something, but it's obvious she's not going to. I guess she thinks what you're going through is more important than what she is, but she's wrong. It's a big deal."

"I have no idea what you're talking about."

"Yes, I know. Glen dumped Ali. The wedding is off."

Finola stared at her. The server returned with their drinks. Finola took a long swallow, then tried to understand what she'd been told.

"It's over? No, it can't be. She never said anything." Not a word. When she'd last seen Ali, her sister had been just like she always was. There had to be a mistake. "When did this happen?"

"The same day Nigel——"

Finola stopped her with a glare. "Not here!"

"Whatever. That same Friday. She called me because she thought you were going to Hawaii and she didn't want to ruin your vacation. When you showed up at Mom's, she made us promise not to say anything so we could just deal with you." Zennie's tone made it clear she thought Ali was an idiot.

"Like I said, I've been waiting for her to say something but

135

when I realized she wasn't going to, I figured you'd want to know. Or not."

"What does that mean?"

"You seem a lot more concerned about someone overhearing your news than worrying about your sister getting dumped a few weeks before her wedding."

"That's not fair. I'm in shock. You just told me all this and I'm taking it in. You've had a couple of weeks to process. Get off me." She took another drink. "Did he say why? Are we sure it's over?"

"It seems that way. Ali's canceled the wedding."

The wedding. "She has to be heartbroken. Have you talked to her? Of course you have. How is she doing?"

"She's coping. It would be nice if *you* talked to her. You two have always been so close. It's just wrong she's going through this by herself to save your feelings."

"That's Ali for you."

"Yeah, and that's you."

Finola glared at her. "What does that mean?"

Zennie shrugged. "You live a very Finola-centric life. I know you just found out what happened, which is on her, but no matter what, life seems to revolve around you. It should be Ali's turn to get a little care and comfort right now. She's lost Glen, she's got the wedding to cancel and she gave up her apartment to move in with him, which means right now she has nowhere to live. Maybe she could move in with you for a few weeks."

Finola still couldn't get her mind around all that was happening. First Nigel, then Glen. Ali canceling the wedding and needing somewhere to live.

"I should go see her."

"You should."

There was something in Zennie's tone. "You mean right now?"

Her sister smiled. "You can finish your drink first."

Chapter Eleven

Thirty minutes later, Finola stood at Ali's door. She'd brought seafood dinner for two from the restaurant and desperately hoped her sister had vodka, soda and ice. She was still trying to shake off Zennie's judgy attitude at their nondinner. It wasn't her fault she didn't know about the breakup. If no one said anything, how was she supposed to figure it out on her own? She wasn't psychic and there hadn't been the slightest hint. She and Ali were texting nearly every day and her sister had never said a word.

She knocked loudly, then realized she'd never bothered to find out if Ali was home. Before she could figure out what to do if she were gone, the door opened. Ali stood there, a chocolate batter-covered wooden spoon in hand.

"Finola! Did I know you were stopping by?" Ali stepped back to let her in. "I was making brownies and then I was going to get some takeout for dinner."

Finola held up the bags she held. "I've brought dinner. Ahi. I hear it's delicious."

Ali looked confused but happy. "Okay, that's really nice. Thank you." She glanced back at the kitchen. "We'll, ah, have to eat at the coffee table. I'm kind of short a table and chairs right now."

"What?"

"Long story. Let me get the brownies in the oven, then we can eat dinner and catch up."

Finola followed her sister into her small kitchen and saw that there was indeed an empty space by the window in the corner. She couldn't remember the last time she'd eaten her dinner while seated on the floor, but as long as there was vodka and later Uber...

"Do you have anything to drink?" she asked as Ali poured thick batter into an eight-by-eight pan.

"Like water or soda or something else?"

"Something else?"

Ali grinned. "There's vodka in the freezer and a choice of mixers in the refrigerator. Limes are in that bowl on the counter."

Five minutes later, the brownies were in the oven and the dirty dishes soaking. Finola had made them each a drink. As she handed Ali hers, she said, "Sweetie, why didn't you tell me?"

For a second her sister looked genuinely confused, then her expression cleared and she wrinkled her nose. "Mom or Zennie?"

"Zennie. You should have said something. I want to know when things happen, especially when your fiancé turns out to be a complete asshole. You've been going through so much. Why didn't you want me to be a part of that?"

"It wasn't that. Finn, your thing is bigger. I mean, come on, you and Nigel? That was magical. You've been together for so long and I knew you wanted to get pregnant. I couldn't mess up that, so that's why I didn't call you right away. Plus, I thought you were on vacation. Then when I found out what had happened, my news just seemed unimportant."

Finola put her drink down and hugged her sister. "It's not unimportant. It matters and I want to be here for you."

Ali hugged her back. "Thanks. It was a shock, although based on what a few people have said, only a shock for me."

"What do you mean?"

Ali leaned back against the counter. "A couple of people at work mentioned they weren't really surprised. I've heard from some of our friends and they weren't shocked, either. I guess everyone knew Glen didn't love me except for me."

Tears filled her eyes. Finola knew that feeling of hopelessness and knew it didn't help make things better.

"I didn't know," she said quickly. "Zennie didn't know. We love you and think you're perfect. If Glen's too stupid to see that, then good riddance. How are you coming on canceling the wedding?"

"It's going pretty well. Daniel's been helping and that's made a difference."

"Daniel?" Finola tried to place the name. "Who is he?"

"Glen's brother. He's the one who told me, actually. Glen wasn't going to do it. He told Daniel he would simply not show up. So Daniel had to do it. He's been amazing."

Finola's gaze sharpened. "Oh, God, you're not falling for him, are you?"

Ali flushed. "What? No. It's not like that. He's helped me cancel the contracts with the vendors and that kind of stuff. He's been a good guy. Just don't go anywhere bad, Finola. Seriously, I couldn't handle it." She turned away. "I know it's not what you're dealing with, but this is still huge to me, okay? I can't take much more."

"I'm sorry. I'm just looking out for you. A rebound guy is one thing, but Glen's brother would be a big mistake."

"As if that would ever happen."

There was a moment of awkward silence. Finola searched for something to say. "How are you on money? Do you need me to loan you some to pay for things?"

Emotion flashed through Ali's eyes. Her voice was controlled as she said, "I'm good."

"What about the apartment? Weren't you moving out? Were you able to change the lease to stay here or do you have to go?"

"I'll be moving out, but it's fine."

Finola thought maybe she'd gone a little too far with Ali, so she smiled and said, "You could always move in with me. There's plenty of room, especially now."

Of course if Nigel did come to his senses and want to come back, having her sister around would be a problem. She supposed if that happened, she could get Ali a hotel room or something. Honestly, it would be easier if Ali turned her down, but she'd made the offer and didn't see how she could get out of it.

"I think me moving in would be too complicated," Ali said quietly. "What with Nigel and all. Don't worry. I have it covered."

Finola started to ask how, then realized she didn't want to know. Because if Ali didn't have it covered, then she was going to have to fix the problem and she was just not in a place to do that. She supposed she could ask Rochelle to help. Her assistant was certainly full of ideas and energy.

Before Finola could offer Rochelle's assistance, Ali said, "Poor Mom. It looks like she's going to have to wait a little longer for those grandchildren of hers."

Finola grinned. "She sure is, unless Zennie turns up pregnant."

They both laughed at the thought.

Ali grabbed her drink and pushed away from the counter. "All right, you. Let's eat dinner. You said you brought ahi?"

"Yes, with salad and a side of broccoli."

Ali made a face. "Seriously? You eat like that?"

"I have to stay thin for TV. You know that."

"But still. Did you at least bring a dinner roll?"

"I'm not eating carbs right now."

Ali sighed. "So fish, salad and vegetables. Oh, joy."

Finola raised her glass. "And vodka, my love. There is always vodka."

Zennie had never been a fan of eating in restaurants, so two meals out in two days wasn't her idea of a good time. Although technically she'd only spent a half hour in the restaurant with Finola the previous night—she hadn't actually eaten there. A thought that should have given her comfort, only it didn't because her unease had nothing to do with the dining out experience, but was much more about the fact that she was on a blind date. Again. Worse, a blind date set up by her mother.

Zennie knew exactly how it had happened. She'd been minding her own business, reading the surrogacy contract Hayes had given her, when her mother had texted the details of the date. Zennie had been flooded with guilt, knowing how upset her mother would be at the idea of one of her daughters finally getting pregnant but not keeping the baby. She'd succumbed to self-induced emotional blackmail, which was the worst kind.

So now here she was, waiting for someone about whom she knew almost nothing. Her mother's description had been brief. "C.J. is in real estate and I think you'll have a lot in common."

Zennie sat in the parking lot, telling herself it wasn't going to be that bad. What was one more blind date? She picked up her phone and texted her mother.

I never asked what he looks like. How will I recognize him?

The answer came back almost instantly. I showed off your picture. C.J. will find you. Have fun.

Not exactly comforting, Zennie thought, getting out of her car and locking it. Meeting Clark had been much easier. No blind date, no expectation. She'd been at the zoo for a fun run and he'd been a volunteer. When she'd finished the run, she'd gone on one of the tours to learn more about the animals. Clark had led the tour. He'd been funny and interesting and they'd ended up talking after everyone else had gone. Before she'd left, he'd asked for her number, then had contacted her right away.

She'd liked Clark, she admitted reluctantly. He was a good guy and she was a little sorry things had ended the way they had. Maybe if he'd given her more time, she thought, then shook her head. No. Better that they'd broken up and gone their separate ways. She wasn't the one for him and she was more convinced than ever that she didn't actually have a one.

She walked into the restaurant and stood in the foyer, not sure what to do. Ask for a table? Wait?

"Zennie?"

She turned and saw a tall, slender Hispanic woman approaching. She was pretty, with long, wavy brown hair and large brown eyes. The woman wore a snug deep-orange dress that outlined every impressive curve. Zennie immediately felt like a plain glass of club soda next to a piña colada in her go-to black capris and loose top.

The woman smiled. "Hi, I'm C.J."

Zennie had to admit she hadn't seen *that* coming. Her mother had set her up with a woman, and not just any woman. Had Zennie been willing to play for the girls' team, she had to admit she would have been tempted. As it was, well, she had absolutely no idea what to say.

"Um, hi."

C.J. stared at her for a second, then started to laugh. "Oh, God, you're not gay."

"I'm more cheerful than gay."

C.J. laughed. "I like that. I'm cheerful, too. So hey, awkward. Why did your mom do this?"

"I have no idea. Where did you meet her?"

"In her store."

Zennie looked over the gorgeous, brightly colored dress that screamed upscale designer. Her mother's boutique in the Sherman Oaks Galleria leaned more toward stylish but affordable work clothes. Dark suits, plain dresses and the like. "Not buying that."

"In my work life, I'm in real estate," C.J. told her. "I wear a lot of black pants and jackets. When I'm not working, I like to take things up a notch. After seeing your picture, I was dressing to impress."

"I am impressed and I'm seriously wishing I was more than cheerful."

C.J. grinned. "You know what? I like you. Let's have dinner anyway. I'll even buy."

"You're on, but I'm paying for my own dinner. I'm just that kind of girl."

"Perfect."

They went up to the hostess and were quickly seated. C.J. ordered a margarita with a tequila shooter on the side while Zennie got herbal iced tea.

When their server had left, C.J. leaned forward, resting her elbows on the table. "So, why does Mom think you're gay?"

"There are a thousand reasons. I don't have a man in my life. I refuse to settle down." Zennie smiled. "I was athletic in high school."

C.J. threw up her hands. "Naturally. I mean everyone knows male athletes are sexy hunks while female athletes have to be lesbos. What is this, the seventies?"

"You asked."

"I did. So no guy?"

"Wow, we are getting right to it, huh?" Zennie thought for

a second, then decided she didn't mind answering the question. "I'm not a two-by-two person. I don't need that. I'm not looking to settle down. I have a great life with great friends. As for the sex thing, which is the next question…"

C.J.'s eyes widened. "Absolutely. I mean at this point, we have to talk about sex."

Zennie laughed. "I don't love it. I just don't. It's nice and yes, I've had an orgasm. It's not a big deal for me. I've decided I'm wired differently than most people. I'm not wrong, I'm simply living my own life."

"Good for you." C.J. shifted in her seat. "I am one of four daughters in a very Catholic household. The whole traditional Hispanic thing. Catholic school, uniforms."

"You looked cute in yours."

C.J. flashed her a smile. "I did. I wasn't supposed to see a boy naked until my wedding night."

"How old were you when you saw your first boy naked?" Because Zennie knew C.J. had to have tried it out at least once.

"Sixteen. It was gross. He was sweet and he tried to do it right, but he was only seventeen and it was over in like six seconds. I just couldn't stand the thought of doing that again. I told myself it was because I was going to live my life in service of God but the truth is I had such a crush on the head cheerleader at the local high school. She was so much more my type."

"So when did you figure it all out?"

"My first year of college. I met this older girl."

Zennie leaned forward. "She was what? Twenty?"

"Nineteen and very worldly. She'd been to France."

"Oh la la."

"I know. It was amazing. The first time she kissed me, I just knew. When we made love, it was perfection. She broke my heart and I was devastated, but at least I knew where I belonged."

"Does your family know?"

"Yes, and while they're not happy, they're supportive, if that makes sense."

Their server delivered their drinks. They toasted each other. C.J. drank her shot of tequila, then picked up her margarita.

"So, Mom says you're a nurse."

"I am. I work in the OR, mostly with cardiologists. It's intense, but I love it. No two days are the same. We save lives—nothing beats that."

C.J. looked crushed. "You're right. I mean all I do is sell real estate." She set down her drink. "What am I saying? I find people their homes. That's important, too. Okay, you get to be the most special, but I'm right there, one rung down."

"Half a rung," Zennie told her. "Where's your territory?"

"East Valley, mostly. I flirt with Burbank but you know that market is pretty specialized. Do you own your own place?"

"I wish, but no. I have a little studio close to the hospital."

"You should buy something. It's good to build equity. The rest of the country's real estate market goes up and down but this is LA. We're always going to be growing." One eyebrow rose. "Unless you're secretly waiting for a man to tell you it's okay."

"Ouch. Not that." Zennie paused. "Okay, maybe that, but only because I wasn't paying attention and wow is that stupid. What have I been waiting for?"

"I have no idea. Maybe you love your place."

Zennie thought about her small apartment. It was where she lived but it wasn't exactly what she'd envisioned for herself. At first she'd liked the convenience, but she supposed that in the back of her mind, she'd always assumed she would…

"I've been waiting for a man," she said, shocking herself with the truth. "I didn't even know. I've been brainwashed by societal pressures."

"It happens to all of us. Awareness isn't easy. So what other dreams have you put on hold?"

"Are you judging me?"

C.J. held up her hands again. "Not me, sister. Career-wise, I kick ass, but in my personal life, I jump into relationships way too fast. If someone wants a second date, I'm immediately planning our lives together. It's awful. I hate being alone. It's like a death sentence. So I'm a mess." She flashed a smile. "But I look good."

"You do. Okay, other dreams put on hold. I want to learn Italian and go to Italy. Not just for a week, but like for a month. I want to experience the rhythm of life there."

"Excellent goal. So start today. Get one of those language apps and learn Italian. You could be ready to go by the fall."

Zennie shook her head. "Not this fall."

"Giving in to fear?"

"I'm hoping to be pregnant."

C.J.'s brown eyes widened. She gulped her margarita, then waved over the server. "I'm so going to need another one of these, then I want to hear the story. You're going to have a baby?"

"Not for me. For a friend."

"That is way more than house-sitting a cat."

Zennie laughed, then told her about Bernie and the surrogacy. "I haven't told my mom yet, so please don't say anything."

"I won't and for the record, I don't hang out with your mom. Not that she isn't lovely, but I have my own mother to guilt me into things. A baby. I don't know that I would do that for a friend. You dazzle me."

"Thanks. I get it's a big deal, but Bernie's been through so much and I know she'll be a great mom. She teaches kindergarten, so she's all prepared."

"Amazing." C.J. looked at her. "All right, I say let's be friends."

"I'd like that."

"Good. I'm going to the restroom. When I get back, we'll order dinner, then talk trash about our exes. How's that?"

"Sounds perfect."

C.J. got up and walked toward the back of the restaurant. Zennie pulled out her phone and texted her mother.

Not a lesbian, Mom. I thought we'd talked about this before.

Just checking. You might have changed your mind.

I haven't, although C.J. is nice. We're going to be friends, so the odds of grandchildren with her are slim.

You're killing me, Zennie. Right now, I'm lying here dead.

Night, Mom.

Dead people can't text.

Zennie was still chuckling when she put her phone away.

Chapter Twelve

Finola arrived home from the studio to find Nigel's bleached and ruined clothes pulled from the pool and neatly folded on the back deck. She had no idea what the pool guy had thought when he'd seen them, but doubted he'd more than blinked. After all, this was Los Angeles and crazy things happened here, even in the valley.

She walked out of the kitchen, formulating her plan for the evening. She would start with a hot shower, then she would redo her makeup, get changed and leave. Traffic would be a mess, but if she got there early, then it was only a win for her.

She'd barely started up the stairs when her cell phone rang. She glanced at the screen, saw it was her stepfather and answered the call as she sank down onto a stair.

"Hey, Dad."

"Hey, yourself. Your mother told me what happened. I wanted to find out how you were doing."

Finola sighed, ready for a little parental comforting. "It's been awful, as you can imagine. What was Nigel thinking? I mean cheating is one thing, but with her? And telling me the way he did. I can't even describe how hard that was."

She felt her eyes fill with tears. "Oh, Dad, he was mean and she was a bitch and everyone's going to know and it's all ruined."

She drew in a breath and waited for him to say something. There was only silence.

"Dad? Aren't you going to say something?"

"I'm sorry you're in pain."

That was it? "I was looking for more sympathy."

"I'm sure you were, but you have plenty of people to give you that. I want to make sure you're asking the right questions."

"What do you mean?"

"Why."

"Why what?"

"Why it happened, Finola." He spoke slowly, as if to a child.

"What do you mean, why it happened? Why did Nigel cheat? I have no idea. Why did he choose that bimbo child? Because he could. Because she's young and beautiful. Did he think about me even once? Did he think about us or our marriage or what's going to happen when it all hits the fan? I doubt it. I had nothing to do with what happened. I'm his wife. I have loved him and taken care of him." She shifted the phone to her other ear. "I wanted us to get pregnant while we were in Hawaii. Now that's never going to happen."

Her stepfather sighed. "You need to ask why. Why did he do this? Why now? Why with her? And how much of it is your fault?"

"What?" She glared at the phone. "My fault? Mine? Are you insane? It's not my fault. I didn't do anything wrong. I've been right here, living our life, while he's been off fucking who knows who. He told me right before the show. Did Mom mention that? He told me five goddamn minutes before I was going to face his mistress on live television. I don't care why he did it. I just want him punished."

And back, a voice in her head whispered. Despite everything, she also wanted him back.

"No breakup is just one person's fault," Bill said quietly. "Very few are even eighty-twenty. There's always shared blame."

She felt fury rise up inside of her. "How nice. When did you get this insight? What is your blame in your failed marriage?"

"I knew from the start Mary Jo didn't love me the way I loved her. I knew she thought she was trading her dreams for someone safe. I could never make your mother's dreams come true, but I married her anyway. The real problems started when I stopped trying to make them come true. The work was too hard and I checked out emotionally a long time before we split up. That's on me."

She hadn't expected her stepfather to be so honest. "Mom doesn't make it easy all the time."

"No, she doesn't, but then neither do I. I don't regret marrying her and I'm not saying we should have stayed together. But I will accept my share of the responsibility."

"Neither of you cheated. You can't know what that's like."

"You're right, I can't. But I do know that cheating is only part of it. The big question is still why, and until you can answer that, you'll never be able to move on." He coughed. "I'm sorry you're going through this, I truly am. But how I feel isn't important. Your feelings are the ones that matter. As long as you're a victim, you're losing."

"That's not fair."

"Maybe not, Finola, but it's true. You think about what I said. I'll check in with you in a couple of weeks."

Before she could agree or scream or tell him he was wrong, he'd hung up on her.

Finola stood, her phone clutched in her hand. "You don't

know what you're talking about," she screamed into the empty room. "You're wrong about all of it."

She raced up to the second floor. Fury gave her energy. Instead of showering, she simply scrubbed off her studio makeup and put on normal makeup, then fluffed and sprayed her hair. She went into her closet and changed into a cobalt blue suit with a patterned silk shell. She hesitated over her shoes before choosing a pair of nude high heels. One killer bag and simple jewelry later, she was ready to leave.

As she drove to Pacoima, Finola did her best to not think about her stepfather. *Screw him*, she thought bitterly. It was easy to give advice when you didn't know what you were talking about. He'd never cared about her, anyway. He'd been all about Zennie. She was his favorite. The tomboy to replace the son he never had. Zennie, Zennie, Zennie.

She made her way through the valley, heading northeast. This time of day there was no point in even attempting the freeway. Besides, surface streets were more direct.

The monthly meetings were held at the recreation center and the group helped fourteen-to-eighteen-year-old girls stay focused to achieve their dreams. Finola had been offered a position on the board more than once, but she'd always refused. She hadn't wanted the commitment. What she did instead was visit a few times a year and spend time with the girls. She talked about the business and how to succeed. She also gave practical advice on how to act in an interview, whether for a job or an internship. She talked about the importance of communication skills, and how you should look people in the eye when you spoke.

Finola pulled into the recreation center parking lot. She was a little early, but knew several of the girls would already be there. They were eager for the information, determined to better themselves. They looked up to Finola, used her as a role model. Last June she'd done a whole segment about the organization on her show and how they were helping local girls.

Finola turned off her car engine and took several deep breaths. She was fine, she told herself. She was going to march in there and share her knowledge. She would be helpful and funny and show the girls that someone believed in them.

Not enough to be on the board, a vile voice whispered in her ear. *Oooh, you did a segment on your show. That's amazing. You go, girl. You're really giving back now. Better be careful or you'll burn yourself out.*

"No," Finola whispered. "It's not like that. I'm a good person. I am."

She was, she repeated silently, then wondered if she was. Or if the rest of her life was exactly like her marriage—a complete and total fraud.

Ali sat on her sofa—the one piece of furniture she was keeping, no matter what—and took stock of her most pressing life issues. She supposed the biggest problem was she had nowhere to live and, thanks to what was still owed on various items for the wedding, she was dealing with crushing credit card debt. She was also feeling oddly uncomfortable about her sister.

Finola had been surprisingly difficult the other night. Ali tried to tell herself it was because her sister had her own pain with Nigel and the affair and all that, but jeez, did she have to accuse Ali of falling for Daniel? That was ridiculous. The man had been a saint and she was grateful, nothing more.

But Finola wouldn't understand that and now Ali was left feeling kind of icky about something she hadn't done, which could be really awkward, considering Daniel was due to arrive in about five seconds.

Right on time, he knocked on her front door. She let him in. He smiled at her as he handed her the ever-present folder.

"Done and done," he told her. "You are released from all your contracts. Glen will live the rest of his life as a moron and years from now, you'll look back on this and be grateful."

Just seeing him made her feel better about everything. "You are so right," she said. "I'm done, too. The gifts are all sent back and my to-do list is reduced to nothing."

They walked into her small living room. Daniel sat on the sofa while she took the chair.

"You doing okay?" he asked, studying her.

"I'm fine. I'm sleeping more, drinking less." She was still eating for twenty, but figured she could give herself another week of indulgence before she had to rein that in. "I've come through the worst of it. Thank you for all your help."

He looked good, she thought absently, with the three-day beard, jeans, a long-sleeved shirt and motorcycle boots. Under other circumstances, she would be pretty excited to have such a dangerously handsome man in her living room, but these weren't other circumstances. Daniel had been sweet to her and they were friends. She wasn't going to be stupid—something she wouldn't have even had to think if not for Finola. Sisters!

"What are you thinking?" he asked.

She flushed. There was no way to tell him, so she mentally scrambled for a lie. "That, ah, I admire your negotiating skills. Mine totally suck. I do okay at work, but I really wish I'd stayed in college and at least gotten my associate degree. Plus I don't really believe in myself and after this whole thing with Glen, I feel even more unworthy." She shrugged. "Like the clock."

"What clock?"

"My mom has this grandfather clock. I know it's old-fashioned and big, but I love it. She's getting rid of stuff because she's moving to a small bungalow, so she wants us to take things. I asked for the clock and she told me no. No one else wants it, so she'll get rid of it one way or the other. I mean seriously? She'd rather give it away than let me have it?"

"Did you take her on?"

She rolled her eyes. "I think we both know the answer to that."

"Does that attitude also explain why the kitchen table and chairs are gone?"

"No!" She stood up and glared at him. "That is so desperately unfair. You're sitting with your back to the kitchen. I did that on purpose. How did you know?"

"I saw they were gone when I walked in."

"And you didn't say anything? You just waited to pounce."

"I'm not pouncing."

"It feels pouncy." She dropped back into her chair. "Fine, yes, they're gone. I couldn't get in touch with the lady who bought them and when she called me, she was so excited. She and her kids have been homeless and now they have a place and she talked about how they would do their homework on that table. I couldn't say no."

She felt both defiant and stupid. Daniel stood.

"Get your purse and your keys. You're coming with me."

"Where are we going?"

"It's a surprise."

She wasn't worried he would take her anywhere bad and it was only five in the afternoon, so it wasn't even late. Maybe dinner, she thought, thinking wherever Daniel picked out would be better than the takeout she had planned. One of these days she was going to have to start cooking again. Once she got her act together, she would go back to the whole cooking on Sunday afternoon so she had healthy food for the week thing she used to do. Okay, not *do*, exactly. But think about doing. Sometimes.

They got in his truck and they headed east. When they reached the outskirts of Burbank, she glanced at him.

"Please tell me we're not visiting my mother. Not that I don't love her and all, but I'll be seeing her this weekend when we have to spend more time going through the house."

He smiled. "We're not going to visit your mother. We're going to my place."

"Oh."

That was unexpected. His place. She'd never been there. She tried to remember what Glen had told her. She knew Daniel's business was a success, plus he'd done well racing. She thought maybe he had a house up in the hills.

Sure enough, a few minutes later, they'd passed through the flatlands and were heading up into the foothills. Condos gave way to small houses. Small houses gave way to bigger ones. The road narrowed and turned and twisted until they were in a very exclusive part of town.

"Well, this is fancy," she murmured as he pulled into the driveway of a large two-story house with a four-car garage. He hit a clicker and one of the garage doors opened.

The first thing she noticed was the motorcycles. There were four parked in two of the spaces.

"You take this motocross thing very seriously," she said as she got out of the truck.

Daniel shook his head. "They're street bikes."

"I knew that."

He looked at her.

She grinned. "I did not know that, but I do now."

He motioned to the empty fourth bay. "This is big enough for all your stuff. Boxes, furniture, assuming you don't give it all away."

She saw what he meant and realized why he'd brought her here. Good thing she hadn't said anything about them maybe having dinner or something.

"You're assuming I'm going to move in with someone, which makes sense," she said. "This is so nice. You're saving me storage fees. Thank you. That's very kind."

"Ali, I'm not just offering you a place to keep your things. I'm offering you a place to live."

"What?"

"Follow me."

Live? As in…live? With him? In his house? With him?

"I don't understand."

He kept moving, forcing her to trail after him. They entered the house through a mudroom. To the left was a large laundry room and in front of them a gorgeous kitchen.

There were huge windows and dark cabinets and an island the size of her former bed and gleaming appliances, some of which she didn't even recognize.

"I don't cook much, but even I could shine in here," she said. "It's massive. This whole house is gigantic. How long have you lived here?"

"A couple of years. It's hard to find a small house with a four-car garage. Plus I figured one day I'd settle down."

Lucky lady, she thought as they continued through the downstairs. There was a big great room just beyond the kitchen.

He went to the far end of the kitchen, down a narrow hall, then pushed open a door.

"Mother-in-law suite," he said, motioning for her to go in.

The small sitting area had a sofa and a TV on a credenza. Beyond that was a bedroom with a queen-size bed, a dresser, another TV and a desk by the window. The closet was huge, as was the bathroom.

"It's yours for as long as you want it," he told her. "My bedroom is upstairs and on the other side of the house, so you'll never hear me. You can use the kitchen, family room, laundry, whatever you want. You can come and go as you please."

She looked at the pretty lavender bedspread and the dresser with big drawers and the bathroom with double sinks and a jumbo shower.

"You're willing to rent this to me?" she asked. "Seriously?"

"Not rent, Ali. You can stay here. I want you to stay here, as my guest, for as long as you'd like." He shoved his hands into his front pockets. "There are no strings. You have my word."

"Strings?"

"I don't want you to think I'm coming on to you."

She laughed. "Trust me, I would never think that. But you can't be serious. I can't just live here."

"Why not? I have the room and you need a place. We get along. I want to do this. I want to know that you're safe."

He was the nicest man ever, she thought, fighting the sudden burning in her eyes. Glen had been so awful and Daniel was his exact opposite.

"Come see the rest of the downstairs," he said.

She took one last look at the beautiful room, told herself she really couldn't, before following him back through the kitchen. He led her into the big great room with a TV over the fireplace.

"There's a media room upstairs," he told her.

She smiled. "Of course there is."

She saw a small formal living room and a much bigger dining room, both of which were empty.

"You're such a guy. You have no furniture in your dining room but you have a media room."

He flashed her a grin. "Priorities."

They went into a good-sized office. There was a desk, a couple of leather chairs and built-in cabinets with bookshelves covering one wall.

The shelves were filled with dozens and dozens of trophies and other awards. On the opposite wall were pictures of Daniel racing or riding, along with photos of him in the winner's circle, looking tired, dirty and triumphant. Ali crossed to the shelves.

"Look at all these," she said, reading some of the plaques. "You're so famous."

"It was a while ago."

She glanced at him over her shoulder. "Please don't downplay your success around me. I'm impressed. I wish I'd known about this before. I feel like when Glen and I were together, I barely knew you at all." She decided to tell him the truth. "Actually, I thought you didn't like me."

His steady gaze never wavered. "Why would you think that?"

"I'm not sure. I guess I wasn't comfortable around you. I am now, obviously. I can gush and fangirl all over you."

"Not necessary. Ali, I meant what I said. Come live here for a few months while you figure out what you want to do next. I'm barely around and you'll have plenty of space and privacy."

"Your women won't mind?" With a guy like Daniel, there were always women.

"I'm between entanglements."

"For now, but later there will be someone." Not anything she wanted to dwell on but there was no point in avoiding reality. Daniel was the kind of guy to have a beautiful woman in his life. Not like a player—she didn't think of him as that. But what was there not to like?

Back to the issue at hand, she told herself. Living here. To be honest, her options were limited. She really didn't want to pick some crummy apartment simply because it was available in her budget. If she had some time to pay off the credit cards and build up her savings, she would sleep easier, that was for sure, and moving in with her mother was not an option. Finola's situation was, ah, fluid and Zennie's place was smaller than hers.

"If you're sure," she began.

"I am. Let's say you can stay here a year, rent-free. After that, I'll toss you out."

"A year? That's too long."

"Then go when you'd like, but as far as I'm concerned, you have a year."

"That's too generous. I'll have to pay something."

"You really don't."

"At least half the utilities. I'd offer to cook, but neither of us want to depend on that."

He hesitated a second. "Fine. Half the utilities," he agreed. "I'll email you a bill."

She worried her bottom lip. It was the perfect solution, at least for her.

"Okay," she said. "Thank you. I'm very appreciative."

"I'm happy to have you here. Now you said you had something going on with your mom this weekend. Let's get you moved in next Saturday. I know a couple of guys who can help. We'll get you packed and moved in on Saturday so you can settle and unpack on Sunday."

"Perfect. I'll need to figure out what I'm keeping out and what goes in storage."

Not that she would need much in his place, which was convenient considering she didn't have that much left.

"Then we have a deal?" he asked.

"We do. Thank you, Daniel."

"No problem, but do me a favor. Try not to sell any more of your furniture."

She groaned. "That wasn't my fault."

He looked at her.

"Fine. It was a little my fault, and yes, I'll stop." She smiled. "Maybe I'll get so inspired by your kitchen that I'll take a class."

"Whatever makes you happy."

You do.

The thought was so unexpected, she tried not to fall over from shock. No, no and no. She was not interested in Daniel. No way, nohow. She had flaws but she wasn't an idiot. Not only were there a thousand reasons not to get involved with her ex-fiancé's brother, it was an awful way to repay someone who had only been nice. Super nice. Nope, she wasn't into him at all. Not even a little. Really.

Chapter Thirteen

"Your blood work results are excellent," Dr. McQueen told Zennie. "You're not on birth control, you've tested negative for any STDs. From a health perspective, there's no reason to think you can't carry a healthy baby to term."

"But?" Zennie asked her gynecologist. "I sense a 'but' coming."

Dr. McQueen was a sensible-looking woman in her early forties. She'd been Zennie's doctor for the past five years. Zennie dutifully saw her for a checkup every twelve months or so, turned down an offer of birth control pills or an IUD and went on her way. She wasn't due for a baseline mammogram for years, never had any "girl" issues and hadn't much thought about getting pregnant until a couple of weeks ago.

"Pregnancy is natural and the majority of women go through their time with only minor inconveniences. Having said that, it *is* a stress on the body. There are major physical and hormonal changes that require support and lifestyle changes. Once you deliver the baby, you'll feel like your old self in a few months but your body will take a full year to heal. There are also risks with pregnancy—I would assume minor risks in your case, but risks nonetheless. And at the end of the day, you will have gone through all that just to give your baby to someone else and it will biologically be *your* baby."

She softened her words with a smile. "Zennie, what you're offering your friend is amazing, but you have to be sure."

"I appreciate the honesty," Zennie told her. "I really do, and you're right—it's a lot for my body to go through. But I love Bernie and I want to do this for her and Hayes. I'm young, I'm healthy and I have no plans to have kids myself, at least not right now. So I don't think giving up the baby is going to be hard for me. I want to do this."

She'd signed the paperwork and dropped it off with Bernie. Now all she needed was a clean bill of health and she would be good to go on getting pregnant.

Dr. McQueen smiled at her. "Sounds like you've made up your mind. All right. I've given you my best 'are you sure?' lecture, so let's move on. I'll meet you in the examination room. After double-checking you're physically good to go, we'll figure out when we next expect you to ovulate. There are a couple of options and we'll go over them. How does that sound?"

"Perfect."

Twenty minutes later, when Dr. McQueen finished the exam, she didn't look happy.

"What's wrong?" Zennie asked. She'd just had her annual four months earlier. Her Pap had come back completely normal. What could have changed in that short a time?

"Nothing's wrong," her doctor assured her. "It's just..." She smiled. "Zennie, my best guess is you're ovulating right now. Not to rush you, but the lab is here. We could confirm you're ready with a quick ultrasound, have your friend's husband come in and make a deposit, so to speak. After the lab does their thing, we could make an attempt right now." Her voice softened. "Or we could wait a month if you need time to process all this. I know it's very quick."

The news was a little disconcerting, but if she was going to do this, why wait another month?

"Let's find out if I'm ovulating," she told the doctor. "After that, I'll decide."

A little warm gel and time with a wand later, she had her answer. Zennie's heart thundered in her chest. She was both scared and excited.

"I want to do this," she told Dr. McQueen. "I'm going to call Hayes right now and have him get over here."

Dr. McQueen grinned. "I'm going to leave you alone for that conversation," she said with a chuckle.

Zennie got her phone and dialed. Hayes's assistant put her through right away.

"Hey, Zennie, what's up?"

Zennie drew in a breath. "Hayes, I know this is really fast, but I'm at the doctor's office. She gave me a clean bill of health, and it turns out I'm ovulating right now. So if you want to get started today, you have to get here right away."

There was a moment of silence. Hayes cleared his throat. "So you're saying I would be, ah, providing the sample."

Zennie sighed. Men were so delicate. "I'm sure they have a room here where you'll be able to make that happen. No pressure."

"Oh, there's pressure. Right now? Okay. I'll clear my calendar and be on my way."

She gave him the address and hung up, then went to tell Dr. McQueen's nurse Hayes was on his way.

Zennie looked at the clock on the wall and knew Bernie would still be at school. Zennie texted her the information, along with the address for the doctor's office, then prepared to wait.

Less than three hours later, Zennie lay flat, with her feet slightly elevated, Bernie holding her hand.

"I can't believe this is happening," her friend told her. "Zennie, thank you so much."

"You know it could take a couple of tries, right? I'm unlikely to get pregnant the first time."

"I know, but still. You just did it, you didn't even think about it."

"I've already said I want to do this. Why would I wait?" She looked at the door. "Hayes isn't joining us?"

Bernie grinned. "He went home. I'm not sure he wants to face you right now."

"It was kind of weird. I did my best not to think about it while it was happening."

They both giggled.

"How do you feel?" Bernie asked. "I heard there could be cramping after artificial insemination."

"There's barely anything. A slight achiness, but it's already fading." She looked into Bernie's eyes. "We're doing this. We're making you a family."

"I know. I can't believe it."

Dr. McQueen knocked once, then entered the room. "All right, Zennie, you're ready to go live your life. I've sent your local pharmacy a prescription for prenatal vitamins. Start taking those right away." She put several papers on the counter. "These talk about what to eat and what not to eat. Also, there's a basic list of restrictions. No alcohol or caffeine. Avoid hot tubs. You can do a home pregnancy test in two to three weeks. Come back and see me, regardless of the results. If you're pregnant, we should talk and if you're not, let's get you going on monitoring your cycle. Fair enough?"

"We have a plan," Zennie told her.

Dr. McQueen smiled at Bernie. "Good luck. I hope I get to see a lot of you at the visits."

"Me, too."

The doctor left. Bernie stepped back. "I'll leave you to get dressed. And once we walk out of here, we're not going to talk about it at all. Not until you take the pregnancy tests. I don't want you worrying that I'm going to overmonitor you. I'm not even going to think about it."

"Me, either." Zennie sat up. "Although we're both lying when we say that."

Bernie laughed. "We both so are. But we'll pretend to be normal. How's that?"

"It's a great plan."

Saturday morning Ali wanted nothing other than to sleep in and be lazy, but that wasn't an option. She'd promised her mother to help finish going through the bonus room. Mary Jo would be working, so it would just be the sisters. If the three of them hustled, they should be able to finish in a few hours, or so Ali hoped.

She parked next to Zennie's car and walked up the front walk, pausing when her phone buzzed.

Zennie joined her on the porch, then let her in the house.

"Did you get a text from Finola?" her sister asked by way of greeting. "She's canceling on us."

"No way." Ali pulled out her phone. Sure enough, there it was.

Sorry to bail. I just can't face more memories today. I'll make it up to you.

Ali wrestled with conflicting emotions. On the one hand she understood her sister was going through a lot. On the other, there was still work to be done on their mom's house and it wasn't as if Finola was the only one going through emotional turmoil.

"Go ahead," Zennie said as they went upstairs. "Tell me why I shouldn't call her a selfish bitch." Her tone was more cheerful than chiding. "You always take her side."

"Not always. Just sometimes. As for today, while I appreciate what she's dealing with, the least she could do was send us a minion to do her share of the hard labor."

Zennie laughed. "I like your style."

They reached the loft and stood staring at the half-open boxes, the mostly empty closet and the cabinets and drawers yet to be tackled.

"Ugh," Zennie said. "This totally sucks. Tell you what. We'll work until noon, then call it a day and go to Bob's Big Boy for lunch."

Ali grinned. "That is a perfect plan. You'll probably get a salad, but I swear, I'm getting a burger and a milkshake."

Zennie wrinkled her nose. "A salad? You're confusing me with Finola. I'm a burger girl all the way."

"You say that now, but Finola eats the way she does to stay skinny. You eat healthy because you're athletic and see your body as a temple or something. It's seriously depressing."

Zennie gave her a strange look but before Ali could ask about it, she turned away and pointed to the cabinet. "Do you want to tackle that first, or finish the closet?"

"Let's finish the closet. That way we'll have space to stack the stuff we think Mom's keeping. We'll keep the junk and giveaway piles out of the closet."

They carried out bins and boxes. Several fancy dresses hung on a rack.

"We might as well leave those," Zennie said. "I have no idea if Mom wants to keep them, but whatever decision we make will be wrong."

Ali agreed. Once the closet was empty except for the dresses, they moved in all the "keep" boxes before sitting on the floor to go through what was left.

Ali opened a bin full of old Halloween costumes. Some were really elaborate while others were the inexpensive store-bought kind. She tossed out the premade ones and saved those her mother had created. She held up a beautiful mermaid dress.

"I never wore this one. Did you?"

Zennie shook her head. "It's Finola's. All the good ones are. I never wanted to be a princess or anything girly, so Dad helped me be a pirate or whatever."

Ali remembered the family discussions around Halloween. Zennie was right—she and their dad would go off to the garage and make something. By that point Finola wasn't interested in going trick-or-treating, so Ali went to the grocery store with her mom to pick out a costume.

Ali fingered the handmade costume with its beading and fringe-fishtail. At some point the costume would have fit her—not that it had been offered and she hadn't known about it so hadn't asked.

For a second she thought about all the times she'd been the odd kid out. Her mother had been all about Finola and her dad had been all about Zennie. There's been no third parent to be on Ali's team.

"How are you doing with canceling the wedding?" Zennie asked. "Do you need help returning gifts or anything?"

"Thanks, but everything is done." She wrinkled her nose. "I honestly don't know what to do about the dress. I'm not excited about selling it or even donating it. I would love to give it to someone I knew needed it, but I don't want to just put it in a donation box somewhere, knowing it will show up in a store and be priced at five dollars."

She looked at her sister. "I don't mean that in a horrible way."

"I know what you mean. It was special and you want it to stay that way."

"I kind of do. Maybe I should look online for a group that finds wedding gowns for women in need or something."

"I have a friend who works in oncology at the hospital," Zennie told her. "There was a patient who was thinking of getting married between rounds of chemo. Want me to check and see if she needs a dress?"

Ali smiled. "I would love that. Just make sure she knows it's going to need alterations." She pulled her phone from her pocket. "I think I still have a couple of pictures of the dress. I'll text them to you and you can forward them to your friend."

Giving the dress to someone in need would make her feel better about having to get rid of it.

She found the picture and studied herself for a second. She'd been so happy to finally find the right gown for her wedding. Even as she'd been excited, Glen had probably been plotting his exit. She wondered when he'd changed his mind about them. There was no way she was going to believe he'd tricked her from the beginning. Even Glen couldn't be that awful, and if he could be, she didn't want to know. She'd reached a place where she was sad but recovering from their broken engagement. The healing had come more quickly than she would have expected, which probably said something about their relationship.

They went through more boxes. They found stacks of books they'd had as kids and put them in the donate pile. Zennie pulled out her letter jacket from high school.

"I'm keeping this," Zennie said, holding it up. "I wonder if I can get it dry-cleaned or something. It has to be dusty."

"Not to mention sweaty," Ali teased. "You were so proud of that thing. You wore it constantly." Given the fact that it was close to seventy degrees, even in winter, thick letter jackets were rarely needed for warmth.

"I worked hard for it," Zennie said, carefully folding the jacket and setting it by the door. "Dad and I were both really upset when I lettered and they told me I could only get a sweater. Seriously, it wasn't the 1880s. Why would only guys be eligible for the jacket while girls got a sweater? Stupid administrators. But we prevailed."

"Dad was always really supportive of you," Ali said. She wasn't bitter—facts were facts.

"He was."

They moved on to another set of boxes. Ali opened the first one and groaned. "I think we're going to have to keep these. You know how Mom is."

She held up several items of baby clothing. Little dresses and onesies, all well-worn but clean. There was a beautiful white dress that Ali didn't remember wearing but knew they all had for their christening.

She waved the dress. "Hard to believe we were ever this small," she said. "Mom is keeping the grandkid dream alive, that's for sure. And we keep disappointing her."

Zennie looked at the dress, then glanced away. She started to speak, pressed her lips together and cleared her throat.

"What?" Ali demanded. "You're acting weird." She tried to figure out why. "Did you get back together with Clark? Oh my God, are you in love with him and thinking of getting married?"

"What? No! Why would you think that? Clark and I aren't together, I'm not in love. The best first date I've had in months was with a lesbian."

Ali made a mental note to come back to the lesbian comment. "So what's going on?"

She half expected her sister to deny anything was, but instead Zennie said, "You have to swear not to tell anyone. I mean it. Completely swear."

"I swear."

Possibilities flitted in and out of her head. She doubted Zennie was sick and if there wasn't a guy, then what? She was moving out of state? She was getting a cat. No, not a pet. That wasn't swear-worthy. Maybe she wanted to go back to school for something.

"You remember when Bernie had cancer?"

Ali's heart sank. "No. Don't tell me it's back."

"It's not. She's doing great. But because of the surgery and stuff, she can't have kids. She and Hayes and I talked and well, I'm going to be their surrogate."

Ali processed the information. "I don't know exactly what that means. Are you going to have a fertilized egg planted inside or are you donating the egg and then having the baby?"

"I'm donating the egg." Zennie's eyes brightened. "I had the procedure yesterday."

"What?" Ali's gaze dropped to her sister's annoying flat stomach. "You're telling me that you could be pregnant right this second?"

"I could."

The news was astounding. "That's incredible, Zennie. What an amazing gift to give your best friend. Or anyone. A baby. You're so generous. I don't know if I could do that for someone. But you are. Are you excited? Or scared? Or both?"

Zennie laughed. "Kind of both. It's not real. I mean I was at the doctor's office and they inserted sperm, but it doesn't feel real. I'll take a pregnancy test in a couple of weeks to find out for sure."

"Good for you. Congratulations. Let me know if I can do anything to help."

"You have enough on your plate, but thanks."

Ali waved away her comment. "I'm doing great. The wedding is canceled, I might have a solution for the dress problem and I'm, ah, going to move in with a friend while I figure out my living situation."

At some point she was going to have to admit she was moving in with Daniel, just not today. Finola's words still stung.

"My point is," she continued, "I'll have plenty of time to help with your pregnancy." She frowned. "Although I'm not sure what I could do. I guess at least offer moral support and buy you shea butter so you don't get stretch marks."

"Do I need shea butter?"

"I have no idea. You should probably look it up."

Zennie reached across the box and squeezed her hand. "Thanks for getting it."

"Of course. Mom's going to kill you, by the way."

"I know. That's why I made you swear. I'm going to wait until I'm sure I'm pregnant before saying anything. I'm afraid she won't understand at all."

Ali grinned. "Not even a little. After years of hounding us for grandchildren, she's finally going to get one, only you're giving it away. I think she might have a comment or two to say about that."

Zennie groaned. "Of that, I'm sure. But for now, you're the only one who knows. Well, you and Bernie and Hayes."

"Speaking of Hayes, how did you get the sperm?"

Zennie's mouth twitched. "Really, Ali? You've been with a guy."

"You didn't have sex." She thought for a second. "Oh no. You're kidding. He had to do *that* at the doctor's office."

"Yup. In a separate room. I tried not to think about it while it was happening."

Ali giggled. "I'm sure he was grateful. I know it's really great that you can do this for them and when they have a baby, they'll be so happy, but sometimes, science is just plain weird."

"Tell me about it."

Chapter Fourteen

Sunday morning Zennie met her friends to go running in Griffith Park. The sky was clear, the air cool. Bernie had texted to say she was sleeping in and wouldn't be joining them. Zennie felt a faint sense of relief. She knew her friend was anxious about the possibility of a pregnancy and would be watching for any signs. As it had been less than forty-eight hours, no one was even sure there was a pregnancy, let alone signs.

Zennie told herself that wasn't fair. Of course Bernie wanted to know what was happening. They all did. It was a big deal. But the only thing they could do was wait. She was determined to put the pregnancy out of her mind as much as possible and just live her life. Somewhere between two and three weeks from now, she would take a pregnancy test and they would all know—unless she got her period first. Regardless, she was not going to dwell on the fact that she might be "with child."

Two more cars pulled up in the mostly empty parking lot.

The friends would run up in the hills, close to the observatory. The path was steep and challenging, but they'd done it before. Zennie enjoyed the change and the fact that there was more focus on running and less on conversation. For most of the circuit, they could only go single file.

Cassie, a short, plump blonde, and DeeDee, a lithe Korean with deep purple streaks in her long hair, had come together. Gina, a tall, fit brunette, got out of the second car and waved.

"How's everyone feeling?"

Cassie pulled on a baseball cap and squinted at the sun. "Hungover. Ugh. I was out too late."

Gina grinned. "Didn't you have a hot date with that new guy? How did it go?"

"The parts I remember were great." Cassie sighed. "He's really sweet. He owns a pool-cleaning business and he's been divorced for two years. No kids."

"I sense a third date in the making," DeeDee crowed. "And we all know what that means."

Cassie and Gina shared a high five. "Sex!" they yelled together. "Woo-hoo!"

"You're all in a mood," Zennie teased, thinking her night of yoga, movies on demand and herbal tea had very little in common with how her friends had spent their Saturday evening.

"One of us is going to get some," Gina said. "Hey, you passed three dates with Clark before it all ended. Did you do the deed?"

"I don't keep to a calendar."

DeeDee put her hands on her hips. "Zennie isn't like us. She doesn't allow herself to be ruled by her base nature. We should admire and emulate her."

"I'd rather get laid," Gina admitted. "I'm in a dry spell and I'm running out of batteries."

They all laughed and headed for the trailhead.

The first mile was on relatively flat ground where they could run abreast. Conversation flowed easily. Most of the talk was about who was dating and who wanted to be. Cassie filled them in on every detail of her date, including the heavy petting before she'd gone home.

"What about you, Zennie?" Gina asked. "What's new with you?"

Zennie thought briefly of her Friday afternoon procedure but knew it was too soon to bring that up. "I spent yesterday morning at my mom's house," she said instead. "She's getting the house ready to sell so she can move to a smaller place by the beach. There's thirty years of crap everywhere. Ali and I finished the bonus room, so at least that's done. But there's still every other room."

"We're entering that stage of life," DeeDee told them. "First they downsize, then they start getting sick."

"That's cheerful," Cassie muttered.

"You know it's true. Soon we'll be the sandwich generation, raising our own families while caring for our aging parents. It's a thing."

"Don't tell me that," Gina said. "I'm an only child. There's no one but me."

Zennie hadn't thought about the next few years, but realized if something happened to either of her parents, their care would fall on her and her sisters.

They reached the next section of the trail, where the path was steep and narrow. Gina took the lead, as she always did. She was an X-ray technician who had run hurdles all the way through college. She competed in triathlons a couple of times a year and often talked about how she should have tried harder to make the Olympic team when she'd been younger.

Gina set a challenging but achievable pace. Zennie was right behind her with Cassie and DeeDee bringing up the rear.

The trail was well marked and well used. There were wider areas for groups to pass and the underbrush was kept trimmed, something Zennie appreciated. She might have grown up as a tomboy, but she still had a deep fear of snakes. The foothills around Los Angeles were home to rattlesnakes and Zennie was convinced that in the rattlesnake community, she was a prize.

They reached a flat area and stopped for water and to catch their breath. The view of the hills and city beyond was amazing. It was early enough that they had the trail to themselves and the only sounds were their breathing and conversation.

DeeDee handed Zennie her water bottle. "Hold this for a second, please." DeeDee put her heel on a boulder and stretched her leg. "I keep getting this stupid tight hamstring."

She straightened and reached for her bottle. Zennie went to hand it to her friend, her arm outstretched.

She wasn't sure what happened next. She knew she stepped on a rock and that knocked her off balance. Zennie's weight shifted, the edge of the hill gave way just a little and the next thing Zennie knew, she was sliding and falling and screaming as she tumbled over before coming to a stop a good twenty feet below the path.

At first she was too stunned to do anything but lie there. She heard her friends yelling her name. Gina scrambled down first, hanging on to bushes and dried grass to slow her descent. By the time she was close, Zennie had pushed herself into a sitting position and was trying to assess her injuries.

She felt shaken but not disoriented. Her upper leg burned. When she looked down, she saw she'd gotten a heck of a scrape from hip to knee. She ignored the oozing blood and dirt and rocks embedded in her flesh. That was superficial and could be dealt with. She was more concerned about serious injuries.

"Lie back down," Gina told her.

"And risk getting a snakebite on the face? No, thank you."

Gina waved to the other two. "She's conscious and still scared of snakes. I think that's a good sign."

"Not snakes," Zennie muttered. "Rattlesnakes. There's a difference."

Gina crouched next to her. "Did you hit your head?"

"No."

"Good. We'll start at the bottom and work our way up."

Gina had her move her toes, her feet, her ankles and so on. They quickly assessed nothing was broken, although Zennie had multiple scrapes with plenty of embedded debris.

"That's going to hurt to get out," Gina said, helping Zennie to her feet.

"I'm trying not to think about it," Zennie admitted as she stood and waited. She monitored herself for dizziness or acute pain, but there was just the dull ache of the abrasions. She was banged up, a little shaken, but nothing more.

She and Gina scrambled up to the trail. DeeDee flung herself at Zennie.

"This is all my fault."

"Don't be ridiculous. I slipped. That's on me, not you."

"You could have died."

Zennie hugged her friend. "You are so weird."

Cassie, a pediatric care nurse, looked at Zennie's leg and winced. "You're going to need to go to an urgent care center. A hospital would be better, but I know you'll balk at that."

"There's one just down the hill," Gina said. "I'll go with her and you two can finish the run."

Cassie snorted. "As if. We are not finishing the run without you two. We'll all go to urgent care and make sure Zennie's okay."

Zennie wanted to protest but she knew there was no way she could clean out the scrapes herself. Not only couldn't she see what she was doing, it would hurt like hell. At least at the urgent care center, they could spray on a topical numbing cream to take the edge off.

Thirty minutes later she was in an examination room. A handsome doctor in a wheelchair entered the room, her chart in his lap. He was in his late thirties, with too-long hair and glasses. He gave her an easy smile.

"Really? You couldn't just sleep in on a Sunday morning?"

"Sorry. I'm not the sleep-in type."

"Fine. Make me work for a living. I'm Dr. Rowell, by the way, but you can call me Harry. Everyone does." He stopped in front of her and looked at her leg. "That's ugly. Okay. I'm going to make sure you're only banged up and not seriously hurt, then we'll clean you up." He picked up her chart. "Any allergies to medication or medical conditions I should know about?"

"No, I'm—" She'd been about to say perfectly fine, only what if she wasn't.

Zennie clutched the edge of the exam room table and stared at the doctor. Horror swept through her as nausea churned in her stomach. Tears filled her eyes.

"What?" Harry asked, his tone gentle. "Zennie, what is it?"

"I might be pregnant. I just got AI last Friday. No one even knows. I'm trying to have a baby for my best friend and I fell." The tears spilled onto her cheeks. "What if I killed her baby?"

"You didn't kill the baby," he told her. "Come on. If you even are pregnant, it's like four cells." He squeezed her hand. "Okay, let's get serious. This early on, the embryo would be embedded in your uterus, surrounded by all your girl parts and internal organs. Fabergé eggs don't get such royal treatment when they're shipped around the world."

She wiped her face and managed a smile. "Girl parts? Are you sure you went to medical school?"

He flashed her a grin. "I think I missed that day, but I totally rocked wound cleaning." He squeezed her hand again. "Zennie, artificial insemination is a simple procedure that doesn't always take. If you're not pregnant, it has nothing to do with your fall. I swear. Believe me?"

She nodded. "I'm not sure I will later, but I appreciate the information." She knew he was right, about all of it, but she wasn't exactly in a rational place. "I just want to give her a healthy little baby."

"I know and I'm sure you will." He released her hand and looked at her leg. "Yup, that's ugly. Okay, let's check you out and find out what's going on, then we'll start the torture."

She laughed. "Sounds like a plan. So are you single?"

He raised his eyebrows. "You work fast."

"Not for me. But I do think you'd like my friend DeeDee. You share a sense of humor."

"I saw your friends and would be open to meeting any of them. Once you're patched up, let's casually introduce me."

"Let's."

Finola knew she had to get her act together. Hiding out in her house was only making her more depressed. She was withdrawing from everything that wasn't work-related and that was not a healthy path.

She was still angry about her stepfather's comments. She knew she wasn't responsible for Nigel's affair and to suggest otherwise was simply cruel. Yet she couldn't let the idea go. Nor could she stop feeling guilty about not joining her sisters to help with their mom's house sorting. She spent a restless night and morning pacing in the house feeling trapped. By noon she knew she had to do something.

She went to the grocery store and stocked up on food for the coming week, then checked the schedule of her favorite workout studio. She saw there was a barre class starting in an hour. She would go to that, sweat out her frustration then come home and make a plan for the next few days. First on her list would be an apology dinner with her sisters.

The Encino fitness studio was both upscale and snooty. Women came to work out and to judge. No jiggle went unnoticed, no slack thigh went uncatalogued. Finola wasn't thrilled with the spirit of the place, but the classes were excellent and many movers and shakers worked out there. Life was all about who you knew.

She had barely started stretching when she heard a familiar voice saying, "Is this space taken?"

She smiled at her assistant. "Hey, Rochelle. You're young and beautiful. Why aren't you on the beach with some hunky guy?"

"I'm always here on Sunday afternoon. You run into the most interesting people."

"Good." Those connections were why Finola had given Rochelle the membership as a Christmas gift. The young woman was going to be someone to be reckoned with in the not too distant future.

Finola let herself relax a little. Having Rochelle in the class would mean she had a buffer. An unexpected bonus, she thought gratefully. While her strict diet had taken care of any lingering effects of the week of carbs and not moving, Finola knew she was still incredibly vulnerable. It wouldn't take much to shatter her like a dropped crystal vase.

For the next fifty minutes Finola couldn't think of anything but keeping up. She scooped, lifted, held and breathed until she was shaking, with sweat dripping down her back. When they relaxed onto mats to stretch, she was pleased to find that her mind had quieted. She was strong, she told herself. She would use the next week to get her act together. She would stop hiding and walk with her head held high.

They finished class and rose. Rochelle was as out of breath and sweaty as she was.

"It kills me every time," she admitted.

"It's supposed to."

One of the women from the class looked out the window. "Huh. There's something going on in the parking lot. I wonder if Jennifer Lawrence is taking a private class again. My daughter just loves her."

Finola's heart sank. *No*, she told herself. She wasn't going to assume anything. She had to remember to be strong.

Several women moved toward the window. Without saying anything, Rochelle joined them, then quickly returned to Finola's side.

"Six photographers waiting by the door. I don't see a news van, so they're freelancers. Jennifer Lawrence really might be getting a private lesson."

The sweat that broke out on her back had nothing to do with the workout. "Do you really believe that?"

Rochelle's gaze locked with hers. "No. How do you want to handle this?"

Finola pressed a hand to her stomach. She had to get out of the studio and to her car. Once she was there, she could make her escape. There was a chance that this had nothing to do with her, but she couldn't count on it.

The problem wasn't the distance to her car, it was the pictures. They would last forever. Oh, why had she worn such an ugly dress over her workout clothes?

"What did you wear in to class?" she asked her assistant.

Rochelle smiled. "A leather skirt and denim jacket. Not practical, I know, but I, ah, didn't come from my apartment."

Despite her terror and the nausea, Finola smiled. "Aha, so there *is* a hunky guy."

"There might be. Let's go get changed."

There was a small dressing area in back. The previous class had cleared out and the new one was heading to the studio. They had the space to themselves.

Rochelle opened her locker and got out her street clothes. She held out the skirt and jacket. Thank God they were both black, as were Finola's leggings.

She pulled on the skirt, then slipped on the sandals she'd worn in. She and Rochelle wore the same size clothes, but they weren't even close on shoes. She pulled a comb from her bag then dug around for a hair fastener. Rochelle had her sit in front of the mirror, then combed her hair back and secured it in a high, perky ponytail. Finola applied lip gloss and put on her oversize sunglasses. Rochelle slipped on her dress.

"I'm sorry it's so ugly," Finola told her.

"It's fine. No one is going to notice me. If the photographers are who we think they are, you're the story. Now let's put the jean jacket over your shoulders."

Finola swung it into place, then stood to look at her reflection.

She looked good. Fit and chic. The sunglasses would hide her wide-eyed stare. She relaxed her face into a neutral expression that showed no emotion. That was her goal. To stay neutral. Pretty, confident and not the least bit upset by what was happening. When there was nothing left to do, they walked toward the studio exit.

"Want me to ask about a back way?" Rochelle asked. "I could get my car and drive around to get you."

Finola managed a genuine smile. "You think they haven't staked out the other side of the building?"

"Oh. Good point. Are you ready?"

Finola nodded because she didn't have much choice in the matter. "I'll walk directly to my car. You do the same. When I pull out, get right behind me. I doubt I'm someone worth following, but just in case, you can block the exit for a few seconds while I blend into traffic."

"Are you all right?"

Finola raised a shoulder. "I'll get through this."

She was so focused on getting away, she didn't have time to think or feel anything else. Probably for the best, she told herself. She had to remember that while she could ignore questions, pictures were forever. She sucked in a breath, then opened the studio door and started directly for her car.

The photographers were on her instantly. The whirring clicks of their cameras were nearly as loud as the questions.

"Finola, when did you find out about the affair?"

"Are you too old to have kids? Is that why your husband's doing this?"

"Have you been in a three-way with Treasure?"

"Does it bother you that she's so much younger?"

"When did your husband stop loving you?"

The questions hit her like poison darts, each more painful than the one before. She kept walking, her head high, her stride confident. She could see her car right up ahead of her. *Neutral face*, she chanted to herself. Neutral expression so no one knows what a bitch this was. She would get through it because she didn't have a choice.

She reached her car. As she touched the door handle, the car unlocked. She slid into her seat, hit the door lock button, then started the engine. The photographers got close, but they didn't crowd her and none of them raced for their cars. Thank God she'd been right—she wasn't that interesting. Just interesting enough. Because of Treasure. If he'd slept with nearly anyone else, none of this would have been news.

She drove out of the parking lot with Rochelle right behind her and merged with the heavy traffic on Ventura Boulevard. She took the long way home, making plenty of unexpected turns, causing other drivers to honk at her. She wove through a quiet neighborhood, even stopping in front of a house for three minutes. No one else drove on the street. Only then did she allow herself to breathe.

She called Rochelle. "I don't think anyone followed me."

"I didn't see anyone after you. Finola, I'm so sorry about all this."

"Me, too."

"It's going to be everywhere by tonight. You're going to have to deal with it at work."

Not anything she wanted to think about. "I know."

"How can I help?"

"I'm not sure, but I'll be in touch."

"Do you want me to get you a hotel room?"

Finola swore silently. Of course—because she probably couldn't stay in her house. Not now.

"Let me figure out my next step," she said. "I'll let you know. And Rochelle? Thank you."

"Of course. You know I'm on your side."

Finola allowed herself a second of self-congratulation. She'd chosen well when it came to her assistant. As to her husband—not so much on the choosing.

She pulled away from the curb. Twenty minutes later her car was in the garage and she was on her laptop. She logged into the TMZ website, then swore when she saw the headlines. News of Treasure's new lover was everywhere along with pictures of the singer with Nigel. Worse, there were clips from the interview on the *AM SoCal* show, showing a very shell-shocked Finola. At the time people had assumed she'd merely had an off show. In hindsight, everyone would know she'd just been told the news and was having to deal on live TV.

Humiliation and anger fought for dominance. Damn Nigel. Why had he done this to her? She hadn't done anything to deserve it. He was a total asshole, but hers was the life that was destroyed. Nobody cared if their plastic surgeon had an affair with a singer. But she was all about home and family. Her brand was smart and fun, without any kind of edge. Her viewers would wonder, much like her stepfather had, how she was to blame.

Her phone started chiming as text messages came in, then it rang. She glanced at the screen. She didn't know the number, so didn't answer. She put it on silent, then watched as it buzzed as if it were being electrocuted.

She needed a plan. It was only a matter of hours until the press found out where she lived. The deed was in both her and Nigel's names, so hardly secure. She really didn't want to go live in a hotel. That would be too depressing and she would feel too vulnerable in such a public location. Anyone could knock on her door.

She dismissed her sisters. Ali was struggling with her own living situation and Zennie's place was the size of a postage stamp. While she loved Rochelle, she wasn't going to violate their relationship by imposing.

Her mother's house was an option. Finola had kept her late father's last name even after her mother had married Bill. She used it professionally and personally. Her mother's last name was different, making her more difficult to trace.

She pushed Ignore on an incoming call, then dialed her mother.

"Finola, darling. How are things? I'm sorry you couldn't come by yesterday but your sisters got so much work done. The whole upstairs is cleaned out."

"That's great, Mom. So I have a situation." She quickly explained what had happened. "Can I come stay with you for a few days?"

"Of course. Your bedroom is always waiting for you, Finola. What a mess. I'm very angry with Nigel. I expected better from him. Pack what you need and come over. I'll be waiting."

"Thanks, Mom. I can't tell you how much I appreciate this."

"It's never a problem."

Finola hurried into the bedroom. She would need to pack enough to last at least a week, she thought grimly. Her work clothes were at the studio. Still, she had to assume she could be photographed anytime she was out in public.

It took her over an hour to pull everything together. Before she left, she called Rochelle and asked her assistant to pick her up a burner phone. When they hung up, she turned off her phone and wondered briefly if it would ever be safe to turn it on again.

Chapter Fifteen

Zennie nearly canceled her blind date Sunday night. She certainly wasn't in the mood—not when she was still sore from her ridiculous fall down the side of a mountain. But Cassie had insisted on setting it up, saying it would take Zennie's mind off her recovery, and Zennie hadn't come up with a reason to say no quick enough. So she dutifully applied mascara, fluffed her hair and pulled on her go-to date outfit.

At least the cropped pants were a soft fabric that didn't irritate her still scabbing wound, she thought as she drove the short distance to the trendy bar in Toluca Lake. Much more important, so far there had been no ill effects of her tumble. No cramping, no signs of bleeding. If she was pregnant, then the tiny life inside of her seemed to have ridden out the fall with no problem.

The bar was small, with bistro tables clustered too close together. The decor leaned toward midcentury modern, with a heavy emphasis on TV shows from the 1950s. She found the old posters and memorabilia just a little over the top.

She looked around for "a guy tall enough to be a basketball player" wearing a black shirt, and spotted a brown-haired guy fitting that description. He looked up, saw her and smiled before coming to his feet and approaching.

"Zennie? I'm Jake."

"Nice to meet you, Jake."

They shook hands and went back to the table he'd claimed. The chairs seemed hard, although maybe that was just because she was a little battered. Still, a little padding would have been nice, she thought, shifting to get comfortable.

"Thanks for meeting me," Jake said when they were sitting across from each other.

The table was so small and his legs so long, their knees were practically touching. Zennie fought against the need to move back to give herself more personal space.

"Cassie tells me you're an OR nurse."

"I am. Most of the doctors I work with are cardiac surgeons, so it's very rewarding work. Cassie told me you're a friend of her brother's and that you're a high school basketball coach."

He grinned. "I am. Recently divorced." His smile faded. "She left to go find herself." He made air quotes. "I've moved on and am ready to start dating again."

Oh, goody.

"What do you like to do for fun?" he asked. "Cassie said you're pretty athletic."

"I run and rock climb. I love surfing and I like yoga. Do you like being a coach?"

The awkward and uninspired get-to-know-you chitchat continued for several more minutes. Zennie tried to stay engaged—Jake was nice enough and attractive, but honestly, she felt nothing. Her faux date with C.J. had been a lot more fun. At least they'd had instant chemistry.

One of the servers stopped by. "What can I get you?" the pretty blonde asked. "Our Old-Fashioneds are really popular."

"I'll have one of those," Jake said. "Zennie?"

Crap. Double crap. She couldn't drink, something she should have thought of before agreeing to meet a guy in a bar. "I'll have a club soda."

Both Jake and the server stared at her for a second before the server shrugged and walked away.

"You don't drink?" Jake asked. "Cassie never said anything." His disapproval was clear.

"It's not that I don't drink," she began, not sure how exactly to explain the situation. "I'm not drinking right now."

He looked her up and down. "You're on a diet?" His tone was doubtful.

"Not exactly." She smiled. "Okay, I need you to promise not to say anything to Cassie because I haven't told her yet and this is way over the TMI line for a first date, but it's really exciting."

Jake looked more wary than interested. "All right."

She quickly explained about Bernie and the artificial insemination. "It's only been a few days, but I don't want to take the chance and drink right now."

Jake stared at her. "You're telling me you're pregnant?"

His voice rose with each word until he was speaking loud enough to cause other patrons to turn and look.

"No, I'm saying I might be. I—"

He stood. "Yeah, this isn't going to work for me. I have no idea what the hell Cassie was thinking. Jesus."

Before Zennie could remind him Cassie didn't know, he was gone, leaving her sitting alone. Seconds later the server returned with their drinks.

Zennie thanked her even as she realized Jake had taken off without paying for his drink. Nor had he wanted to listen to her explanation. As far as first dates went, it certainly wasn't her best.

She took care of the bill and left. As she drove home, she replayed the disastrous few minutes, finding the situation more humorous than disappointing. Her mood lightened even more as she realized that she had the perfect excuse for not dating: she might be pregnant.

"I might be pregnant," she whispered aloud, taking the concept on a test drive. Really, she might be and if she was, she couldn't be dating. No one would understand—Jake was proof of that. So where did that leave her?

Alone, she thought as she pulled into her parking space. Happily and blissfully alone. She didn't have to date anymore, not until she knew if she was having a baby and if she was, then hey, not for months and months.

She hurried inside, practically giddy with a sense of freedom. No more small talk, no more worrying about what to wear or if she'd shaved her legs that day. She could do what she wanted and the hell with a man. She could learn Italian or spend more time with her friends or figure out what she wanted from her life. She was free!

As Zennie stood in the center of her apartment, she wanted to spin or cheer or do both. What she did instead was to really look at the small space and wonder if she should start thinking about buying a condo. Just her, for her. She could get exactly what she wanted and not wait for some guy to transform her life. Because if she needed changing, by God, she was going to do it herself!

Word of Nigel's affair seemed to be spreading more slowly than Finola would have thought. Apparently not everyone hung on TMZ's every word. Of course not everyone had a husband sleeping with Treasure, so there was that.

Monday she got through her show without anyone saying anything. Afterward she had an uncomfortable meeting with her producers where she was forced to tell them what had happened. They said all the right things, offered support and promised to talk to her should anything change, which was about the best she could hope for.

Rochelle did research on personal bodyguards, something Finola didn't want to deal with but knew she had to consider, if the press got out of hand. She took the information and promised to contact one of the companies the second she felt threatened. Rochelle made it clear she thought Finola should have one on call before then, but Finola wasn't ready to make the decision.

By three o'clock, she'd left the Burbank studio and was heading southwest toward Beverly Hills. She'd taken a second to log into Nigel's work computer to check his surgery schedule. She didn't know if he was back from his South American ski trip or if he hadn't left yet and she didn't care. All that mattered to her was the bastard was in town and she was going to confront him.

She left her car with the medical center's valet and took the elevator up to Nigel's plush offices, grateful there weren't any photographers around. Apparently Nigel wasn't stalk-worthy.

She'd looked up what kind of surgery he was doing that day and knew when it was going to be finished. The first thing Nigel always did after surgery was to go to his office and dictate his notes. He might be a shitty husband, but he was a good doctor, something that didn't give Finola the least amount of comfort.

She breezed into the waiting area, waved at the perky receptionist and kept on walking. While she was fairly sure that everyone on staff knew about the affair, she was still his wife and there was no way they would try to keep her out. Not at first anyway. By the time they came up with a plan, she would be long gone.

She heard the receptionist scramble out of her seat, but ignored the movement and headed directly for Nigel's corner office. She pushed on the partially open door and saw her husband at his desk, dictating into a small recorder. When he spotted her, he paused the recording. She closed the door and let the rage overtake her more sensible emotions. Power and strength would be required, she told herself. The next few minutes would be difficult but she was going to survive them.

"Finola, what are you doing here?" Nigel asked, coming to his feet. "I'm at work."

His emphasis on the last word made her smile.

"Really, Nigel? Are you at work? Is this where you do your work things and have I violated that?" She waved her hand. "By the way, the office is lovely. The color scheme, the tasteful art. Hmm, who decorated this office for you? Your wife?"

"Stop it," he growled. "What are you doing here? You can't just waltz in here like this."

"Your days of telling me what I can and cannot do are long over. At least I had the courtesy to wait until you were done with surgery for the day. I could have come early—shown up right before you had to do something important, but I wasn't that much of an asshole. Only you are."

"You're comparing a television show with surgery?"

"I'm comparing work and what matters to each of us and being thoughtful and trusting the person we were married to. Things you've forgotten about." Her anger grew and she reveled in the power. She took a step toward him. "The tabloids know. I was confronted by photographers yesterday. Word is out and it will be spreading. First you blindsided me on my show and now this. You're a monster."

She expected Nigel to push back. He surprised her by returning to his seat and waving her into the one opposite. She hesitated, then sat down.

"We need to talk about this reasonably," he told her, obviously trying to keep his temper under control. "We are where we are."

"That's easy for you to say. We are where you put us. You're not the one being chased by photographers."

"Oh, please. As long as it helps the ratings of the show, what do you care?"

Tears burned, but she refused to show weakness. "Is that what you think?" she demanded. "That this is a game to me? You're wrong. This is my life. Our life. You're the one playing games, Nigel. You're the one destroying everything we have."

His gaze was steady. "I may be the one who cheated, but I'm not the only one who destroyed things. You had your part."

"I'm not sleeping with Treasure."

"I didn't go looking," he yelled. He lowered his voice. "I wasn't searching for anything on the side. Yes, I was unhappy, but I lived with it. She's the one who came on to me, and to be honest, it was nice to have the attention."

"Nice to have the attention?" she shrieked, not caring who heard. "That's how you excuse yourself?"

"I'm not excusing and I'm not apologizing. I'm telling you what happened. You can think what you want. You always do. Treasure was interested. She pursued me. She reminded me what it was like to feel young and vital and attractive to the woman in my life."

"You're blaming me? You're saying I wasn't doing things the way you wanted? You never once said you were unhappy. You never once asked for anything to be different. What exactly did I do wrong? Not read your mind? We had a good marriage. We cared about each other. We had plans." They had been on the verge of getting pregnant, although he didn't know that.

"This is not about me," she told him.

He leaned back in his chair. "So I'm the bad guy here? You have no part in it? You're not going to take even a little blame?"

"Why should I?"

"That's an interesting question." He pulled his cell phone out of his desk drawer and tossed it onto the desk. "Remember that time we accidentally synced up our calendars?"

"What does that have to do with anything?"

"You unsynced with mine, but I was still connected with yours. I saw all your appointments. I figured out the code, Finola. I saw the little icon you use to remind yourself to have sex with me."

She felt herself flush as she stared at him. "I have no idea what you're talking about," she lied. *Shit. Shit. Shit!*

He shook his head. "Don't pretend. I can show you the calendar now, if you'd like."

"I thought us having sex is a good thing."

"It would be if you really wanted it. But you didn't. You scheduled it like the dry cleaning. No one wants to be a chore."

She remembered her father's words that part of the breakup was her fault. She'd told him he was wrong, but listening to Nigel, she thought maybe, just maybe, he'd been partially right.

"It wasn't like that," she whispered. "It was never like that." Only it had been *exactly* like that.

"I didn't go looking for Treasure," he repeated. "She came looking for me. I was flattered and lonely and maybe later I'll regret it but right now she's the best thing that's ever happened to me. I can't explain how I feel when I'm around her, but it's like a drug." He stood. "I didn't mean to hurt you and I'm sorry about the tabloids, but I can't undo either."

And he didn't want to, she thought. Or wouldn't want to if the price was giving up Treasure. He didn't say it, but he didn't have to. She knew him well enough to guess what he was thinking.

She looked at him. "It's not going to last and then what? Do you expect me to take you back?" A question that presumed he wanted to come back in the first place.

"I guess we'll have to see where it goes."

"Just like that?" She stood. "You're willing to risk everything?"

"For her? I am."

Ali found herself scrambling to be ready for her Saturday move. There had been an unexpected work crisis in quality control on Thursday and Friday. Ali had gotten the first call from a disgruntled customer Thursday morning. It had taken her the better part of the morning to figure out what had gone wrong.

Friday had been a series of meetings with lots of yelling. As Ali hadn't been part of the mistake, she'd only had to listen, but the problem had sucked up any chance of leaving work early to get ready for the move.

She'd stayed up late Friday, organizing as much as she could. When she'd texted Daniel, he'd told her not to worry—the guys who were helping would finish the packing. All she'd needed to do was sort her belongings into two piles: the things she was storing in Daniel's garage and the items she would want with her, conceivably for the next year.

She had gotten to bed shortly after midnight. Saturday morning she was up early to double-check her decisions and try to be awake enough to be both perky and collaborative as she finished packing up her bedroom. On a usual day neither feeling was especially hard to muster but for some reason and despite two cups of coffee, Ali couldn't helping feeling a little…sad.

She supposed the reasons were obvious. She was leaving her apartment after living there for three years. Although moving had always been the plan, it was supposed to be because she was marrying Glen and taking the next step in their relationship. Instead she found herself forced out of her home and into a living situation that was admittedly lovely but not of her choosing. Okay, sure, technically she'd chosen to move in with Daniel, but only because she couldn't afford a decent place of her own. She accepted the relationship with Glen was over, she just wished there weren't daily reminders of how sucky things had gotten.

The date of the wedding was rapidly approaching. As she studied the sealed boxes and the stuff yet to be packed, she wondered how she was going to feel on the actual day. Would she be sad, angry, depressed, resolute or some combination of a thousand other emotions she couldn't predict? And while she was on the subject, what was Glen feeling? Did he miss her at all? Miss them? Did she want him to? She'd been so caught up in logistics that she hadn't spent a lot of time on her own emotions. Or maybe she'd been hiding from them. Either way at some point she was going to have to deal. Not just with the loss she felt, but also the lack of loss. The truth was she didn't miss Glen much at all.

She hated admitting that, but what choice did she have? She'd been sad at first and humiliated because hey, who wouldn't be, but not devastated. She wasn't crushed or thinking she would never again be happy. What was up with that? She wanted to tell herself she was in shock, but she wasn't sure she was. And if she wasn't—if she'd really gotten over him so very easily—what did that say about her, about them? If she hadn't been in love with him, why on earth had she agreed to marry him?

All difficult questions she didn't want to think about but until Daniel and his guys showed up, she didn't have many distractions. She walked through the half packed, half empty apartment, as if she could find the answers somewhere in a closet or drawer. There were pieces of her life with Glen, items from the life they were going to have together, but no real pain, no heartbreak. She'd been so sure he was the one…but he wasn't.

Before she could go down the path of wondering what she'd done wrong, she heard a knock at her door. She opened it to find Daniel flanked by two massive guys. He was at least six feet so his friends had to be six-five or six-six. They both had shaved heads and lots of tattoos. Ali stared at a beautiful swirling tattoo design and wondered if she should get a tattoo herself. Something to signify her life taking a new direction or…

"Morning," Daniel said, holding out a take-out coffee. "All ready for us?"

"Not as ready as I wanted to be. There was a crisis at work. But at least I'm sorted."

Daniel nodded at the guys with him. "Sam and Jerome. They're helping us today. This is Ali."

"Ma'am," they said together.

"We're happy to help you," Sam added. "Just show us what you want done."

She stepped back and led them through her suddenly tiny apartment. She'd packed up her bedroom and living room, but there were still some things in the kitchen cupboards. Jerome went downstairs and got boxes and tape while Sam went to work on the furniture. He pushed her sofa and coffee table to the center of the room.

"I should do something," she said to Daniel.

"Drink your coffee."

"I should do something more."

"They've got it handled."

The two men did. Sam moved to the kitchen. He expertly packed dishes and glasses, using plenty of paper to wrap each breakable item carefully. Boxes were sealed and labeled, then stacked in the living room. At the same time, Jerome wrapped her sofa in plastic wrap. He took apart her coffee table and wrapped it up, as well, then took her lamps apart. By ten o'clock, everything she owned was in neat piles or sealed in boxes. The guys began to move the items out to the truck Daniel had rented.

As the rooms were emptied, she vacuumed the carpet. She'd already cleaned out the refrigerator and freezer, and had tackled the bathroom a few days before. It didn't take long for them all to be done, then she was standing in what had been her home, wondering when everything had gone wrong.

"Ma'am," Jerome said from the open front door. "We're loaded."

She smiled. "You really can call me Ali."

"Yes, ma'am. Whenever you're ready."

She looked around. "I wasn't sure if it would be hard to leave or not."

"Is it hard?"

She drew in a breath. "More sad, I think. Starting over isn't easy, even when it's the right thing to do."

"That's true, but if you don't start over, you stay stuck where you are. Sometimes that's worse."

She wondered what Jerome was starting over from. Not that she would ask. Repaying his hard work with prying questions seemed rude.

"Thank you for all your help, Jerome."

"You're welcome, ma'am."

She put her hands on her hips. "Seriously? You're not going to say my name?"

Instead of answering, he winked at her, then walked out of the apartment. Ali took a last look around before stepping onto the landing and locking the door behind her. She went to the front office where she turned in her key before heading to her car to drive to Daniel's and what an optimist would call the first day of the rest of her life.

Chapter Sixteen

At Daniel's house, the unloading went quickly. The furniture and boxes for storage went into the far bay of the garage with plenty of room to spare. Jerome and Sam took the other boxes into the room she would be using. She and Daniel carried in the clothes she'd left on hangers. Well before noon, she was moved.

"You're going to let me pay for the truck and the guys' time," she said when they were done.

Daniel shook his head. "It's already taken care of. Sam and Jerome work for me so they're getting paid through the company and I borrowed the truck from a friend. There's nothing to pay."

She insisted on giving each of the guys forty dollars. Daniel went and got sandwiches while she started the process of moving into the oversize bedroom and bath. When he returned, he put the food on her dresser and left.

It took her less time than she would have thought to unpack.

She had more closet space and more drawers than she'd had before, which made fitting in her clothes super easy. The bathroom had tons of storage, and everything else—her laptop, bill file and checkbook—went into the desk. She even had a small linen closet with plenty of sheets and towels. She made the bed, adding a pretty patterned blanket across the foot of the mattress, then opened up her laptop and checked her email.

Nothing except for a few email ads. Her phone was just as quiet. No texts from anyone. She sent Finola and Zennie each a "thinking of you" text, then stood in the center of the room and wondered what she was supposed to do now. And for the next fifty years.

It was kind of a daunting question. What was she going to do? Get her own place, for sure. But what about the rest of it? There was no Glen, no wedding, no yet-to-be conceived children. Did she want to start dating again? Change jobs? Go to college and get a degree? Start working out?

She told herself that her mini life crisis was about all the upheaval of the past few weeks. She would give herself a little time to get settled, then she would come up with a plan.

She wandered into the kitchen and got a glass of water, then decided to explore the downstairs. That should be safe and allowed. She was surprised to find Daniel reading in the living room. And not a tablet, either. The man was holding a book.

He looked up when he saw her. "All unpacked?"

"Yes. It was easy. There's plenty of storage. Going from small to bigger is much easier than the other way around. Thanks again for letting me move in. I appreciate having the transition space."

He put down the book and motioned for her to take a seat. "It's going to take you a while to get used to living here," he told her.

"I think that's true for both of us." She smiled. "You don't strike me as the roommate type."

He flashed her a smile that had her stomach doing all kinds of flippy-over things. "I've had my share."

"I'm talking roommates, not girlfriends."

"I know you are." His humor faded. "Ali, I meant what I said. I want you to take your time when it comes to finding a place. You're welcome to stay here as long as you want."

"I appreciate that. I'm going to wait a few weeks and then figure out a plan. I don't want you to get sick of me."

Something flashed in his eyes, something that she couldn't define although she didn't think it was bad. "There's no chance of that," he told her. "You're strong. You'll have decided what you want long before that's an issue."

"You think I'm strong? Is that how you see me?"

"Of course. Look at what you've been through in the past few weeks. You had a couple of bad days after you found out about Glen, then you handled it all."

"Actually, I completely fell apart then asked a virtual stranger for help."

His smile was gentle. "You reached out to friends. That's the healthy thing to do."

"You make me sound way better than I am."

"Is that bad?"

"No. It's nice. I'm just…" She looked away, then back at him. "I'm going to say something and I want you to just listen. No judging."

"I don't think I've ever judged you."

She hesitated. "I'm not sure I was ever in love with Glen."

Daniel didn't say anything and his expression was unreadable.

"When he dumped me, I was so angry and hurt and embarrassed, and I had to cancel the wedding." She twisted her fingers together. "Since then, I've been busy with work and looking at apartments and helping my mom and stuff. I'm still pissed at him and I think he's a jerk and I can't believe I was so stupid to fall for him, but I don't long for him or think about what we would have had if he hadn't dumped me."

"Is that bad?"

"No, but I don't get it. My sister is devastated by what's happening in her marriage. Shouldn't I be feeling at least a little of that? And if I'm not, why did I want to marry him in the first place?"

"You were in a relationship and it progressed. That's pretty natural."

"I guess. What I don't know is where it all derailed."

His gaze sharpened. "You know that whatever went wrong is his fault. You didn't do anything. Glen is the one who walked away."

"Obviously he didn't love me and while it hurts to say that, I'm not broken by the concept. I don't feel much of anything. So what happened? Was I fooling myself? Taking the easy way out? I don't want to be a shallow person."

"You're not. Ali, you believed him and trusted him and he betrayed that. Maybe you weren't as in love with him as you thought, but I don't think that makes you shallow. Sometimes love grows over time and sometimes it fades. Maybe your love faded."

"You're putting a very nice spin on it considering I was going to marry him," she said, kicking off her shoes and tucking her feet under her. "I think I was impressed by Glen in the beginning. Not crazy about him, but I liked him and then as the relationship continued, I went along with it. I thought he was a nice guy who cared about me and that was appealing." She hesitated again. "I'm not a super visible person."

"What does that mean?"

"I got overlooked a lot as a kid. My mom totally focused on Finola, and Zennie was my dad's favorite. There wasn't a parent left for me." She sighed. "That sounds so dramatic, but it was true. I had friends and stuff, but…" She looked at him. "Too pathetic?"

"Not pathetic at all. We are all the product of how we were raised. If your parents had been different, you would be different."

"I'd had boyfriends before, but nothing really serious. Glen noticed me at a fund-raiser my sister hosted. He came right up to me and started talking to me. Nothing like that had ever happened before. He was funny and had a good job."

She wrinkled her nose. "That's not very romantic, is it? Shouldn't I have said he swept me away? That I couldn't imagine life without him? Did I want to be with him because that's the stage we were at? I mean he broke up with me, so why did he propose in the first place?" She looked at Daniel. "I saw a comedian on TV once, talking about how the reason people get married is they reach a place in their relationship when there's nothing left to say so one of them says let's get married and then they have a lot to talk about. I don't want it to have been that."

"It wasn't."

"You can't be sure."

"I know you. You wanted what most people want—a connection. A partner who will love you back and be there when you need him. You wanted to be a part of something, you wanted to love and be loved. You wanted kids."

She smiled. "Apparently Glen talked about me more than I thought. You're right. I did want all those things. I wanted to be like everyone else. Not famous or anything exciting. I just wanted to belong."

She felt tears burning in her eyes. "You know what? I miss that. I don't miss Glen but I miss being a couple. What's up with that?"

"I think it's really normal."

She managed a strangled laugh. "You're really good to me, Daniel. Thank you."

"You're welcome." He looked at her. "You didn't do anything wrong—I know. I was married before. We went into our relationship with the best of intentions and then it all went south. I can't say she was a total bitch, because she wasn't, and I didn't cheat or do drugs or even hang out with my friends too much. We just weren't happy together."

"We both know Glen wasn't happy with me."

"We both know Glen's a dick."

She smiled. "There is that. Okay, let's talk about something else. Do Jerome and Sam really work for you?"

"Sure. Why?"

"I don't know. They were very polite but they didn't seem like typical motocross guys and I'm not sure why."

He surprised her by looking away. "I, ah, have some employees that, ah…"

She put her feet on the floor and scooted to the edge of her seat. "What? Are they undercover cops or something?"

"No. They're part of a program run by the state to help former felons find their way in society. I hire a couple of guys at a time in a work-release program."

She felt her mouth drop open and carefully closed it. "Really?"

"You were never in any danger."

"I never felt in danger. That's really cool. So you're helping them."

"Yes."

"Why?"

One shoulder rose and lowered. "I've been given a lot of opportunities. It seemed reasonable to give back."

"Just like that?"

He nodded.

"Wow. Glen wouldn't ever leave more than a twelve percent tip in a restaurant. It always bugged me. Sometimes I'd sneak back and leave a few dollars. How did you two get to be so different?"

"I have no idea."

"Don't take this wrong, but I'm pretty sure I like you better."

The sexy grin returned. "I like you better than Glen, too."

She laughed. A prison-release program. Daniel was kind of a cool guy.

"I loved their tattoos. I was thinking maybe I should get one. Except they do it with needles, right?" She shuddered. "I have trouble getting a flu shot."

"Then you might want to avoid the whole tattoo thing."

"You have several." Glen had mentioned it, in a disapproving way.

"A couple."

He was wearing a T-shirt over jeans and from what she could tell, there was no ink on his arms.

"Where? Oh, man, please don't tell me one is on the small of your back. That would change everything."

"Not on the small of my back and maybe another time."

What did that mean? That they were in places not usually seen in public? The idea of exploring Daniel's body, searching for the tattoos had instant appeal. His skin would be warm, his muscles honed. What would happen if she got up and sat next to him, then put her hands on his…

Stop, she told herself firmly. She had to stop. She was not going to repay his generosity with some creepy move. Coming on to him would totally change their dynamic. Worse, he would pity her and she honestly didn't think she could stand that.

"Your wedding date is coming up."

His statement was so not what she'd been thinking about that it took her a second to catch up.

"Yes, it is."

"We should plan something for the day. We can do something you've never done."

"Like skydiving?"

"I was thinking of something a little more earthbound, but yes."

"I have a morning of beauty planned. I kept my spa appointments because I figured I'd want to be pampered, but I'm free after that. What did you have in mind?"

"A dirt bike lesson and dinner."

Nice, nice and more nice, she thought. If she was willing to be the least bit stupid, she would so throw herself at him. He was totally irresistible offering to spend her would-be wedding day with her.

"A dirt bike lesson and dinner sound perfect," she said. "Thank you. But after that, you have to get back to your real life and stop worrying about me. I'm going to be perfectly fine."

His dark gaze settled on her face. "Ali, you do realize I enjoy spending time with you, don't you?"

"Um, sure. But you don't have to, you know, take care of me or anything."

Was it just her or was it getting awkward in here?

"So we have a plan for your wedding day," he confirmed.

"We do. I will come back from my appointments looking like a princess and then you can dirty me up." She winced. "You know what I mean."

One corner of his mouth turned up. "I do."

"Great." She pointed back toward her end of the house. "I'm going to make a graceful escape while I still can."

He chuckled. "Probably a good idea."

Finola couldn't stop feeling weary. Her days weren't any longer, her commute was actually shorter, but the ever-present sense of being exhausted only grew.

She knew it was a combination of stress and emotional pain. The news about Nigel and Treasure had exploded into the tabloids and she was pretty much under siege. The studio had put on more security to keep the photographers away and she was being deluged by interview requests. Her producers wanted a sit-down with her, and her agent was furious that she'd gone this far without letting the agency know what was happening. Finola knew she was right—her excuse was she had simply wanted it to all go away.

She drove to her mother's and parked in the garage. Her mom was working late at the boutique so Finola had the house to herself. She went inside through the kitchen door, then paused to breathe in the familiar scent. Every house, it seemed, had its own smell. This was a combination of years of lemon Pledge and a hint of her mother's perfume.

Finola couldn't remember exactly how old she'd been when she and her mom had first moved into the house. After Mary Jo and Bill had married, for sure, so maybe she'd been six or seven. She'd loved the house—having her own bedroom and a big backyard with a swing set left by the previous owners. She was pretty sure her mom had been pregnant at the time. Finola had been excited about having another kid in the house. Being an only child was lonely.

She walked through the kitchen and into the living room. The house was so normal, so ordinary. It had been built for a family, she thought. She'd lived here, grown up here, left for college from here. It wasn't that she minded her mom selling the house, it was that her mother moving was one more change to deal with.

She looked at the worn sofa and love seat, the matching coffee table and end tables. The style wasn't hers at all, but it was familiar, comfortable.

Nigel didn't want to be with her anymore. The truth couldn't be avoided forever. She could dance around it, scream, run, she could even hide, but she couldn't change the truth. There would be no baby, no happily-ever-after. Nigel had thrown away their future with his affair and from what she could tell, he'd done it without giving the consequences any thought.

She wanted to say Treasure had bewitched him, that he was under the influence of some sex drug and one day he would resurface. She wanted to believe that with counseling and therapy and maybe some kind of rehab program, her old husband could come back to her. The only problem was deep in her gut, she didn't think he wanted to. Nigel liked who he was with Treasure and she couldn't be with someone like that.

She tried not to hear him accusing her of scheduling sex with him. Why was that so awful? Why did that make her a bad person? They were busy. Yes, they loved each other, but after so many years of marriage, the reality was it was difficult to always find the time. So she'd made sure their lovemaking didn't slip off the radar. Why did that make her a bad wife?

But in Nigel's eyes, she'd committed an unforgivable crime and when Treasure had come along... She admitted she wasn't sure if he'd taken revenge, seen no reason to resist, or both.

Her bedroom was at the front of the house, with a big bay window and a walk-in closet. Her old full-size bed, dresser and desk were where they had always been. There were posters on the wall, but hers had never been of movie stars or rock bands. Instead she had pictures of Jane Pauley, Andrea Mitchell, Diane Sawyer and Elizabeth Vargas. All her heroes. While her friends had been glued to E!, she'd watched news reports.

Shelves were crammed with her awards from both high school and college. She'd worked hard to be a good journalist. When she'd landed her first job as a TV reporter in Bakersfield, she'd known she was going places. The offer from the LA station had been even more exciting. Hosting *AM SoCal* had sent her in another direction but one that challenged her. Everything had been so great and then it had all come crashing down around her.

She walked over to her desk where she'd already set up her laptop. Next to it was the mail she'd collected from the house.

She flipped through the handful of bills and ads, and saw a thick envelope. After opening it, she stared at the invitation and groaned.

The charity gala to benefit children with cancer was a big deal. The local station was a corporate sponsor. There was no way not to go and no way to go with Nigel.

She sank onto the chair and covered her face with her hands. What had happened to her hopes and dreams? How had she lost everything without warning? And even though she knew it was over, why did she so desperately want her husband to come back?

"I can do this," Zennie murmured to herself. It was two weeks and one day after her artificial insemination procedure. She'd had a big glass of water, had three different pregnancy tests lined up and was simply waiting for the urge to pee.

She felt good. Not pregnant or in any way different, just good. She'd been eating from the approved list of foods, drinking plenty of water and taking her vitamins, although all of it felt more like going through the motions than for any real purpose. She wondered if "real" mothers felt any differently while they were waiting to find out the good news.

She walked around her apartment, trying to think about anything but having to go to the bathroom. After a few minutes of flipping channels, she found herself caught up in a *Love It or List It* episode on HGTV. Half an hour later, she got up at the commercial and walked into her bathroom. It was only when she saw the sticks carefully laid out on the counter that she realized she'd totally forgotten about the test.

"This is ridiculous," she murmured with a laugh and prepared to do her thing.

She followed the instructions and when she was done, she put the tests on the paper towel and waited. It didn't take long for them to change. Each test had a different kind of indicator, but the results were exactly the same. According to the sticks, she was pregnant.

Zennie stood in her small bathroom, not sure what to think. She stared at herself in the mirror, noting she looked wide-eyed and more than a little scared. She was pregnant. Pregnant, as in with child. There was a baby growing inside of her. Holy crap!

She ran and got her phone, then took a picture of the sticks and texted Bernie. She didn't have to wait very long for her phone to ring.

"I knew you were going to do it today," her friend said, her voice thick with emotion. "I just knew it. Really? Really?"

"I'm just telling you what the plastic said."

"Oh, my God!" Bernie shouted. "We're having a baby!"

Zennie grinned. "So it seems."

"I'll be right over."

"I'll be here. Do you want me to keep the sticks or can I—"

"Don't you dare throw those out. I'm keeping them forever."

"You know I peed on them, right?"

"I know and I'm so happy. Give me fifteen minutes. Maybe twenty."

Zennie was still smiling when she hung up.

She put the sticks into a small plastic bag then tried to figure out what she should do while she was waiting. Before she could pick something, Bernie was at her door.

Bernie dropped her purse and a grocery bag onto the floor and flung herself at Zennie.

"Thank you," she said, hugging her so tight she couldn't breathe. "Thank you, thank you, thank you. I would have loved you forever no matter what, but now I love you more."

Zennie laughed and hugged her back. "I'm happy, too. I mean that."

"Yay." Bernie stepped back. "I brought you a couple of gifts." She picked up the shopping bag and pulled out a jar of pickles.

Zennie grinned. "Clichéd but appreciated." There was also a pint of chocolate chip ice cream and two copies of a thick book.

"For us to read together," Bernie said, handing her one. "Everyone says this is the one to really read. It goes month by month through the pregnancy. I'll make up a schedule so we're reading at the same time. It's going to be great."

Zennie took the book and flipped through it. As Bernie had said, there were chapters on each month with a drawing showing how big the baby was and lots of questions and answers. The word *hemorrhoids* caught her eye and she quickly closed the book.

"Thanks. I'll start reading it today."

"Me, too. Hayes is super excited. I called him on the way over. We want to take you to dinner. There's a great new vegetarian place that doesn't serve alcohol so you won't feel deprived. Just make sure you eat plenty of protein at lunch so you get in enough for the day. They have great cheese dishes for calcium." Bernie hugged her again. "This is going to be great."

"Uh-huh."

Zennie told herself it would be. That there was no reason to feel overwhelmed or confused or just a little sense of misgiving. Of course Bernie was excited and Zennie really needed to know what was happening to her body. More information was always better than less.

"So dinner tonight?" Bernie asked.

"Absolutely. I'm looking forward to it."

"No hot date?"

"You know there isn't. No guy wants to deal with a pregnant woman and I'm in a good place right now." Zennie laughed. "The best first date I've had in months was with a woman, so what does that tell you?"

"That this pregnancy was meant to be. If you'd stayed with Clark, he would have been upset and in your face about what you were doing."

The comment surprised Zennie. "I don't think he would

have at all. I mean, we were just getting to know each other, but Clark wasn't like that. He was really supportive."

"I'm sorry." Bernie touched her arm. "I didn't mean anything by that. I'm just saying, now it's not a problem."

Zennie actually preferred being alone to being in a relationship, but she wasn't sure she liked Bernie thinking of her being with someone as an impediment to her having their baby.

"So better for me to be alone so I can focus?"

Bernie's lower lip trembled. "Zennie, I'm sorry. I'm saying everything all wrong."

Zennie shook her head and hugged her friend. "No, you're not. It's me. I'm sorry. I don't know why I said that." She started to laugh. "I think it was hormones."

"Really?"

"Aren't I your most levelheaded friend?"

"You are." Bernie clutched her arms. "You're really having our baby."

"I really am." She opened the front door. "I love you, now go celebrate with your husband. I'll see you two later."

"I'll text the time. Love you bunches. Bye."

Zennie closed the door behind her friend, then sat on the sofa. Pregnant. She was well and truly pregnant and had no idea what to do with the information. She had so many people to tell. Her mother for one, and her dad. She was going to keep quiet at work as long as possible. Ali knew about the procedure but not the results.

Zennie got her phone and quickly texted her sister, then sat back and tried to wrap her mind around the information. Pregnant.

I'm super excited for you, Ali texted back. Congrats.

Zennie smiled. She scrolled through the contacts list, hesitating when she saw Clark's name. No way, she told herself. She didn't want to tell him. Besides, it would be a little too weird to text him to let him know she was pregnant. Jeez—what a crazy idea. Why on earth would she be thinking…

She flopped back on the sofa and grinned. Oh, yeah, she was pregnant and it was going to be a heck of a ride.

Chapter Seventeen

Post-show fan greetings were a tradition on the show. Those who wanted to meet Finola stayed after for a quick meet and greet. Finola usually enjoyed spending time with her viewers but ever since the news had hit, she'd been reluctant to have any one-on-one time. Even smiling and shaking hands seemed risky, and she'd kept Rochelle close to whisk her away if necessary. But it had been more than a week and no one had said anything, so she was more relaxed as she worked her way through the line of fans, and Rochelle had retreated to the dressing room.

"Thanks for coming," she said, shaking hands with an older couple. "I appreciate it. Are you locals?"

"Yes, we live in Huntington Beach," the gray-haired man said. "Bought our first house there nearly forty years ago."

Finola chuckled. "And it's worth a whole lot more now."

"It is." He winked at her. "You're sure pretty. Just as pretty in person."

"Oh, Martin, you're such a flirt." Martin's wife rolled her eyes. "As if she'd been interested in an old coot like you." Her tone was teasing, her smile friendly.

"You're charming, Martin," Finola said, chuckling before turning to the next guests. "Hello. Thanks so much for coming to the show."

The next couple was what looked like a mother-daughter pair, with the mother in her midforties and the daughter college age.

The daughter smiled. "Your clothes are great. I try to get my mom to dress better, but she won't listen to me. Do you do your own hair, or does someone do it for you?"

Before Finola could answer, her mother narrowed her gaze. "I don't understand why you'd want to air all your dirty laundry out in public like that. What's the payoff to you? Are you that hungry for attention? Is that why Nigel left?"

Finola felt the judgment and slap all the way down to her soul. She wanted to run away but there was no escape and no one to protect her. She looked around, but most of the crew had disappeared and the other guests had left. These were the last two.

"It wasn't my choice," Finola said before she could stop herself. She knew there was no point, that she should simply thank them for coming and walk away, but she couldn't seem to move. "Not the affair or the publicity. There are photographers stalking me. They found out where I live and they chase me in their cars, making me feel scared and unsafe. It's a nightmare and it's humiliating."

She was saying too much but she couldn't seem to stop. She wanted this woman to know that it was all Nigel. All him and that whore Treasure. Finola was the innocent party. She'd done nothing wrong.

She opened her mouth to say that, then shook her head. She was a fool. Whatever this woman thought of her was her business.

Finola forced herself to smile pleasantly at both of them.

"Thank you so much for coming. I hope you enjoyed the show." Then she turned and walked away, heading for the hallway where there would be people to make sure that awful woman didn't follow her.

Behind her she heard the daughter saying, "Mo-om, why'd you say that? It was really rude."

"She thinks she's all that because she's on TV."

"She's doing her job."

"She chose this."

Finola turned another corner and the words were lost. She made her way to her dressing room and went inside. Once the door was closed behind her, she leaned against it, as if keeping out everyone else.

Rochelle looked up from her laptop. "You okay?"

"Yes, of course. Just dealing with fans. You know how they can be."

Rochelle's gaze sharpened. "Did someone say something?"

Finola used her hand to flick away the question. "Do we have the segments for next week's shows?"

"So that's a yes."

"It doesn't matter. There's no way to keep this sort of thing from happening. Everyone has an opinion, even if they don't actually care about me or Nigel or even Treasure. Right now we're interesting. Next week everyone will tune in to watch a surfing dog."

"Do you know how many views you've had?" Rochelle asked softly. "Of that segment with Treasure?"

"Tell me."

"Over two million."

Finola collapsed on the sofa. "We're just not that interesting. How can anyone care?"

She didn't expect an answer and Rochelle didn't say anything. Finola closed her eyes. "Isn't it enough that we've had meetings discussing what segments we can and can't do on the show? My agent yelled at me when she found out. She reminded me that when anything like this happened, she was my first call. The producers all huddle together and stop talking when I walk by." She opened her eyes and stared at her assistant. "I'm not the bad guy."

"I know. I'm sorry. Let me get you some tea."

Because Finola couldn't go home yet. She had fittings for the next quarter's wardrobe and after that she had to work out for two hours to stay thin enough to be on TV and be attractive so people wouldn't think Nigel had cheated on her because she was a hag.

"Thanks," she said gratefully. "I swear I'll get this figured out and quit whining."

"You're not whining," Rochelle told her as she stood. "Finola, you've been through a lot. You're dealing and it's damned impressive."

"Thank you."

Finola told herself she would hang on to the kind words of support. She would stay strong and get through this, whatever it took. And when things were sorted out, she would—

Honest to God, she had no idea what she would do, but she was determined to be stronger than she had been. Honed by fire or whatever the phrase was. Because she was so tired of feeling broken.

Midmorning Ali finished the semiannual inventory of Mustang parts. The process controls she'd suggested a few months ago had turned out to make a big difference. She had a few more ideas she was going to discuss with Paul once she got her thoughts down in writing. As she made a few notes to review later, she thought about the possibility of going to college.

She hadn't—after Finola and Zennie had gone, her parents had told her there wasn't any money. She didn't have a burning ambition to do anything specific, so she hadn't really minded.

Now it occurred to her she should have protested a little more than she had. Both her sisters had four-year degrees and she had nothing. They both had well-paying careers and she worked in an auto-parts warehouse. Yes, she'd moved up, from stocking to shipping to inventory control, but did she want to do this for the rest of her life? Didn't she want to grow and be challenged and maybe contribute more than making sure there were plenty of headlights in stock? Not that she didn't pride herself in her work, but was this where she saw herself in twenty years?

She knew her restlessness was as much about her breakup as her job. She was in transition and that was never easy. Even good change was stressful. So fine, if she didn't have direction, she would figure it out. In the meantime, she could go to community college and start taking her general education classes. At least she would be moving forward instead of standing still.

She entered her inventory results into the computer, then went to the shared printer to pick up the paperwork. On her way, she saw Ray. Instead of his usual jeans and T-shirt, he had on black pants, a dress shirt and sports jacket.

"Ray, what's going on? Hot lunch date?"

He rolled his eyes. "Yeah, Ali. I have a date." He tugged at his collar. "Man, I hate dressing like this, but it's for a good cause, right?"

"I don't know what you're talking about."

Ray frowned. "You haven't heard? Paul has given notice. He's finally retiring. I'm interviewing for his job. The owner asked me to. Wish me luck."

"Good luck," Ali said automatically. "Let me know how it goes."

"Sure thing."

Ali stood there, unable to move. No one had asked *her* to interview. No one had said a word. She was working by herself right now but in her previous positions, she'd had people working for her. When Paul went on vacation, she was the one who took over for him. She'd been doing that for two years. Wasn't she the more obvious replacement? Ray was gruff and moody and he frightened people. Not exactly great management material. So why not her? Was it because she didn't have a degree? She wasn't sure of Ray's academic status, but she thought maybe he might have a few years of college. Or was it something else? Her age? The fact that she was a woman? Or was it because she'd never once talked to anyone about wanting to grow in her career? She'd never expressed any desire to take on more responsibility.

She didn't have an answer and she wasn't sure where to get one. All she knew was that just when she'd finally found a little peace, everything had turned crappy again.

Saturday morning Finola risked the grocery store. She figured the busy shoppers wouldn't really care that she, too, was buying bread and cantaloupe—they had schedules to keep and lives to live. Her mother had gone to work—weekends were always busy at the mall in general and the boutique in particular. Young women looking for clothes to make them feel powerful would be on the prowl and Mary Jo's successful store was a go-to stop.

In an effort to distract herself and to avoid spending the day alone and moping, Finola texted her sisters, inviting them over to lunch. There was just enough time between their answers to make her wonder if they were texting with each other first. She told herself she was being paranoid only to have them reply at exactly the same time using nearly the same phrasing.

Can't wait. Want to see you.

So excited. Want to see you.

She didn't know what was up with that, but honestly, it was more than she could deal with so she ignored it. That was her new mantra. Just ignore it. Maybe not as spiritually healing as finding the good in the world or inviting in kindness, but for now it was working and that was enough for her.

She'd shopped with the idea of company. She had ingredients for curried chicken sandwiches, along with green salad fixings and everything she needed to make her famous basil ranch dressing.

She spent the morning getting everything ready, then went for a walk in the neighborhood. With her hair pulled back in a ponytail, a baseball cap and dark glasses, she figured she was fairly unrecognizable. Three miles later, she was slightly out of breath and feeling much better about herself. She showered and dressed, then checked on the food. She'd just finished setting the table when Ali arrived.

"Hey, you," her baby sister said, hugging her tight. "How are you doing?"

"I've been better."

"I'll bet. I still hate Nigel so much and I'm never listening to a Treasure song again in my life. I hate her, too." Ali rubbed Finola's arm as they walked into the kitchen and took seats at the table there. "Are you doing okay being back here? Mom would drive me crazy but you two get along okay."

"It's not exactly where I saw myself, but it's helping. Turns out, having a different last name is a good thing."

"As long as you're safe," Ali told her, looking concerned.

"I am. Word was bound to get out. Treasure is a paparazzi magnet, so's everyone in her circle." Finola fought against tears. "I just don't understand why he did it. An affair is one thing, but an affair with her? Did he have to? It's so public and everyone knows. They're all talking about me and judging me. I hate it."

Ali hugged her. "Of course you do. I'm sorry. I wish I could do something to help."

"Having you here today is nice."

"Good. I'm glad."

Zennie arrived. She breezed into the house looking tall and fit, as per usual. There was something about her air of confidence that always made Finola feel as though she had to work harder. Not a competition, exactly, more of a challenge. Zennie could be stunning, but she never bothered to try. She wasn't interested in makeup or dressing up or being noticed.

"How's it going?" Zennie asked, hugging them both. She looked at Ali. "Still getting through it?"

"I'm managing. Every day is easier."

In that second, Finola realized she hadn't bothered to ask how Ali was doing. In a way they were going through similar circumstances, although a case could be made that a broken marriage was a lot bigger than just a broken engagement. Still, Ali was her sister and it wasn't as if she'd even bothered to check on her. How had that happened?

"Have you heard from Glen at all?" she asked, as if she'd been worried about her all along.

"Nothing. He sent me that check and that's it."

"Bastard," Zennie grumbled, setting her bag on the floor and joining them at the table. "He's a nightmare. He should definitely pay for at least half the wedding. Maybe all of it. He's the one who proposed and he's the one who walked."

Finola hadn't realized Glen hadn't helped pay for the canceled wedding. "Do you want to talk to a lawyer? I could get you a name."

"No, it's done. I took care of everything myself. I, ah, managed to negotiate a decent deal on most of the contracts. Now I just have to pay off my credit cards, build up my savings and I'm good." She shrugged. "Honestly, I don't want to talk about it." She smiled at Finola. "Thanks for inviting us to lunch. I feel as if we haven't been together in a while." She rolled her eyes. "Cleaning out Mom's house doesn't count."

Zennie sighed. "It's going to take forever." She looked at

Finola. "You could do it in little bits every night. I mean, you're here already."

"Thanks, but no. I think it should be a group activity." Finola ignored the fact that she'd ducked out the last time they were supposed to be finishing up the bonus room. "If it's just me, Mom will want me to take everything and that's not happening." She leaned toward Ali. "She's trying to pawn off that hideous old clock on me. I keep telling her you're the only one who wants it."

"She's giving away my clock? No! Why would she do that? I'm going to have to talk to her. That should be my clock. I swear, I really am going to have to steal it." Ali looked at Zennie. "So, what's new with you?"

If Finola hadn't been looking at her sisters, she wouldn't have noticed anything going on. But there was something between them. As Ali spoke, Zennie's mouth twisted, as if she were being called out on something. Zennie hesitated before speaking.

"What?" Finola asked, glancing between them. "You know something I don't."

Zennie smiled at her. "So, funny thing. I'm pregnant."

The information was so unexpected, Finola couldn't quite understand what Zennie was saying. "You're what?"

"Pregnant."

"But you're not even in a relationship."

"Yes, there is that. I can explain."

Pregnant? Zennie was having a baby? Finola thought of the gift she'd had for Nigel—the sexy toys and baby booties. They were supposed to have gone to Hawaii together. She was supposed to have been pregnant by now. They were supposed to have been happily married to each other forever.

"You remember my friend Bernie," Zennie began.

"What does she have to do with any of this?"

Zennie explained about Bernie and the cancer and the artificial insemination. "I'm their surrogate. I'll carry the baby and when it's born, they take over. Oh, Mom doesn't know. I'm going to tell her but I would appreciate it if you didn't say anything."

Finola couldn't believe it. "Are you insane? Who does that? My God, it's a potential legal nightmare. What if they break up? What if one of them dies? What if there's something wrong with the baby? Will you be stuck with it? Did you even think this through? I know she's your friend, but you've made a huge mistake. Are you sure you're pregnant? Do you have to keep it?"

Finola stopped talking when she realized both her sisters were staring at her with similar looks of confusion and distaste.

Ali spoke first. "This is a great thing. It's a wonderful gift to give someone she loves. I think Zennie's amazing for taking this on."

"Then you're as much of a fool as she is."

Ali flinched. Finola immediately felt guilty.

"I'm sorry. That came out too harshly. All of it. I'm just surprised. It's a huge step and there are legal ramifications to be considered."

"Yes, there are," Zennie said, her voice cool. "Hayes is a lawyer. We went over all of them and it's covered. I might not be as calculating and self-absorbed as you are, but I'm not stupid. I know there's a chance it could go badly but there's also a chance everything will work out. I love Bernie and I want to help her and Hayes have a baby. It's fine not to agree with my decision, but I would appreciate it if you'd at least respect it and not be so negative."

They were both looking at her with such disapproval, Finola thought, feeling uncomfortable and a little attacked.

"Of course. I didn't mean to upset you. It was a bit of a shock." She cleared her throat. "Congratulations. You must be very excited."

"I'm still getting used to the news," Zennie admitted, relaxing a little. "It's a lot to take in. Bernie got me a book to read."

"*What to Expect When You're Expecting*?" Finola asked eagerly, wanting to change the mood and not be the bad guy. "It's the one everyone talks about whenever we're doing a pregnancy segment on the show. It's supposed to be brilliant."

"That's the one. The information is month by month, which makes it easier to read. So far I'm afraid to get started but I really should."

Ali smiled at her. "I'm so impressed you're doing this. It's the most selfless act, right up there with donating a kidney."

Zennie flushed. "It's not like that."

"It kind of is."

Finola wanted to scream that she was impressive, too, and Ali had always liked her best. When they'd been kids, Ali had been her shadow. Ali had been the one to admire her and tell Finola how she was going to be a famous journalist, that she would go into dangerous places and do incredible investigative journalism. That had been Finola's dream, too. When she'd gotten the job at the LA affiliate, she'd hoped to start digging deep into complicated stories that would change people's lives. Instead she'd been the weekend anchor and then she'd gotten the job on *AM SoCal* and well, it had been a while since she'd reported on anything.

"I hope everything goes well for you," Finola said, fighting a sour taste in her mouth.

Zennie smiled. "I'm sure it will. Now what's for lunch?"

They ate the sandwiches and talked about everything from work to their mother's determination to downsize to a beach cottage.

"Her commute to work is going to be awful," Ali said. "Now she only has to go from Burbank to Sherman Oaks, but getting into the valley from the beach is going to be a nightmare."

Finola had to agree. The whole "going against traffic" thing didn't exist—not in LA.

"Maybe she's going to quit her job and do something else,"

Finola offered. "She never wanted to go into retail in the first place. Managing the boutique had never been her dream."

Ali looked doubtful. "Do you think she wants to get into acting?"

Mary Jo had always talked fondly about her brief acting career, when she'd been young. She'd moved to Hollywood like so many other young women, hoping for a big break. Instead she'd gotten walk-ons and the occasional line in a movie. But at one of those jobs, she'd met a handsome young actor named Leo and they'd fallen deeply in love. They'd married quickly and Finola had come along. Leo's career had taken off and Mary Jo had been happy to take care of her daughter and go on location with Leo. When he'd unexpectedly passed away, Mary Jo had been devastated.

Finola knew all that secondhand. While in theory, she'd been around for some of it, she didn't remember her biological father. She had no flashes of memory or bits of recollections. She'd seen the pictures her mother had kept and had listened to the stories and watched his movies, but for her, Leo was nothing but a story her mother told and an actor she saw in old movies.

"She doesn't talk to me," Zennie said cheerfully. "Maybe she could get a job managing a boutique by the beach. There are lots of stores there. She has her theater group she hangs out with. They might be able to help her find something closer to home."

"I'll let you discuss that," Ali said with a grin. "I'm not brave enough to have that conversation with Mom."

"Not me," Zennie said, pointing her fork at Finola. "That would be your job. You two are the tight ones."

"That's right." Ali shrugged. "You and Mom, Zennie and Dad and me by myself."

Zennie bumped shoulders with her. "We all love you, little Ali."

Something flashed in Ali's eyes, then disappeared. "Yeah,

that's what I hear. Anyway, let's not plan her life for her. I say we leave her to figure it out herself."

"Good idea," Finola said quietly, thinking how estranged she felt from her entire family. It was as if she only knew them from a distance.

When her sisters left, she cleaned up the kitchen, then walked into her bedroom. Her room was a mess, with her computer open on the table and clothes scattered everywhere. She told herself she should clean up but instead collapsed on the bed and rolled onto her back. She pulled an old, tattered teddy bear to her chest and wrapped her arms around it as tears spilled from her eyes and rolled into her hair.

She wasn't a bad person, she told herself. She *wasn't*. She was smart and funny and kind. The problem was there was so much going on and she just couldn't seem to get her mind around how everything had changed. With Nigel, of course, but also with her sisters. She couldn't believe Zennie was a surrogate for one of her friends. It was an insane decision and one that had so many opportunities for disaster. Seriously, what had she been thinking? Only Zennie was certainly at peace with her decision and Ali was acting like Zennie had just walked on water. It was disconcerting and uncomfortable and strange.

Finola told herself it was okay for Ali to admire Zennie for this and that it was no reflection on her as a person. But she knew in her gut she could never be as selfless. She just couldn't. If she was going to have a baby, she was going to keep it herself.

Without wanting to, she remembered what her stepfather had said. That regardless of what had happened, some of the failure of her marriage was her fault. She didn't want to believe that, only she couldn't seem to dismiss his point. The stupid concept kept coming back to her, as if daring her to admit some of the fault was hers. But even if she did admit the premise had some merit, what could she have possibly done to deserve Nigel cheating on her like that?

She sat up and swung her feet onto the floor. What if, she thought reluctantly, not wanting to entertain the idea but unable to let it go. What if Nigel had cheated with a normal person? How would this all be different? What if he hadn't cheated at all? What if he'd just left her?

Pain ripped through her, but she ignored the searing across her heart as she tried to figure out how she would feel under those circumstances. What if Nigel had just told her he was unhappy in their marriage and wanted out? Then their situation wouldn't be about him or Treasure or betrayal. It would be about her.

It would be her fault.

She held the bear closer. No, she told herself. It wouldn't be. He was still the one who... It was him. All him. It had to be. She was just...

She thought about what he'd said about scheduling sex and felt herself flush. As for the rest of his complaints, that she was too busy and too focused on her career, the same could be said about him. His work mattered more than anything. They were successful, driven people.

But Nigel had been unhappy. She didn't want to think about that, but the words refused to go away and she couldn't stop hearing them. And if she accepted the premise that without Treasure, without cheating, it was all on her, where did that leave them? Were there any pieces to pick up or were they past the point of redemption? Had they gone all this way only to end up with nothing?

Nigel was the only man she'd ever loved—she couldn't have lost him. And yet, it seemed she had.

Chapter Eighteen

Ali sat in the dark. It wasn't even ten o'clock, but it felt later. Or maybe it was just her mood. She knew she should get up and get ready for bed. Or go eat ice cream.

No, she amended, still not stirring from the sofa in Daniel's huge living room. She *shouldn't* eat ice cream but she probably would. Maybe a nice sugar rush would distract her from the hamster wheel that was her current thoughts. She wouldn't mind the spinning so much if she was thinking something nice about herself, but she wasn't. Words like *loser* and *stupid* and *insignificant* kept tumbling around and around.

She pulled her knees to her chest and told herself she was fine. Or would be fine. That these feelings would pass and she would be—

A light clicked on in the hallway. Seconds later Daniel walked into the room.

He was in silhouette so she couldn't see much more than the

shape of him. He looked big and strong, as if he could easily handle whatever life threw at him. He was so together. He had a beautiful house and a great business and a wonderful future to look forward to. By contrast she was homeless, stuck in a dead-end job with an employer who didn't think she had any potential. And if she kept eating ice cream she was going to be even more overweight than she was now.

"Want to talk about it?" he asked, settling in one of the chairs opposite the sofa.

He turned on the table lamp next to him, looked at her and waited.

"I'm feeling whiny," she admitted. "Trust me, you don't want to be a part of this."

He smiled. "Give me your best. I can handle it."

She really didn't want to fall apart in front of him. She'd done too much of that already. But somehow his words seemed to loosen whatever self-control she had until she found herself blurting, "It's awful. You have no idea. I figured Glen dumping me was the worst of it, but it's not. Or maybe that was just the beginning of my unhappy revelations."

She dropped her feet to the floor and put her hands on her lap. "Did you know that my dad and I haven't actually talked in six months? We don't ever talk. We text every now and then. When he found out about Glen, he texted me. There was no supportive phone call. Just a text. My mom was slightly more supportive, but it's a really low bar. She and I did have a conversation during which she asked me what I'd done wrong to lose Glen."

She paused, waiting for him to say something, but Daniel only watched her, as if expecting her to continue. She drew in a breath.

"I thought things were great at work. I thought I was doing a good job. I'm in charge of inventory control and I've implemented a lot of changes that are making a difference. I've run other departments, I've had people working for me. When the warehouse manager goes on vacation or gets sick, I'm the one who fills in."

She glared at him. "And you know what? He's retiring and they've interviewed Ray for his job but not me. Why not me? I know more about the warehouse. I'm a better manager. Ray was invited to interview and I've heard nothing. Nada. It's like they don't see me. Zennie's having a baby for her best friend. She's giving Bernie and Hayes a baby. A baby! That's amazing. She's amazing and I'm not. I want to be amazing, too."

Daniel shifted slightly. She thought he was going to say something, but he didn't so she continued.

"Adding insult to injury, and I know this won't make sense to you, but it's a big deal to me," she said, doing her best to keep the whine out of her voice, "there's the clock I told you about. I've loved it since I was a little girl. I know it's silly and who needs a grandfather clock, but it means something to me and you know what? The woman is downsizing. She's begging us to take things and she doesn't want the clock, but she doesn't want me to have it either. She would rather donate it to a charity than let me have it."

She pressed her lips together. "I feel small and overlooked and useless. Just when I thought I was getting my life together, I realized it's all falling apart and I don't know what to do." She found herself fighting tears.

"I swore I was done being the victim," she said, angrily brushing her cheeks. "I don't want to feel that every eight seconds my life is falling apart, but I also don't know how to make things better." She sniffed. "So if you want to give me a bracing pep talk, this would be a good time to do that."

One corner of his mouth turned up. "Is that what you want?"

"I want *something*. Anything that isn't feeling like a fool all the time. What am I doing wrong? Why can't I get my act together?"

"It's more together than you think."

She sighed. "Daniel, while I appreciate the words, honestly, just give me some tough love. I swear, I can take it. Please."

She wasn't sure why she felt his advice would be the right advice, but deep in her gut she had the feeling he saw her more clearly than most people.

"Okay," he said, his gaze steady. "I don't know what to say about your dad. He sounds like a jerk and I'm sorry he hasn't been there for you. Do you need his support or do you just want it?"

"Oh, that's a good question. I've never considered that like that before." She thought for a second. "I've managed this long without him. I guess I thought he'd call me about Glen breaking off the wedding. I put a couple of calls in to him but I didn't hear anything back after that first text. I guess I want his support but don't need it."

"You could confront him."

"I could, although I'm not sure what I'd say. 'Hey, Dad, it would be nice if you pretended to love me.'" Her eyes filled again. "Stupid emotions."

Daniel shifted, as if he was going to move to the sofa. Maybe to offer comfort, maybe to hold her close. For a second she was caught up in the idea of him taking her in his arms and…

Back the truck up, she told herself. Daniel was her friend and there wasn't going to be any taking anyone in anyone else's arms. She was smarter than that.

She returned her attention to the topic of her father. "Okay, Dad's a jerk and when I grow a pair, I'll tell him exactly that."

He tilted his head. "You do that a lot—put yourself down. Why do you have to grow a pair? You're not weak, Ali. You've been through a lot the past few weeks and you've held it together. You should be proud of that. Maybe you don't need one more thing right now. Maybe when you've recovered from all this crap, you'll be ready to deal with your dad."

"Oh." She smiled. "That's good, too."

"Now, work."

She groaned. "Yes?"

"You're working in a man's world. The cars, the warehouse, all of it is dominated by men. If you want to get ahead, you have to play by their rules."

"I hate that. It's not like they post them or anything. How do I know what the rules are?"

"They're simple. Be visible. If you want the promotion, tell them. When they ask why you should get it, be prepared with a list of your accomplishments. Be specific. Tell them how you've saved the company money, time, whatever. Speak up at meetings. You don't have to be rude, but you do have to be noticed. Don't let them take you for granted. When you do something right, talk about it. When you do something wrong, fix it."

She fell across the sofa, her body and head landing on the cushions. "No," she groaned. "Don't make me talk about my accomplishments and be all braggy. It's not me."

"Then you won't get the promotion and you'll grow old and bitter monitoring inventory."

She sat up. "That was harsh."

"It's true. Ali, you're more than qualified, but you have to act like it. It's very possible your boss knows you'd be the best person for the job, but has no idea you're interested. You've never discussed advancement or even a five-year plan."

"How do you know that?"

"You don't have a five-year plan."

He was right, of course, she just wished he hadn't said it so bluntly. *Tough love*, she reminded herself. She'd been the one who wanted it.

"Fine," she grumbled. "I'll come up with a plan and a list of accomplishments, then I'll go talk to my boss."

"Are you sure you even want the job? It's going to be a lot more work and responsibility."

"Of course I want the job. I'd be good at it and it would be interesting. Plus, I'm not working at the warehouse for the rest of my life, despite what you said. The promotion would look great on my résumé."

The smile returned. "Bring that attitude to the interview and you'll do fine."

"You're right. Thanks. Sometimes it's hard to remember I have to be like them when I really just want to be like me."

"Don't change too much. I kind of like how you are now."

"A mess?"

"Sweet, funny, kind, interesting. Don't lose that."

"Is that how you see me?" she asked before she could stop herself. "Because those are not the words I would use."

"You should. Stop putting yourself down." His gaze sharpened. "Why don't you accept compliments more easily?"

She blinked at him. "Yes, well, isn't that a fascinating question? And look at the time. You're probably ready to turn in for the night."

She waited, but Daniel didn't move. She sighed.

"You're right. Compliments make me uncomfortable and I don't know why."

"So if I said I thought you were beautiful…"

She flopped down on the sofa again and covered her face with her hands. "I'd know you were lying. I'm completely average and on a good day can pass for pretty, but otherwise, no. Just no."

He chuckled. "I see we have some work to do."

"There is no 'we' in the work department. It's all on me." She sat up. "You are such a good guy. Thank you. And for what it's worth, your ex-wife was really stupid to let you go."

"I could say the same thing about Glen."

She waved her hand. "Don't. He was totally wrong for me. I see that now. It's over and I'm glad."

"Ditto."

"Do you think about getting married again?"

He nodded. "I still want a traditional life. A wife, kids, dog."

"And a kitten?"

He smiled. "Yes, Ali. And a kitten."

He stood. For a second she thought he was going to walk toward her and maybe pull her to her feet and… Okay, she had no idea what would come next but whatever it was, she was all in.

But instead of kissing her senseless or kissing her at all, he just looked at her.

"It's late. I'll see you tomorrow."

She did her best to keep her disappointment from showing. "You will," she said brightly. "Thanks for the pep talk. You've given me a lot to think about. I'm going to make some notes, then talk to my boss on Monday."

"That's my girl. Night."

She watched him leave. His girl. If only, she thought with a sigh. Because being Daniel's girl would actually be kind of nice.

Zennie had debated meeting her mother at a restaurant, but that seemed unfair to both of them, so instead she texted, asking if she could stop by after work. As she walked up to the front door, she told herself that whatever happened, she would be fine. She was doing exactly what she wanted to do, and for the right reasons. If her mother didn't understand, then that was Mary Jo's problem.

"Hey, Mom," Zennie called as she let herself into the house.

"In the kitchen. I'm pouring wine."

Zennie braced herself and walked into the outdated kitchen. "Hi, Mom."

Mary Jo smiled at her and poured a second glass of chardonnay. "Just getting off work? You must be tired. I know how my feet feel at the end of the day." She pointed to the kitchen table. "Have a seat. Are you hungry? I could fix something."

"I'm fine, but thanks."

Her mother sat across from her. She picked up her glass. "I'm sorry about the blind date with the lesbian. I was just trying to help."

Zennie relaxed. "Don't apologize. C.J. and I actually had a good time." She held up her hand before her mother could speak. "No, I'm not a lesbian, but I think we're going to be friends, which works for me."

"Have you met anyone since then?"

"Mom, please. You have to stop fixing me up."

"Why? I want you to be happy. I want you to have someone in your life. You're young now, but time passes quickly and before you know it, your life is more than half over and then what? Don't you want a family? Don't you want to be part of something? Surely there's some handsome doctor at the hospital who could sweep you off your feet. If you don't do something, you're going to die alone."

"I'm not alone. I have lots of friends."

"You don't have a *husband*." Her mother stretched across the table and put her hands on Zennie's. "I want you to be happy."

"I am happy, Mom. You have to believe me."

"I wish I could." Mary Jo straightened and sipped her wine. "Fine. I'll be quiet for now. So what's new?"

Zennie told herself it was going to be okay. She knew she was lying, but she repeated it anyway. "A few things. Do you remember my friend Bernie?"

"Of course. What a lovely girl. And her husband's a lawyer. You could do worse."

"Thanks, Mom. Well, because of her cancer, Bernie can't have children, but she and Hayes want a family, so I'm going to be their surrogate."

Her mother stared at her. "What? You're what?"

"I'm going to be their surrogate. I'm providing the egg and Hayes is providing the sperm and then I'll carry their baby to term and—"

"Are you insane?" The words were a shriek. "Have you totally lost your mind? You're going to get pregnant and have someone *else's* baby? No. No! You can't. It's ridiculous. My God, Zennie, you've always had strange ideas, but that is ridiculous. I won't allow it. Have you thought this through? It's what, a year out of your life. You have no idea how challenging pregnancy can be. It's not like in the movies. It's back pain and hemorrhoids and stretch marks and my God, no. Just no. You could die in childbirth. It happens. No. The whole idea is madness. She can have a baby another way."

Zennie stared longingly at the glass of wine. If there was ever a time to drink…

"Mom, I'm already pregnant."

Her mother burst into tears. "Pregnant? How could you? You didn't even talk to me first. You're having a baby and you're just giving it away? Who does that? You know I want grandchildren. How could you be so cruel? You always were the selfish one, Zennie. Always."

"Mom, I—"

Her mother glared at her. "No. There's nothing you can say to make this right. I can't believe you'd do this." Her mother stood. "Go. I don't want to see you right now. You're a disappointment to me. More than I can say. I used to be proud of you, but I can't be anymore. I can't believe this. Go. Just go."

Zennie wasn't sure she would have been more shocked if her mother had slapped her.

"We're not going to talk about it?"

"There's nothing to say, is there? You've done what you wanted to do, just like you always did when you were a little girl. My opinion didn't matter before and it doesn't matter now."

She'd known her mother wouldn't be happy but she hadn't expected this. She stood and got her bag, then walked out of the house. On the drive home she told herself that she would be fine, that her mother would come around. It might take a while, but they were family.

By the time she got home, she'd nearly convinced herself everything was going to be fine. She ate her healthy dinner and had just started her prenatal yoga video when her phone buzzed. She looked at the screen and saw a text from her dad.

Is it true?

For people who had been divorced more than a decade, her parents appeared to have no trouble communicating, she thought grimly.

If you're asking if I'm going to be a surrogate for my best friend, then yes.

Of all the dumb-ass things to do. You're having a baby for a friend? Have you thought about what's involved? Jesus, Zennie, what's wrong with you? How could you be so impulsive?

Her healthy dinner suddenly didn't feel very good in her stomach.

I wanted to help my best friend, Dad. I can give her this.

Give her a goddamned gift card. Not a baby. You're destroying your life and for what? She's just a friend. Is it too late to get an abortion?

She dropped her phone as his words hit her like a slap across the face. She picked it up again.

Dad, no. Don't be like this. Even if you don't understand, you have to accept my decision. You've always said I had a good head on my shoulders. Well, I thought this through and I'm doing this.

What I see is my beautiful daughter ruining her life. You used to be so sensible and together. I used to be proud of you. What happened?

Her mother had mentioned being proud of her, too. Zennie had expected this from her, but not her dad.

You used to be someone I could depend on to support me, no matter what. What happened?

For a couple of minutes, she didn't see a reply, then three dots appeared on her screen as he typed.

You're going to regret this, and when you do, don't come running to me.

Zennie tossed down her phone without answering. *So much for parental support*, she thought, trying to hold herself together. Her mother's reaction had been over the top but not completely unexpected, but her dad… It had never occurred to her he wouldn't get it.

She put her hand over her still flat belly. "I'm going to take care of you," she whispered. "I don't care what anyone else says. We'll figure this out together."

It wasn't as if she was alone. She had Bernie and Hayes, and Ali. She was strong and healthy, and she knew in her gut she'd made the right decision. As for her father, she supposed every daughter had to face a time when her father broke her heart. She just didn't think it would hurt so much or be so sad.

Chapter Nineteen

Finola pulled into the gas station on Ventura Boulevard. If she were honest with herself, she was stopping to fill her tank more as a delay tactic than because she actually needed fuel. Zennie had texted her a warning that Mom knew about the pregnancy and that she hadn't taken the news very well.

Hardly a surprise, Finola thought, inserting her credit card into the machine. What had Zennie been thinking?

Finola put the nozzle into her gas tank and pressed the lever to start the flow. It was only then she noticed the two teenage girls on the other side of the pump. They were whispering and pointing at her.

Finola instantly wanted to jump in her car and drive away. She ignored the urge, telling herself she was imagining things. There was no way they had any idea that she was—

"You're her, aren't you?" the shorter of the two teens asked, her blond ponytail swinging as she spoke. "You met Treasure on your show."

They were both wearing school uniforms, no doubt from one of the expensive private schools in the area.

Finola watched the gallons click by on the gauge and wished the fuel would flow faster. Realizing there was no escape, she forced a smile. "Yes, I did meet her. Are you fans?"

The girls looked at each other, then back at her. The taller teen rolled her eyes. "Of course we are. She's just amazing. So talented and beautiful. She could have anyone. Is she really sleeping with your husband? Isn't he like really old?"

The blonde nudged her friend. "Don't."

"What? I'm just asking. I would hate my boyfriend to cheat on me, but with Treasure I guess it would kind of make sense." She smiled. "My mom says you've had work done, but not enough to keep him happy. I'm thinking of getting bigger boobs, but I just can't decide."

The blonde shook her head. "Don't do it. Wait until you're her age to have surgery. You look great the way you are." She turned to Finola. "So do you mind he's sleeping with Treasure? I mean do you not care anymore when you get old, or does stuff like that still hurt? You know—being left and laughed at and stuff."

Finola told herself they weren't deliberately cruel, they were just young and thoughtless. At least she hoped they were because otherwise the next generation was going to be a disappointment.

Not caring that she didn't have a full tank, she flipped off the nozzle and put it back in place, then screwed on the gas cap.

As she walked toward the driver's door, one of the girls called. "You're really not going to say anything, are you? Man, you totally are a bitch. You deserve it, you know."

Finola started the engine, then drove away. She was careful to check for traffic before merging onto the street. It was only once she was safely away from the gas station that the shaking started, an aftereffect from trauma, she thought grimly.

There was no escape. There was nowhere to go where she wouldn't be recognized and humiliated. Everyone had an opinion on her marriage, the affair, her appearance. Telling herself she didn't care wasn't helpful, because she did care. She wanted to be liked. More important, she *needed* to be liked to be successful at her job. It was so damned unfair—six weeks ago everything had been fine, and now it was all crap.

She drove back to her mom's place in Burbank and thought wistfully of her own beautiful house. *If only*, she thought as she walked inside and called out, "Hey, Mom. I'm back."

"In the kitchen."

Finola set her bag on the entry table and kicked off her shoes. As she entered the kitchen she saw at least half a dozen boxes stacked by the back door. One was open with the contents spread on the table. Her mother brushed a stray strand of hair off her face.

"After Zennie left I was so upset, I had to do something so I dragged these boxes in from the garage. It was that or sit around and drink." Mary Jo sighed. "Not that there won't be wine later, but at least I'm doing something constructive first. Did you know?"

The question was direct enough that Finola knew there was no point in pretending she thought her mother was asking if she knew there would be wine later.

"Zennie told me a few days ago."

"And you didn't tell me?"

"She wanted to be the one to share the news." Finola walked over to the table and looked at the collection of odds and ends. There was a photo album, some old dress-up clothes and a few books. She glanced back at her mom.

"I think she's an idiot," Finola said flatly. "She's all caught up in the romance of the moment—giving her best friend a baby—but what if something goes wrong?"

"That's what I said. This is so much bigger than she thinks.

She'll be carrying that baby, she'll feel it growing inside of her and start to care. I remember how I felt when I first found out I was pregnant with you." Mary Jo's expression softened with a smile. "Your father and I were so happy. It was a dream come true."

Finola couldn't imagine being anyone's idea of a dream, but it was nice to hear.

"What a mess," her mother said. "Nigel cheats on you with that ridiculous singer, Glen dumps Ali and now Zennie's having a baby for someone else. I swear, I must be the worst mother on the planet."

"I'm happy to put all the blame on you," Finola said without thinking.

Her mother stared at her for a second, then burst out laughing. "It's always the mother, isn't it?" Mary Jo pointed to the pile of junk on the table. "Let's get this cleaned up. We'll go through the other boxes, then drink the wine I opened."

They sorted through the first two boxes quickly. The dress-up clothes were assessed for wear. Those still viable were put in the giveaway pile while the rest went into the trash. The books were sorted and the photo albums stacked to be gone through later.

The second box was more of the same, with the exception of several pairs of painted wooden spoons.

"Those are ugly," Mary Jo said, reaching for the spoons. "They should be tossed."

"No way." Finola grabbed them and waved one in the air. "These are our fighting spoons."

Her mother looked at her blankly.

"We used to have sword fights," Finola explained. "Upstairs. The three of us battled." She smiled at the memory of time spent with her sisters. She'd been older and not as interested in play but they'd always been able to entice her into joining them with the fighting spoons. "Trust me, Zennie and Ali are going to want to keep these." She plucked out the two dark green spoons. "These are mine."

"If you say so."

There was a box of old summer clothes from when the sisters were young and a very dusty and slightly moth-eaten fur stole. Mary Jo shook it out before wrapping it around her shoulders.

"Your father bought this for me." Mary Jo smiled sadly. "Your biological father, I mean. We were so poor, but so happy. We'd been invited to a fancy party and wearing fur was all the rage." She pursed her lips together. "It wasn't like today when any kind of fur has a stigma. Back then it was all good. Your dad found this at a thrift shop." She sighed as she walked back and forth in the kitchen, the fur contrasting with her T-shirt and yoga pants. "I felt pampered and oh so beautiful." Her smile turned wistful. "Your father had a way of doing that. He could turn any occasion into something special."

"Do you still miss him?"

"Less than I used to, of course. He was a wonderful man. I'm sure over time we would have had our ups and down, but he was gone when everything was still perfect." She looked at Finola. "Then it was just you and me."

She draped the fur over a kitchen chair. "I know it's silly, but I think I'll keep this. Maybe I can get it cleaned. It's not in horrible shape."

Memories were powerful, Finola thought, wondering what she would want to keep from her marriage when—

No, she told herself firmly. Her marriage wasn't ending. She and Nigel were going to get through this and come out stronger than before. They had to.

She put the next box on the table and opened it. Her mother was still stroking the fur so didn't notice the box until Finola pulled out a large green-striped hatbox.

"This is nice," she said. "But I don't remember it."

Mary Jo looked up. "Oh, there it is," she said, almost to herself. "I'd wondered… You shouldn't open it."

"Really?" Finola laughed. "You're keeping secrets."

Her mother surprised her by running her hand across the box. "I suppose it doesn't matter now. It's been so long. Go ahead. I'll get the wine."

"Now I'm intrigued."

Finola quickly cleared off the table and set the hatbox in the middle. She sat down, then carefully removed the lid. Inside was a hodgepodge of greeting cards, jewelry boxes, folders and several scripts.

Her mother returned with an open bottle of pinot grigio and two glasses. "Go ahead. Go through it, then ask your questions."

Finola opened one of the robin's-egg blue boxes with the words *Tiffany & Co.* embossed on the top. Inside was a beautiful starfish brooch encrusted with diamonds.

"Holy crap, are these real?"

Mary Jo poured the wine. "They are."

"You can't keep something this valuable in the garage, Mom. It should be insured and in a safe-deposit box."

"I suppose." She took the brooch and held it in her hand. "It's pretty, but not me. Still Parker insisted."

"Parker?" Finola pulled out one of the folders and opened it. Inside were head shots of Parker Crane.

The actor was much younger in the pictures, all handsome with a sexy smile and a twinkle in his eye. Parker Crane had been as famous for his reputation with the ladies as for his movies, she thought, trying to remember what else she knew about him. But he'd been way before her time. Now he was a successful TV character actor who still had a roguish air about him.

"You knew Parker Crane?" she asked, looking from the pictures to her mother. "No, you were involved with him. When?"

"After your father died. For months I was too stricken with grief to do much more than take care of you. There wasn't enough money to support us forever so I had to do something. When I started looking for a job, a few friends insisted I go with them to a big Hollywood party first. Just to get my spirits up. Parker was there. He swept me off my feet. You and I moved in with him. We traveled the world. It was very romantic."

"I don't remember any of this."

"You were still just a baby. Probably about a year old."

"You met a guy at a party and took off with him?"

Her mother smiled. "I'm sure I made him work a little harder than that, but in essence, yes. I was so grateful not to be sad anymore. I knew it would never go anywhere. Parker was the consummate playboy and it wasn't as if I truly loved him. Your father still had my heart. But it was fun while it lasted."

Finola took a drink of her wine. "How did it end?"

"I woke up in a hotel room in Rome and he was gone. The bill was paid and he'd left two tickets for us to fly home. I remember lying in bed thinking I had to start living a real life. That I was done with pretend and done with Hollywood."

She picked up a small ring box and opened it. Finola gasped when she saw the large ruby surrounded by diamonds.

"You could have sold the jewelry and lived off the proceeds for a few years."

"Oh, I was going to, if it became necessary." The smile returned. "I wasn't foolish enough to think Parker's gifts were to be kept sacred. But I wanted to see if I could support myself first. I did sell a couple pairs of earrings to pay for secretarial school, then I got a job as a receptionist at the ABC television studios and that's where I met Bill."

Finola thought about her handsome, movie star biological father, and then Parker, a man from the same mold. "Did you marry Bill because he was a regular person?"

"I thought things would be better if I admitted to being ordinary. And for a while, they were. We had good years." She drank more wine. "But I could never give him what he wanted."

And vice versa, Finola thought. She would guess Bill had seen Mary Jo as an exotic flower. He would have admired her but not known exactly what to do with her.

"In the end," her mother said, "I couldn't make him happy. I suppose after a while I stopped trying."

"That's what he said," Finola told her. "Dad called me when he found out about Nigel. He wanted to tell me that even though Nigel cheated, I still had some fault in the failure of the marriage."

Her mother looked at her, her expression sympathetic. "Not what you wanted to hear."

"Of course not. Nigel humiliated me. He didn't just cheat, he made it public."

"He did all those things and he's a horrible person for doing it, but Bill isn't wrong."

"Mo-om, you're saying it's my fault?" She didn't care that she sounded like she was seven. "I'm the injured party."

"You are if you think you are." She slipped on the fur wrap and slid the ring on her right hand. "But being the injured party is an easy trap. If you spend too much time feeling sorry for yourself, you never act." She looked at Finola. "It took me until I was fifty to figure that out. You might want to learn the lesson a little sooner."

Zennie and Gina stood by the bar area, searching for an open table. It was nearly five and The Cheesecake Factory at the Sherman Oaks Galleria was starting to fill up.

"There," Gina said, pointing.

Sure enough there was an empty booth in the back by the bar. They hurried over, each sliding onto the bench seats.

"I claim this for me and my friends," Gina said with a laugh.

"It's an interesting choice for us." The group tended to go out to local bars rather than brave the Galleria.

"DeeDee's been talking avocado egg rolls for two days," Gina admitted. "After a while, I caved. I mean, who can resist those?"

"I'm in." Zennie might not be drinking these days, but she was still eating. And after days of following her prenatal diet perfectly, she figured she was due something fried.

Cassie and DeeDee joined them, DeeDee sliding in beside Zennie.

"You're lucky you didn't scrub in today," DeeDee said with a sigh. "Dr. Chen was on a tear. He had Rita in tears before we'd even opened up the patient. I missed having you there to act as a buffer." She grinned at Gina and Cassie. "Zennie's his favorite."

"Oh, we know," Gina said. "He makes it very clear."

"Why didn't you scrub in?" Cassie asked.

"There was an emergency bypass this morning around five. I was on call." Her phone had gone off at four o'clock and she'd been in the OR by five. Six hours later, their patient was in recovery and doing well.

Their server appeared to take their orders. Everyone got cocktails, DeeDee ordered two plates of avocado egg rolls and then it was Zennie's turn.

"Club soda," she said, bracing herself for the onslaught.

"What?"

"You're not drinking?"

"We're going to Uber home. Come on, Zennie, forget that it's a school night."

She smiled at the server. "Club soda," she repeated.

When the server left, Gina looked at her. "What's up? You're not feeling well?"

"I, ah, had an early morning."

No one looked convinced, which was not a surprise. Four wasn't really that early, not when her alarm typically went off at five. She drew in a breath and quickly explained about Bernie and the surrogacy and the fact that she was pregnant.

All three of her friends stared at her. DeeDee recovered first and grinned. "That is the coolest thing. Congrats. I can't believe you're doing something so wonderful for a friend. I mean I knew you were amazing but this is—"

"Too dumb for words," Gina said flatly. "What were you thinking, Zennie? Having a baby you're not even keeping. What if something goes wrong? What if they change their mind?"

The questions stung. "You sound like my mother."

"Maybe because your mother's right."

The attack shocked Zennie. DeeDee came to her rescue.

"Back off, Gina. What Zennie's doing is fantastic."

"No, it's not." Gina's expression was serious. She shook her head. "How long until Dr. Chen takes you off rotation? You might be his favorite, but he's not going to want you in surgery if you're pregnant. What if you get nauseous or pass out or something?"

Zennie hadn't thought of that. "He can't do that. It's illegal."

"He'll find a way," Cassie said gently. "Zennie, what you're doing is really wonderful for Bernie, but have you thought about how it's going to screw up your life?"

"I'm having a baby, not taking on a terminal illness."

"Pregnancy's hard," Cassie continued. "I've watched my sisters go through it and it truly sucks. You have no idea what you've signed up for. I hope it's worth it."

DeeDee glared at both of them. "Don't listen to the sourpusses. You're my hero. Good for you, Zennie. Dr. Chen isn't going to do anything about your being pregnant. He's a sweetie."

All three of them stared at her. She blushed. "Okay, maybe not a sweetie, but he's not that awful."

"You said he had Rita in tears," Gina muttered. "Rita was a Marine."

Zennie did her best to process her friends' reactions. Having her parents object was one thing, but she'd really expected her friends to be more supportive. And what if they were right about Dr. Chen? What if she did get thrown off the team?

"You know the worst part?" Gina asked. "What if you find the right guy? How are you going to explain being pregnant?"

"I'm not looking for a guy."

"That's when you always find him," Cassie pointed out. "Oh, Zennie, I wish you hadn't done this."

Zennie glared at the two of them. "You know what I wish? That I had friends who could be happy for me and support what I'm doing." She turned to DeeDee. "I need to go."

DeeDee slid out of the booth. Zennie followed. She faced the table.

"I can't begin to tell you how much you've disappointed me," she said before hugging DeeDee. "Not you, my friend."

"Thanks. You don't have to go."

"Yes, I do."

She threw twenty dollars on the table to cover her drink and share of the egg rolls, then walked out.

As she got to her car, she was overwhelmed by nausea. She didn't know if it was mistimed morning sickness or just because she was upset. Regardless, she took deep breaths until the sensation passed, then drove home.

When she was safely in her apartment, she threw herself on the sofa and decided she was perfectly justified in having a mini pity party—at least for a couple of hours. Her parents objecting was one thing, even though she was still mad about what her dad had said, but Gina and Cassie chastising her was harder to deal with. So far she only had Ali and DeeDee on her side. She'd been hoping for a larger contingent in the support department.

She did a few breathing exercises, then tried to gather some enthusiasm about dinner. She knew she had to eat. Maybe she would feel better if she texted with a friend. Only who? DeeDee was still out with Gina and Cassie, and Zennie couldn't discuss her problem with Bernie—it would only upset her.

She started to text Ali, only to stop herself. She was stronger than this—she didn't need to bother anyone. If only she didn't feel so alone.

Maybe she needed a pet, she thought. Not a dog—she wasn't home enough. How about a cat? Cats purred and that would be nice. She could go to a local shelter and adopt a nice adult cat who would be there for her. A cat would—

She swore under her breath. Hadn't she read something about cats and pregnancy? A parasite or something? She eyed the pregnancy book on her coffee table, confident the answer was in there, but not wanting to look.

Great. She couldn't eat sushi, she couldn't have coffee or wine or go in a sauna and now she couldn't even get a cat. She wasn't willing to admit to second thoughts, but being pregnant was a much bigger drag than she'd ever thought possible.

Chapter Twenty

"You need to go on a date." Rochelle's voice was firm, as if she actually expected Finola to listen.

Finola stared at her assistant over her mug of coffee. "Are you kidding? A date? Really? Because I need one more thing?"

"You'll feel better, I swear. Nothing serious. Just a nice, happy revenge date with a great-looking, younger guy who has a mad crush on you."

Finola thought about how she still wasn't sleeping very well and how putting on enough concealer to look refreshed was becoming an art form.

"And where would we find such an amazing guy? On Amazon?"

They sat across from each other at the small table in Finola's dressing room.

"You've had dozens of offers," Rochelle said eagerly.

"You're making that up."

"I'm not. You forget, I have your old phone. You're working off a burner. I get your messages every day."

And cleared them out, Finola thought. Rochelle was deleting the cruel comments, the requests for interviews and all the other crap designed to make her feel worse than she already did.

Rochelle smiled gleefully. "Trust me, there are plenty of men eager and willing to help you get over Nigel, and some of the offers are pretty tempting."

"Then you go out with them."

"They're not interested in me."

"They would be if they saw you." Rochelle was young and beautiful—filled with possibility. Finola was simply used-up and tired.

"I'm not ready for a revenge date."

"Are you waiting for Nigel to come back?"

"Of course not. I was at first. I had no clue anything was going on. I was devastated." She still was, she admitted to herself. "I wanted things to go back to the way they were." She clutched her coffee, recognizing a truth she hadn't articulated before. "I just don't think they can."

Her voice was so small, she thought. So powerless. Nigel hadn't just cheated on her, he'd stolen the very essence of her. He'd ripped her bare and left her with nothing but wounds. She knew, excluding the public nature of what had happened, her situation wasn't unique. She wasn't the first woman to be cheated on and she wouldn't be the last. But that knowledge didn't take away the pain or sense of loss. She was truly broken and she didn't think she would ever feel whole again.

"They can't be the same," Rochelle told her. "But maybe they could be better."

Finola looked at her assistant. "Do you really believe that?"

"What I believe doesn't matter. This is about you."

"What is the purpose of a revenge date?"

"I think the name kind of says it all."

"Yes, but that presumes Nigel would care. He wouldn't. So where's the revenge?"

"It's not about him. It's about you remembering who you are. It's about realizing there are men out there who think you are beautiful and smart and Nigel is simply a stupid man who's going to regret what he's done."

Regret would be nice, she thought wistfully. Regret, remorse and maybe a painful, oozing rash.

"I have a list of guys I think you'd like."

Finola stared at her. "You have a list?" She couldn't help laughing. "Of course you do. Let me guess—it's in a spreadsheet and you've sorted them by age, appearance, appropriateness and what else?"

Rochelle grinned. "Income, and how good I think they'd be in bed. The latter is subjective, but I felt it was important." Her smile faded. "Finola, you've got the gala coming up. Wouldn't you like to go with a date?"

"I couldn't. There would be too much speculation." She hadn't decided what she was going to do. "I'll be fine if I go alone."

"You won't be fine. I'd offer to go, but everyone knows I'm your assistant and that would just be weird."

Finola knew that was true.

Rochelle's phone buzzed. She glanced at the screen and then at Finola. "I have to take this."

Rochelle walked out of the dressing room. Finola thought about the gala and who would be safe. For some reason, she zeroed in on Zennie, who would look gorgeous in an evening gown. Everyone would wonder who she was.

A sister was safe, Finola thought. A sister made for good press.

She picked up her phone only to realize the last time she'd talked to Zennie, she'd totally freaked out about the surrogacy. Not exactly her best example of being supportive. She hesitated for a second, then started to type on her phone.

Sorry I was such a bitch the other day. Your news caught me off guard and in my current mental state, I seem to be defaulting to the dark side of things. What you're doing really is amazing. I know Bernie and her husband are going to be really happy.

She pushed Send and knew she would hear from Zennie later. No doubt her sister was in surgery this morning. Because that was what Zennie did—she saved lives, and was pregnant with a baby for her best friend, while Finola hosted some ridiculous TV show and worried about being photographed by the press and gossiped about.

"I'm a completely shallow person," Finola whispered aloud. She didn't want it to be true, but the truth was kind of hard to avoid. She was shallow and self-absorbed and both her sisters were nicer people than she ever was. She'd apologized to her sister for the sole reason of getting her to come to the gala—not because she thought she was wrong.

The realization was uncomfortable. She felt slightly sick to her stomach and her skin felt weird—as if it were suddenly too small. Her cheeks were hot and the sense of being less than everyone else returned. Not sure where to put all the unwelcome emotions, she quickly turned on the TV.

The Today Show came on with a well-dressed woman talking to one of the hosts. "Yes, I do think that there is always blame on both sides."

"Even when one partner cheats?"

Finola froze. This was not happening, she thought, reaching for the remote control. But before she could silence the words, she heard, "Yes, even then. While there is the occasional partner who is compelled to be unfaithful, in most relationships, there's an underlying reason that needs to be addressed."

Finola pushed the off button and the screen went dark, but it was too late. If the universe was trying to get her attention, it had succeeded, and she didn't like it one bit.

Ali spent two days surreptitiously observing the men she worked with. They were good-natured and funny, always insulting each other. Everything was a competition, with the winner crowing about his victory. Their style of communication was completely different from hers.

She remembered when she'd first started at the company—how she'd been the only female, and she'd known nothing about cars. She'd been overlooked, dismissed and bypassed. It had taken a lot of hard work to learn the inventory, then prove herself to the team, but she had. Now the new guys always came to her with their questions and when something went wrong, she was put in charge of fixing it. She was respected and appreciated, but she wasn't sure she was ever seen as ambitious.

She didn't talk about her successes or what she'd done right that day. She didn't brag or put anyone down. She didn't play pickup basketball at lunch. She wasn't one of the guys, but she was part of the team.

She knew there was a difference between the two and her gut told her that her problem wasn't not being one of the guys. She suspected the issue was her natural reticence. She did a good job and expected that was enough. Given what had happened with Ray, it obviously wasn't. She was going to have to start talking about what she did for the company on a daily basis. She was going to have to come up with a plan and fast because if she didn't, she would never be considered for the promotion and wouldn't that suck.

She used her lunch break to write up what she'd accomplished the past year above and beyond her job description. Then she walked through the warehouse and made notes on what she thought should be done differently. Later she would back up her ideas with tangible suggestions connected to cash flow. She had time—the owner was going on vacation and not picking up the job search until he was back.

She'd just returned to her desk when her phone rang. She didn't recognize the number, but it was local. "This is Ali."

"Hi, it's Betty from All Occasion Bakery. Your cake's ready for pickup. Just a reminder, it's in several boxes that you won't want to stack. You don't want anything happening to your beautiful cake before your special day."

Ali closed her eyes and groaned. She'd totally forgotten about the cake. She hadn't canceled it, which meant she was going to have to pay for it and then what? She had a cake for several hundred people. And her canceled wedding date was this weekend—a fact she'd been doing her best to avoid.

"Okay, thanks," she said with a sigh. "I'll be by later to pick it up."

"We're open until six."

Ali hung up and thought about banging her head against her desk, but she knew that wouldn't accomplish anything. Instead she thought about the massive cake Glen had insisted on. They'd needed one for only a couple hundred people but he'd liked the look of the five-layer one, so that was what they'd bought.

Five layers, she thought grimly. That would never fit in her car.

She picked up her phone and quickly dialed Daniel.

"Hey," he said when he answered. "What's up?"

"Any way I can borrow your truck?"

"Sure. What for?"

"I totally forgot to cancel the cake. It's huge and I'm afraid it won't fit in my car."

"Not a problem. I'll meet you at the house after work. What are you going to do with it?"

"I don't know. I guess donate it. You don't happen to know someone who's getting married and forgot to order a cake, do you?"

"No, but I know a good food bank. Let's take it over there."

"Done," she said firmly. "At least it's going to a good cause."

"See you tonight."

"See you."

She hung up and wished just once she could be something other than inept around Daniel. Was it too much to ask that just one time she was together and confident and sophisticated? Even though she already knew the answer, she couldn't help wishing for a miracle.

As promised, Daniel was waiting when she got home from work. She pulled into the garage, then climbed into his truck.

"Thanks for doing this," she told him. "I really appreciate it."

"Happy to help. Plus, cake. Where's the bad?"

She laughed. "There is that. So how's the world of moto-cross?"

"Good. There are a lot of promising young guys who want to make it happen. We'll see if any of them can do it."

"Just guys?"

He looked at her. "Sometimes there are girls, but not very many. It's physically challenging and…" He returned his attention to the road. "I'm going to stop talking now, before I get myself in trouble."

"Probably for the best. I'm sure the sport is physically grueling, but still, you should support girls."

"I do my best to be supportive."

She believed him. He'd sure been there for her. "I've been watching the guys at work, trying to understand their communication styles."

"And?"

"They do talk about themselves a lot. It's interesting. I can see how it would be easy to overlook me. Not in a deliberate way, but just because I tend to blend into the background."

"What are you going to do about it?"

"I already have an appointment with my boss when I'm back

from my week off and he's back from his vacation. I'm working on my plans to improve the warehouse and I'm listing my accomplishments for the past year." She held up a hand. "By that I mean I'm figuring out how much money I've saved the company or how I've brought in new business, not just that I'm a good worker bee."

"Excellent. If you want to run anything past me, I'm happy to be a sample audience."

"You mean for a practice interview?"

"If you'd like. I do hire and fire."

She winced. "Firing can't be fun."

"It's not. Screwing with someone's life is the worst. But sometimes it has to be done."

They arrived at the bakery. Ali braced herself for the hit on her credit card, then led the way inside. Betty, a middle-aged woman wearing a bright yellow apron, smiled when they entered.

"Can I help you?"

"I'm Ali Schmitt. I'm here for the cake."

"Of course. It came out beautifully." Betty looked at Daniel and winked. "I can see you're going to have lots of gorgeous babies."

Ali flushed, not sure what to say. Explaining who Daniel was seemed too complicated, but she didn't want him to think she was... Well, she didn't know what she didn't want him to think, but nothing bad.

Before she could figure out a response, he chuckled and said, "I hope that's true. Now let's get a look at the cake."

Betty already had the five boxes on a cart. The biggest box had to be nearly three feet in diameter and two feet high. Holy crap, that was a lot of cake!

While Daniel loaded the boxes into his truck, Ali passed over her credit card and tried not to wince when she saw the total.

She walked outside. "You know what I hate more than having to pay for that cake myself? It's spice cake. I hate spice cake, but Glen wanted it so of course I said yes."

He loaded the last layer of cake, then closed the back of the truck. "You wanted to do right by him."

"Of course I did, but why didn't he do right by me?" She stomped her foot on the ground. "I hate this. All of it. Dealing with the wedding, the money I'm spending, where my life is. I need an apartment that's clean and doesn't bankrupt me and a promotion and I need a better quality of fiancé for sure. I have to stand up for myself and I'm just not sure I can but I hate feeling like this and I don't know what to—"

Before she could finish her sentence, Daniel cupped her face in his large, strong hands and kissed her. Just like that—in the bakery parking lot, with the sun beating down.

He kissed her softly at first, a gentle kind of kiss that made her feel cherished. She was just getting into the feel of his mouth on hers and the softness of his beard when everything changed. He pressed a little harder and moved his mouth against hers. Unexpectedly she found herself putting her hands on his back as she somehow moved closer. Or maybe he moved—she wasn't sure and it really didn't matter.

He dropped his hands to her shoulders, then slid them around her so that he was holding her as tightly as she was holding him. He tilted his head and stroked her bottom lip with his tongue.

Heat exploded everywhere. Liquid, sexy, take-me-now heat that had her breasts suddenly taking notice and her girl parts murmuring that they liked this new guy a lot. She welcomed the feel of his tongue against her own. He kissed her like he meant it, with lots of tingles and promise and just enough demanding to make her swoon.

Kissing Glen had been perfectly fine but kissing Daniel was taking off in a rocket headed for Mars. Maybe it was tacky to compare the brothers, but she didn't care, because hey, Mars.

He dropped his hands to her butt and gently squeezed, then slowly, seemingly reluctantly, he stepped back.

She stared up into his dark eyes and blurted, "If I got all that for a cake, I can't help wondering what you would have done if I'd been unable to cancel the catering."

He laughed, then kissed her again until they were both breathing hard. Then he drew back again.

"I'm confused," she whispered.

"Me, too."

"We should probably pretend that never happened."

"If that's what you want."

Was it? She was so disoriented. How much of this was real and how much of it was because of her breakup?

"Any part of that a pity kiss?"

His dark gaze was steady. "Did it feel like a pity kiss?"

"That's not an answer."

"It was not a pity kiss."

Then what was it? Only she didn't ask because she honestly didn't want to know.

"It's probably best to pretend that never happened," she repeated, knowing that was the sensible decision, but secretly hoping he would insist they go directly to his bedroom and close the deal.

But that wasn't Daniel's style. He lightly touched her cheek and said, "Smart and beautiful. I like that in a woman."

Which sounded great, but left her slightly squishy girl parts desperately unsatisfied.

Later, when they'd delivered the cake to the food bank and then gone home, she'd wondered if she was being sensible or cowardly when it came to Daniel. While he obviously liked her enough to kiss her and he'd been so sweet and nice, she couldn't shake Finola's warning about him. Getting involved with her ex-fiancé's brother was dumb and getting involved so quickly was dumb and not knowing how she felt about him and how he felt about her was dumb, so she was making the right decision, wasn't she?

Around ten, she wandered into the kitchen to get a snack. There she found a pink bakery box on the counter, with her name scrawled on top. When she opened it, she saw a two-layer chocolate cake with chocolate icing.

Of course, she thought, fighting a thousand feelings she couldn't begin to define. The only thing she knew for sure was that when it came to Daniel and Glen, she'd absolutely picked the wrong brother.

Zennie and Bernie sat across from Dr. McQueen. Dr. McQueen looked at the tablet, then up at them, only to smile.

"All right," she said. "I'll admit it. This is a first for me. I've had heterosexual couples and lesbian couples, but I've never had a surrogate and her friend in here before. It's going to take a little getting used to."

Bernie grabbed Zennie's hand and squeezed. "I'm only here as long as she's comfortable. The second she wants me out, I'm gone."

A sentiment Zennie appreciated, even if it was strange. Why wouldn't she want Bernie with her? She was having Bernie's baby.

"Your blood work looks excellent and there's no sugar in your urine, so we're good there. You're taking your vitamins?"

"Every day, and drinking extra water and eating from the list. I haven't had any alcohol or caffeine."

The doctor smiled. "I recognize the wistful tone. I want to tell you it gets easier, but instead I'll say in a few months, you can eat and drink what you want."

Bernie released Zennie's hand and turned to the doctor. "Hayes and I were thinking about a meal service. Food for Two. Do you know it?"

"I don't," Zennie said. "What is it?"

"A meal delivery service that specializes in food for pregnant women," Dr. McQueen said. "Several of my patients find it very helpful. Perfectly balanced meals are delivered every couple of days. All you have to do is heat them up and eat."

Bernie smiled at Zennie. "We just want to make things easier for you. Please let us do this."

"I can cook my own dinner. It's no big deal."

"No, but shopping and preparing can be. You're busy at work. This way you don't have to think about what you're going to eat. We were thinking of the full package, so three meals and two snacks a day."

Zennie wasn't thrilled with the idea of someone else deciding what she was going to eat, but she didn't want to disappoint Bernie.

"Let's talk about it later," she said cautiously.

"Absolutely."

Dr. McQueen nodded. "All right, so now let's discuss exercise. Zennie, I know you're a runner and you surf. What else do you do?"

"Yoga every now and then. I lift weights, of course. Go rock climbing. I hike with my friends in Griffith Park. I snowboard, but we're coming up on summer so that won't be an issue."

"That's impressive," the doctor told her. "You already know about avoiding saunas and Jacuzzis. I want you to stay away from hot yoga, as well. For now I'd like you to limit your runs to three miles. You'll have to back off completely but not for a while. Surfing is also a risk. There are just too many ways you could damage your midsection and holding your breath because you're underwater is also a problem. The hiking is all right for now. Once you get bigger, you'll have balance issues. Look at walking more or using the elliptical. Also, let's stay away from the rock climbing wall. You wouldn't want to fall."

Zennie remembered what had happened on the hike and how scared she'd been. "I can certainly put off rock climbing until after the baby's born." As for the rest of it, she did her best to look happy and not as if the doctor was taking away all her fun.

"You need to start wearing support hose at work," the doctor continued. "They will make your legs feel less tired and avoid problems with varicose veins later. Get plenty of rest. When you get the chance, get off your feet. You don't need it now, but you will, so let's develop the habit."

The conversation continued with more restrictions and admonitions. Zennie reminded herself it was natural to feel overwhelmed and the restrictions were temporary. In a few short months, or eight, she would get her life back.

Eight months! She blinked as she took that in. She was going to be pregnant for another eight months.

When the appointment was over, she and Bernie walked out together.

"That was so exciting," her friend said. "There's so much to learn." She linked arms with Zennie. "I'm so glad you've agreed to the meal service. I'll send you the link so you can put in your preferences. They'll deliver the food right to your door. Oh, and let me know when you want to go shopping for support stockings. Hayes and I will be paying for those, too."

"You don't have to," Zennie protested, wondering when, exactly, she'd agreed to the meal service.

"They're expensive," Bernie told her. "You'll need a few pairs because they have to be washed by hand and they need time to hang dry."

"Oh. I didn't know that."

Bernie smiled. "I've been reading up on your pregnancy. You can ask me anything."

Zennie ignored the image of her small bathroom filled with old-lady stockings and told herself this, too, would pass. She was having a baby. Compromises had to be made. Eight months wasn't all that long and in the end, when she handed over their happy, healthy baby, she would know she'd done a good thing. Until then, she was going to suck it up and eat her greens. And, apparently, wear support hose.

Chapter Twenty-One

Finola found it more and more painful to check on the house. Every time she drove the familiar streets, she had to admit that she was alone, she'd been chased out of her home and was now living with her mother. Hardly the description of someone at the pinnacle of her success. She lived in fear of being recognized, of having someone point and laugh. Showing up to work had become increasingly difficult and she no longer slept at night.

She'd done enough shows on mental health topics to guess she was dealing with a bout of depression. She'd read about it but wasn't prepared for the sense of heaviness that pervaded every part of her day—as if there was suddenly more gravity. She felt sluggish and ugly and sad nearly all the time. And hopeless, she thought as she pulled into the garage and carefully closed the door behind her.

She walked into the house and stood in the silence. Everything looked as it had the last time she'd been here and the time before that. Mail was neatly piled on the entry table. The housecleaning service kept things clean, and she'd canceled the meal service. The gardener and pool guy kept the outside of the house looking tidy. The only thing missing from this life was her and Nigel, and without him, what was the point?

She flipped through the mail. Most of the bills came electronically, so she didn't have to worry about that. Nigel hadn't emptied their bank account and she had her own checking account, so money wouldn't be an issue. Not in the short term. Even her mother wanted her to talk to a lawyer, but Finola couldn't imagine it. What would she say? The lawyer would ask her what she wanted and she honest to God had no idea.

She walked through the kitchen, the family room, then down the hall. The pictures still hung where they always had. The cracks from the last 5.0 earthquake looked exactly the same. She touched the textured walls and wished the house could touch her back, that it would tell her all would be well. Only it couldn't and even if it could, she doubted it would lie.

She took the stairs to the second floor. After bypassing the master, she walked into what they had always said would be the baby's room. The walls were a pale yellow and the wood trim was painted white. There was a window seat and a nice-sized closet.

How many times had they talked about having a baby? How many times had Nigel said he was ready, that he didn't want to be seventy when his kid graduated from high school, and how many times had she put him off? Soon, she'd promised. Next year for sure. But one year had bled into another until Nigel had stopped asking.

She looked out onto the backyard. He'd stopped asking, she repeated to herself. When was that? Six months ago? Eight? Why hadn't she noticed? His silence had been a sign and she'd ignored it. No, not ignored, because that implied she'd recognized it and had deliberately not paid attention. She'd never seen it in the first place. What else had she missed?

She went back downstairs and walked into her office. Her sleek desk was tidy, as always. She didn't like clutter in here. The room was entirely hers, with pale pink walls and a beautiful floral carpet that she'd chosen herself. The only visitor's chair was deliberately uncomfortable. She didn't want anyone else to linger—when she was working from home, she'd been all about avoiding distractions.

She looked at the photographs and awards on the walls. There were dozens of each. Pictures of her with various dignitaries and celebrities, along with a few framed magazine covers. There were no photos of her and Nigel, or even just of him. Not on the wall and not on the desk. She'd always told herself she wanted to keep her career separate from her personal life. That was why she'd kept her maiden name after they'd married. Nigel had said he never cared. She used his last name socially, of course, but not for anything legal or important.

She crossed the hall and went into his office. Here the colors were darker, the decor more masculine. His desk was piled with papers and across from it was a huge black leather sofa. It was the kind of place that invited you to curl up and read, or stretch out and take a nap. More than once they'd had sex on that sofa. She knew the feel of it against her bare skin. They'd talked and laughed and fought on that sofa.

He had art on his walls. His professional degrees and awards were at his office. Behind his desk was a large photo from their wedding. Several pictures of her littered his desk.

Without knowing how her brain got there, she thought about the spa she'd visited the previous year. She'd taken a week off and had gone by herself to unwind. She'd read and slept and gotten massages. The time had been heavenly and she hadn't really missed Nigel. Not enough to invite him to join her.

What must he have thought of her going away without him? She wasn't worried he would think she was having an affair, but she'd just gone off, leaving him behind. They weren't joined at the hip and he went to medical conferences and symposiums, but the spa retreat was different somehow. Not that she couldn't or shouldn't do things for herself, but it was more than that, and she couldn't put her finger on what it was.

She walked back into the hallway, then headed for the kitchen. She checked for water leaks and that the refrigerator was working, all things the cleaning service would have done. She was restless. Afraid to stay and not ready to go. Her father would say it was guilt. That she was being forced to admit that while the affair was all on Nigel, his unhappiness before that was at least partially her fault. She was slowly starting to wonder if maybe she'd taken too much for granted. Had been too involved in herself and not involved enough in her marriage.

Ali had said she would be hard to live with. Zennie, however misguided, was willing to give up nearly a year of her life to have a baby for a friend. Even her mother used her spare time to work with that ridiculous theater group down by the beach. What did she have beyond her work? Not real friends. She had Rochelle, but her assistant, however loyal, would get a better job offer one day and she would be gone. Not her volunteer work. She didn't do any. She showed up—she was the face—but she didn't get involved.

She'd thought she would have Nigel for always. That they would be happy together. She'd thought they would love each other until they were old and gray and waiting to die. But they weren't doing any of those things.

She returned to her car. Before opening the garage door with the remote, she sat in the darkness and wondered if she'd really brought this all on herself. Was she the cause of her unhappiness? Was she really that horrible a human being?

Terrified the answer was yes, she opened the garage door and started the engine, then turned on the radio so loud, she couldn't possibly think.

Zennie ached all over. She was hungry, her feet and back hurt and she was desperately thirsty. The ten-hour surgery had been stressful from start to finish. The patient had come through all right in the end, but he was going to have a hell of a recovery.

She'd managed to change into street clothes, but that had used up the last of her strength. She wanted someone to carry her to her car while offering her some energizing elixir and a big, stacked high pastrami sandwich. Instead she would drink plain water and go home to eat whatever disgusting protein and kale delight was on for this night's dinner.

"That's a face."

Zennie turned and saw Gina approaching. She hadn't seen her friend since their disastrous evening out. Cassie had texted an apology, but Gina had been quiet.

Now, seeing her, Zennie felt herself stiffen as her hackles went up and she braced for more criticism.

"Just thinking about the healthy meal waiting for me at home," she said evenly. "Bernie, the baby's mother, arranged for a food delivery service that specializes in food for expectant mothers."

Gina leaned against the lockers and offered a faint smile. "So no chocolate-covered graham crackers with a tequila chaser?"

Zennie's mouth twitched. "Probably not. I've been eating plenty of green vegetables, though."

"Fried?"

"No such luck."

There was a moment of silence between them. Zennie let herself get her hopes up.

Her friend drew in a breath. "I'm sorry I upset you."

"Which isn't the same as apologizing for what you said."

"No, it's not." Gina worried her lower lip. "Zennie, I know you think you're doing the right thing, but I don't. I think you're taking a huge risk. You're my friend and I love you, but I also think you're wrong."

It wasn't exactly a kick in the gut, but it was close. "Then we're going to have to agree to disagree," she said, opening her locker and pulling out her backpack. "I'm not sure what that means about us being friends."

Gina winced. "You can't let my opinion go?"

"Not when you can't keep it to yourself. You're right—something could go wrong, but you know what? Everything might work out just fine. This time next year, they could have a happy, healthy baby and I'll be back to my life, having given my friend the most incredible gift ever. Even if there's a chance for disaster, I want to try. I want to do this and if you can't support me, then I can't be around you."

She hadn't meant to say all that, but somehow the words came out.

"This is hard," she admitted. "Way harder than I'd thought, and from everything I've read it's going to get worse. I have to keep up a brave face for Bernie and her husband, so I really need my other friends to help me through this." She opened her backpack and dug out a T-shirt that had been left in a bag on her doorstep. She held it up.

"Do you see this?" She pointed at the ridiculous cartoon stork instructing her to glow and grow. "My self-absorbed older sister left this for me sometime in the night. I'm not asking you to show up twice a week and rub my feet, but I need you to respect my decision. You've said you disagree and that's fine, but if you can't let that go and get on board, then I can't have you in my life right now."

Even worse than the verbal diarrhea were the tears that suddenly filled her eyes.

"This is ridiculous," she muttered, brushing them away. "I swear, I will not get hormonal."

Gina stared at her openmouthed. "You've never talked to me like that before."

"I've never talked to anyone like that before. I'm sorry. I want to say I'll love you no matter what, but apparently my love has conditions."

"Okay," Gina told her. "That's clear. I'm not ready to make that decision. I guess I'll see you later."

Her friend…her possibly *former* friend…turned and walked away. Zennie felt the telltale pressure of more tears, but she ignored them. She just had to get home. She would eat, drink water, then go to bed and sleep. Everything would be better in the morning. Zennie tried to tell herself if Gina couldn't support her, she was better off without her, which sounded very strong and brave, but in truth made her feel completely lost, alone and scared. Just one more thing that was different, now that she was going to have a baby.

Ali woke up early the morning of her wedding-that-wasn't. She wrapped herself in a blanket and crept silently to the patio off her room to watch the sunrise. She had no idea how she felt about herself or her circumstances or anything else, but she knew one thing for sure—she wasn't sorry she wasn't marrying Glen.

She had an early hair appointment followed by a mani-pedi. When she got back, Daniel had promised her a day of fun. She knew he was going to take her out to the track so she could try motocross. Anything to keep her mind off what the day was supposed to be. She might be grateful she wasn't marrying Glen but that didn't mean she wasn't feeling a little regretful about the day itself.

Two hours later, she had highlights, a new, flattering bob, along with freshly painted nails. She'd gone with a bright aqua on her toes and a pale pink on her fingers. She felt sassy and sexy and more than a little adventurous.

"I'm ready for my motocross lesson," she said as she walked into the house.

Daniel stood in the kitchen. He stared at her from across the kitchen island, his eyes wide.

"What?" she demanded, then remembered her haircut. Her heart instantly sank. Did it look bad? Did he think she'd made a mistake? No! She loved her new hairstyle and if he didn't then he was stupid.

"You look incredible," he said, setting down the coffee mug. "Your eyes look bigger and your face is just..." He motioned vaguely in her direction. "You look great."

"Thank you. I feel good. Now let's go conquer some motorcycles."

He put his coffee mug in the sink and pointed to her flip-flops. "You're going to need closed-toe shoes. Also a long-sleeve T-shirt. The jeans are fine."

She collected tennis shoes and socks, along with a jersey, then met him by the truck.

"My pedicure will have dried by the time we get there," she said. "I'll put on my shoes and socks then."

"Beauty over safety."

She wiggled her toes. "Duh!"

He grinned and held open the door for her.

On the way to the track, he talked to her about the class she'd be taking. "It's for beginners, so expect there to be little kids."

"How little?"

"Seven or eight years old."

She groaned. "Great. I'll feel large and uncoordinated. That's perfect."

He grinned at her. "You'll do fine. The instructor will take you over the safety basics, then we'll get you your protective gear. You'll need body armor, goggles and a helmet."

"Body armor? Seriously?"

"We dress for the crash, not the ride."

"Oh, that's a cheerful saying. Note to self—avoid crashing."

They got on I-5 and headed north to Sun Valley. Ali had been to Daniel's business a couple of times with Glen. She knew there were three different tracks, a grandstand, a service center where bikes were repaired and modified, along with several buildings that were used for everything from classrooms to locker rooms to the office staff. From what she'd been able to piece together, the business had been a lot smaller when he'd inherited it. Daniel had worked hard to grow it into a success.

She was impressed by how he'd taken something good and made it better—not that she was surprised. She glanced at him out of the corner of her eye, remembering their kiss. She still wasn't sure what it had meant, but it had been pretty fantastic. She was willing to admit there was something between them. At this point, she had no idea what, but whatever it was, she liked it.

Two hours later she'd gone through a forty-five-minute safety class, been fitted for gear and had survived her first two laps of the track. She stopped by the instructor and pulled off her helmet. Eight-year-old Brandon pulled up next to her and give her a high five.

"You were really good, Ali," he said with a grin.

"Thanks. You were better. You went so fast."

His chest puffed out a little. "I'm going to be the best. You'll see. When I'm famous, we can hang out if you'd like."

She did her best not to smile. "That would be very cool."

Daniel strolled over. "Hey, my man," he said to Brandon. "Have a good time?"

"The best! My mom's gonna sign me up for the summer session. I can't wait."

"I look forward to seeing you around."

Brandon flipped his visor closed, then headed off for another circuit. Daniel leaned close.

"It seems I have competition."

She laughed. "When he's famous we're going to hang out, so yes, I would say you do."

"How'd you like it?"

She thought about the speed, the dirt track, the way the bike had leaned into the turns. "I was scared and I loved it. I want to come back and learn more."

She stood up and felt her legs protest. Muscles not used to that kind of workout were going to be sore later.

"I'm glad," he said, taking her bike from her and walking it toward the rental building. "Motocross is intense. You really have to concentrate, which means it's a great way to clear your head. When you're out on the track, you can't think of anything else."

He returned the bike while she stripped out of her protective gear. Her clothes were covered in dust and she felt a little gritty all over.

"I need a shower," she said.

"That is a hazard of the sport. Let's head back to the house. You can clean up, then pack a bag."

She looked at him. "For what?"

His dark gaze met hers. "We'd agreed we were going to fill the day."

For a second she had no idea what he was talking about. Learning how to ride the bike and navigate the track had taken all her concentration. There'd been no room left for anything else, including remembering that today was supposed to be her wedding day. And the fact that he'd promised her dinner.

"We did," she agreed.

"I thought we'd head up to Santa Barbara for the weekend. I've booked us a couple of rooms at a great hotel. We'll walk around town, have a nice dinner, drink a little too much wine and call Glen names."

She was kind of stuck on the "couple of rooms," then told

herself not to be greedy. Daniel had been fantastic to her in more ways than she could count. And he was a gentleman—of course there would be two rooms.

"You don't have to do that," she told him. "I mean it. This morning was plenty. You probably have lots of other things you'd rather be doing than spending the day with me."

"Not a one," he said lightly.

Her natural inclination was to push back again, only she didn't want to be that person anymore. He'd offered, she'd given him an out and he'd refused. She was going to take him at his word and go with him to Santa Barbara. They would have a great time together because they always did.

"Sounds wonderful. It won't take me long to pack, then we can be on our way."

The weather was LA movie perfect, with beach temperatures in the low seventies and the skies a stunning California blue. They took the coast road north, passing through Ventura, then Carpinteria on the way to Santa Barbara.

They stopped at a little hole-in-the wall taco place for a late lunch and ordered a half dozen pulled pork tacos with extra avocado. The tortillas were homemade, as was the salsa. The juices dripped down their chins and onto the plates but were delicious enough to be worth the mess. They took their beers down to the patio by the beach and sat in the shade, watching the ocean.

"This is bliss," she said, resting her feet on the railing and closing her eyes.

"I agree."

"What time is it?" she asked.

"Three."

"Let's see. I would be getting ready right now, and the makeup lady would be doing her thing. I'd be nervous, but not scared. My mom and sisters would be with me."

She opened her eyes and looked at him. "Is it weird of me to say that?"

"No. I'm sure talking about the wedding helps."

"The whole situation feels really surreal. Like the engagement and breakup happened to someone else." She sipped her beer. "Daniel, I can't thank you enough for what you've done for me. From the first second you told me about Glen until now, you've been amazing. I'm not sure I would have gotten through this without you."

"Happy to help."

She studied him, taking in the firm line of his jaw and his broad shoulders. "Tell me why you've done it. I get the first part—Glen put you in a horrible position and you were being a great guy. But why do you keep rescuing me?"

"I'm not rescuing you. I'm being a friend." His gaze was steady. "I like you, Ali. I thought I made that clear."

What did that mean? He liked her as in she was cute like a puppy and they had fun together? Or he *liked* her the way a man liked a woman?

One eyebrow rose as if he guessed what she was thinking. She waited, hoping he would cough it up, but he was silent.

"You're going to make me ask, aren't you?"

"You're the one who complained about agreeing to spice cake when you didn't want to. Maybe it's time to demand a little chocolate."

She went hot, then cold. Embarrassment battled with frustration. He wasn't wrong, she thought, as resignation joined the emotional stew. She didn't ever ask for what she wanted—she took what was offered and was often disappointed, be it at work or with her mother and the stupid clock or in her personal life. She always had.

"What if I'm invisible because that's how I want to be?" she blurted. "What if I'm making a choice? It's not that people can't see me, it's that I don't want them to?"

She had no idea if she was right, only that the concept *felt* right. Empowering, even. She had to take charge. If she wanted something, she should go for it. She should respect herself and demand the same from others.

"I want to steal the clock."

"Good. When we get home, we'll come up with a plan. Anything else?"

He was watching her carefully, as if he was hoping for something else. Something more. She thought about the initial question, screwed up her courage, sucked in a breath and asked, "What do you mean when you say you like me?"

His expression relaxed. He leaned back in his chair, his posture very "I am the man," in a sexy kind of way.

"I enjoy your company. I like spending time with you. I look forward to seeing you. I like how you look and move and talk. I like the sound of your laugh and I like kissing you."

"Oh."

She opened her mouth to say something else, then couldn't think of a single thing. Her mind was too busy turning over his words, looking for a meaning beyond the obvious, which was he *like* liked her. As in boy-girl like. As in there could be more kissing.

Feeling both empowered and incredibly shy, she ducked her head, then looked at him from under her lashes. "I like you, too," she whispered.

"We probably should have gotten that out of the way before heading off for the weekend," he teased. "But at least we know now."

She laughed. "Yes, we do."

He tossed his bottle into the recycling bin, then took hers and did the same. He pulled her to her feet, then tugged her against him and lightly kissed her.

"Ready to go?"

She nodded. Anticipation quivered in her belly. She had no idea what was going to happen, but she knew whatever it was, it was going to be good.

Chapter Twenty-Two

The Four Seasons Biltmore, an old Spanish-style compound, had been built around the turn of the previous century. Still elegant, with an old-world air, it was a celebrated piece of Santa Barbara history.

After leaving the car with the valet, Ali and Daniel went inside and checked in. A bellman led the way to their rooms. The two-bedroom bungalow had been decorated with plenty of Oriental rugs and botanical prints. There was a large sofa and a coffee table, and on one end was a dining room table that seated six. Outside was a patio with comfortable seating, along with a fire pit and the ocean beyond.

There was a brief argument over the master bedroom versus the smaller, second bedroom. Ali thought Daniel should take the master, and she wanted him to have it. He was insistent and she acquiesced, hoping against hope that come the night, they would share it.

Once they'd unpacked, they headed into town to walk around. They strolled along State Street and wandered in and out of stores.

Daniel insisted they buy a kite to fly on the beach in the morning, then they spent time in a little bookstore. He surprised her by buying a couple of biographies on Civil War generals while she bought a workbook to help her decide on the next stage in her career.

They returned to the hotel and went back to their room. Ali spotted an ice bucket filled with champagne next to a tray of what looked like delicious appetizers.

"I thought we'd eat in," Daniel said. "Is that all right?"

She looked from the champagne to him. Courage, she reminded herself. It was going to be her new mantra. "Are you trying to seduce me?"

"Yes."

She smiled. "Okay, then. Good to know. I'm going to go put on something seduction-worthy."

She put on her dress and touched up her makeup, then smoothed her new bob and hoped Daniel had brought condoms. Anticipation danced with her nerves, making her stomach jumpy. She was scared and excited and wondering if this was all really happening.

Back in the living room, she found Daniel had turned on music and opened the champagne. He handed her a glass and they went out onto the patio.

He pulled two chairs close together with a small table in between. They sat next to each other, watching the ocean rush into the shore. He was the first one to break the silence.

"I always knew I was the marrying kind," he said with a quick shrug. "Given my profession, you'd probably think I was a player, but that's never been my style. I'm conventional. There were women, but only one at a time. Volume was never that important to me." He flashed her a smile. "I guess I burned up my restlessness on the track so I could be steady everywhere else."

"Good to know."

"I meant what I said before about my first marriage. There was no great drama. We fell in love and then we fell out of love. I think we were more interested in getting on with the next part of our lives than figuring out if we could actually spend the rest of our lives together. She's a good person, we weren't awful during the divorce. I don't miss her. But I do want to find the right person. I'm not looking to play around."

It was a lot of information, she thought, not sure what to do with it.

"You know my sad history with Glen," she said, hoping her voice sounded light instead of stunned. "Before him, I'd had a few boyfriends but nothing that lasted a long time. I want to say they didn't really see me, but with my recent revelation that maybe I've been trying to be invisible, now I'll tell you maybe I was the one afraid to want more than I had. Maybe I'm the one who always kept myself so protected that no one could get in."

"Until Glen."

"Yes, until Glen. I'm not sure why I was more comfortable with him." She looked at him. "Honestly, I wonder if maybe it was because there wasn't any real passion between us. Being with him was comfortable, but not exciting. I think maybe I've been afraid of exciting."

"Are you still?"

She smiled. "I'm willing to take a chance."

"Good."

She couldn't believe they were talking like this—putting it all out there. She felt vulnerable, but strong, too. She trusted Daniel. She knew in her gut that even if things went south, he wouldn't be a jerk. He would never send his brother to break up with his fiancée.

The background music—a soft jazz version of old standards—

went silent for a second before starting up again with "I'll Be Seeing You." Daniel rose and held out his hand.

"Dance with me."

She rose. He led her inside and pulled her close. They swayed together with the music.

"The first time I saw you was on a Sunday morning," he said.

"I remember. We had brunch with your parents. You barely spoke to me. I thought you hated me."

He drew back just enough to look in her eyes. "You wore jeans and a white sweater with a V-neck. You had your hair in a braid and your perfume smelled like vanilla. The second I saw you, it was like being kicked in the gut. I couldn't think, I couldn't breathe. I sure as hell couldn't talk. Not without saying something inappropriate."

They'd stopped dancing. Ali was having trouble processing what he was telling her.

"You liked me back then?"

"I wanted to run away with you. I'd never felt a lightning strike before, but I felt it with you. I wanted to take you somewhere so we could talk for hours. I wanted to throw you over my shoulder and find a quiet corner to make love with you. I wanted to challenge Glen to a fight to the death over you. Instead I ate quiche."

Her chest was so tight and her legs were shaking. Nothing he said made sense, but there was an intensity in his gaze that told her he was telling the truth about all of it.

"Me?" she asked, her voice a squeak.

"You. Glen telling me he was calling off the wedding was the best and worst day of my life. Finally you were free of him, but first I had to break your heart. I hated him for what he was doing to you and at the same time, I was relieved you would be single."

She couldn't quite connect the dots. Daniel had liked her all along? He thought she was a lightning strike?

"You never said anything."

"What was I supposed to say?" He ran his hand through his hair. "Hey, Ali, I'm crazy about you. Dump my useless brother and run off with me."

She heard the frustration in his voice, and the pain. She had no idea what to say, so she decided to act instead. She put her hands on his face and kissed him. He responded instantly, his mouth hungry against hers. Then they were a tangle of arms pulling close and tongues stroking. Want and need flared, melting every part of her.

She stepped back and stared at him. "Please tell me you brought condoms."

His slow, sexy grin had her quivering. "I did, indeed."

It took only seconds to get to Daniel's room, then they were pulling off clothes, even as they kissed and touched each other. When they were naked, he explored her everywhere, first with his hands and then with his mouth. He kissed the very heart of her, loving her until she cried out her release. Then he entered her and she came again, surging against him as he climaxed inside of her.

When they were done and lying together on tangled sheets, she raised herself up on one elbow.

"I had no clue about how you felt about me."

"I didn't want you to know."

"But you were so stealthy. You were—" She hesitated, then decided to dodge the *L* word. It wasn't as if *he'd* said it, and she didn't want to assume. "You were crazy about me and never hinted. I feel dumb."

"Don't." He stroked her bare arm, shifting slightly to tease her nipple. "I didn't want you to feel uncomfortable around me. Better to be the friend than rejected."

He'd been afraid she would reject him? Seriously? She straddled him.

"Still worried about rejection?"

He smiled. "It's less on my mind." He squeezed her butt before reaching for another condom. "You're okay with being on top?"

"Yes. Or my side or any way you'd like." Knowing how he felt about her made her feel safe and free and sexy.

"Interesting. I wouldn't have guessed you were the adventurous type."

"I'm not. I mean I wasn't." She shook her head. "Okay, we are not going to talk about my sex life in detail. It's too weird. I'll just say with you, it's different. I want to play."

He looked into her eyes and smiled. "I want to play, too."

Finola wasn't sure that an upscale Beverly Hills bar was any more interesting than an upscale bar in the valley, but this was LA where things like location really mattered. So she fought Saturday evening traffic over the pass and guided her car to the valet. After taking the claim ticket, she squared her shoulders and walked inside.

For reasons still not clear to her, she'd agreed to meet a man for drinks. Rochelle's insistence and her own misery had combined to convince her she had to do something. Maybe an hour or two with an adoring man would be just the thing she needed. The problem was the second she'd agreed to the invitation, she'd been filled with regret, but there was no going back now.

Chip Knipstein was a sportscaster for the local news. He was barely thirty, incredibly good-looking and ambitious. The LA market wasn't big enough for him. It was commonly known he wanted to make the jump to a national show on ESPN and she'd heard rumors it was going to happen.

According to Rochelle, Chip had left more than one message on her phone, asking her out for dinner or drinks or a weekend in Maui—whichever she wanted. She'd met him only a handful of times, but he'd seemed innocuous enough and he photographed well, so she'd agreed to drinks.

She spotted him at a small corner table. He stood up, all six-feet-two of him, and smiled as she approached.

"Finola," he said, kissing her cheek. "You are even more beautiful tonight than usual. Something I didn't think was possible. Thanks for joining me."

He gestured to the chair opposite his. There was a glass of white wine waiting there.

"I took the liberty of ordering," he said. "You seemed like the white wine type."

She was less interested in the drink than getting the evening over with. Why had she thought this was a good idea? But before she could say that white wine was fine, she remembered that she wasn't supposed to drink anything that had been left on a table. That Chip could have put in some kind of date rape drug.

As soon as the thought formed, she dismissed it as ridiculous. Really? Sportscaster Chip drugging her? Only she couldn't shake the thought, which increased her growing need to bolt.

She told herself to suck it up and act normal. She could get through a few hours. Women went out on dates all the time—except she hadn't been on a first date in over eight years and back then she'd been much more focused on her career than getting "the guy," so she'd never been one for the whole flirting-call-me-let's-go-out circus. She was woefully unprepared for how the dating world had changed and now she had to deal with whether or not to trust the drink in front of her. Ack! When had life gotten so complicated?

A question she knew the answer to, but asking it wasn't going to help her one bit.

"White wine gives me a headache," she lied, looking regretful.

Chip immediately flagged a server. "No problem. I'll know for next time."

She forced a smile, thinking she would rather prep for a colonoscopy than go on another date.

He handed back the white wine, ordered red, then leaned

closer. "Did you hear that Steve and his wife are expecting twins? That's got to be great for them, and terrifying."

Steve was the local evening weather guy. "I hadn't heard. Thanks for telling me. I'll be sure to send them something."

At least one marriage was working, she thought, trying not to feel bitter.

"Everything okay?" Chip asked.

She held in a sigh. "Sorry. I'm struggling a little here. I feel so awkward."

His expression was serious. "Is it because I'm so good-looking?"

The unexpected question surprised her. She burst out laughing. "No, it's not that."

"Hey, you could have at least thought about it for a moment." His voice was teasing. "I'm genuinely crushed."

"You'll get over it."

"Not without years of therapy." He pressed a hand to his chest. "My heart is shattered."

"No one believes you."

He smiled at her. "Okay, so here's the thing. I know you're going through some stuff. It takes a while to get back out there. I'm glad you agreed to meet me, so I'm going to mentally give myself high fives all night, but that's as far as it goes. I'm going to spend the next ten or so minutes talking about myself so you can figure out how uncomfortable you are and if you want to stay or bolt. Then we'll assess and take it from there."

The server appeared with her wine. Finola took her glass and stared at Chip.

"I don't think you've been married before," she said slowly. "So this incredible insight into the separated woman's psyche must come from practice."

"Years of it."

"You like women who are newly separated or divorced."

"Guilty," he said cheerfully. "It's the sex. Revenge sex is very in right now and I'm happy to be the means of making that happen. So if you want to get back at Nigel, let me be clear. I'm all in." He leaned close. "I mean that in every sense of the words, for as long as you want, Finola."

She tried not to laugh. "I don't know if I should be impressed or appalled."

"I'd say impressed, but it's not up to me. Oh, and just so you know, I don't overlap. It's one woman at a time for me. Nothing serious, of course, but I am monogamous."

"For both minutes?" she asked drily.

He winced. "I'm more of a twenty-minute guy."

"That's what they all say." She sipped her wine. "Now tell me about yourself."

Chip talked about growing up in San Bernardino and how he had always been interested in sports. She nodded at what she hoped were all the right places even as her mind began to wander.

Chip was a nice enough guy. He was more fun than she'd expected and plenty good-looking, but she didn't want to be here. Nothing about this felt right. In her heart, she wanted to be with Nigel and in her gut, she felt like she was cheating. Even her head, which was starting to believe her marriage was at the bleeding-out stage, wasn't the least bit intrigued by Chip.

She'd rather be home watching TV or reading or doing anything that wasn't having a drink with a man. She wasn't ready. She wasn't interested.

She interrupted him midsentence. "Chip, I'm sorry but I can't do this."

"I understand. If you change your mind, you know how to reach me."

She didn't, but Rochelle did, which was enough. She nodded.

They both stood. Chip tossed a couple of bills on the table, then escorted her outside. He handed her ticket to the valet, then returned to her side, where he put a hand on the small of her back and leaned close.

"Let me know when you're ready for revenge sex," he murmured. "No strings. Just me making you happy while you punish the bastard who cheated on you. You'll like it, Finola. I promise."

She got in her car and waved, then merged into traffic to start the journey home. At the first stoplight, she felt tears on her cheek.

She was sure he'd meant his words to be sexy or even tempting, but to her they felt like a slap across her face. Worse, his words shamed her, because this was what her life had become.

The magic of Ali's weekend with Daniel lasted right up until they got back to his place and walked into the house. Daniel set both their bags on the living room floor and looked at her, as if asking what happened next.

They'd had an amazing time at the hotel. They'd ordered in dinner, sipping champagne and enjoying their meal while dressed in fluffy robes. Later, they'd made love again, this time in the big bed in the master, where they'd spent the night. Every time Ali had woken up, she'd felt Daniel pressed up against her, his arm around her waist.

Sunday morning they'd slept late, then gone on a leisurely bike ride before heading to brunch, followed by the drive home. She'd loved every second with him, but was also still trying to take it all in. Six weeks ago, she'd thought he didn't like her very much. Now they were involved and he'd made it clear he'd had a thing for her from the start. She needed a second to catch her breath.

"It's whatever you want," he told her when they got home. "We had a great weekend, but that doesn't have to lead to something else. We can go back to what we had before. I know you've been through a lot and I'm not going to push."

"Thank you. It's just everything happened so fast."

Emotions darkened his eyes, but they were gone so quickly, she wasn't sure what she'd seen. Maybe disappointment, maybe something else.

He started toward the stairs that would take him to his room on the second floor. With each step he moved farther and farther away from her.

"Wait!" she called. He stopped and turned back to her.

She thought about all she'd been through. All the times she hadn't asked for what she wanted, hadn't risked not going along. She thought of the way Glen had treated her, of how she'd been left to deal with everything while he'd just disappeared. Only Daniel had stood with her, shouldering the burden. She thought of how he'd invited her into his house and kept her safe and how he'd held her all night long. She thought of the wedding cake she'd had to pay for. Spice cake instead of chocolate, because she'd always been afraid to ask for what she wanted. No, not ask—to demand it. Because sometimes it took a demand for the world to pay attention.

She walked up to him. "I want us to be together. I want us to start dating and I want it to be exclusive. I want us to be lovers and boyfriend and girlfriend and I want to learn how to ride a motorcycle for real."

His gaze was steady, even as one corner of his mouth turned up. "That's very direct."

"It is."

"And specific."

"I want what I want." Some of her courage faded. "What do you want?"

He cupped her face in his hand. "You, Ali. I've always wanted you." He brushed her mouth with his. "Want to move your things upstairs?"

She wrapped her arms around his neck and smiled. "In a little bit. First I think we should have sex."

He grinned. "You do, huh?"

"Yes. Right now." She looked around. "On the kitchen table."

He chuckled. "It's gonna be cold."

"I trust you to keep me warm."

She trusted him with a whole lot more than that, but keeping her warm was a great place to start.

Chapter Twenty-Three

Zennie didn't like being pregnant. There—she'd said it. Okay, not out loud, but she'd thought it. Actually, being pregnant was fine, it was the hormones that were going to do her in.

She felt *fragile*. She'd never felt fragile in her life. She was emotional spun glass, with tears always ready to rise to the surface and a heart that felt broken. She'd cried twice the previous day. Twice! Who did that? Gina and she still weren't speaking, which was hard, but so was everything else in her life. Deciding what T-shirt to wear to help out her mom on a Sunday afternoon seemed impossible. Commercials made her weepy. She wanted to hold kittens and save whales and have someone big and strong hold her tight and promise everything would fine.

Not anything she wanted to dwell on, she told herself as she drove to her mom's place to help with yet more sorting. Zennie hoped they wouldn't find anything emotionally significant because she didn't want to have a meltdown in front of anyone. Bad enough to sob at home.

When she got to the house, she found her mom was out and only Finola was at home.

"Mom's off with her theater friends and Ali's not coming," she said by way of greeting. "She went up to Santa Barbara for the weekend. Probably for the best. Getting away would make things easier."

"What things?" Zennie asked.

Finola surprised her by smiling. "Thank you for not remembering. I have felt like I go from bitch to bigger bitch lately. It's good to know you can be thoughtless, too."

A normal sister kind of comment that would have been fine any other time in her life, but not right now, Zennie thought, tears filling her eyes.

"How was I thoughtless?" she asked, her voice shaking.

Finola stared at her. "What's wrong with you? Are you crying? You never cry."

"It's the hormones," Zennie said, wiping her cheek. "I'm a mess. I've gone through more boxes of tissues in the past three days than in my entire life. I hate it."

Finola surprised her by pulling her close. "You are a mess. I kind of like it."

The hug felt good. Zennie hung on longer than she would have before, and Finola didn't let her go until she was ready. When they stepped back, Zennie promised herself she was going to power through.

"The hormones are supposed to get better in a few weeks," she said. "They're what cause morning sickness. It's the surges or some such crap. So far my stomach's a rock, but I'm crying twenty times a day. It's humiliating." She tried to shake it off. "So what did I forget?"

"Yesterday was Ali's wedding day."

Zennie collapsed on the sofa and covered her face. "I'm the worst sister ever."

"You and me both. Only Mom remembered. I thought about

sending flowers, but seriously, what would the card say? Sorry you got dumped and now it's your wedding day? Maybe we should just take her to dinner later this week."

Zennie nodded. "Poor Ali. She has to feel terrible. She's all alone, living in pain, knowing Glen walked out on her. I can't believe I forgot her wedding day."

Finola eyed her. "Yes, it was awful. Now let it go."

"How can I?"

"I liked you a lot better when you were stuck-up and sanctimonious. I'm just saying." Finola motioned for her to stand. "Are you going to be like this when we go to the gala together? I'd really rather not have you sobbing every five seconds. People will start to talk."

Zennie followed her sister into the dining room. The table and chairs would be easy to get rid of, but the massive hutch was another issue. The upper cabinets were all filled with dishes and glasses and serving pieces, while the cabinets and drawers below overflowed with crap from their lives.

"I won't cry at the gala," Zennie said. "I'll take a supplement."

Finola stared at her. "They make supplements for that sort of thing?"

Zennie rolled her eyes. "Of course not. I'm pregnant. I can't take anything. I can barely drink almond milk without worrying I'm damaging the fetus. It's hell. If the baby were mine, I think I could relax a little, but it's not mine and yet I'm completely responsible. Every decision I make has to be considered with the baby in mind."

Finola grinned. "You're regretting the pregnancy."

"I'm not and don't sound so gleeful. It's just a little harder than I thought. The crying and my boobs hurting and Bernie monitoring every single thing I eat or breathe. We've had the most perfect surfing weather and I can't go. It's hideous. But once I stop crying, I'll be fine."

"You want coffee."

Zennie groaned. "Yes, and a glass of wine and I don't usually care if I drink. But yes, wine and sushi. I want to go in a sauna. I want to run until I'm so exhausted I barf. I want to not be careful." She looked at Finola. "It's only been a few weeks. I have months to go."

"It will get easier."

"How do you know that?"

"Because the human spirit is amazingly resilient. This will become your new normal and you'll move on. Look at me. I still can't decide if I would sell a kidney to get Nigel back or if I want him dead, and last night I met a man for drinks."

Zennie stared at her. "You didn't. How was it?"

"Awful. He offered to sleep with me, either for revenge or to clean out the plumbing. He was pretty open to either."

Zennie shuddered. "Sex sounds awful right now."

"Sadly, it does to me, too. And I'm not pregnant." She touched Zennie's arm. "I know I wasn't on board before, but there's a very good chance you're doing the right thing."

"You sound surprised."

"I kind of am. I made the statement to be nice, but now I realize I actually mean it. You're a good person, Zennie. I'm sorry you're suffering. Now let's start with the drawers."

Zennie grinned. "Could I have a second to enjoy the compliment?"

"I don't think so."

They each pulled out a drawer and set it on the dining room table. Zennie sorted through half-used pads of paper and a couple dozen pens. There were paper clips, old circulars, playing cards, some batteries and a hair clip in the shape of a butterfly. She found old report cards and sorted them into three piles, then held up a roll of pennies.

"We're rich," she said, waving the roll.

"Good to know. Oh, look." Finola passed over an envelope. Zennie opened it and saw ticket stubs to a Kelly Clarkson show, along with backstage passes. She turned the tickets over, remembering how much she and Ali had wanted to go to the concert. Zennie had begged and somehow her dad had come through. The three of them had been in the fifth row, dead center. After the show, they'd gone backstage where they'd met Kelly. She'd been sweet, posing for pictures and signing autographs before offering them cupcakes from the crafts table.

"Don't start crying," Finola ordered.

"Too late." She held up the tickets. "This was my first concert. Ali's, too. We got to meet Kelly and the band." She managed a strangled laugh. "I remember wearing my backstage pass lanyard around my neck for a week until my teacher made me leave it at home. I thought I was so cool and special."

"You were both those things."

Zennie sniffed. "Don't be nice to me. It's dangerous."

"Sorry. You were a spoiled little brat who didn't deserve a backstage pass."

Zennie nodded. "Better. Thanks."

Finola laughed. "Wow, hormones really are powerful. I had no idea. I have a lot more respect for Mother Nature than I did, let me tell you."

"Me, too."

They finished with the drawers. Finola went into the kitchen to make them a snack while Zennie sat at the table, fingering the passes.

She missed her dad. Was this what Ali meant when she talked about Dad not being there for her? Zennie had to admit it sucked.

She pulled out her phone and took a picture of the tickets and passes, then texted it to him.

Remember these? What a great night and a great memory. Dad, you're wrong not to support what I'm doing. I can only help out a friend this way because of how you raised me, so you're as much to blame. Not talking to me is ridiculous. I'm your favorite—we both know it. So stop acting like this. I'm pregnant and I need my dad.

There were a couple of seconds of silence, then she saw the three dots that told her he was typing.

Imogene isn't talking to me. She's pissed and let me tell you, it's hard to fight with someone when you live in a boat. There are no corners to retreat to. While I won't admit you're my favorite, you are a terrific daughter. I just hate to see you taking a chance like you are. What if something goes wrong?

She thought for a second. What if something doesn't?

Point taken. I love you, Zennie, and I miss you. You're right—I should be there for you. But really? A baby?

She sniffed. Yes, Dad. A baby. Let it go.

It's gone. Love you, baby girl. We'll talk soon.

She smiled. There were more tears—of course—but these were the happy kind. There were still multiple issues—Gina, her mother, work, telling her coworkers, actually being pregnant for eight more months, delivering the baby, recovering, eating kale—but they were doable, she told herself. Everything was going to be just fine.

Ali spent the first part of her vacation week working on her notes for her conversation with her boss when she returned to the warehouse the following Monday. She wanted facts and figures easily accessible. Once that was done, she had lunch with Finola, helped her mother empty a few cupboards and spent her evenings and nights with Daniel. The man was a god in bed and she didn't care who knew it.

On second thought, she did care, which was why she didn't mention the shift in their relationship to anyone, but she knew and that was enough. Their time together was amazing. He was funny and kind. He always wanted to know what she was thinking. He wanted her with him and he liked her sleeping with him.

Glen had never wanted to spend the night at her apartment and he hadn't wanted her staying over with him. Ali hadn't figured that out until recently. They'd usually had sex at her place and then he left. She wasn't sure how they were supposed to have transitioned into an actual marriage, she'd thought when she'd put the pieces together. Had Glen expected them to have separate bedrooms or something? Not that she cared—the only significance was that there was another check mark on the list of reasons it was never going to work.

Thursday morning she headed for the motocross track. She had a lesson that afternoon but she wanted to spend the morning getting more familiar with Daniel's business. She was meeting him for lunch, but before that, there was much to explore.

The tracks themselves were open seven days a week, as were the extra trails. The rentals and concession stands were only available on weekends during the winter months. In a few more weeks, they would stay open every day through the summer.

Ali walked into the huge garage area. Guys with bikes could rent space to do repairs or they could use the on-site mechanics, for a price, of course. There were plenty of tools, a lot of light and advice available.

She went through the swinging doors into the back where the parts were kept. This was her world, she thought with a smile. Long rows of metal shelves filled with parts for the rentals or for owners doing repairs. Only as she walked around she saw the layout was disorganized at best. Multiple-piece components were not clustered together, and refurbished parts were mingled with new. Some of the closest shelves were dusty from disuse while the parts she knew had to be used nearly every day were in the back. In a word, Daniel's parts inventory was a mess.

She walked to a nearby computer and discovered it wasn't password protected. She got into the inventory system and did a quick printout. After that, she played around and discovered that she could easily change inventory numbers, meaning theft would be a snap.

"Oh, Daniel," she murmured. "We so need to have a talk."

She took pictures and measurements, then started studying the printout. When he showed up with sandwiches and sodas, she'd taken over a desk in the back and had papers spread out all over.

"Homework?" he asked, his voice teasing.

She looked up. "Is it lunchtime already? I've been working."

"I can see that. Want to tell me about the project?"

"Give me a second and I'll meet you in your office."

She retreated to the restroom to wash her hands, then grabbed her notes and joined him in his office.

"You look serious," he said, sounding more intrigued than annoyed.

"You have a big inventory problem," she said as she sat down and stuck a straw in her cup of soda. "No wonder you always need me to rush you parts. Your computers aren't password protected and anyone can get into your inventory control. For all you know, hundreds of parts are just walking out the door every month. There's no system for how parts are stored. If I didn't know better, I would say you simply throw them on whatever shelf is available."

He shifted in his chair. "It used to be like that, but I've made some improvements."

"No, Daniel. *I've* made some improvements." She shifted her chair to his side of the desk and showed him what she'd been working on.

"First I listed your parts by sales volume. Like every business,

20 percent of your inventory makes up 80 percent of your business. You need to keep those up front where they can be found and distributed easily."

They went through her notes. She talked to him about doing spot checks and making people sign out parts.

"There are some high-end items that should be locked up."

"I trust my guys," he said.

She looked into his dark eyes. "Yes, but it's not just your guys back there. The public can wander around at will. I know you're losing money from theft. You need to figure out how much."

He handed her a sandwich. "Smart and beautiful. I'm one lucky guy. What else would you do differently around here?"

She gave herself a second to enjoy the compliment. Daniel was always generous with them and she was actually starting to think he might mean what he said.

"The concession stands need to be fixed up. They're looking old and tired. A fresh coat of paint would help and maybe some new signage. Nothing fancy. Also, you have a ton of land out here and not all of it is chewed up by the tracks."

"Chewed up?"

"You know what I mean. You have natural wilderness. This is LA. We love the outdoors."

"You don't."

She smiled. "I tolerate it. My point is, you're not making any money from the unused land."

"What do you suggest?"

"Spend a couple thousand dollars to section off an area, put up some inexpensive fencing and rent it out."

His brows drew together in confusion. "For what?"

"Weddings, parties, corporate retreats." She felt her eyes widen. "Oh, wow. You should offer corporate bonding exercises. That would be a great way to grow the business. Corporations are always looking for stuff like that for their executive teams. It's way more interesting to ride a bike than do some trust exercise. And you already have classrooms and decent bathrooms. They could make a day of it."

He stared at her. "You've given this a lot of thought."

"Not really. I'm just brainstorming. My point is your inventory control sucks and it's costing you a lot of money. Fix that. Then we can talk about ways to grow the business. I think you could even have weddings up here."

"The bikes are loud."

"The bikes stop running around six. So all the weddings would start at seven. No biggie."

"Ali, you've come up with a half dozen ideas in ten minutes. You're good at this."

"Thank you." She waved her sandwich. "Oh, what about a Christmas village? You know with cute shops and reindeer and Santa."

"No Christmas village."

She slid onto his lap and wrapped her arms around his neck. "You say that now, but I'll bet I can convince you."

"You probably can." He kissed her. "The confidence is very sexy, just so you know."

Confident? Her? She nearly laughed out loud only to realize she was feeling kind of confident. Inventory was her thing, so that wasn't a surprise, but the rest of it had just come to her.

"You're good for me," he said right before he claimed her mouth with his.

As she kissed him back, she realized he was good for her, too.

Finola told herself she wasn't going to faint. She'd had a protein drink a couple of hours ago and later tonight there would be actual food. She would be careful, though. After five days of no solid food, she didn't want to get sick. That would hardly support the image she was presenting to the world.

She was buffed, spray-tanned and had endured a painful facial that had left her skin glowing. All that was left was for her to finish her makeup, then put on her gown.

Her mother stood in the doorway to her room. "I'd forgotten what it was like to get dressed up," she said with a sigh. "So much work, but it's worth it." She crossed to the mirror over the dresser and studied herself. "Not that I would look like I used to."

Finola put her hands on her mom's shoulders and kissed her cheek. "You look great." She paused. "Mom, are you dating?"

Mary Jo met her gaze in the mirror. "My goodness, no. Dating. At my age."

"You're in your fifties. You could live to ninety. Are you sure you want to be alone all that time?"

"I'm not alone. I have my girls and my friends." She sighed. "Besides, love is complicated."

Finola smiled. "It is, but sex can be easy."

"Finola Louise!"

"Come on. You can't tell me you don't miss it. Find some nice man and take him for a test drive. You know what they say. Use it or lose it."

They were still laughing when Zennie arrived. Finola saw that her sister had actually put on mascara and used hair product so her short cut was spiky. She carried a dress in a plastic garment bag.

Zennie and Mary Jo looked at each other for a second. Finola felt the rising tension in the room.

"Mom."

Finola willed her mother to try to let it go.

"How are you feeling?" Mary Jo asked. "I never had morning sickness when I was pregnant, but I was an emotional mess. Show me a kitten and I would cry for hours."

Zennie laughed. "That's what I'm dealing with, too. Everything is drama and I can't handle it."

"Wait until your boobs start hurting. It goes away in a few weeks but until then, it's like knives."

"Thanks for the warning."

They smiled at each other and Finola relaxed. While they chatted, she wrestled her way into shapewear, then slid on the Rachel Gilbert black-and-silver sequined gown. The sucker weighed several pounds, but she didn't care. It was gorgeous and suited her. She wanted to make an entrance and photograph well—nothing else mattered.

"You look great," Zennie said, stripping off her clothes and stepping into the bridesmaid dress she'd bought for Ali's wedding.

Of course the simple, inexpensive gown looked stunning on her. Oh, to be that tall, that fit and that genetically blessed, Finola thought with only a tiny bit of rancor.

While Mary Jo zipped up the dress, Finola handed her sister a small navy evening bag. They'd just stepped into their shoes when the doorbell rang.

While Mary Jo greeted the driver, Finola checked that she had everything, then she and her sister stepped into the limo.

"Thanks for doing this," she said as they pulled away from the curb. "The station is a big sponsor of the charity so I couldn't get out of going but I really didn't want to face the hordes alone."

"Happy to help," Zennie told her. "It's not my idea of fun but lately I'm feeling unsettled and out of sorts, so this is a nice distraction."

Finola studied her. "No regrets?"

"The occasional surprise, but no regrets."

Impulsively, Finola squeezed her hand. "I'm glad."

It didn't take long to get to The Beverly Hills Hotel. They waited in a line of limos before reaching the red carpet. Zennie stared at the crowd of photographers.

"I wasn't expecting this. What should I do?"

"Smile and head inside. I'll be right beside you."

"What if I trip?"

"Then you'll be on the news."

Zennie grinned. "Good to know."

They made it inside without mishap. Finola led the way to the registration area where she checked them in. The night was a fairly traditional event with cocktails and a silent auction followed by dinner and a live auction. She was at one of the station's three tables where she would be surrounded by people she knew and trusted. Zennie would sit on one side of her and she'd arranged for Rochelle to sit on the other. But first she had to get through the cocktail party.

She linked arms with her sister. "Ready?" she asked.

"I'm not sure for what, but okay. Let's do it."

They walked into the huge ballroom. There were dozens of pairs of photographs of children on the walls. The picture on the left showed a sick, sad child while the one on the right showed the same kid, but healthy and happy. Everywhere banners proclaimed *You can make miracles.*

As they made their way to the bar, they passed too many people Finola knew. Women stopped her with a concerned expression.

"How *are* you?" a tall redhead asked. "Really, Finola. How are you?"

Finola smiled. "I'm doing great, Maddie. How are you?"

"I just feel so *awful*. Everything was so *public*. You really didn't know at *all*?"

Finola stepped back. "We're parched. Let's talk later, all right? Right now a vodka martini is calling my name."

Maddie nodded sadly, as if concerned.

"She seems nice," Zennie offered.

"She's a heartless bitch who hates my guts."

"She hides it well."

They reached the bar. Zennie ordered a club soda. Finola did the same.

"What happened to the vodka martini?" Zennie asked, sounding confused.

"I haven't eaten in five days. I'd get sick. I'll have some wine with dinner."

"Five days?" Her sister stared at her. "So you could look good here?"

"Absolutely. Everyone wants to know how I'm doing. If there's any sign of weakness I'll be ostracized and that's a best-case scenario."

Zennie looked around at all the well-dressed people in the ballroom. "So why do you do it?"

"I love my job and it's worth it to endure this so I can show up at work on Monday and love my job again."

They wandered around the silent auction. Zennie started to bid on martial arts lessons from a celebrity instructor only to realize the opening bid was five thousand dollars. She tucked her bag under her arm.

"So, only looking," she said, looking shell-shocked.

"You're pregnant, sis. No martial arts for you for a while."

"Right. I forgot."

Several more women came up and offered Finola the sympathetic half hug-air kiss. One acquaintance's husband walked by, pausing only to hand her a business card without saying anything. When he'd moved on, she turned the card over. He'd handwritten *Call me* followed by a number.

Zennie peered over her shoulder. "Am I imagining things, or is he offering you sex?"

"I think he's offering me sex."

"I had no idea your world was like this. No offense, but I'm not sure I like it."

"It was easier when I had Nigel."

"I could get you a really big stick. That might help."

Finola laughed. "Thank you for coming."

"You're welcome. Do you know what the menu is? I'm dying for a meal without kale or yogurt."

"Healthy food getting to you?"

"You have no idea."

Finola pointed to an auction. "That's a brownie and cookie package delivered every quarter for a year. I'm going to buy you that and I don't care what it costs."

Instead of laughing, Zennie stared at her with tear-filled eyes. "That is so sweet." She hugged her. "You're the best sister ever."

"And you're easy," Finola murmured. "Come on. Let's get you another club soda. Later, you can get wild and have a ginger ale."

They headed for the bar. As they moved through the crowd, she realized that while she'd talked about Nigel a few minutes ago, she wasn't missing him, not even as a buffer. Apparently she was getting used to being without him—something she wouldn't have thought was possible a month ago. What she didn't know was if emotionally moving on was good or bad. Or if it was simply inevitable.

Chapter Twenty-Four

Despite having worn flats to Finola's fund-raiser, Zennie's feet still hurt Sunday morning. While she was used to standing all day, she wasn't used to doing it in ballet flats that pinched her toes. She was pretty sure that if she'd been wearing heels, she would be crippled for days. She thought about Finola's four-inch stilettos and wondered how her sister did it.

More than just the shoes, she thought as she went through her yoga stretching routine. The whole evening. The beautiful people really were different from the rest of the world. Some of Finola's supposed friends had acted supportive, but a whole lot of them had been looking for an open wound they could exploit. It wasn't Zennie's idea of a good time.

She'd just finished her video when her phone buzzed. She was surprised to see a text from C.J.

It's a beautiful day. Let's go do something.

Zennie considered the offer. She would love to spend time with C.J. They'd gotten along so well and since she and Gina weren't speaking, she felt a little vulnerable in the friendship department. But she also couldn't deal with one more disapproving person. While not telling C.J. about her "delicate condition" made the most sense, she found herself typing, First you should probably know I'm pregnant.

C.J. didn't answer for a couple of minutes. I was thinking we'd just hang out, but sure, be pregnant.

That made Zennie laugh. Give me some time to take a shower and get dressed. Meet in an hour?

Sounds great. C.J. named a restaurant that served brunch.

Zennie got there at the same time as her friend. They hugged, then settled at a table. C.J. waited until Zennie had looked over the menu to say, "Pregnant? So the procedure was successful? I'm both impressed and shallow. No way I would do that for anyone. How's the world taking it?"

"My boss doesn't know yet. My mother's pissed but she's coming around. My dad was also upset, but I've shamed him into loving me again. I've lost a couple of friends over it."

Zennie found herself fighting tears. "Honestly, being emotional is the worst of it. I'm not an emotional person."

C.J. smiled. "All evidence to the contrary?"

"Exactly."

"I have a solution. Let's go look at some open houses. There are a couple of cute condos that just came on the market. When I saw the listings I thought of you."

"You mean condos for sale?"

"Uh-huh."

Zennie stared at her. "I'm not ready to buy a place. By myself? I couldn't possibly…" She forced herself to stop talking. Of course she could. In fact, she should!

She grinned. "Yes, I'll go look at condos with you. It will be fun. Just promise me we don't have to talk about the baby."

"The baby is the last thing I want to talk about. We'll lament LA traffic and groan over bad carpeting because there's always bad carpeting in at least one."

Zennie smiled at her even as she had the oddest thought that Clark would enjoy looking at condos with her and C.J. She picked up her menu as a distraction, all the while telling herself that there was no reason Clark should be on her mind. They were done. Long done. Besides, if she were to fall for someone, it wouldn't be him. Sure he'd been nice enough and interesting, but not for her. Clark, Schmark.

"What?" C.J. asked.

"I can't wait for my hormones to calm down. My mom swears it will happen soon and when it does, I'm having a party."

Ali was willing to admit it—she felt good. Better than good. She'd had the week off for her honeymoon and instead of feeling depressed and stupid, she'd spent the time figuring out her career and hanging with Daniel. She'd laughed with him, talked with him, made love with him and slept snuggled in his arms. Just as amazing, it turned out that keeping as busy as she'd been had meant eating less. Over the past couple of weeks, she'd noticed her clothes feeling a little looser. A quick step on the scale shocked her with the information that she'd lost ten pounds.

On her first day back at work she was wearing cute dark-wash jeans she hadn't fit in for maybe eight months and a chunky open-knit sweater over a tank top she'd almost forgotten she had. One of the upsides of moving—aside from her yummy roommate—was going through all her clothes and reminding herself of what she owned. Something she should do more often, she told herself as she drove to the warehouse.

Losing a little weight had even inspired her to get up early and spend thirty minutes walking up and down the hills in Daniel's neighborhood. She'd brought her lunch to work rather than going to the taco truck. Not that she would give up tacos forever, but a little protein on a salad every couple of days wouldn't kill her and might keep the downward trend going.

"I feel good," she whispered to herself as she parked, and she was determined that feeling should last. She had a nine-thirty meeting with her boss and once that was done, she was going to focus on her job and her responsibilities.

She got to her desk a few minutes early and plowed through her email. After printing out the weekly sales reports, she ran her inventory control program and collected the printouts before heading to see Paul.

She knocked on his open office door right at nine thirty. He looked at her and raised his eyebrows.

"Vacation agrees with you," he said, motioning for her to come in and take a seat.

She closed the door before sitting in the chair and setting a folder on his desk. "I enjoyed my vacation," she admitted. "I thought I'd be upset about Glen, but I barely thought about him."

"I'm glad. He was never good enough for you. So, what can I do you for?"

Ali felt the first flicker of uncertainty, then told herself to suck it up. She was prepared with all her information and arguments. If Paul didn't think she was ready to take over his job, then that was good information to have. She would make her plans accordingly. Either way, she was going to make her case.

"I heard you're retiring," she began, looking directly at him. "Congratulations."

"Thanks. It's been a long time coming, but I'm ready. The missus and I are going to buy a place in Arizona and hide out from our kids."

She smiled. "I happen to know you adore your kids and love your grandkids even more, so I know that's not true." She cleared her throat. "It's taken you a while to find someone, which makes me wonder if the job is going to be more difficult to fill than anyone had considered. There might be a reason for that. I was disappointed not to be asked to interview for your job. I have the skills. I know how the warehouse functions, I'm good with the people and when you go on vacation, I'm the one who runs things."

Paul looked surprised. "I never thought you'd be interested, Ali. You don't talk about getting ahead. For the past six months you've been all about your wedding. I thought you'd see the promotion as too much work."

His words hit her like a slap. Seeing herself from someone else's point of view was instructive, but painful.

She wanted to say that wasn't true, that she hadn't been all about the wedding, only she thought maybe he was right. Once Glen had proposed, she'd kind of floated through life, spending her time planning and dreaming and writing her new last name on random pieces of paper.

"I don't want to manage inventory for the rest of my life," she said, keeping her voice steady. "I would like to be considered for the job. I've prepared information on what I've done to decrease theft and reduce shipping costs, along with the controls I've put in place for inventory." She pushed the folder toward him.

"Ali, I know what you've done for the company."

"Probably not all of it," she said, keeping her tone light.

"Good point. Thanks." His expression was kind. "I really didn't know you'd be interested. Now that I do, I'll be in touch to set up an interview with me and the owner. We'd rather promote from within and I think you'll be an excellent candidate."

"Thank you."

She spoke calmly, but on the inside she was cheering. They spoke for a few more minutes, then she returned to her desk where she forced herself to act completely normal. Dancing in place would be too hard to explain.

At lunch she headed to the post office box she'd set up before moving out of her apartment. She collected a couple of circulars and her VISA bill, opening the latter when she was back in her car. She stared at the five-figure balance and felt all the blood rush from her head. How had it gone *up* from last time?

Her hands shook as she studied the transactions. There were only two, and one was huge. The cake, she thought grimly. That had been a big hit, and the interest because she hadn't been able to pay much more than the minimum amount. Even being able to use rent money to pay down the balance, it was going to take a year for her to work her way through this. Dammit, canceling the wedding wasn't her fault and she shouldn't have to pay for all of it.

Without considering what was going to happen when she got there, she drove directly to Glen's office. She had no idea if he was even in town or not, but she was going to take the chance. Assuming he was sitting at his stupid desk, being his stupid self, she was going to confront him once and for all.

She stormed into the building and went directly to the third floor. Glen's assistant, a mousy woman in her fifties, stared wide-eyed as Ali approached.

Ali motioned to the half-open door. "He in?"

The assistant nodded without trying to stop her from entering.

"Good. This won't take long." Ali pushed open the door.

The second she was face-to-face with her ex-fiancé, she realized she hadn't seen Glen since before he dumped her. All their communication had been via text or over the phone. For a second she worried that being close to him after all this time would hurt her, that she would realize she missed him and that she was devastated by the loss. Only that didn't happen.

As she stared into his light brown eyes, she realized he was a much smaller version of his brother, and not just physically. While before she wouldn't have cared that he was shorter, slighter and paler, now she found herself just a little smug that she was sleeping with the much better brother. But even more important than looks were temperament and character. Where Glen was demanding, Daniel was easygoing. Glen had a short temper while Daniel was patient. Glen was critical and his brother was a sweet, funny, kind man who made her feel like a princess.

"Ali!" Glen's eyes widened in alarm as he pushed up his glasses. "What are you doing here?"

"Confronting you."

He reached for the phone on his desk. "If you're going to get violent, I'm calling security."

She rolled her eyes. "Really? Violent? When has that ever happened?"

"You're a woman scorned."

That nearly made her laugh—then she remembered the credit card bill. She walked over to his desk and waved the envelope.

"What I am is dealing with a lot of debt from the wedding. You proposed to me, Glen. You helped plan the wedding, then you walked away without bothering with your responsibilities. I'm willing to pay for half, but that's all. I'm going to stand here until you write me a check for twelve thousand dollars."

He blanched. "I'm not going to do that and you can't make me."

His voice was petulant. As she watched him, she tried to figure out what she'd ever seen in him. Had she really been so lonely and desperate that she'd wanted to spend the rest of her life with him? The answer was obvious and embarrassing. Thank goodness he'd dumped her—what if he hadn't? She might have married him.

"Glen, be a human being and give me the money. You know it's the right thing to do."

She waited. After a couple of seconds, he muttered, "I, ah, don't have my checkbook with me."

She sighed. "You always have it in your briefcase, Glen. Come on. Don't play this game with me."

He made a face, then reached under his desk for his briefcase. It only took him a second to write out the check and hand it to her.

"What about the ring?" he asked as she tucked the piece of paper into her back pocket. "I want it back."

She smiled. "Funny you should mention that. You know what? Per the state of California, the ring is an implied conditional gift. Had I broken the engagement, you would certainly be entitled to the ring back, but as *you* ended things, it's mine to keep." She smiled. "And just in case you try to pretend things happened otherwise, let's all remember you didn't have the balls to break up with me yourself. You had your brother do it, so there's a witness."

He stood and glared at her. "You're different. I'm not sure I like it."

"Glen, what you like and don't like about me is no longer my problem." She offered him an insincere smile. "Thanks for the check. Have a nice day."

She walked out without saying anything else. When she got to her car, she was both elated and shaking. The combination was unsettling, but she was going to go with it.

She opened her banking app and deposited the check. Once it cleared, she could pay off a good chunk of her credit card and get on with her life. Even better, in less than five hours her workday would be done. She would go home to Daniel and have some hot monkey sex to celebrate her newfound backbone.

When Zennie's mother had said her boobs would hurt, Zennie had not understood the truth in the statement. They didn't just hurt, they ached and burned and were uncomfortable enough that she wanted to whimper.

"I thought we had a deal," she said to herself as she got her things out of her locker and headed for her car. "I've always taken care of you. I eat right and exercise. I'm just pregnant, can't you cooperate a little more?"

Before her body could answer—or not—she was close enough to her car to see something tucked under her windshield wipers. While she prayed it was a circular for a new car wash or even somebody leaving a note after denting her car, she knew her luck wasn't that good. Not anymore.

She unfolded the piece of paper and groaned when she recognized Bernie's handwriting.

Just a gentle reminder that you need to be taking your calcium every day. Oh, and I have a coupon for a couple's massage. I thought maybe I could set up an appointment for the two of us. I could make yours a prenatal massage. Wouldn't that be fun? Love you.

She got in her car, dropped her backpack on the passenger seat, then leaned her forehead against her steering wheel.

"I can't do this," she said aloud, not caring that talking to herself was becoming a thing. "I just can't."

The changes to her body were hard enough, but dear God, Bernie was getting on her nerves.

It wasn't just the meal service or the very ugly and tight support hose she'd dropped by. It was the email reminders of her next doctor's appointment and the little notes like the one left today, and texts about whatever Bernie had just read in the pregnancy books and understandable interest that a nicer person would like but that Zennie was finding overwhelming and intrusive.

She reminded herself that Bernie was her best friend and of course she cared about the baby, but Zennie desperately needed a break. And a hug. And someone to listen to her whine. And the other kind of wine.

She ignored the inevitable tears that were a daily part of life now and started the car's engine. All she had to do was drive home and then she would be fine. She was always happy to head to her own place and decompress from a long day in surgery, but suddenly she felt less excited about, well, everything.

It was just the note, she told herself. And the stupid food that was waiting for her, she thought with a sigh. Every dinner came with a healthy salad with dark green vegetables and lots of crunchy raw things and beans and a dressing that tasted like road tar. She was tired of plain white fish or plain chicken breasts and two servings of vegetables and unsweetened yogurt because she needed dairy but God forbid she have a little Brie and a hot fudge sundae.

"This sucks," she admitted. She was only two months along and there were seven-plus months to go. She wasn't going to make it. She would snap and go on a bender in Target, running down the food aisles, ripping open bags of cookies and spraying Reddi-wip directly into her mouth while begging someone to give her coffee with a shot of vodka in it.

The truth was, and she really hated to admit it, she'd been impulsive about the pregnancy and while she wasn't sorry, she sure as hell wasn't happy.

Her phone rang. She answered it without looking at the screen, then shuddered when she realized it was probably Bernie.

"Hello?"

"Hi, Zennie, it's Clark."

She blinked as the name sank in. "Clark, wow, that's so strange. I was just thinking about you the other day. How are you? How are things?"

She heard the enthusiasm in her voice and was surprised when she realized she *was* happy to hear from him. He'd been a good guy and she had a feeling she might have been a little too judgy when they'd been going out.

"Things are good. I, ah… I'm calling because I still miss you. I know it's over—you were clear enough on that—but I can't seem to forget you and I wanted you to know."

She stared out the window as she processed his words. He

missed her? Instead of annoying her, the news was kind of nice to hear. In fact, if she dwelled on it for very long, she thought she might start to cry for possibly the third time that day.

"I know you were really clear on things," he continued, "But I wondered if you might consider being friends."

Friends? What did that mean? She'd never had a lot of guy friends—not as an adult. She wasn't sure of the ground rules, then found herself thinking it didn't matter. She wanted to see him.

"I take it that's a no." His voice was soft.

"It's not. Sorry. You caught me by surprise. I think your offer is an interesting one, it's just there's something you should know first."

"You're seeing someone."

"What? No. God no. I'm pregnant."

She hadn't meant to just blurt it out, but she had. She heard his sharp intake of air followed by his hurt tone as he said, "That was fast. Look, I won't keep you any—"

"Wait. Don't. It's not what you think. It's not anything you could imagine."

"Because you didn't hook up with some guy?"

"I didn't hook up with anyone." She quickly explained about Bernie and Hayes and the turkey baster.

"You're having a baby for a friend? You're going to be pregnant for nine months, then give the baby away?"

"That's the plan, yes." She closed her eyes, hoping he would get it because she honestly couldn't deal with one more mean person in her life.

"That's amazing. Zennie, I don't know what to say. You're incredible."

Tears filled her eyes. "I'm not. I'm a mess. My hormones have me crying every fifteen seconds, my boobs hurt and if I have to eat another salad, I'm going to go screaming into the night. Being pregnant sucks."

"Sounds like it. Look, how about I bring by Chinese and we'll talk? Would that be okay?"

She thought about the hideous dinner waiting in her refrigerator. She would have it for lunch tomorrow, she promised herself. While Bernie had insisted on buying all three meals a day, Zennie had talked her down to breakfast and dinner only.

"That would be great," she said. "You remember where I live?"

"Sure do. Anything you can't eat?"

She gave him a brief list, then agreed they would meet up at her place in about forty minutes. She hung up smiling.

Thirty-five minutes later she'd showered and changed. She set the table and put on some music. The quivers in her stomach were unexpected, as was the sense of anticipation. She supposed that while she wasn't interested in Clark romantically, she was happy to see someone who wasn't going to tell her what to do or be upset with her. Plus, the man was bringing over Chinese—what was there not to like?

When he knocked on the door, she raced to open it, then stood there staring at him. He was a little taller than she remembered and slightly more handsome. She smiled.

"Hi," she said, stepping back to let him in. "It's good to see you."

"It's good to be seen."

They laughed and she led him into the kitchen.

It took a few minutes to unpack all the food. She offered him a beer, which he refused.

"Just because I can't drink doesn't mean you have to suffer, too," she said.

He raised his water glass. "In solidarity."

They settled across from each other at the table. She breathed in the delicious smells and tried not to moan.

"This is so bad," she murmured. "All the sodium and the

spices, but I don't care. It's just one night and then I'll go back to my regular food in the morning."

He handed her a serving spoon. "Dig in."

She filled her plate, then took a bite of kung pao beef. The flavors exploded on her tongue.

"I can't thank you enough for this," she said when she'd swallowed. "You have saved me. I was having an actual meltdown in my car when you called. I didn't think I could do it."

"Eat your healthy food?"

"Have the baby." She waved her fork. "Sorry. I don't really mean that. I'm sure everything will be fine, it's just hard right now. I'm getting used to things and I'm emotional all the time. Bernie is so attentive and I know she means well, but she's driving me crazy and it's not like I can tell her. Plus the whole list of shoulds and shouldn'ts. I don't actually drink very much and I've never been that fond of Brie, but I would kill for both. Or coffee. Or sushi. I can't remember the last time I was in a Jacuzzi but now that I'm not allowed, I daydream about them. It's ridiculous. I can't go surfing, I can't do hot yoga. I'm a strong, motivated person. I want to do this for my friend, so what's wrong with me?"

He reached for an egg roll. "It happened pretty fast, Zennie. Not you saying yes, I would have expected that, but actually getting pregnant. Most people would have more time to get used to the idea. But you got pregnant right out of the gate."

"How would you know?"

He smiled. "I know how long it's been since I've seen you and I can do simple math."

"Oh, right. It was quick." She told him about the appointment and how she'd been ovulating. "Hayes came in and did the deed and here we are."

Clark looked uncomfortable. "I'm not sure I could have handled the pressure of knowing several people were waiting on the, ah, sample."

She giggled. "That's what I thought, too, but I guess he was motivated."

They talked about Clark's work and the improvements that were planned to the orangutan exhibit and the grant money his department had received. She talked about her family, bringing him up to date on Finola and Ali.

"It turns out we all got dumped on the same weekend," she said, serving herself more fried rice. As soon as the words were out, she groaned. "I'm sorry. I didn't mean it to come out that way."

"If you're not upset, I'm not either."

She looked at him and had no idea what he was thinking. "There wasn't anyone else," she told him.

"I know. And you swear you're not a lesbian."

"I'm not. In fact my mom fixed me up with one. C.J. She's great. If there were going to be girl-on-girl sparks they would be with her, but nope. Maybe I'm just meant to be alone."

Words she'd thought before but saying them now made her feel sad. Did she really want to be alone for the rest of her life, with no one to depend on? Maybe it was the pregnancy making her feel more vulnerable than usual, but for once, she didn't want her future to be so empty.

"You're not meant to be alone," he told her. "You simply move at a different pace than other people. There's nothing wrong with you." He hesitated. "I meant what I said before. I'd like to be friends, if you're interested."

She felt shy as she smiled at him. "I'd like that, too, but you have to be okay with the pregnancy thing. It could get messy."

He smiled. "I think I can handle it."

"Even when I'm moody?"

"Especially when you're moody."

"Then I'm in. Want to stay and watch a movie?"

"There's nothing I'd like more."

Simple words, she thought, but the exact ones she wanted to hear.

Chapter Twenty-Five

"You're sure?" Daniel asked.

"Yes." Ali hoped her voice sounded more confident than she felt. "It's the right thing to do. Okay, not the *right* thing, but the correct thing." She paused, not sure there was a difference. "You know what I mean."

"I do. I just want to make sure you're up to it." He backed his truck into her mother's driveway, then turned off the engine. "You could ask her again."

Ali shook her head. "I have literally asked her five times and every time she's said no. Apparently I'm not mature enough or whatever. She would rather give the clock to charity than let me have it. I don't care. No one wants it but me and we're going to take it."

Steal it, actually. She and Daniel had driven over on a Saturday when Ali knew her mother would be at the boutique, for the express purpose of stealing the clock. Ali had texted her intentions to Finola so her sister could not be home and therefore avoid having to take a stance on the issue. Her sister had also left the front door unlocked for her.

Armed with tools and instructions for dismantling downloaded from the internet, she and Daniel walked into the house. He paused in the living room and looked around. She glanced at him.

"Second thoughts?" she asked.

"No, just getting a sense of what it was like when you were little. You grew up here."

She tried to see the living room as he would, with worn furniture and too many small tables and lamps. It was a comfortable house in a pleasant enough neighborhood, but she'd never felt like she belonged. The downside of being the third child with parents who could only have one favorite.

It wasn't a new concept for her, but for the first time she could remember, she was more understanding and less bitter. She hadn't heard from her father since that one pathetic text and she knew she wasn't going to—not unless she reached out to him. Her mother was friendly enough but Mary Jo had never really been that involved in her life. Ali had her sisters and a few friends, but had never felt connected to anyone. Not the way other people did.

That was why she'd wanted to marry Glen, she thought suddenly. Because with him, she would be the most important, the first, the one he loved best. She'd been so enamored with the concept of finally being like everyone else that she'd overlooked some pretty big red flags, including the fact that she'd never truly loved him. She'd been that desperate and she'd paid the price for it.

Daniel walked over and put his hand on the side of her face. "What?" he asked, his voice gentle.

"Just having a bit of an emotional revelation. I know why I got engaged to Glen even though I wasn't in love with him. I wanted to be special to someone."

He kissed her. "You are special."

To him, she thought, letting his caring wash over her. "Now," she said, her voice teasing. "Not so much before."

"You were always special." He kissed her. "Come on. Let's go commit a felony."

She chuckled as she followed him over to the clock. It was huge and old-fashioned with an ornate face and hadn't been wound in years. The finish was dull from years of neglect and she was sure it needed a good tune-up or whatever it was clocks required to stay working.

"I know what you're thinking," she began.

"I doubt that."

"I know it's ugly and not what most people want in their houses. It's just, I love this clock."

He frowned. "Ali, you really don't get it, do you? If you love this clock, then I want you to have it. My house is huge. There's plenty of room. I was thinking we'd put it in the dining room."

She'd been thinking the same thing. "On the shorter wall by the opening to the kitchen?"

"That's the one."

"That's perfect. It has to be on an interior wall so there's no sudden change in temperatures and it can't be near an air vent and…" She pressed her lips together. "Sorry. I'm enthused."

"You are, now let's get going."

They laid out the instructions on the coffee table. Daniel went to work taking apart the working parts of the clock while Ali unscrewed the hinges for the glass door.

Daniel took pictures as he went to help them with reassembly, and separated the small pieces into plastic bags. Ali got the hand truck. Together they carried all the pieces out and laid them on the truck's back seat, then returned for the main housing. The wood frame was heavy but they got it outside and into the back of the truck where Daniel tied it down.

They drove slowly back to his place and reversed the process to bring the pieces inside. It took a couple of hours to assemble the clock in the dining room. When they were done, Ali carefully wound the clock, then adjusted the time. She waited anxiously to see if the pendulum would stay in motion. They stood in silent anticipation until the quarter hour when the familiar chime sounded.

"Perfect!" she said, clapping her hands together before throwing her arms around him. "I'll find someone to give it a nice clock spa treatment so it can keep going. Thank you for helping me."

"You're welcome. This crime thing is kind of fun."

She laughed. "Maybe we can do something else bad."

His expression turned knowing. "I'm all in." His phone buzzed.

Ali stepped back. "I hope it's not the police," she teased.

"Your mom won't be back from work until tonight," he reminded her, then checked his screen and read the message. His expression turned sheepish as he looked at her. "Ali, we need to talk about something."

Her good mood vanished as her stomach tightened. "What? It's bad, isn't it?" Had something happened? Was he breaking up with her? Did he want her to move out and—

"That was my mom. I told her about us."

He'd what? She hadn't told anyone. Not because she was ashamed or anything but it was kind of weird that she'd gotten involved with her ex-fiancé's brother. Socially it was kind of a no-no.

"She hates me," Ali moaned. "She has to. Or she thinks I'm a slut. I liked your parents when I met them and I thought they liked me."

"They do like you," he told her. "They understand it was all Glen." He hesitated. "My mom guessed how I felt about you a while ago. She never said much, but she knew. So she's happy that I'm happy."

Ali let some of her panic fade. "You're sure?"

"Yes. They want us to come over to dinner. I thought we'd set something up in the next couple of weeks."

Dinner with the parents? Wasn't it too soon? Although they weren't strangers, but still. "It's going to be awkward."

"Yes, it is."

She shrieked. "How can you say that? You're supposed to reassure me."

"It's going to be awkward and then it's going to be fine."

"You could have started with the fine part and then moved to awkward."

He smiled. "I'll remember for next time."

"Glen won't be there, will he? Because that's a level of weird I can't handle just yet."

"No Glen. Although at some point—"

She raised her hand. "Daniel, you're great and I can't tell you how much I appreciate the help with the clock and everything else you've done and all, but I am not ready to hang out with your brother just yet. I need you to be okay with that."

One corner of his mouth turned up. "I am very okay with it."

"You swear?"

He pulled her hand to his chest and pressed her palm against his T-shirt. "I swear. So dinner with my parents?"

"Uh-huh." She sighed. "And I'll tell my mom and my sisters. I really hate being mature."

"Maybe so, but it looks good on you."

The emotional resiliency of human beings was a marvel, Finola thought as she walked back into her dressing room after a long planning meeting. She and her team got together every quarter to look at upcoming holidays, blockbuster movie openings and social events so they could be prepared with appropriate segments. The back-to-school fashion shows did not plan themselves.

She'd gotten through the meeting with no problem, making suggestions and noting when key team members would be on vacation. She could do her job, laugh, even think about things like back-to-school without relating it all to Nigel. He was always there, of course, lurking in the back of her psyche, but she was dealing.

It helped that the press was no longer interested in her or her life. Treasure was being surprisingly low-key about her ongoing affair and without a new scandal, Finola was no longer interesting. She'd taken advantage of the lull to move back into her own house and had even taken possession of her cell phone again.

At some point his affair with Treasure would fizzle and he would be free to return to his marriage. The question was, did she want him to? Two months ago she would have sold her soul to have him back but now she was less sure. Not only because of how he'd betrayed her but also because she'd taken a hard look at what she'd been willing to put into the marriage and, to be honest, it hadn't been much. She wasn't sure if her disinterest was about him or her or both, but it was something she had to consider. If their marriage had been so flawed before, was it worth saving now?

Just as important were the questions about herself. Why hadn't she been more involved with her husband? Maybe she'd fallen out of love with him or maybe she was simply too selfish to truly love anyone. She didn't want it to be the latter, but she had recently discovered she was not the warm, loving, giving saint she'd always imagined.

She understood the foolishness of planning for a future when she didn't have enough information but that didn't stop her from searching for marriage counselors in the area as well as divorce lawyers. So far she hadn't called either.

Rochelle burst into the office, her eyes wide. "Did you see it? It's online."

"Did I see what?"

"You have to see it."

Rochelle grabbed Finola's computer and typed in an internet address. Seconds later a video appeared of Nigel being interviewed by a reporter Finola didn't recognize.

He looked thinner, she thought absently. As if he hadn't been eating enough. And tired. He seemed very tired. She waited for a sense of happy revenge or elation that he, too, was suffering, but there wasn't any. Just concern for him and sadness. A lot of sadness.

Rochelle turned up the volume. He was talking about being in the spotlight and how it was unexpected.

"You and Treasure make an interesting couple," the reporter said. "Things started rather quickly between you."

Nigel shifted uncomfortably in his chair. "Yes, they did."

"You were married at the time?"

His jaw tightened. "I still am."

"How does your wife feel about the affair?"

His eyes narrowed. "I'm sure you can imagine."

"Do you still love your wife?"

The question took Nigel by surprise—she could see it in how he stiffened and looked away. It startled her, as well. She instinctively took a step back, as if distance could protect her. Rochelle grabbed her arm.

"Don't worry. He has a good answer."

Nigel looked straight at the camera then and nodded. "Yes, I love my wife. Very much."

"Was it worth it?" the reporter asked.

Finola pressed her arms to her midsection and turned away. "Shut it off. I don't want to hear any more."

"Are you okay? I thought you'd be happy. Nigel loves you. I'm sure he's tired of the drama with Treasure and wants to come home. Of course he's been an ass and will have to do a lot to earn your trust…" Her assistant's voice lowered. "I'm sorry. I thought you'd be thrilled."

"I mostly don't know what to think," Finola admitted. "He hasn't been in touch with me in weeks. I don't even know where he is. I've had to deal with all this without him."

There were still wounds, but some were less fresh. The bleeding had stopped. She turned the words over in her mind. Nigel said he still loved her. He'd said it in public, as if he wanted her to know.

"Treasure's not going to be happy," she said.

"I know. Isn't it great?"

Finola was less sure of the greatness of the moment. Two months ago she would have been giddy. Now she was just confused.

She glanced at Rochelle only to see her assistant looking both guilty and resigned. As if she'd been hoping for a different reaction. Her senses immediately went on alert. Something was up—she knew it in her bones. She and Rochelle worked closely together nearly seven days a week. Their relationship required trust. They'd always been honest with each other. The rules were simple—be all in while she worked for Finola and in return Finola would teach her about the business, introduce her to the right people and when the time came—

The kick in her gut was sharp. She grabbed the back of a nearby chair to keep from stumbling. It was happening, she thought, even as she wanted to scream she wasn't ready. Normally she didn't care when her assistants left her, but this was different. She was so vulnerable right now, so exhausted from the roller coaster of emotions she'd been on. She couldn't do it on her own, and hiring a new person was always so much work. It wasn't the training that sucked up her energy, it was figuring out if she could trust the person. That took time.

She looked at her beautiful assistant. Rochelle was smart, savvy and ambitious. They had a deal and Finola knew she was going to have to abide by it, no matter how much it hurt.

She sat in the chair she held and motioned for Rochelle to take a seat opposite.

"So what's the job offer?" Finola asked.

Rochelle's dark brown eyes widened. "I have no idea what you're—"

Finola raised her eyebrows. "Don't start lying to me now. You know someone is going to call me for a reference."

Rochelle ducked her head. "Associate producer on *Late Night LA*."

"Impressive. That's a big job."

Late Night LA was a fast-paced, hip show about the city after dark. Some of the segments were devoted to hot spots and great dining, but there were human interest segments along with some investigative reporting. The ratings were excellent, especially in the 18 to 34 demographic. The network paid attention to the local show. If all went well there, Rochelle would quickly move up the food chain.

"How long have you been sitting on this?" she asked.

Rochelle drew in a breath. "A few weeks. I didn't want to leave when everything was going down like it was. You needed me and you've given me so much. I wanted to be here for you."

Finola smiled. "I appreciate that. I couldn't have gotten through this without you, but it's time for you to go. Take the job."

"But if you and Nigel aren't getting back together then—"

"Take the job."

Of course Finola wanted her to stay, but she wasn't going to have someone she cared about give up the opportunity because Finola's heart was still shattered. That would be ridiculous.

"You have names for me?" she asked, because part of Rochelle's responsibilities would be helping her find a replacement.

"Three." Rochelle's voice was soft. "But we don't have to—"

"Call them today and we'll start interviewing tomorrow.

We'll get the list down to two by end of day. After that, I want you to talk to my lawyer to get the background checks started."

Rochelle stared at her. "You ran a background check on me?"

"Of course and one day you'll do the same when you have an assistant you trust with your life."

"A background check. I never knew."

There was a lot she didn't know, Finola thought enviously. She had so much life ahead of her. So much to learn and experience.

Impulsively she grabbed Rochelle's hand. "Listen to me. This is a tough business. Be strong, be smart and be determined. Watch your back. Make people earn your trust, but don't be a bitch about it. And no matter what, always remember to be a decent human being."

Tears rolled down Rochelle's cheeks. "I can't do this. I can't leave. I'll stay."

"No, you won't. It's time. Past time. I should have noticed. That's on me, but with everything going on, I forgot our deal. I'm sorry." She released her hand. "Tell whoever's interviewing you that they can call me whenever they'd like. I'm happy to talk about you."

Rochelle nodded and stood. She crossed to the closed door, then looked back. "I can never thank you."

"I know and you don't have to. Just pass it on. Do for someone else what I'm doing for you. And when you're incredibly famous and I'm just someone you used to know, take my call."

More tears fell. "I'll always take your call."

Rochelle left. Finola did her best to ignore the sense of dread sweeping through her. The start of training a new assistant was overwhelming, but she didn't have a choice. She'd screwed up nearly every other part of her life. She wasn't going to screw up her career or her deal with Rochelle.

She glanced at her computer and thought about replaying the

video. Nigel still loved her. She was fairly confident she still loved him. And while that should be enough, deep in her heart she knew that it wasn't. Not anymore.

Chapter Twenty-Six

Ali enjoyed the feel of the bike racing around the track. She'd taken the first couple of laps slowly, wanting to get a feel for what was happening, but as she gained confidence, she picked up speed.

Even with ear protection and a helmet, she could still hear the roar of the engine. Dust blew around her as some of the more experienced riders passed her. She wanted to increase her speed to keep up but reminded herself this was a practice session, not a race. She still didn't know exactly what she was doing.

She completed another lap and decided she could go a little faster. As she went into the turn, she remembered what the instructor had said about leaning into the curve rather than turning the bike. She experimented by shifting her weight and was shocked when the bike moved in a smooth turn.

Elation joined the adrenaline already racing through her. No wonder Daniel loved what he did—this was exciting.

On the straightaway, she gave the bike even more gas. She was about to pass a slower rider when she saw a bike up ahead take the curve too fast. The bike twisted, the driver fell off and rolled right into the path of the rest of the pack.

Ali immediately slowed down, all the while telling herself to keep control. She was doing all right until another biker bumped her, sending her right for the barriers on the inside of the track.

She knew she was going to crash and forgot what she was supposed to do. She hit the brakes too hard, then slammed into the barrier. One second she was absorbing the impact and the next she was flying over the barrier onto the hard ground. She landed with a thud that knocked the wind out of her. Pain exploded from so many places, she didn't know what to focus on first. The sky seemed to swirl and shift and then everything started going dark.

This was bad, she thought hazily. Really—

"Ali? Ali! Can you hear me? Ali?"

She opened her eyes and saw Daniel bent over her. He was pale and frantic as he began examining her.

"Ali?"

"I fell," she murmured, wishing the pain would settle in one or two places so she could figure out what she'd done.

"I saw. It wasn't your fault. That jackass ran into you."

"That jackass is eight, Daniel. It's not his fault, either."

She shifted on the ground. Okay, her legs worked and her back wasn't too bad. She didn't think she'd hit her head that hard, so maybe she was—

"Yikes!"

Moving her left arm had been a mistake, she thought, glancing down at it. With all the protective gear, she couldn't tell what was wrong, but it hurt bad.

She wiggled her fingers and they were fine, then raised her right arm. Just an okay kind of ache. She carefully lifted her left arm and rested it across her body. The pain increased. Still holding it against her, she managed to raise herself to a sitting position.

She looked at Daniel. "I think I broke something."

He swore. "That's what I was afraid of. You also might have a concussion."

"I'm fine."

"You blacked out."

"For one second."

"That's all it takes." He stared at her. "Look at me. I want to see if your pupils are dilated."

She wanted to protest, but figured he'd taken a bunch of first aid classes and probably knew what he was doing. She did as he requested, then answered basic questions about what day it was and where she was.

"I should call an ambulance," he said, pulling out his phone.

"Don't you dare." She shifted onto her knees. "I'm okay. It's just my arm. Help me up and you can drive me to the hospital."

When he didn't move, she added. "I'm getting up with or without your help."

"You're so damned stubborn."

"So I'm just like you."

He helped her to her feet. She took a second to get her balance but was pleased when the world stayed firmly in place. He removed her helmet and her gloves. They left the rest of her gear in place.

As they walked back to the buildings, she saw that everyone else had survived the pileup just fine. One of the guys from the repair shop had taken her bike and was walking it in. Laps had already resumed.

"Does this sort of thing happen all the time?" she asked.

"You play, you pay."

"That's just so macho."

"It's a macho sport."

She wanted to keep bantering with him, but her arm hurt too

much. She waited while he grabbed her handbag, then they went to his truck. He helped her into the passenger seat and carefully clipped her seat belt into place, then started for the hospital.

Ninety minutes later the doctor showed them an X-ray that confirmed what Ali had suspected. She'd broken her arm. It wasn't a bad break, but it was going to take a few weeks to heal and she would need a cast from her wrist to her elbow.

At the news Daniel went white and for a second, she thought he was going to pass out.

"It's just a little hairline thing," she said when the doctor had left. "I don't have a concussion and the break is clean and easy. I'm fine."

Daniel crossed to her and held her tight. "Dammit, Ali, I love you and I'm supposed to take care of you. Not let you get beat up."

He loved her? He loved her? She stared up at him. "What did you just say?"

His dark gaze met hers. "I love you. This is my fault."

Happiness filled her. Happiness and a floaty, giddy feeling that made the pain in her arm disappear. Daniel loved her. Based on what he'd said before, he probably had for a while. The whole time she'd been with Glen, about to make the biggest mistake of her life, Daniel had been loving her.

She thought about how much they'd been through together and while she wanted to blurt out she loved him, too, she didn't say it. She needed a little time to think things through. She and Daniel hadn't been together that long, at least from her side of things, and she wanted to be sure.

"It's not your fault," she began, thinking she would then ease into telling him that she liked him a lot—a lot and was totally on her way to being crazy in love, but things had happened so quickly and—

"Ali?"

She turned and saw her mother in the doorway. Her mother?

"Mom? What are you doing here?"

Her mother, dressed for work because it was Saturday and Mary Jo was always at the boutique on Saturday, hurried to her side. Her mother who had screamed at her over the phone for a full twenty minutes because of the stupid clock.

Mary Jo stared at Ali's swollen arm and then touched her face. "You're in the hospital. Where else would I be?"

"But how did you know I was here?" Ali turned to Daniel. "You called my mother?"

"No," he said firmly. "Your phone rang while you were having your X-ray. I saw it was her, so I answered it."

"Yes, yes," her mother said. "While that's fascinating, what happened? How did you break your arm?"

"I was riding a dirt bike and some kid ran into me and I went flying. It's not bad, Mom. I'll wear a cast for a few weeks and then I'll be fine."

"You were riding a motorcycle?"

"A dirt bike, but yes."

Her mother's gaze shifted to Daniel. "I know you. How do I know you?"

"I'm, ah, Daniel Demiter." He hesitated. "Glen's brother."

"Glen, as in your former fiancé Glen?"

Ali saw the flaw in her decision not to share much about her life with her mother. "So, it's a funny story. When Glen broke off the engagement, he didn't have the balls to do it himself, so he sent Daniel tell me. Daniel helped me deconstruct the wedding and we, um, became friends. I wanted to try something new and he was a professional motocross guy so I was on a dirt bike."

Her mother looked between them before settling on Ali. "I appreciate that you think I'm old and feeble, but a blind squirrel could see you're sleeping together. Really, Ali? Your fiancé's brother?"

Ali held in a whimper. "Mom, don't. Just don't. Daniel's a

great guy. Even if you don't believe me, I just broke a bone and I deserve sympathy."

"Mrs. Schmitt," Daniel began, "I assure you that I would never put Ali in any danger."

"All evidence to the contrary?" Mary Jo asked. "I just don't understand any of this. One minute you're marrying Glen and the next you're breaking bones and sleeping with his brother and stealing people's grandfather clocks. Ali, what's gotten into you? I barely know you."

"Mom, it's not like that."

"It's exactly like that. You're becoming someone else and I don't like it. Who is this Daniel person?"

"He's standing right there," Ali said frantically. "Please, can we talk about this later?"

"No. I want to talk about it now. He stole his brother's girl, Ali. What does that say about his character?"

Daniel headed for the door. "I'll be right outside."

"Don't go."

"It's okay, Ali. She's your mom."

Ali had no idea what that meant, but she knew it wasn't good. Not any of it. She leaned back against the pillows and wondered why now, of all times, did her mother suddenly have to give a damn about her life.

"She's *sleeping* with him," Mary Jo said for the fourteenth time since Finola had arrived at the house on Sunday morning. "It's a nightmare."

"Mom, just stop. Ali's a grown woman who knows what she's doing," Finola said, trying to take in everything her mother had said without getting distracted by the fact that her sister had apparently moved in with a guy she'd fallen for and hadn't said a word. Although her first instinct was to get mad at her sister, she had a feeling that the real problem was more about her. In truth she'd barely been in touch with Ali over the past few weeks. They'd once been so close, but somehow that had been lost.

Finola assumed they were equally to blame—each of them had been dealing with so much upheaval and there hadn't been a lot left for reaching out. Still, she should have made more of an effort.

Oh no, she thought, remembering the last time Ali had mentioned Daniel was helping with canceling the wedding. She'd talked about him in glowing terms and Finola had warned her not to make a fool out of herself. No wonder she hadn't heard from Ali.

"You're not listening to me," her mother complained as they sorted through dishes in the large hutch. The estate sale was fast approaching and there were still cupboards and closets to be sorted. Finola had promised they would finish the dining room today.

"I'm listening, Mom, but I'm thinking, too. I'm thinking Ali was with a guy who didn't love her the way he should have, and we should be happy that she's with a good guy now."

"But we don't know he's a good guy. What if he's worse?"

Finola thought about what her sister had said about Daniel. "He was there for her from the first moment Glen dumped her. He stepped in and took care of things. He's a good guy." Which her sister had been trying to tell her for a while, only she hadn't been listening. "Ali knows what she's doing. We should give her a little credit."

"Knows what she's doing?" Mary Jo's voice rose two octaves. "She practically got stood up at the altar."

"Yes, and my marriage is in shambles and you got a divorce, so let's not cast stones."

Her mother glared at her. "You're being very magnanimous all of a sudden."

"Let's just say I'm trying to make up for past behavior."

"Fine." Her mother sniffed with displeasure. "Think the best.

It's all going to fall apart. I just don't know where I failed my daughters."

Finola decided not to get into that. She shifted the subject to how they were going to advertise the estate sale and managed to get through the rest of the morning. When she left around noon, she sat in her car and texted her sister.

Mom told me about your broken arm. Please let me know how I can help. Finola hesitated before adding, I heard about Daniel, too. I was wrong before about what I said. I'm glad you're together and I hope he makes you happy. Love you.

She'd barely pushed Send when her phone buzzed with a text. How on earth had Ali answered so quickly? Only it wasn't Ali. The text was from Nigel.

Can we talk? I'd like to come by. Are you free today?

She went hot and then cold. Her insides flipped and she didn't know if she should cry or just throw up.

I'm at my mom's. Give me an hour and I'll meet you at the house.

See you then.

Finola sucked in a breath, not sure what to think. She backed out of the driveway and made her way home. She thought about changing her clothes, or putting on makeup or something, then decided that what she should do was breathe. The rest would take care of itself.

Nigel arrived fifty minutes later. She heard the garage door open. She thought about going into the living room, but that seemed too formal. Instead she poured herself a cup of coffee and sat at the kitchen table.

He walked in seconds later. He looked as he had on the interview—older and thinner. Tired. Part of her wanted to go to him and hold him. Part of her wanted to bolt. But nowhere inside did she feel smug or pleased that things had obviously gone badly for him with Treasure. She didn't want him punished—not anymore. Mostly she wanted not to feel sad.

He got himself a cup of coffee and sat across from her. They stared at each other for several minutes until he finally spoke.

"Hell of a thing."

"I saw the interview," she said. "I assume if it's not over, it will be soon. Treasure doesn't strike me as the type to take that kind of information well."

"It's over." He dropped his gaze to his coffee. "I was a fool. It's the oldest story in the book. I thought I was getting something better, something that would last, and I was wrong on both counts."

Finally, she thought, waiting for the sense of relief, of rightness. At last they could pick up the pieces of their marriage and start over. They could go into counseling and forgive each other. She could even get pregnant.

Only there wasn't much of anything. It was as if she'd felt so much over the past weeks and months, she was drained of all emotion.

"I don't know how much you want to know," he began.

"I don't want to know anything. It doesn't matter."

He looked at her then. "I know what I did was unforgivable. The things I said to you." He shook his head. "How I blindsided you. How I acted about the ski trip—all of it. I'm ashamed, Finola, and broken. I'm sorry. I can't say that enough. We were so good together and I screwed that up. I destroyed something wonderful and precious. I ripped our lives apart and for what? An affair? It's pathetic."

He was visibly shaking. She found herself feeling bad for him, but also a little dispassionate, as if she weren't truly in the moment.

"I know there were problems in the marriage," he continued. "But that's not an excuse. I should have talked to you. I should have told you how I was feeling. I've been doing some reading on infidelity. I'm a fairly classic case, it turns out."

He wrapped his hands around his mug and looked at her. "Say something, please. Tell me we can try or that I should go to hell. Whatever you want. Scream at me, throw something. Tell me I'm a bastard and you'll never forgive me. I deserve it all."

"Just like that," she said, more curious than upset. "A month ago she was a drug and now you want to come back?"

He nodded. "Yes."

"Nigel, you were wrong. Not just the affair but how you didn't have my back. You undermined me and you mocked our marriage publicly."

"I did. You're right."

"How am I supposed to trust you not to follow the next flirty woman who promises you the world? How can I ever believe that I matter?"

"Trust has to be earned. We'll get help. Finola, I want to make this right."

She wanted to believe him—she wanted to know that the pieces could be put back together. That the broken bits weren't unmendable, that instead they would heal as scars, that in the end, they would be marred but still together and stronger for what they'd endured.

But even if she could get over what had happened, what about the rest of it?

"Do you know what's in my office?" she asked, surprising herself with her words. "Pictures of me with politicians and celebrities. Awards, certificates. Do you know that I have never bothered to serve on a charity board? I'll show up to events. I'll sign a check, but God forbid I commit to doing actual work on a regular basis. I put my career first, Nigel. It was more important to me than our marriage. You should have told me you were unhappy but I should have seen it for myself. I should have guessed there were problems."

"My practice has suffered," he told her. "My partners are pissed at me and I'm going to have to work to build back their trust. They're giving me a chance, Finola. Can't you give me one, too? I'll do the work. I'll show up and take the steps and be here."

"Did you even hear me?" she asked gently. "I'm saying some of this is my fault."

"No, it's mine. All mine. I see that now." He stretched his hands toward her. "We're a team, Finola. We're so good together. Give me a chance. Please."

She placed her hands on his, feeling the familiar warmth of his skin. She thought of all she'd been through, of how her life had been shattered. She thought of her behavior and who she'd become. There were only a handful of relationships she could be proud of. She'd done right by Rochelle and she'd been a decent daughter. She was going to do better with her sisters. As for Nigel…

"You were wrong," she said, releasing his hands. "But let's be honest. Treasure's a symptom, Nigel, but she's not the real problem. We both know that."

His eyes filled with tears. "Don't. Don't say we can't make it. Don't say it's over."

She wasn't going to. She'd never been going to say that. She wanted them back together. They had so much history and potential and she'd wanted them to get back together from the second he'd first told her about the affair. And now she didn't.

The truth was soft and unexpected, flowing into her brain like a cool breeze. She had no idea what she did want, but it wasn't her marriage. Maybe there had been a time when the damage could be fixed, but that time had passed. They'd both gone in different directions.

"You've already decided," he said, wiping his face. "I ruined everything."

"No, Nigel. We ruined it together. Both of us. We let it slip away and now it's gone. I'm sorry."

He nodded.

She rose and went around to his chair. He got to his feet and then they were holding on to each other. She gave in to tears and they stood there, crying for what they had once had and what had been lost.

It took a few minutes for them to recover. They returned to their seats and looked at each other.

"We're really doing this?" he asked.

She nodded. "Where are you staying?"

"In a hotel."

"That's expensive. Why don't you move in here? I'll go back with my mom. We'll get the house ready to sell."

It wouldn't take much—not only was the market always hot for this neighborhood, the place was beautiful and in perfect condition. She would miss the house, she thought sadly. She would miss a lot of things.

"Thank you," he said. "Let me know when you're ready and I'll check out of the hotel."

"I can be out by tomorrow. I just need to let her know and grab my things. We can sort out the rest of it later."

She spoke so calmly, she thought, somewhat surprised by her lack of emotion. She was probably numb. The shock and pain would come later, but for now she was just in the moment, watching her marriage end and wishing things had been different for both of them.

"I'm not going to be an asshole about the divorce," he said. "We'll split what we have and walk away."

"I agree."

And there it was, she thought with resignation. The end.

They went upstairs. Finola packed the suitcases she'd so recently unpacked. Nigel wandered around. He came out of his closet holding a wrapped package she'd nearly forgotten about. For the first time since they'd started talking, she felt a stab of pain in her gut.

"What's this?" he asked.

She shook her head. "Don't. I bought that back when I thought we were going to Hawaii. Don't open it, Nigel. You don't want to see—"

He didn't listen. He pulled off the bow and ripped the paper, then lifted up the cover of the box. Inside were yellow booties, a small jar of flavored body dust and a silly fluorescent vibrator. He looked at her.

"I don't understand."

She felt the pieces of her shattered heart crumble and turn to dust. "It was for our week in Hawaii. I thought we could work on getting me pregnant."

He sat on the edge of the bed and broke into sobs. Finola gently laid a hand on his shoulder. So much had been lost, she thought grimly. They could have had it all and now they had nothing, and they were each very much to blame.

Chapter Twenty-Seven

Regret didn't begin to cover what Zennie was feeling. She still had months to go and already her body was turning into something she didn't recognize. Her boobs didn't just throb, they were growing. Her emotions continued to simmer just below the surface. That morning, in the OR, she'd been so caught up in the beautiful dance that was heart surgery that she'd nearly started to cry. She was a mess and she was pissed at herself for agreeing to have Bernie's baby in the first place.

Who did that? Who did it without considering the consequences? That would be her. She'd blithely agreed to something momentous without a second thought and now she was paying the price. She was trapped with a baby growing inside of her and there was nothing she could do about it.

Dr. Chen watched as new team member Dr. Kanji carefully closed after the surgery. Zennie collected the dirty instruments and equipment. On her way past, Dr. Chen said, "Zennie, would you meet me in consult room three in ten minutes?"

Her head snapped around as she stared at Dr. Chen over her surgical mask. She nodded once and hurried out of the OR.

Ten minutes later, she was a swirling mass of nerves. What if he was going to fire her? What if he yelled at her? Dr. Chen didn't like change or incompetence or any disruption to his OR. He was a perfectionist and demanding and while she'd always prided herself on being his equal in her own way, she was filled with doubts.

She returned to wheel the patient to the recovery room and passed on Dr. Chen's instructions. He would check on him several times before he was taken to the cardiac care unit. Zennie left recovery and went directly to the consult room where Dr. Chen waited.

She did her best not to look wary and defensive as she closed the door behind her. Dr. Chen motioned for her to sit down across from him at the small desk.

The consult rooms were used for just that—consultations with the family before surgery—usually in an emergency. They offered some privacy, although they were far from soundproof. Zennie told herself to be grateful Dr. Chen wasn't a screamer and made a mental note to not cry. As if a stern instruction would make a difference to her wayward hormones.

"There's something going on, Zennie," Dr. Chen said flatly. "I'm not much of a people person, but even I've been able to guess that. So far it's not affecting your work, and I'm grateful, but I would like to know what the problem is. Maybe I can help."

The unexpected offer made her smile. Dr. Chen helping her while she was pregnant. Um, no.

"I'm fine," she began.

He raised his eyebrows. "I've always trusted your integrity. Don't make me doubt it now."

Ouch. "I'm fine," she repeated. "But there has been a change in my life." She hesitated, wondering if she could put off the conversation a few more months. That had been her initial plan, but now she was stuck.

"I'm pregnant," she said, meeting his steady gaze. She explained about the artificial insemination and Bernie and how far along she was.

"I'm healthy and I have excellent medical care. There's no reason to assume I won't be able to continue working in the OR for several more months."

She'd meant to stop there. That was all the man needed to know. But somehow she found herself continuing to talk.

"It's just so much harder than I thought it would be," she admitted. "I feel emotional all the time. The smells aren't getting to me, so that's good, and I don't have morning sickness, but my body is changing and the food I have to eat is disgusting. I thought I ate fairly healthy but I am so sick of being told how many servings of dairy I need in a day. I have to cut back on my running and I miss coffee and wine and I know this is a good thing and I love my friend, but sometimes I feel really alone and scared and then I start crying."

On cue, tears filled her eyes. "See? It's a nightmare and now I'm worried you'll take me out of rotation."

Dr. Chen opened a drawer and pulled out a box of tissues. She grabbed one and blotted her eyes.

"Are you wearing support stockings?" he asked.

"Huh?"

"Support stockings. You're at risk for varicose veins and the support stockings will help with that."

"I'm wearing them." And they were one more insult to her life. "I thought I'd be a better person. I thought I'd get pregnant and be happy the whole time and I'm not. I don't want an abortion or anything, but this is a lot harder than I thought. My mom isn't very understanding and some of my friends have been awful. Clark's back in my life, which is weird, but nice. He's a good guy. We're just friends this time, and I like that."

"I have no idea who Clark is."

"I know. Sorry. I'll stop talking now." She consciously pressed her lips together in an effort to silence the flow of words.

"Zennie, you're the best nurse on my team. I don't want to lose you. I'm glad you told me what's going on." He leaned toward her. "You're doing a good thing. Of course you have doubts—you're human and this is a huge thing to take on. But you'll get through it. As for work, I'm going to trust you to tell me when you aren't comfortable handling the long hours on your feet. Given how fit you are and your age, I'm guessing you can go several months, but at some point, you're going to have to transfer out of the unit."

More tears. "I don't want to."

He smiled. "I don't, either, but it will just be temporary. Trust me, I'll be counting the days until your return."

"You promise?"

The smile widened. "Yes. Now to get yourself through this, work on strengthening your core and your back. That will help you manage the standing. Also, get Clark to rub your feet for twenty minutes a day. Studies show it helps with lower leg circulation." He winked. "And I've heard it feels nice."

Zennie had wild thoughts about Dr. Chen doing just that with Mrs. Chen. The man had depths. Who knew?

"Children are a blessing," he continued. "Not many people can do what you're doing. Remember that. You're an amazing person."

"I mostly feel crabby."

"That's okay, too. Anything else?"

"Nope. I believe in one big secret at a time and I already have mine."

"I'm proud of you, Zennie. You should be proud of yourself, as well."

His words touched her. "Thank you. I'll try." And if that didn't work, there were always the foot rubs.

Ali closed her eyes as Finola applied eyeliner. "I could have done this myself," she said. "It's my left arm that's broken, not my right."

But she wasn't complaining. It was nice to have her sister fussing over her, like she had when they'd been kids.

Finola had texted both her sisters to talk about the motorbike accident. That exchange had led to a three-way conversation about Ali's broken arm and Mom showing up in the ER. Her relationship with Daniel had tumbled out. While Ali had expected to be scolded, both her sisters had been supportive. When Finola had learned of the dinner with Daniel's parents, she'd insisted on coming by to help Ali get ready.

"I want to be here." Finola added more eye shadow. "I'm sorry about what I said before. About Daniel."

Ali involuntarily opened her eyes. "It's okay."

"It's not. I'll make an excuse and tell you I was in a bad place, but that's not good enough. I should have been more supportive." She smiled. "Obviously I was wrong about how he felt about you."

Ali felt herself flush. "He's, um, pretty into this."

"Then he's a lucky guy." Finola's smile was kind. "You're happy. Really happy. I can see it in your face. Don't take this wrong, but you weren't like this with Glen."

"I know. The breakup was awful, but honestly the logistics of canceling the wedding were harder than losing him."

"We all make mistakes. You learned from yours and you're moving on with your life."

Ali smiled. "I made Glen pay for half my VISA bill. I marched into his office and stared him down. When he asked about the engagement ring, I quoted California law—I get to keep it."

"Good for you."

"I'm not going to. I'm waiting a bit before I return it. I have no interest in what he gave me." Plus she saw returning the ring as proof that she had moved on. Things were looking up, she thought happily. Finola had come around and even her mother had texted a semi-apology for how she'd been at the emergency room.

"Look at you," Finola teased, as she reached for the mascara. "All grown up and happy in your new life."

There was more, Ali thought with a bit of pride. Daniel had said he loved her. She wasn't ready to share that with the world, not until she was sure her feelings were true love and not just a combination of hot sex and gratitude. Also, she'd killed at her interview, and starting in two weeks she was officially the new warehouse manager. She'd also decided to get her degree. Come September she would be taking two night classes at community college. She would get her degree in business management then conquer the world, with Daniel at her side.

"How are you doing?" Ali asked.

Finola finished with the mascara. She picked up an eyebrow pencil. "I'm dealing."

"Mom said you'd moved back in."

"Yes, well, Nigel's at the house."

Ali sat up straighter. "He's done with Treasure?"

"So it seems."

"Are you two…"

Finola wrinkled her nose. "We're not getting back together." She held up a hand. "We shouldn't get into this now. You have your dinner and I don't want you thinking about me. I'm okay. Sad and disappointed in both of us, but okay."

"You're getting a divorce?"

Finola nodded. "We've already talked to our respective lawyers. The house will be going up for sale. I'm going to stay with Mom until she lists her place, then I'll find a rental near the studio."

Ali hugged her. "I'm sorry. I'm so mad at him."

"Thanks, but you don't have to be. He was wrong to have the affair, but I screwed up, too. Just not so publicly."

Ali was surprised. This Finola was different. Less brash, more thoughtful. Tragedy had a way of burning away the surface of a person, leaving what was underneath. In her sister's case, that was a good thing.

"Let me know how I can help," she said.

"Thanks. I'm okay. Like I said, I'm sad, but I'm okay. Now enough about me. We're going to talk about how great you look and how much Daniel's parents are going to adore you."

Ali bit her lower lip. "Yes, well, they've already met me. As Glen's fiancé."

"You're right. I'd forgotten that. Do you have any idea how it's going to go?"

"Other than awkwardly? Not really."

Ninety minutes later, as Ali and Daniel walked up the front walk to his parents' beautiful Calabasas home, she hadn't changed her mind.

"This was a bad idea," she said as he knocked.

He squeezed the hand he was holding. "Too late now, unless you want to run for it."

But before she could consider that as an option, the front door swung open.

Marie Demiter stood in the doorway. She and her husband, Steve, were a perfectly nice couple. Steve was an architect and Marie owned a small chain of nail salons in the West Valley. They'd raised two boys, were active in the community and until tonight, Ali had always thought they kind of liked her.

Now, looking at her former mother-in-law-to-be, Ali realized she couldn't do this. Couldn't be Daniel's girlfriend after being engaged to Glen. It was ridiculous. She was a fool to think it would ever work.

"Hi," Marie said, her voice falsely bright. "Come on in."

They stepped into the huge, two-story foyer. Marie called out, "Steve, they're here."

"Good." Steve, as tall and dark-haired as Daniel, joined them. Everyone shook hands. Marie hugged her son and asked about Ali's broken arm.

"I fell off a bike on the track," she said. "It was just one of those things. I'm fine."

"She was very brave." Daniel put his arm around her. "Scared the crap out of me, though."

Marie and Steve both looked at the draped arm, then at each other. Ali's stomach sank. This was not going well.

Marie urged them all into the living room. There was a plate of appetizers waiting. Steve got them all drinks, then they sat opposite each other on the two oversize sofas in the giant and perfectly decorated room.

Ali looked at her glass of white wine, at Marie and Steve, then told herself she'd gotten through worse. She couldn't remember what, but there had to be something.

"We should talk about it," she said quietly. "Otherwise the elephant in the room is going to squish us all and the evening will be horrible."

Marie looked relieved. "That's an excellent idea, because this is a very unusual situation."

"Why don't I—" Daniel began, but Ali put her hand on his.

"I'll do it," she said. "This is my thing."

"So that's all I am?" he teased. "A thing?"

She managed a slight smile before telling herself to be strong as she looked at his parents.

"I had no idea Glen was unhappy," she said. "He never said anything. My first clue was when he ended things."

Marie and Steve exchanged a glance. Ali knew she had to keep talking or she would crumble under the pressure.

"I was devastated, of course. The wedding was less than two

months away, I'd already mailed out the invitations. I couldn't seem to grasp what was happening."

She avoided mentioning her meltdown, the drinking, the phone throwing and other details that did not paint her in the best light.

"Canceling the wedding was a lot of work. Daniel stepped in and helped me with that. Then I had to deal with getting a new place because I'd given notice and the management company had already leased out my place. We were spending a lot of time together and we became friends."

Make that *more than friends* but she was pretty sure his parents could read between the lines.

"I don't understand why Daniel was there when Glen broke off the engagement," Steve said.

"Oh. I thought you knew."

"I didn't tell them," Daniel admitted. "Sorry. I forgot about that."

"Forgot about what?" Marie asked. "What don't we know?"

"Mom, Glen didn't break up with Ali himself. He came to me and told me he didn't want to marry her. He wasn't going to tell her, so I had two choices. I could do nothing, in which case she would be stood up at the altar, or I could tell her myself. I chose to tell her."

Marie's eyes widened as she turned to Ali. "Glen didn't tell you himself?"

"No. When I texted him, he confirmed he was done with me, but that was it." She thought about mentioning the five-hundred-dollar check, but figured his parents already knew enough.

"I saw him a couple of weeks ago and we hashed out the last of the details." Which was her way of describing how she'd made him pay her what he should. "Oh, except for this."

She opened her small handbag and pulled out a ring box. "If you'd see that Glen gets this. I didn't have it on me the last time we spoke." Which was technically true, but not the reason she hadn't told him he was getting the ring back. But again—no need for the parents to know.

"Like I said," Ali continued. "I know this is really awkward. You're going to need some time to process everything. I'm not a looking to disrupt your family. Daniel was there for me when my life was falling apart. He was a good friend who helped me. What's happened since then grew out of that friendship." She smiled. "He's a really great guy, but it's a weird situation and not one I expected to find outside of reality TV."

Marie smile. "That's a little of how we feel. I can't believe Glen didn't tell you to your face. I don't want to believe he wouldn't have said anything, but now I just don't know." She looked at Daniel. "He put you in an impossible situation."

"I had to tell her what Glen was doing. I didn't want her to be played."

"He made you break her heart."

Their brief exchange told Ali that his mother knew about his feelings for her. The entire situation was complicated and crazy and she honestly didn't know what they must think of her.

"I'm sorry," Ali began.

"No," Steve told her. "You don't have anything to be sorry about, although it does sound as if we need to speak to our other son." He glanced at his wife. "Marie?"

Marie smiled. "Now that we all know what happened, we can put the situation behind us. I always liked you, Ali. I still do. It's going to take a bit for our mind-set to shift, but I think we're up to it. Now why don't you come help me in the kitchen and we'll leave the men to talk about sports?"

Ali felt a rush of gratitude for the gracious acceptance. "Thank you. I'd like that very much."

Finola spent much of Thursday and Friday afternoon and evening pricing the items for the estate sale. She'd thought she might feel sad about seeing bits of her life put up for sale, but she was oddly excited about the fact that they would soon be gone. She was releasing the past and moving on. She wasn't sure what she was moving on to, but steps were being taken.

She and Nigel were still playing nice. The paperwork had been signed to sell the house and the For Sale sign would go up in a week. They'd divided the bank accounts and were beginning the process of conscious uncoupling, as it was called these days.

Finola carried boxes into the garage. Her mother had borrowed folding tables from a friend for the smaller items. There were racks with clothing ready to be wheeled onto the driveway and stacks of books and games, along with boxes of old toys. Finola had written up a list of furniture available so people could know what was for sale before tracking into the house. Once items were sold, they would be crossed off the list.

Ali had taken care of advertising the estate sale. She'd used both social media and the *Los Angeles Times* website to let people know what was available. This being the land of Hollywood and movies, there would be a special interest in all the Parker Crane memorabilia, and she'd made sure to highlight that.

Zennie and Ali would be at the house by six thirty and the estate sale would start at eight. It would be a busy day. Finola was hoping to move everything on Saturday so they didn't have to deal with a second day. With luck, all she and her sisters would have to do was run whatever didn't sell over to a donation center. Once that was done, their mother would get the carpets cleaned and put the house up for sale.

Finola returned to the house for another load of boxes. Her cell phone rang. She glanced at the screen and recognized her agent's number.

"You're working late on a Friday."

"I am and only for you," Wilma said dramatically. "Because you're my favorite."

"You say that to all your clients. We've talked about it and none of us believe you anymore."

Wilma chuckled. "I'm all right with that. So, I have news."

"Based on your tone, I'm going to assume it's the happy kind." Which she believed she was due for, she thought with a smile.

"It is. It's fantabulous and I don't say that lightly."

"Tell me."

"The network wants you to guest cohost the 10:00 a.m. hour of the national show. For a week."

Finola walked over to the sofa and collapsed. Her heart thudded in her chest and there was a ringing in her ears.

"Are you serious? They're asking me?"

"They are. I've been hearing rumors that one of the morning show hosts was leaving so everyone moves up a rung on the ladder, leaving a spot open for someone and I want that someone to be you. This is an audition, Finola. You need to kick ass that week."

Going from *AM SoCal* to the ten o'clock hour of a network show was huge. Bigger than huge.

"I'll do it. Of course I'll do it. When is it?"

"In three weeks. Can you be ready?"

"Yes. I'll have to call my producers and let them know."

They wouldn't be happy but they also couldn't refuse a network request.

"There's more," Wilma told her. "They're going to let you produce a weeklong series, if you want. One segment per show per day. You pick the topic. It will be a lot of work, but you can show them what you're capable of."

"I'll do it," she said without considering any other option. Because she didn't need to make a decision. "I already have a topic. Why marriages fail."

Wilma gasped. "That's insane. You can't talk about that."

"Why not? It's relevant. Everyone knows someone who has

gotten a divorce. They'll be thinking about my marriage anyway. Why not get it out in the open?"

"That's a gutsy move, Finola. It's going to take a lot of strength."

"I can handle it," she said. Yes, it would be painful and yes, she would feel exposed, but she had a feeling she would feel a lot lighter and more free when she was done.

"I'll email you the details," Wilma told her. "Take the weekend to think about the topic and get back to me."

"I'm not going to change my mind."

"Take the weekend."

Finola grinned. "Yes, ma'am. Talk to you on Monday."

They hung up. Her mind was spinning with possibilities. She started to dial Rochelle only to remember her assistant was moving on. She had a great opportunity here. Dangling New York would be a distraction. Better for Rochelle to become an associate producer here than be Finola's assistant in New York, assuming the audition turned into an offer.

"I can do it myself," she said aloud, mostly to hear the words. She had plenty of free time. She would put together an outline for the segments, then talk to the booker about getting the appropriate guests. She was interested in a thoughtful, informative series that helped the viewers. If she got closure herself, well, that was just a bonus.

Chapter Twenty-Eight

"Go back to bed," Zennie said with a laugh as she drove through the quiet streets of Burbank, just after six in the morning. She adjusted the volume on her speakers so she could hear the Bluetooth call more clearly. "Clark, it's Saturday. Why are you even awake?"

"You're pregnant and Ali has a broken arm. That's going to limit the workforce."

"It's an estate sale, not ditch digging. And me being pregnant doesn't change anything. I'm on my feet all day at work, so I'm used to it."

"You're on your feet all day at work, so you should stay off your feet on the weekends. I want to come help."

"We discussed this at dinner."

"Yes, we did and you told me no. I'm pushing back."

Since getting back in touch with her and offering friendship, Clark had been around a lot more than she would have expected.

Even more surprising, she kind of liked it. He was steady and calm. Given her current emotional state, those were both qualities she needed right now. True to his word, he hadn't pressured her about anything. They were hanging out—nothing more.

"Fine," she said. "Come by around ten and you can man the cash register while I take a thirty-minute break, but then you have to leave."

"Great. See you at ten. Want me to bring doughnuts?"

She thought about the whole wheat waffle barely covered by nut butter and organic berries she'd had for breakfast and the gross protein shake she'd brought with her.

"I would kill for a maple bar," she whispered. "But you can't tell."

"Your secrets are safe with me. See you soon."

Zennie was still smiling when she pulled onto her mother's street. She parked down several houses to give the shoppers the prime spots, grabbed her smoothie and a twenty-ounce BPA-free water bottle Bernie had given her, then walked the quarter block to her mom's house.

Lights were on and the garage door was open. Zennie spotted Ali sorting contents of boxes onto tables while Finola rolled out racks of clothes. Both sisters smiled at her.

"What time did you get here?" Zennie asked, hugging Ali, then examining her cast.

"I was here at six," Ali told her with a smug smile. "I'm better than you."

"I guess so. Let me put all my stuff in the refrigerator, then I'll be out to help."

"You can help me carry the tables," Finola said, then wrinkled her nose. "Can you help me carry the tables?"

Zennie looked at the folding tables stacked in the garage. "They weigh like ten pounds each. Yes, I can manage that."

She walked into the house and stored her things. Her mother came into the kitchen just as she was heading back to the garage.

"Good," Mary Jo said. "You're here. I want to give you something before the estate sale starts."

"Sure." Zennie kept her tone upbeat, even as she imagined old posters that were supposed to be donated, or a membership to Match.com. But instead, her mother handed her a box.

Zennie opened it and saw it was filled with baby clothes. There were onesies and dresses with matching frilly hats, tiny shoes and a beautiful crocheted blanket done in different shades of pink.

Her mother watched her. "Those were yours. I rescued them from the sale because, well, I thought you might want them. For the baby."

Zennie didn't know what to say. "Mom, I'm not—"

"Keeping the baby. Yes, I've accepted I'm never having grandchildren. Finola's getting a divorce and you're having a baby for someone else. Ali's with Daniel now, so maybe they'll get busy, but with my luck, I just don't know." She glared at Zennie. "You girls are not easy. First Ali and Glen break up, then Finola and Nigel. You refuse to commit to a man. God forbid you should fall in love, but have a baby for a friend? Sure. Why not?"

Zennie impulsively hugged her mother. "I love you, Mom. I'm sorry I'm making things hard for you. That was never my goal."

Her mother hung on tight for a second. "Yes, well, that's too bad, isn't it?"

Zennie touched the baby clothes. "Thank you for these. I'm sure Bernie will love them."

"I don't care if she does or not. I'm doing it for you. To say that while I'll never understand, I'm your mother and I love you, too."

"Good. Now we should probably go supervise what's going on."

Zennie and her mom went out into the garage. They spent

the next ninety minutes getting the estate sale set up, and the first shoppers arrived at seven forty-five.

Two cranky-looking old guys blew through wanting to look at jewelry. When they found out that it was all costume, they left.

"As if I would sell my good things like this," Mary Jo fumed. "How ridiculous. I took every valuable piece of jewelry to the bank last week to store in my safe-deposit box. I'm not an idiot."

"Mom, you should probably go inside," Finola told her. "That way you can make sure no one goes where they shouldn't or takes anything."

The big pieces of furniture were in the house, along with the displays of Hollywood memorabilia.

"Good idea. People are vultures. All of them."

When she'd left, Ali grinned. "So she wants to sell her stuff, but she resents anyone who wants to buy it?"

"Don't look for logic," Zennie told her. "She means well, though."

"She does."

That was the last chance they got to talk for a while. More customers arrived and began looking through things. The furniture went quickly. By the time Clark arrived with doughnuts, the dining room table and hutch were being loaded into the back of a small box truck and two women were arguing over the living room furniture.

Zennie found herself oddly happy to see the curly-haired man in glasses and even as she told herself it was more about the doughnuts than him, she knew she was lying. This Clark who didn't ask for much and was just a friend was way more to her liking than the one who wanted to date her. Although if truth be told, she wouldn't object to the occasional kiss or two, which was really strange considering how she hadn't been upset when they'd broken up before.

But there was no time to think about that. They barely had time to finish their doughnuts and for her to explain to her sisters that while she and Clark weren't back together, they were friends, before more people arrived, wanting to look through everything.

The clothes went quickly, as did the toys. The artwork sold fast, but the kitchen stuff just sat there. Clark stuck around, helping carry items to people's cars. Around eleven, a sleek two-seater Mercedes convertible pulled up in front of the house and a handsome older man got out.

"I saw online you had some Hollywood memorabilia," he said to Zennie. "Can you point me in that direction?"

She stared at the guy, frantically trying to place him. "It's inside." She pointed to the open front door. "My mom's in there. She can show you."

Finola walked up to them. "You're Parker Crane."

That's *who he is,* Zennie thought. He'd been in a lot of movies when he'd been younger and now he had a successful detective series on TV.

"I am." Parker smiled. "I keep an eye out for sales like this. I'm always curious what fans have collected. Sometimes they have things I don't."

Finola opened her mouth, then closed it. "My mom's not a fan. What I mean is you, um, you knew her. After my father died." She shook her head. "Sorry. I'm not sure why this is hard to say. My mother is Mary Jo Schmitt now but you knew her as Mary Jo Corrado."

Parker's eyes widened and he swung his head toward the house. "Of course I remember her. She and I... Well, you girls don't want to hear about that. I always regretted how things ended. Is she, ah, married?"

Finola grinned. "Divorced. Why don't you go inside and talk to her?"

Parker nodded and slowly approached the house. Zennie pulled Finola into the garage and motioned for Ali to join them.

"Mom had an affair with Parker Crane?" Zennie asked. "When, and how do you know this?"

"What?" Ali yelped. "Are you serious?"

"It was before she married Dad," Finola said. "I just found out a few weeks ago when we were going through boxes. She has a bunch of stuff he gave her. Apparently it was hot and heavy and he just walked out on her."

"So he's a dick," Ali said firmly.

"It was a long time ago." Finola glanced toward the house. "He said he had regrets and it's been a long time. This could be interesting."

"So we don't hate him?" Ali asked. "Doesn't it seem like we should hate him?"

Zennie hugged her baby sister. "Times are changing. We're going to have to change with them."

Monday morning Ali was wrestling with the fact that her mother had gone off for lunch with Parker in the middle of the sale and had not returned. Around three she'd texted that they should shut down the estate sale at four and close up the house. Oh, and anything that didn't sell could just be donated.

The sisters had done as she'd asked. Daniel had come by with his truck. He and Clark had loaded the remaining items into the back of it, then Daniel and Ali had taken it to a donation center.

By noon on Sunday, all three sisters were texting each other to see if anyone knew where their mother was. Mary Jo had finally responded to their increasingly frantic texts with a brief, I'm at Parker's, I'm fine. You all need to get a life. And that was that.

Ali told herself that of course she wanted her mother to be happy. It was just all so strange and a little uncomfortable to think that her mother would have sex with some guy she hadn't seen in decades. When she'd said that to Daniel, he'd pointed out that at least she had a little ammunition the next time her mother got judgy about her life.

Ali spent Monday morning moving into Paul's office. The owner of the company had surprised her with new furniture and carpeting, which was unexpected and nice. Paul would stay on as a consultant for a month, to make for a smooth transition. With the new responsibilities came a nice raise. Ali had run the numbers and figured she would be out of debt in six months. After that she could start saving and figuring out what she wanted to do about her living situation.

Daniel was a big piece of that. While he hadn't said the *L* word again, she thought about it a lot. She wanted to say it back to him, but before that, she wanted to be sure. Given what had happened with Glen, she wanted to be super, super sure. Her feelings for Daniel were totally different and they got along so much better, but was that—

"Hello, Ali."

She looked up and saw Glen standing in the entrance to her office, as if thinking about him had conjured him.

"What are you doing here?"

"I wanted to talk to you."

Well, I don't want to talk to you. Words that were both petulant and immature, she told herself.

She motioned for him to take a seat, then carefully closed the office door before returning to her chair.

"What's up?" she asked.

He looked around. "This is new."

"The promotion? It is, but it's all good. I'm excited about the opportunity."

He looked the same as always. Funny how she now saw him as a lesser version of Daniel. Lighter hair, lighter skin, thicker through the middle. She'd never cared about appearances, but having spent time with Daniel... Well, it was hard to think about going back.

He pushed up his glasses. "I went by your apartment over the weekend. You don't live there anymore." His tone was faintly accusing, as if she'd done something wrong.

"Of course I don't live there. I gave notice because I was going to move in with you, remember? I'd already sold half my furniture when you dumped me. When I tried to get my apartment back, I couldn't because they'd upped the rent to the point where I couldn't afford it *and* they'd already leased it out to someone else. So I was stuck with nowhere to live."

She paused for breath and to dial down the energy. She wasn't mad at Glen, exactly—it was more that he simply didn't seem to get all he'd done to her.

"You dumped me without warning," she said, her voice more calm. "You didn't have the decency to tell me yourself or give me an explanation. To this day, I don't know why you ended things. You didn't handle one single detail. Instead you left everything to me. I had to do it all, Glen. I had to make the calls and let our friends know and give away a wedding gown that wasn't returnable. I did everything because you just disappeared."

He shifted in his seat. "You don't have to make it sound so awful."

She was just about to shriek at him, then told herself it didn't matter. Getting angry was too much energy and honestly, she didn't care. Not anymore.

"It was awful," she told him. "All of it, but that's not why you're here. Tell me what you want." *So then I can ask you to leave*, she thought to herself.

"You have a new apartment?"

The question was so at odds with what she'd been thinking, it took her a second to figure out what he was asking. "What? No. I'm living with Daniel."

She realized a second too late she should have phrased that differently, but oh, well.

"What? With Daniel?" His face flushed. "I knew it. He always had a thing for you. He wouldn't admit it, but I could tell.

I should have guessed he would do this. He's so damned sanctimonious all the time while he was planning on stealing you away from me. That bastard."

"Hey," she said, her voice icy. "Stop it. There was no stealing. I'm not a vase on a shelf to be stolen. As for what happened, you ended our engagement and didn't have the balls to tell me to my face. Daniel was a good friend. He helped cancel the wedding—something you couldn't be bothered to do."

"I'll bet."

She had figured out Glen was a jerk, but until this exact minute, she'd never realized how jerky. She'd been lucky that he dumped her. Lucky to get out in time.

While Glen got worse the more she learned about him, Daniel was the complete opposite. He was kind and thoughtful and sexy and funny and smart. When she was around him, she felt good about herself. They brought out the best in each other. He was... He was...

Ali half rose out of her seat, then sank back down. Holy crap, she was in love with him. Completely in love with Daniel.

"What?" Glen asked.

She smiled. "Nothing." No way she was telling jerk Glen before she told Daniel. "You never said why you were here. It can't be about the ring. I gave that back to your mother."

"She told me. It's not about the ring." He leaned toward her. "I thought we could try again."

Words genuinely failed her. She stared at him and could not make a sound, which apparently he took as a positive sign.

"Ali, I know this has been hard and I had some part in it. I felt really trapped and I wasn't sure we were right for each other. You were always so meek and you did everything I wanted."

"What a horrible thing to have to deal with," she said, her voice returning.

He ignored the sarcasm. "But this new version of you, it's very powerful. You yelled at me and you have direction and I like who you are now. I miss you. I miss us. We were good to-gether. We can be again."

She really should remember to keep a vase in her office. A big one she didn't care about so she could have it to throw at Glen's head.

"No," she said, proud of how calm she sounded. "No. I am not in love with you. I'm ashamed to say, I'm not sure I ever was. We were not good together, neither of us was happy. I don't want to be with you. I'm with Daniel and I want to stay with Daniel. You were wrong to break up with me the way you did, but right to end things. It's over, Glen. We are finished."

His shoulders slumped. "You don't mean that."

"I do. You're not interested in me anymore. You're just upset I'm with Daniel."

He stood. "You're making a mistake. He's never going to love you the way I did."

She wanted to say she didn't need his kind of love in her life, but then remembered if all went well, Glen would be her brother-in-law, so best to keep things civil.

"Goodbye, Glen."

He started to say something, then shook his head and walked out. Ali stayed in her chair, making sure she felt okay, then pushed all thoughts of Glen from her mind and went back to work.

Chapter Twenty-Nine

Finola double-checked her appearance in the well-lit mirror in her temporary dressing room. Every hair was in place, the makeup was understated and the sleeveless dress had been tailored to fit her perfectly. She touched the bouquet of flowers Zennie and Ali had sent and smiled at the spray of balloons from Rochelle and the team back in LA. She was really doing this. In less than thirty minutes, she would be live on a national show.

She sat in her chair and closed her eyes before inhaling for a count of four. She held her breath as she counted to eight, then exhaled slowly.

When her breathing exercises were done, she walked out of the dressing room and found the sound guy to help her feed the microphone under the front of her dress and around to the rear of the armhole before he clipped the pack on the back of her belt. One of the producers, a young, thin guy in his early thirties, rushed over.

"You ready?" he asked, sounding anxious.

"It's going to be fine."

"If you say so. I wouldn't have picked this topic in a million years, but it's too late to change your mind now."

She smiled. "Don't worry. I've got this."

Finola walked onto the set and faced the cameras. There were three and they were remotely controlled, which made it seem as if they were alive and moving however they wanted. She told herself not to be distracted, that she was going to be great, then smiled as she was given the count.

"Five, four, three—"

The two and one were done silently, then the red light went on.

"Good morning. I'm Finola Corrado, filling in this week, and welcome to our ten o'clock hour." She focused on staying relaxed and reading from the teleprompter.

"In recent months, as many of you know, my personal life was in the news. My husband had an affair with a famous singer and I found myself being part of the story instead of reporting the story. This was a change for me, and not a very fun one."

She paused to flash a rueful smile. "I was scared, I was angry and I was hurt. I spent a lot of time feeling sorry for myself and maybe drinking a little too much wine. But then, as the wounds stopped bleeding quite so much, I started thinking. About my marriage and the other relationships in my life, about what it takes to make another person happy while staying true to ourselves."

She paused. "If you're hoping for salacious details about my personal life this week, I'm afraid you're going to be disappointed. But what I would like to talk about instead is what makes a good marriage and how marriages go wrong. Unless there's abuse, no relationship failure is just one person's fault. Even mine. I might not have cheated, but I wasn't the wife I could have been. I'm hoping the guests I've invited to join us will be informative and interesting and that we're all going to learn something. So let's get started."

She turned toward the sofa and chairs as her first guest walked out.

The hour passed in a blur. Finola kept to her notes when she could, but there were a couple of times everyone got off on a tangent. She went with the conversation, then returned them all to the point of the segment. Without audience feedback, she had no idea how the show was being received, but she told herself she knew what she was doing and to trust her gut. When the camera light went off at four minutes to the top of the hour, she felt as if she'd run five marathons.

The skinny producer was back. He stared at her in disbelief.

"That was incredible. Really honest and raw without being maudlin. The psychologist was perfect. I don't, as a rule, like shrinks, but she knew her stuff. If the other shows are this good, you've got a winning series, Finola."

"Thank you."

She walked back to her temporary dressing room. People congratulated her, but as she didn't know who they were the praise wasn't all that meaningful. She missed her regular crew where she knew what they were thinking by the looks on their faces.

When she picked up her phone, she saw dozens of texts. She scrolled through them until she found one from Rochelle.

You kicked ass, lady! I'm incredibly proud of you and I had nothing to do with it. LOL. Miss you.

There were warm congratulations from her sisters and an unexpected text from Nigel.

Thanks for not making me the asshole.

Finola changed into jeans and a T-shirt. She planned to walk around the city for a couple of hours before returning to her hotel room to put the final touches on tomorrow's show. The guests were confirmed, so all she had to do was review her notes.

She slipped on sunglasses and made her way outside. No one had any idea who she was and if they did, they didn't care. She blended in with the pedestrians, heading north, toward the Peninsula Hotel.

The midday air was warming up rapidly. By five it would be close to eighty. The sky was blue and the hustle and bustle oddly comforting.

She'd come a long way, she thought. She'd been reduced to emotional rubble and she'd built herself back up, stronger this time. On the way, she'd lost her marriage and her innocence, but she'd learned a lot and she liked to think she was a better person for it. If only there had been an easier way. If only she could have read a self-help book instead. Except life didn't work that way. Most people avoided the difficult and painful until it was forced upon them. Most people learned by going through the trial, not just reading about it. Most people didn't realize the cost until it was too late.

Zennie told herself there was no reason to be nervous. Friends were allowed on the Sunday morning runs and she'd invited a friend. So while she hadn't technically violated the rules, she still felt guilty.

Cassie arrived at the Woodley Park/Lake Balboa loop parking lot right after her.

"Hey," Cassie called as she got out of her car. "I'm glad we're meeting early. It's going to get hot today and you know I hate sweating. How are you feeling?"

"Good." Zennie hugged her. "The pregnancy thing might be getting easier."

"I'm happy to hear that. Now what's up?"

"What do you mean?"

Cassie rolled her eyes. "You're obviously hiding something. It's not gonna be that you're pregnant, so what is it?"

"I invited Clark to join us."

DeeDee drove up just then, giving Zennie a thirty-second reprieve that lasted until Cassie yelled, "Zennie invited a boy."

"And in your delicate condition," DeeDee said with a laugh. "Is this a new boy or an old boy?"

"That is the strangest question."

"An old boy." Cassie grinned. "Cla-ark." She drew the name out in a singsong tone.

"The zoo guy? He broke up with you a couple of months ago, didn't he?"

"Note to self," Zennie muttered. "Say less to you two. Yes, we broke up, then he got in touch with me and suggested we hang out as friends. So we are. I'm also friends with C.J. and you never say anything about her."

"You hanging out with a woman isn't as interesting," DeeDee said. "So is it serious?"

"We're just friends."

Cassie and DeeDee exchanged a look. "If you say so," Cassie said as Clark pulled up.

"Be nice," Zennie told her girlfriends. "Please, I beg you. Don't say anything..."

"Embarrassing?" Cassie asked. "Or mention the fact that, while you and your two sisters all got dumped the same weekend, you're the only one back together with the guy?"

Zennie groaned. "Yes, saying that would be a problem."

Cassie and DeeDee shared a high five.

Zennie knew that however much they teased her, they wouldn't embarrass her. They cared about her and would be there for her. Unlike Gina who had disappeared from her life. And although Zennie didn't like to think about it, while her mother had come around, her father hadn't. Oh, he'd said all the right things, but things between them were different.

The rejection hurt her, but she knew there was nothing to do about it. She'd confronted him and told him what she thought. What he did with that was up to him. Funny how getting pregnant had helped her see who she could trust and who she couldn't.

Clark joined them, looking especially cute in shorts and a T-shirt. Zennie introduced him and they all shook hands.

"Just so we're clear," he said cheerfully, "I expect you all to leave me in the dust and I'm okay with that. Strong women don't intimidate me."

"Oooh, good answer," Cassie said. "But we're not really running that fast these days. Someone is in a delicate condition. We make allowances because we love her."

Zennie knew her friend was just being herself, but somehow the words caught her off guard with their heartfelt support. She fought against tears, telling herself the stupid hormones would not control her life.

"Let's get this over with," DeeDee said. "Because when we're done here, I want to go to The Cheesecake Factory. They have a Sunday brunch and I want that giant Belgian waffle they have. And a mimosa."

"When you go, you go big," Cassie said.

"I can't help it. That's just who I am."

"Shall we?"

Zennie jogged to the path, then set the slow warm-up pace. They quickly sorted themselves into two pairs of two, with Clark next to her.

"This is nice," he said. "Thanks for asking me."

"You're welcome."

"We should probably get all our talking done now because in about fifteen minutes I'm going to be out of breath."

She smiled. "You'll do fine."

He glanced at her and grinned. "I'm doing my best, Zennie."

He was, she thought happily. And so far, it was really good.

★ ★ ★

Ali loved Daniel's kitchen. It was big, there was tons of counter space and while she'd never had real feelings for a range before, she was pretty sure she could do three full minutes on why this Viking range was amazing.

She happily unpacked the groceries she'd picked up on her way home from work. That night she was going to get wild and try chicken marsala. The recipe she'd found online looked easy enough. She would serve it with mashed potatoes and the fresh green beans she'd bought.

Since she and Daniel had taken things to the next level, she'd found herself wanting to cook more. Nesting, she assumed. Staking out her place in their couplehood by doing kitchen things. It was old-fashioned and traditional and she honestly couldn't help herself. Besides, cooking dinner made her happy.

She'd chosen a nice bottle of wine and had even picked up some frosted cookies for dessert. Tonight was going to be special, she thought with a smile. Tonight, over chicken marsala and mashed potatoes, she was going to tell Daniel she loved him.

It was time, or possibly past time. She'd suspected her feelings for a while, but had been waiting to be sure. Her confrontation with Glen had made everything clear. Daniel was the right guy and she loved him and she wanted him to know.

After collecting everything she would need, she pounded the chicken breasts flat, then went to work on peeling the potatoes, her cast and broken arm barely slowing her down. She'd just finished that when Daniel got home.

She heard the sound of the garage door and had to laugh as her stomach immediately started fluttering. What that man did to her. She washed her hands and hurried to meet him, only to come to a stop when she saw his serious expression.

"What?" she asked, in the hallway by the kitchen. "What happened?"

When he didn't answer right away, she knew something was

wrong. She could see it in the tense set of his mouth and the way his shoulders were tight.

"Daniel, you're scaring me."

"I don't think we should see each other anymore."

The blunt words hit her like a two-by-four, knocking the air out of her and nearly sending her to her knees. She had to grab the wall to stay on her feet.

"What?"

He looked away. "Glen came by to see me this afternoon. He said he made a mistake when he ended things with you. He said he was sorry and that he wanted another chance with you." He returned his attention to her, his gaze stricken. "He's still in love with you."

"He's not."

"Ali, I saw him, I talked to him. He's broken. You two were together a long time. You were going to get married. You have a history with him and—"

Disbelief and anger and pain battled for dominance. "No," she said loudly. "No. Stop talking. Just stop."

She sucked in air as she tried to make sense of everything. She'd just seen Glen. Yes, he'd talked about them getting back together, but he hadn't been serious. He didn't like that she was with Daniel.

She snapped up her head. "This is not what you think. Glen is playing both of us. He came to see me, as well, and I made it incredibly clear that he and I are done. He was a mistake and while I'm willing to be polite for your sake, in a perfect world I would never see him again."

She moved toward him, stopping when they were only a couple of feet apart.

"Daniel, I swear, I can't decide if you're the nicest guy on the planet or a complete moron. You know I don't care about him. You've been amazing to me. You've been there for me, you've been a friend and a lover and you said you were in love with me. Wasn't any of that real?"

"Of course it was real," he said with a growl. "I gave you all I have."

"Then why would you let me go?"

"Because I want you to be happy."

"But I'm happy with you. We're happy together. I'm cooking you chicken marsala so that I can—" Realization dawned. He didn't know. She'd never said the words back and he didn't know. While he could hope for the best, he could very well be thinking she assumed he was her rebound guy.

"Oh, Daniel, I'm sorry." She closed the distance between them and took his hands in hers. "I was making dinner because I wanted tonight to be special when I told you I loved you."

She stared into his dark eyes. "I love you. I waited to say it because I wanted to be sure. Because Glen was such a mistake. I love you, Daniel. I think we're great together but not if you won't fight for me. Not if you're willing to just walk away."

"I would only walk away if that was what you wanted."

He hauled her against him and held her so tight, her ribs hurt.

"I thought you weren't sure," he admitted, his voice shaking. "I've loved you for nearly two years, but this is all new to you. I wanted to give you time and space. I was okay with you not saying anything back until today when Glen showed up. He made it sound like you wanted to get back together with him."

She raised herself up on tiptoe and kissed him. "Never. Never, never, never. I swear. I love you, Daniel."

He kissed her back, stealing her breath in the best way possible.

"I love you," she repeated between kisses.

"I love you, too."

After a few minutes, they managed to catch their breath. He brushed the hair off her face.

"You're cooking?"

"Yes, and I bought wine and dessert and the whole thing. It was going to be very romantic."

"It still can be."

She smiled. "I was hoping you'd say that."

They went into the kitchen where he admired everything she'd bought, then excused himself to wash up. When she was alone, Ali took a second to point out to herself that honesty was always the best policy and that in the future she would say what she was thinking. Daniel could take it.

She'd just put the chicken in the frying pan when Daniel returned.

"Ready for me to set the table?" he asked.

"That would be nice."

He got out plates and flatware, then opened the wine. When it was time, he mashed the potatoes while she put everything else into serving pieces. It was only when they carried everything into the dining room that she saw the small blue Tiffany ring box sitting by her place setting.

The platter of chicken marsala started to slip from her hands.

"We can't have that," he said, grabbing it from her and putting down.

Ali stared from the box to him and back. "You, ah, bought me a necklace?"

He led her over to her chair. Once she was seated, he knelt in front of her and took her hands in his.

"Ali, I love you. I'm a traditional kind of guy. I want a wife and kids and a dog and a house." He smiled. "And a kitten."

Her heart beat so fast, it sounded like hummingbird wings. "You already have a house."

"I do and it's a nice one. I hope you like it."

"Yes. A lot."

His gaze locked with hers. "I want to spend the rest of my life making you happy. I want us to grow old together. Ali, will you marry me?"

Yes. Yes! Only… "What about your parents? It's going to be weird. You have to admit it will be weird."

"They know and they're fine with it. They liked you before and are happy to have you in the family. Speaking of parents, I talked to your mom. She gave me her blessing."

"She's sleeping with Parker Crane."

"The guy on TV?"

"That's the one. I can't explain it but there it is. Apparently the affair is quite torrid. I don't like to think about it."

"Good. Any other concerns?"

"Glen will make comments."

Daniel's grin was smug. "Let him. I got the girl. Marry me, Ali. I will spend the rest of my life loving you."

She flung her arms around him. "Yes, Daniel. Happily. For always." Because this time was right.

He opened the box and showed her a diamond solitaire the size of a bus. She nearly fell off the chair.

"No," she whispered, even as she slid the ring on her finger. "Oh, wow. Just wow. It's stunning."

"So are you."

He kissed her then, and kissing turned to other things, and it was a very long time before they ever got around to dinner.

Chapter Thirty

The Encino house sold quickly. Finola and Nigel weren't asking for the moon, pricewise, and the place was in excellent condition. The new buyers were a young family—she was a TV writer and he was a stay-at-home dad. They bought most of the furniture and what they didn't want, Nigel took.

Finola left the escrow office after signing the papers and drove directly to the house to look around one last time. She pulled into her spot in the garage and then walked inside.

She felt strange looking at familiar sofas and the dining room set, knowing they weren't going to be hers anymore. All the personal items were gone. She and Nigel had split up the artwork. She'd packed up her pictures and a few bits of memorabilia and put them in a small storage unit in Burbank.

She'd sorted through her clothes and had culled those down to the very basics. She would be buying a new wardrobe once she was settled in New York. The rest of her clothes and shoes and accessories, she'd donated to a women's shelter.

She walked into what had been her office and looked around. The desk was still there, but everything else was gone. She studied the empty places on the wall, the view of the pool and the small cracks from the last earthquake.

She pressed her hand against the drywall, as if she could feel the cracks or somehow mend them. Little ones were okay but if they got too big, if they expanded, there was trouble. That was what had happened to her and Nigel, she thought sadly. Small cracks had led to something much worse. She'd been so busy living her life, she hadn't noticed and now it was all gone—the house, her marriage, the very way she had defined herself.

The job in New York had come through. She'd rented a midtown studio apartment for a ridiculous amount of money but it had a huge walk-in closet and an in-unit washer-dryer. Both a rarity in Manhattan. She'd negotiated keeping some of her LA staff and had lured Rochelle away from her late-night gig. Associate producer on a national show was a big deal and Finola knew they would make a good team.

She went upstairs to the master bedroom. The bed was gone, but the dresser and nightstands remained. She closed her eyes, remembering how things had been with Nigel. How they'd laughed and talked and made love in this room. She thought about how she'd assumed that by now she would be five or six months pregnant. She'd expected her life to change, and it had— just not in the direction she'd hoped. She'd lost her husband and her marriage. Maybe they were never going to be forever, but she hadn't known.

She gave in to the threatening tears, crying for what had been and how everything was different now. She was excited about the opportunity in New York and sad about leaving her family. They would stay in touch, of course. Ironically, because of all she'd been through, she'd grown closer to her sisters than ever. As for Mary Jo—well, she'd given up on moving into a bungalow by the beach. Instead she was living the dream in Parker's

Beverly Hills estate. They were wildly in love and the Burbank house had pretty much been abandoned. Ali and Zennie were planning on getting it listed in the next couple of weeks.

Life was all about change, she thought ruefully. Whether we wanted it or not, things happened. She brushed the tears from her face. She'd been forced to grow as a person. The process had sucked, but she hoped she was better than she had been. Less selfish, more aware of the people she loved. Maybe those life lessons would make her a better journalist, but even if they didn't, she wanted to continue to strive to be a better person.

She went downstairs and into the garage, then headed toward Burbank. She was donating her car to the girls' group she'd been reluctant to fully support with anything other than the occasional visit. Honestly, giving them the value of the car was the least she could do. She would stay with Ali and Daniel tonight, then they would take her to the airport in the morning and she would fly to New York to start her new life.

A better life, she promised herself. It had to be.

Zennie had decided to deal with her pregnancy by telling herself she was simply a vessel. Whatever happened, her vessel self would be fine. She would eventually return to the vessel she had been before and if, in the meantime, she was forced to eat disgustingly healthy food and give up things she loved and grow a basketball, well, it was for the greater good.

The fact that the hormones had died down as promised helped a lot. Her breasts hurt less and she was starting to feel a lot more normal. Maybe the second trimester would be better than the first, she thought as she walked into Dr. McQueen's waiting area.

Today was her three-month checkup. Bernie and Hayes would join her to hear the baby's heartbeat for the first time and see the ultrasound. It was too early to determine gender, but at least they would know that everything was fine.

Zennie told the receptionist she was there, then checked her phone again. The only cloud on the horizon, so to speak, was the fact that she hadn't heard from Bernie all morning. They'd texted last night and Bernie had been wild with excitement, but this morning, there hadn't been a word.

She texted again, saying she was already checked in and waiting for her appointment. There was no response. The nurse called her in. Zennie explained the situation and asked if she could wait for a bit.

"Sure," the other woman told her. "But if you give up your appointment, we'll have to fit you in and that might take a bit."

It was Friday so Zennie had the day off. "I can wait. I really want them here."

Twenty agonizing minutes went by. Zennie texted Bernie again, then tried to call Hayes. There was no answer. Panic started to set in. What if something had happened to them? What if there had been an accident or a house fire? What if they had changed their minds about the baby and didn't know how to tell her?

She told herself to stay calm, but once the panic was established, it would not be denied. She felt herself starting to hyperventilate. How could this be happening?

She walked out into the hallway so she could pace without disturbing the other clients. She tried calling Cassie and DeeDee, but they were both on shift and couldn't take a personal call. Finally she texted Clark.

I'm having my ultrasound. It's three months and a big deal, but Bernie's not here and she's not answering her texts and I can't get Hayes on the phone.

It took only a couple of seconds for the little dots to appear on the screen.

Are you going to keep your appointment?

Yes. Even if they're not here, I need to know the baby's okay.

Then I'll be there in thirty minutes. If they show up in the meantime, let me know and I'll go back to work. If not, I'll be a friend.
Ah, there's nothing scary to see, is there?

Despite everything, that last question made her smile. Nothing scary, I promise. Just the heartbeat and an ultrasound.

Cool. Be there soon.

She continued to pace and worry and try not to imagine the
worst, although at this point she wasn't sure which was more
upsetting—that Bernie and Hayes had been in a traffic accident
or that they'd changed their mind about the baby.

Just when she thought she was going to have to go into the
appointment by herself, the elevator opened and Clark stepped
out. Zennie ran to him, her arms outstretched.

"They're still not here. I don't know what's going on, but it
has to be bad. What am I going to do? My best friend is dead
and I'm pregnant. I know it sounds horrible, but I wasn't looking
to have a baby. I can't do this. I can't. I know everyone thinks
I'm strong, but I'm not."

Clark held her until she finished talking, then put his hands
on her shoulders and stared into her eyes.

"There is a perfectly logical explanation for what has happened. I don't know what it is, but it's something. We will find
out and we will deal. You're not going to have the baby on your
own. All the legal issues were covered in the paperwork."

"You don't know that," she said frantically. "I might want
kids someday but I'm not sure and definitely not like this. Not
now. Not with Hayes."

"Zennie, calm down. Breathe. It's going to be fine."

"You don't know that," she repeated.

"I do. Whatever happens, we'll get through it. I meant what I said before. We're friends and you can count on me. How long have you been waiting?"

"Nearly an hour."

"Let's go inside and get to the procedures, then we'll manage the rest, okay?"

She nodded, still unable to catch her breath. "I don't understand."

"I know. It's okay. Whatever is happening, you have lots of support. If it's bad, DeeDee and Cassie will be with you as soon as they're off work. You have your sisters and your mom."

"Thank you," she said. "I'm sorry to be such a mess."

"You're fine. Now let's go in and torture me with whatever this is."

She managed a smile and led the way back into the waiting area.

It took another forty minutes for her to be called. Clark waited outside while she put on a gown and robe, then stretched out on the table for the ultrasound. When the technician let him in, Bernie raced in with him and hovered by Zennie's side.

"I'm sorry," her friend said, the right side of her face swollen and puffy. "I'm so sorry. I woke up in horrible pain and went to the ER this morning. They sent me to my dentist where I had to have an emergency root canal. It took forever and they knocked me out with something and I never thought to text because I didn't think it would take four *hours*." Bernie grabbed her hand. "And Hayes is in court so he couldn't contact you but he's on his way and oh, Zennie, I'm sorry. I hope we didn't scare you."

The relief was sweet. Zennie held on to Bernie's hand. "I'm okay," she said. "I was worried that something had happened." She glanced over her friend's shoulder to see Clark giving her an "I told you so" smile. She smiled back.

Hayes walked in and hurried over.

"Everyone okay?" he asked. "Sorry I got stuck in court. Bernie, you look awful."

"I feel awful. They drugged me. I had to Uber over, so we'll need to get my car later, but none of that matters." She squeezed Zennie's hand again. "Let's see our baby."

"We'll do the heartbeat first," the technician said, pulling a container of gel out of a warming oven.

Zennie held out her free hand to Clark, so he could join them. Bernie looked between the two of them, but didn't say anything. Later Zennie would tell her about the meltdown and they would all laugh, but for now, she was grateful for the support.

"Here we go," the technician said.

For what felt like the longest time, there was nothing. Zennie knew that finding the heartbeat this early could take some doing. It all depended on the position of the baby in her body and the—

The sound of tiny galloping horses filled the room. Bernie cried out and clutched Hayes. Clark squeezed Zennie's hand.

"Let me get Dr. McQueen," the tech said with a smile. "She'll want to count the beats."

Zennie knew that one hundred and twenty to one hundred and sixty beats per minute was normal. The beats were strong and regular and there really was a person growing inside of her.

"Thank you," Bernie said, with a shaky smile. "Oh, Zennie, thank you for everything."

"Of course. You're my friend."

"And you're a miracle."

"I've never been a miracle before," Zennie admitted, telling herself to remember this moment for when it got hard. Because this made it all worthwhile.

Chapter Thirty-One

Six months later…

Ali studied the brochure from the Four Seasons in the Bahamas. It was a beautiful resort with every possible amenity. She didn't dare imagine the price, but it was tempting.

"Are you sure?"

Daniel looked up from his desk. They were in his home office on a lazy Saturday morning, debating what to do after Mary Jo and Parker's destination wedding on Valentine's Day. The happy couple was flying everyone to Jamaica for the ceremony at one of those all-inclusive resorts. The timing worked out—Zennie would be recovered from having Bernie's baby and Finola could easily fly in from New York.

"Ali, I want what you want. You know that. I love you and I want to get married, but the how is up to you. It was just a suggestion. If you don't like it, we can have a big wedding somewhere here, if you'd like. The beach or a hotel. The Ritz Carlton in Marina Del Rey is beautiful."

It was and yes, they could have a big wedding. Only she kind of felt she'd already done that. And Daniel's first marriage had started with a blowout wedding. This time she wanted something smaller. Something that felt like them.

Valentine's Day was a Friday and Parker and her mom were putting everyone up through Sunday. Daniel's idea was to fly from Jamaica to the Bahamas and get married there. Just the two of them.

Ali had been in touch with the resort's wedding planner and the process was fairly simple. A couple could apply for a wedding license after being on the island twenty-four hours and get married one day later. If she and Daniel arrived Sunday morning, they could apply Monday afternoon and get married on Wednesday. The wedding planner had told them that a midweek wedding would be available with no problem. One of the gorgeous beachfront suites was available for the week. The wedding planner would handle all the details, including providing the required two witnesses. Easy peasy.

There were a lot of advantages to eloping, she thought. It spared everyone wedding awkwardness. While Glen had come around and was even dating someone else, Ali didn't relish the thought of walking down the aisle only to see him standing next to Daniel. Not having his brother as best man was an option, but also a difficult decision. Tying the knot in the Bahamas seemed like the perfect solution.

"Let's do it," she said.

He grinned. "You sure?"

"I am."

"All right. Let's make our reservations. I'm getting married!"

His excitement was gratifying. Every day, Daniel made it clear how much he loved her. They were happy and looking forward to their future together. Ali was thinking that she just might talk to Daniel about her going off birth control so that they could start trying to get pregnant on their honeymoon. Wouldn't that be fun?

Her cell phone buzzed. She glanced down and read the text, then jumped to her feet.

"Zennie's in labor." She grabbed her phone. "She's been in labor all night and they're on their way to the hospital right now. We should go, too."

"By 'they' you mean Zennie and Clark?"

"Yes. Who else?"

"But they're not dating."

"They're friends."

"He practically lives there. They're together all the time." Ali didn't understand why Daniel couldn't get it. "But as friends."

"So no sex."

She smiled. "Not everyone wants it as much as you do."

"And you."

"And me," she said, standing and heading toward the garage. "Some people don't do it much at all."

"From what I hear, Parker and your mom do it all the time and they're old."

"Let's not talk about my mother. Zennie and Clark have a different kind of relationship."

"That poor guy must take five cold showers a day."

Ali climbed into the passenger side of the truck, then leaned over and kissed Daniel. "Something you never have to do."

"I know. I'm a lucky, lucky guy."

She was the lucky one, she thought as he backed out of the driveway and headed for the hospital. Finding Daniel was the best thing that had ever happened to her. She glanced at him, then smiled. Okay, it was actually the second-best thing. The first best had been finding herself.

"I. Can't. Do. This."

Zennie stared up at the ceiling and wanted to kill someone. Anyone would do. A random stranger, a member of her family. She just wanted to lash out, preferably with a baseball—

"Nooo!" she screamed as the pain ripped through her. "Dammit, somebody do something."

The delivery nurse shook her head. "You waited too long, honey. The baby's on his way and there's no time."

Zennie grabbed the side of the bed as her entire body twisted, those damned muscles she'd been so proud of betraying her now with a force that could crush a planet.

"I hate this," she screamed.

"We're not having fun, either," the nurse said calmly. "But we're not complaining."

Zennie saw Clark's lips twitch. "Do not smile at me, mister. This is all your fault."

He was undaunted by her display of temper. "You're the one who refused to go to the hospital. You said you didn't want to be one of those whiny women who showed up six days early, complaining about the pain. You said you knew best."

All of which was true, but he didn't have to say it. "I'll hate you forever," she growled.

"Tough talk, Zennie. Tough talk."

She was grateful he wasn't offended. She had no idea where her rage came from, except maybe it was her way of dealing with the pain. Holy crap, how did women survive this? It was her worst ever menstrual cramps times a million. It was so bad, she'd thrown up, but now there was only enduring the hideousness of it all.

Bernie and Hayes burst into the room. "Oh, Zennie, is it really time?"

Zennie opened her mouth to yell that it was all their fault when Clark caught her eye. He shook his head as if warning her that Bernie was her friend and she loved her and, dammit, why did it have to hurt so much?

Another contraction ripped through her. She screamed, knowing she was frightening everyone, but she couldn't help it. She'd had a relatively easy pregnancy and now she was paying for it.

"I can't," she gasped, as Bernie squeezed her hand. "I can't do this."

"Seems like a silly time to give up," Clark said calmly.

She glared at him. "You will pay for this later."

"Bite me."

That almost made her laugh, but then the pain was back, even stronger this time. Dr. McQueen walked into the room, already in her gown.

"Someone told me you're about to have a baby," she said cheerfully. "Ready, Zennie?"

"Get it out of me. Get it out now!"

Zennie lay in her hospital bed enjoying the light sedative she'd insisted on after giving birth. She still hurt because hey, she'd just passed something the weight and size of a boulder through her vagina, but it was done. She'd delivered a seven-pound, eight-ounce healthy baby boy.

"You did a good thing," her mother said, smiling at her. "I'm proud of you."

"And disappointed?" Zennie asked.

"No. Bernie's going to be a wonderful mother and she said I could visit him anytime I want. When she's more comfortable with me, I'll even babysit, because technically, he's my grandson, isn't he?"

"I never thought of that," Zennie admitted.

"Parker pointed it out. So I am getting a grandchild after all."

Mary Jo glowed—not just from the news about her grandson, but also because of her relationship with Parker. They were truly in love and while it was kind of weird, it was nice, too.

Apparently the wedding was on. Her mother had mentioned something about Valentine's Day and Jamaica. That was five weeks away. Zennie figured she would be almost back to normal by then.

Her mother left so Zennie could rest, but she was too wound up. The hospital room was filled with flowers. Finola had sent a bunch and promised to visit in a couple of weeks. Bernie and Hayes had delivered a huge bouquet. Dr. Chen had also sent an arrangement with a card that said he was literally counting the days until she was back at work.

Zennie smiled as Clark walked into the room. He had a take-out bag in one hand and carefully closed her door with the other.

"You got it?" she asked eagerly, raising her bed.

"Anything for you."

She ripped open the bag and unwrapped the cheeseburger from In-N-Out Burger. The smell was heavenly, as was the first bite. She held in a moan.

Clark put a milkshake container on her tray. "Chocolate, just like you asked."

She felt a rush of emotion and knew the stupid hormones were back. From what she'd read, they would be with her for a while, but then they would fade.

"You've been very good to me," she said as he pulled up a chair.

"I'm kind of a saint, huh?" His voice was teasing.

She thought about how he'd been her friend for the past seven months, how he'd rubbed her feet and indulged her cravings and listened to her rant as her body had changed. She thought of how she'd kept him company at the zoo when he'd been worried that one of his orangutans was sick, and all the movies they'd been to. She thought of how he'd listen to her agonize for nearly forty-eight straight hours when she couldn't decide which of two condos to buy and how he'd helped her move, basically doing all the packing, lifting and unpacking. And best, best, best of all, how he stayed with her all night when she'd been in labor and how he hadn't gotten upset when she'd screamed at him in the delivery room.

She'd never wanted a man in her life. She'd never understood the whole pairing up thing. It just seemed unnecessary. She had family and friends, and her work and her life was full. No man required. Only…only…it just didn't seem right. Not without Clark.

Somehow, when she wasn't looking, he'd become a part of her life. A part of *her*. He was always there and she liked that. She depended on him and she hoped he depended on her.

And as she was figuring all that out and eating her burger, it occurred to her that he'd never once tried to make a move on her. Not once. Not a kiss or an inference or anything.

"Are you seeing anyone?" she asked.

He stared at her. "What? You mean like dating?" He chuckled. "Zennie, I'm with you nearly every second I'm not working. When would I find the time?"

That was a relief. "What about sex?"

"Sometimes I take long showers. What do you do about sex?"

"I've been pregnant. Trust me, it hasn't been on my mind for a while."

"And before that?"

"It was never that interesting."

"I remember you saying that."

She supposed she was one of those people who simply didn't have a very strong sex drive. Although now that she thought about it, she could kind of see the appeal of that kind of intimacy. Not now—every part of her hurt—but maybe later, when she was healed.

"I always thought I wanted to be alone," she admitted. "That the pairing up thing was for everyone else."

His humor faded. "I know. You made that clear."

Was that disappointment in his voice? Did he want more? Did she?

She wiped her hands, then sucked on her milkshake. The combination of ice cream and chocolate and just plain goodness was magical.

"Can you sneak in wine later?" she asked.

"I thought we'd wait until you were discharged, then I'd bring over a nice dinner and a bottle of wine."

"I'm so getting drunk. And drinking coffee. And going in a Jacuzzi." Although she was pretty sure she couldn't do the latter until her stitches were healed, but absolutely right after that.

She looked at him, at his familiar face, and thought about how much she liked him and how she didn't want to lose him. She thought about kissing him and touching him and wondered if the problem hadn't been lack of interest but not realizing she needed the right person.

She put down the milkshake. "Clark, will you go out with me? On a date?"

Instead of answering, he stood up and moved close to the bed. Seconds later, she realized he planned on kissing her.

"I just ate raw onion," she murmured, more flustered than she would have expected.

"I genuinely don't care."

He pressed his mouth against hers. She waited, wondering what, if anything, she would feel. And then it happened. A little quiver down low. A need to put her arms around him and hang on. Desire flickered and grew and before she knew it, he'd pushed the tray aside and somehow they were both in the bed, kissing and holding on and wow, she just never wanted to let go.

When they came up for air, she was smiling.

"So yes on the date?"

"Yes."

"I can't have sex for six weeks."

Clark chuckled, then shifted so she could rest her head on

his shoulder. "You can't have intercourse for six weeks, Zennie. There's a difference."

"Really. That's an interesting notion."

"I was hoping you might say that. So about Italy. I think we should go together."

"I'd like that."

"Me, too."

★ ★ ★ ★ ★

California Girls Stuffed Scones

Treat your book club to these super-delicious scones as you settle in for a cozy chat about the book! Best when served with hot tea or coffee. Or, if you're feeling wild, serve them with fresh strawberries and a side of bacon for a decadent breakfast.

With all these almonds and raisins, these scones were inspired by my great home state of California.

Filling:
4 oz cream cheese, room temperature
2 tbsp sugar
¼ tsp vanilla

Scones:
2 cups flour
3 tbsp sugar
1 tbsp baking powder
½ tsp salt
4 tbsp very cold butter, in 16 small pieces
¾ cup heavy cream
1 egg, beaten
1 tsp almond extract
2 oz sliced almonds
½ cup raisins

Combine filling ingredients and mix well. Set aside.

Preheat the oven to 425° F. In a mixing bowl, combine the flour, sugar, baking powder and salt. Cut in the butter until the mixture looks like coarse crumbs. I did this with the flat paddle attachment of a stand mixer. You can also use a pastry blender or two knives. I don't recommend you use your fingers, as that will warm the butter too much.

Add the cream, egg and extract and mix by hand or by machine on low speed just until a dough forms, then gently fold in the almonds and raisins. Turn the dough onto a floured surface and knead lightly 5–10 times, just until the dough is smooth. Do not overwork.

Divide dough into two balls. Pat one ball into a 9-inch circle, smoothing the exterior edges. Plop half the filling in the center and spread into a circle, leaving a 1-inch border around the edge. Fold the circle in half and press the borders together. Cut into 6 wedges. Place on a baking sheet lined with parchment paper. Repeat with the other ball of dough. Bake until golden brown, about 12–14 minutes.

Questions for Discussion

*These questions contain spoilers about the story, so it's
recommended that you don't read them until after
you've finished* California Girls.

1. Finola was the first of the sisters to be dumped, and in a
    truly jolting way. What did you think of the way she reacted
    to her husband's pronouncement, then Treasure's? How do
    you think you would have reacted in those circumstances?
    Did you admire Finola's professionalism, or did you wish
    she had reacted differently?

2. What were the similarities and differences between each
    of the three sisters' breakup moments and the days that fol-
    lowed?

3. How would you describe the sisters' relationship? How did
    it evolve as the story developed?

4. At the start of the book, Zennie is annoyed that the world
    seems to insist that people pair up two by two. Do you think
    that a romantic relationship is essential to a happy life? Why
    or why not? Do you know people who are happily single?

By the end, of course, Zennie has found true love. How did you feel about that?

5. Would you ever carry a baby for someone else? Why or why not? What would you think if your daughter, sister or close friend agreed to carry someone else's baby? How would you advise her? How would you support her?

6. Ali struggled with feelings of invisibility all her life. Could you relate to that? Do you think her parents really did each have a favorite child, or did Ali misinterpret that? Explain your thoughts. How did falling in love with Daniel change her view of herself?

7. What did you think about Daniel when he first appeared in the book? Did your feelings about him change as you continued to read?

8. What surprised you about *California Girls*? What made you laugh? Which scenes brought tears to your eyes?

9. With which sister do you share the most in common? Give some examples.

10. Although Mary Jo wasn't a point-of-view character in the book, she certainly made her perspective very clear. Why do you think she wanted grandchildren so much? What did you think of the way the story resolved for her, reuniting with a lost love and getting a grandchild in a most unexpected way?

11. What lessons did you take away from this book, if any? Did it make you think about your own life in a different way? How so?

12. Susan Mallery has a long-standing promise to her readers that every book she writes will end in a satisfying way, with

the main characters in a better place at the end than they were at the beginning (and lots of surprises along the way). Unusually, in *California Girls*, that meant that Finola got a divorce. Do you think that was the right ending for Finola's story? Why or why not? What about the other sisters? Did Zennie and Ali get the endings they deserved?

#1 New York Times *bestselling author Susan Mallery delivers a heartfelt new novel about twin sisters overcoming their disastrous love lives and finding their true happiness.*

Enjoy this preview of
The Summer of Sunshine & Margot

Chapter One

Social interactions fell into two categories—easy or awkward. Easy was knowing what to say and do, and how to act. Easy was witty small talk or an elegant compliment. Awkward social interactions, on the other hand, were things like sneezing in your host's face or stepping on the cat or spilling red wine on a white carpet. Or any carpet, for that matter. Margot Baxter prided herself on knowing how to make any situation fall into the easy category. Professionally, of course. In her professional life she totally kicked butt. Personally—not so much. If she were being completely honest, she would have to admit that on most days her personal life fell firmly in the awkward category, which was why she never mixed business and pleasure and rarely bothered with pleasure at all. If it wasn't going to go well, why waste the time?

But work was different. Work was where the magic happened and she was the one behind the curtain, moving all the levers.

Not in a bad way, she added silently. Just that she was about empowering her clients—helping them realize it was all about confidence, and sometimes finding confidence required a little help.

She turned onto the street where her nav system directed her, then blinked twice as she stared at the huge double gates stretching across a freeway-wide driveway. She'd been told the private residence had originally been a monastery built in the eighteen hundreds, but she hadn't expected it to be so *huge*. She'd been thinking more "extra-big house with a guest cottage and maybe a small orchard." What she faced instead was a three-story, Spanish-style former church/monastery with two turrets, acres of gardens and an actual parking lot for at least a dozen cars.

"Who *are* these people?" she asked out loud, even as she already knew the answer. Before interviewing a potential client, she always did her research. Overdid it, some would say, a criticism she could live with. Margot liked being thorough. And on time. And tidy. And, according to some, annoying.

Margot pressed the call button on the electronic pad mounted perpendicular to the gate and waited until a surprisingly clear voice said, "May I help you?"

"I'm Margot Baxter. I have an appointment with Mr. Alec Mcnicol."

"Yes, Ms. Baxter. He's expecting you."

The gates opened smoothly and Margot drove through onto the compound. She parked in one of the marked spots, then took a moment to breathe and collect her thoughts.

She could do this, she told herself. She was good at her job. She liked helping people. Everything was going to be fine. She was a professional, she was trained and she was calm. *Calm-ish*, she added silently, then reached for the glasses she'd put on the seat next to her briefcase.

Margot stepped out of her car and smoothed the front of her slightly too-big jacket. The outfit—gray suit, sensible pumps, minimal makeup—was designed to make her appear professional and competent. The glasses, while unnecessary, did a lot to add gravitas to her appearance. She was thirty-one, but in shorts and a concert T-shirt, she could pass for nineteen. Even more depressing, in said shorts and T-shirt, she looked ditzy and incompetent and just a little bit dumb, and that didn't reassure anyone.

She walked up the stone path to the enormous front door. Although she knew nothing about Spanish architecture, she wanted to trace the heavy carved wood doors where angels watched over Christ as he carried the cross toward a hill. Yup, the big-as-a-stadium building really had once been a monastery and apparently the monks had been sincere in their worship.

Before she could get her fill of the amazing craftsmanship, the doors opened and a tall, broad-shouldered, dark-haired man nodded at her.

"Ms. Baxter? I'm Alec Mcnicol. It's nice to meet you."

"Thank you."

She stepped inside and they shook hands. She had a brief impression of two-story ceilings and intricate stained-glass windows before Alec was leading her down a hallway into a large office lined with bookshelves and framed maps of lands long forgotten.

She did her best not to gawk at her surroundings. While she was used to working with the rich and famous, this was different. The books made her want to inhale deeply to capture their musty smell and the maps had her itching to trace a path along the Silk Road.

She'd taken a step to do just that when her host cleared his throat.

She glanced at him and smiled. "Sorry. Your office is incredible. The maps are hand drawn?"

He looked slightly startled, his eyebrows coming together in an attractive frown. "They are."

She looked at them one last time. If she got the job, she would have to ask permission to study the framed drawings. She reluctantly pulled her attention away from the distractions around her and took a seat across from him at the wide desk.

When he was settled, he said, "As I explained on the phone, you're here to help my mother."

"Yes, Mr.—"

"Please call me Alec."

She nodded. "I'm Margot, and yes, I understand she will be my client."

"Excellent. She and I decided it would be easier if I conducted the preliminary interview to see if you and she are suited."

"Of course."

Margot relaxed. Hiring someone like her was often stressful. Her services were only required when something had gone very wrong in a person's life. Or if the potential client was anticipating something going wrong. Or was overwhelmed. Very few people looked around at their happiest moment and thought, *Hey, I should find someone to teach me social etiquette and how not to be odd/uncomfortable/weird or just plain nervous.* There was always a trigger that made a client realize he or she needed her services and it rarely grew out of an uplifting event.

Alec glanced at the papers on his desk. They were arranged in neat piles, which Margot appreciated. How could anyone find anything on a messy desk? Her boss, a man whose desk was always covered with folders and notes and half-eaten sandwiches, was forever sending her articles on how messy desks were a sign of creativity and intelligence, but Margot would not be swayed in her opinion. Disorder was just plain wrong.

"You know who my mother is?" Alec asked, his voice more resigned than curious.

Margot filed away the tone to review later. The dynamic between mother and son could be significant to her work.

"I do. Bianca Wray was born in 1960. Her father died when she was an infant and she was raised by her mother until she was twelve." Margot frowned. "Why she was put in foster care isn't clear, but that's where she ended up."

She flashed Alec a smile. "She was literally discovered while drinking a milkshake with her girlfriends, propagating the myth that in Los Angeles anyone, at any moment, is just one lucky break away from being famous."

"You've discovered my deepest wish in life," Alec said drily.

"Mine, too," Margot said, allowing her mouth to curve slightly at the corners. "After a career in modeling, your mother turned to acting. She preferred quirky roles to the obvious in-genue parts that would have helped her have a more successful career. She had one son—you—when she was twenty-four. She and your father, a Swiss banker, never married, but you were close to both your parents."

As she spoke, she sensed tension in Alec's shoulders as if he were uncomfortable with her reciting the facts of his personal life. He might not be her client, but he was her client's son and therefore of note, she thought, but didn't bother explaining her-self. Her methods were excellent and if he couldn't see that, then this was not the job for her.

"Bianca is a free spirit and despite facing her sixtieth birth-day, is still considered a beauty. She acts in the occasional proj-ect. From what I could see, there doesn't seem to be a pattern in why she chooses the roles she does. She enjoys remodeling homes and has made a lot of money flipping upscale houses. She gives generously to charity and has many lovers in her life, but has never married. She is currently dating a man named Wesley Goswick-Chance. Mr. Goswick-Chance is the youngest son of an English earl. His parents divorced when he was an infant and he grew up in both England and the small European country of Cardigania. He is currently their senior attaché to the United States. He is stationed at the consulate here in Los Angeles."

There was a lot more she could have mentioned about Alec's mother. There was the time Bianca had been presenting at the

Academy Awards and had dropped her dress on national television. Or her sex tapes that, back in the 1990s, had been quite the scandal, although they were fairly tame by today's standards. Bianca was a colorful protestor, a woman who slept with kings, movie stars, artists and, according to some gossip that was never confirmed, had once had a torrid affair with the wife of the world's largest yacht builder. While Margot would never admit it to anyone, she was equally intrigued and terrified by the idea of working with Bianca.

"That was very thorough," he said with a sigh. "And thank you for not mentioning all the salacious bits I'm sure your research uncovered."

Margot nodded. "Of course."

He looked at her. His eyes were very nice—dark, with thick lashes. She could see traces of his mother in his appearance—the eyes she'd admired, the curve of his mouth.

"My mother has recently accepted a proposal of marriage," Alec said, his voice stiff. "From Wesley. He's a nice enough man and he makes her happy, so I have no objection to the union."

Margot waited quietly, not showing her surprise. How unexpected that after sixty years and countless lovers, Bianca had finally gotten engaged.

Alec's gaze was steady. "If Wesley were a shipping magnate or a movie star, there wouldn't be an issue. But he is a diplomat and as such, he moves in the kind of circles that will not be very accepting of my mother's somewhat, ah, eccentric ways."

"She wants to learn how to fit in."

"Yes. To be clear, hiring you was her idea, not mine. I'm not pushing her into anything. She's worried that her impulsive behavior will be a problem for Wesley and she claims she loves him enough to want to change for him."

"What do you think?" Margot asked.

Alec hesitated, his gaze shifting from hers. "I believe most people are who they are. Asking Bianca to be a staid, polite and unobtrusive person is like asking the sun to shine less brightly. Ambitious, but unlikely."

She'd wondered if he would say it was wrong for Wesley to not accept his fiancée as she was. Interesting that Alec had gone in a different direction. "You're saying she can't change."

"I'm saying it's improbable." He returned his attention to her and leaned forward. "My mother is funny, charming and generous to a fault. I'm confident you will enjoy her company but if you take this job thinking you're going to succeed, I'm concerned you'll be very disappointed."

Margot smiled. "You're warning me off?"

"I'm suggesting you consider the possibility of failure."

"Which only makes me want to take the job more, Alec, if for no other reason than to prove myself."

"Not my intent, but I can see how it would happen."

He relaxed as he spoke. Margot found herself as curious about her client's son as she was about her client. She'd done preliminary research on Alec, in the context of him being Bianca's only family. She knew that Alec was a scholar who studied ancient texts. When he'd inherited the monastery nearly six years ago, he'd done extensive remodeling, turning much of the space into a research center for the study of obscure written works. He was reclusive, had never married and was rarely photographed. A few people had described him as stodgy and boring, but she knew they were wrong on both counts. Alec was a man who kept tight control over his emotions—a trait she could respect. To her mind, order was a kind of meditation that should be embraced by all.

"Shall we?" he asked, coming to his feet.

She rose as well and followed him out of the office and down a long hallway that opened onto the grounds. The hallway ceiling was fifteen feet high and all hand-carved wood. The stone floor was smooth and she could see faint grooves from the thousands of feet that had walked this same path. She wanted to ask about the history of the monastery and what it was like to live here. She wanted to know if sometimes, in the quiet of those hours after midnight, he heard the whispered echoes of so many prayers. Margot didn't consider herself religious but she admired those who were. Faith must be a wonderful thing. She was just a little too pragmatic to believe that any divine force was going to help her with her life. As such, she believed in being self-reliant.

To her right were huge gardens. The well-kept grounds went on for acres—a private paradise in the middle of Pasadena. She recognized several of the flowers and plants but many were unknown to her.

"The grounds are lovely," she said, wishing she had time to explore the paths she could see weaving through hedges and by trees.

"Thank you. They were in disrepair when I inherited the place but I hired a landscape architect to clean things up. He's done a good job."

He paused by a stone path and turned to her. "My mother recently sold her house and has moved in with me until the wedding," he said, his voice carefully neutral. "Should you take the job, she would like you to stay here, as well, for the time you're working together." He glanced at her. "Just to be clear, my mother sometimes keeps odd hours."

"Many clients do," she assured him, thinking of the business executive who had wanted to work on his Chinese etiquette between four and six in the morning.

"She's not—" he began, then pressed his lips together. "My mother is…" He shook his head. "You'll have to see for yourself."

He started across the lawn toward the garden. Margot followed him along the stone path that was just as worn as the open hallway had been. They passed between two flowering trees onto a huge patio created with paving stones. Stone benches lined the perimeter while hundreds of pots of various sizes over-flowed with exotic flowering plants.

The scent was divine—sweet without being cloying. If she had to pick a single word, she would have chosen *alive* as the fragrance. She found herself longing to sit on one of the stone benches and turn her face to the sun. Farther on, she spotted a table and chairs and desperately wished for a slow-paced din-ner at sunset.

"This is the most incredible garden I've ever seen," she admit-ted, unable to hold in the comment. "It's magnificent."

"I can't take credit." He gave her a slight smile. "But it is very nice."

Nice? Iced tea was nice. This was stupendous!

She reminded herself that she was here for an interview and reluctantly let go of her garden lust. As they moved toward the table and chairs, Margot saw a woman seated in a small, hidden alcove, reading a magazine. The woman glanced up when she noticed them and waved a greeting.

Margot rarely worked with celebrities. Her area of expertise was the corporate arena. If you had a quick trip down to Argen-tina, for example, she was the one who could give you a crash course on things like greetings—while the first greeting with a client or customer involved a handshake, in subsequent meet-ings, the greeting was likely to be a kiss on the cheek, even if the business meeting was between two men. She could advise that good posture was important and that dinner rarely started before nine. She found comfort in rules and knowing the right thing to do in any situation.

Each employee in her company had a profile that was made available to prospective clients. Coming to an understanding of who worked best with whom was a mutual decision. Movie stars and those in the music business rarely picked Margot and she was fine with that. She'd been on a couple of jobs with di-rectors looking to be more successful in obtaining financing in

China, but that was different. Which probably explained why she was unprepared to meet Bianca Wray in person.

Oh, she'd seen pictures of the actress and had watched three of her movies the previous weekend. She was familiar with the sound of her voice and the way she moved, but none of that had equipped her for the reality of seeing her up close.

Bianca was far more delicate in person. Slim, but also small boned. There was a glow to her bare skin, a grace to her movements. Her deep blue eyes were wide and her light brown hair was wavy, just past her shoulders.

Taken individually, the features were nice enough but unremarkable. Yet there was something about the way they were put together. Something…breathtaking. She supposed that was the difference between the chosen and the ordinary. An undefinable quality that couldn't be manufactured, only recognized and worshipped.

Her great-grandmother had talked about star power. She couldn't say what it was, but she'd been able to recognize it when she saw it. Bianca had star power. When she smiled, Margot instantly felt like the most special person on earth. Even as she reacted viscerally, the intellectual side of her brain cataloged how Bianca stood, smiled and moved toward them. She was looking for clues to the problem, along with any information that would help her do her job to the best of her ability.

"Have you thought about what I said, Alec?" Bianca asked as she approached. She wore jeans and a loose T-shirt. Nothing out of the ordinary, yet both suited her perfectly. Her feet were bare, her toes painted with little American flags. "I'm sure they would enjoy it."

Alec exhaled. "My mother thinks I should invite a few nuns over for lunch."

Margot glanced at him. "You know nuns?"

"No. She wants me to find a local convent and ask them over."

"Why?"

He looked at her, his expression clearly indicating there was no reasonable explanation and with luck, this, too, would pass.

Bianca stopped in front of them. She was maybe five-four or five-five, at least three inches shorter than Margot.

"Because of what Alec has done with the monastery," she said, her voice light and happy. "They would be delighted to see how you've kept the spirit of the building while modernizing it."

"The master bedroom is in what used to be the church," he said drily. "I doubt the nuns would approve."

Bianca linked arms with him. "Oh, darling, don't worry about that. It's not as if you're having sex there." She winked at Margot. "Alec goes out for that sort of thing. He's a little bit like a groundhog. Once a year he makes an appearance, so to speak, then retreats to his regular world."

Margot wasn't sure if the comment was meant to shock her or test her or humiliate Alec. Given the warm tone and loving expression, she doubted it was the latter. Still, it was an unusual thing to say to a stranger—especially about her own son.

"I'm Margot. It's nice to meet you." Margot held out her hand.

Bianca shook it. "It's nice to be met." Her smile broadened. "I'm a fairly hopeless case, as I'm sure Alec has told you. I'm impulsive and reckless and not the sort of person who should be marrying a professional diplomat. But here we are, trying to make it work." Her smile faltered. "It's just that Wesley is all I've ever wanted. I love him and I don't want to be the reason he loses his job."

For a second her eyes were no longer bright but instead filled with fear and uncertainty. Margot studied the flash of emotions and saw the exact moment self-preservation kicked in.

"Imagine falling in love at my age!" she said with a laugh. "What a ridiculous thing. Until now I've only really loved one person and that's Alec." She smiled up at him. "I'm sure he'll be delighted to have someone else share that burden."

Margot nearly felt dizzy from the emotional ping-pong. Bianca had shifted from the odd comment about Alec's sex life to a flash of honest vulnerability with a quick return to fact, all couched in a protective shield of humor. There was a lot more going on here than the desire to learn which fork to use.

One of the advantages of being socially awkward—not that there were many—was the ability to recognize it in others. Bianca might be more beautiful than 99 percent of the population, but that didn't mean she was comfortable in her own skin. She was obviously afraid of disappointing everyone she cared about. Perhaps she thought she'd been doing it for years. *How intriguing,* Margot thought, suddenly itching to get on her computer and begin working on her development program.

Alec squeezed his mother's hand. "I just want you to be happy."

Bianca flashed him a smile that was brighter than the sun Alec had mentioned earlier, then turned to Margot. "Shall we have a little talk to see if we suit?"

"I'd like that."

Bianca led her to the table in the center of the paved garden while Alec retreated to the house. When they were seated across from each other, Bianca studied her for a second.

"You don't need to wear glasses, do you?"

The question surprised Margot. "No. How did you know?"

"I've worn prop glasses before. Why do you do it? No, don't tell me. Let me guess." Her gaze turned probing. "You want to look smart. Oh, because you're pretty. You must be very serious about your work. I never was. I liked acting but I was never passionate about it." The megasmile returned. "However, they do pay me a ridiculous amount of money for it, so why not?"

One shoulder rose and lowered. "Tell me. Can I be fixed? Do you have the skills to make me just like everyone else?"

Margot saw the trap in the question immediately. She sensed that Bianca was testing her in a hundred different ways and wasn't sure what that meant. If she was the one who had requested assistance, then surely she was motivated to change. Yet the way she phrased the question…

"I can certainly teach you how to behave in formal occasions, whether social or political," she began. "As for fixing you, I'm afraid that's not my job. I want to make you feel comfortable so everyone can get to know who you really are."

"I'm not sure that's a good idea," Bianca said quickly. "They couldn't handle the real me."

"Then the you you want them to know."

"What's your background?"

Margot smiled. "I started in hotel management. I received training to work with our international clients and loved it. I was recruited by my current employer and have moved to help-ing people deal with our ever-shrinking world."

"Hmm, yes, that's fascinating, but what's your background? Where are you from? Who raised you?"

A different question than "tell me about your parents." It was almost as if Bianca knew there hadn't been parents. "My mater-nal great-grandmother," she said slowly. "She owned a beauty and charm school for nearly fifty years. She trained pageant contestants."

"Were you in pageants?"

"No. I'm lacking certain skills." Like the ability to speak to a group. Margot still remembered the first time Francine had made her get up on the mock stage they had in the workroom and address the group. She'd barely taken her place when she'd projectile vomited and promptly fainted. It had been a fairly quick end to any hopes her great-grandmother had had about Margot taking the crown.

Margot had forced herself to overcome her deficiency and could now give a decent lecture, but she would never be a natural up on stage. Not that she'd ever aspired to be a beauty queen. She just wanted to do her job and live her life. Oh, and not be dumb about men, because she'd already done that enough already.

"Alec picked you," Bianca said. "He looked over all the people at your agency and he picked you. Now I see why."

Did she? Margot hadn't known he'd been the one to make the decision. Why her? She wasn't an obvious choice, was she?

"Can you do it?" Bianca asked before Margot could question her statement. "Can you help me be who I need to be so I don't embarrass Wesley?"

"Yes."

"You promise?"

Margot leaned forward. "I will use every technique I have, and if those don't work, I will create new ones. I will work tirelessly to get you to a place where you are comfortable in Wesley's world."

"That's not a promise."

"I know. I don't make promises when I can't be sure of the outcome."

Bianca looked away. "I make promises all the time. I rarely keep them. It's just that in the moment, I want the person to be happy."

"And later?"

Bianca shrugged again. "They always forgive me. Even Alec." The smile returned. "All right. Let's do this. Alec thinks I need about two months of instruction. You'll have to move in here. There are a few guest rooms upstairs. I have the big one and I'm sorry but I'm not moving out for you."

"I wouldn't expect you to." Margot looked at her potential client. "Bianca, I don't live that far from here. I could easily drive over—"

"No. You have to stay here. It'll be like we're on location. Alec doesn't care. He rarely looks up from his work to notice anything. The house is beautiful. You'll love it and I'd feel better if you were close."

Margot nodded slowly. She'd lived in before. She didn't prefer it but when the client insisted, she agreed.

"As you wish. I'll send over the contract as soon as I get back to the office. Once it's signed and you've paid the retainer, I'll be in touch to discuss a start date."

"Monday!" Bianca sprang to her feet and raced around the table. She crouched in front of Margot, took both her hands and smiled. "We'll start Monday. Oh, this is going to be fun. We'll be best friends and have a wonderful time."

Bianca rose and twirled, then ran to the house, her laughter trailing after her.

Margot watched her go. There was something, she thought, some secret driving Bianca. Margot wasn't sure if she was running to something or away from it, but whatever it was, it was the key to the problem. Finding out what it was would be difficult, but she knew in her gut if she could figure out the mystery, she could teach Bianca what she needed to know and be gone in far less time than two months.

She glanced around at the beautiful gardens and the monastery's worn, red-tiled roof and reminded herself that whatever she might have to deal with while helping Bianca, at least her living quarters were going to be extraordinary. Perhaps, if she were lucky, she might even run into a ghost monk or two.

Chapter Two

Sunshine Baxter was done with love at first sight. *D. O. N. E.* More times than she could count, she'd looked deeply into a pair of—insert any color here—eyes and immediately given her heart. The relationships had all ended in disaster and she'd hated herself for being so incredibly stupid over and over again, so she decided she was finished with the falling in love concept. Over it. Moving on.

Except…

"I've decided," Connor said, pushing up his glasses, his dark brown eyes staring intently into hers.

Sunshine leaned close, knowing that once again she'd foolishly fallen for an inappropriate guy. "Tell me."

"Ants."

Sunshine smiled. "Are you sure?"

"Yes. I've read three books on ants and they're very smart and they work hard. I want to build the world's biggest ant farm."

"Okay, then. That's what we'll do. We should probably start small," she told him. "Get a regular-size ant farm and see if we can make it work. Then we'll add on."

His mouth began to curve in the most delightful smile. "I thought girls didn't like ants."

"I don't want them crawling in my bed, but I think an ant farm is super cool."

The smile fully blossomed. Connor ran toward her. She pulled the eight-year-old close and hugged him, telling herself if adoring her new charge qualified as breaking her no-heart-giving rule, then she was willing to live with the disappointment. Connor was irresistible.

He released her and stepped back, nearly slipping off the path and into a tall, aggressive-looking succulent that no doubt had an impressively long, Latin name. Sunshine shifted her weight, gently grabbed his arm and spun him out of the way of impalement. Connor barely noticed.

"You're going to tell me that you have to ask my dad, huh?"

"I am. We're talking about being responsible for several hundred life-forms. That's a big deal."

"You're right." He paused, then giggled. "Can I be their king?"

"Of course. Maybe we can teach them to chant *All Hail Connor.*"

Connor laughed. The desert garden section at The Huntington's acres of gardens was his favorite. Given that Connor's father was a landscape architect, Connor and Sunshine both had memberships and in her three weeks of employment as Connor's nanny, they'd been four times. So far all they'd visited was the desert garden, but she was okay with that. Eventually Connor's interests would broaden.

He squatted in front of a reddish plant apparently called *terrestrial bromeliad* and studied it.

"You start school on Monday," he said.

Something Sunshine didn't want to think about. Part of her plan to avoid bad relationships and shift her life onto a happier and more positive course meant going to college. Not back so much, as that implied she'd been at one in the first place.

"I do."

He glanced at her. "Are you scared?"

"I am. Well, maybe scared is strong. I'm nervous."

"Do you think all the other kids will be smarter than you?"

She grinned. "I wouldn't have put it like that, but yes, in part. And they'll be younger."

He stood up. "As young as me?"

"I think a little older, but certainly not my age."

She was thirty-one and had absolutely nothing noteworthy to show for her years on the planet. How sad was that?

Connor took her hand. "You don't have to be scared. You're smart, too, and we can do homework together."

She touched his nose. "You're in third grade. You don't have much homework."

"I'll sit with you and read about ants."

And this, she thought with a sigh, was why he'd won her heart. Connor was a good kid. He was funny and kind and affectionate. He'd lost his mother to cancer a few months ago and while his father obviously cared about his son, he had a big, impressive job that took a lot of time. Declan had hired a series of nannies, all of whom Connor had rejected within a week. For some reason, the two of them had clicked.

"Come on," she said, wrapping her arms around him. "Let's head home. I'm going to make lasagna roll-ups for dinner."

"What's a roll-up?"

"It's all the lasagna goodness rolled up in a noodle."

His gaze was skeptical. "You're going to put vegetables in the recipe, aren't you?"

She grinned. "Yes. Zucchini. Skinny little zucchini French fries."

"How skinny?"

She thought for a second. "Ant size."

He sighed. "Okay, but I won't like it."

"As long as you eat it."

An hour and a half later, Sunshine put the completed salad into the refrigerator and glanced at the clock. According to a text from Declan, he was planning on joining them for dinner. She'd set the table for three, but honestly, she wasn't holding out much hope. Her boss was in the middle of a big project—something about designing the gardens of a new five-star hotel just north of Malibu. Not only was the job time consuming, there was actually no good way to get to Pasadena from anywhere by the beach without dealing with miles of gridlock and hours stuck in traffic. More than once he'd texted to say he would be home in time for dinner only to call her an hour later to say he was still on the freeway and to start without him.

Sunshine didn't mind when it was just her and Connor, but she knew the boy missed his father when he wasn't around.

Once he got home, Declan spent the rest of the evening with his son and he was the one to get Connor ready for bed. They were obviously close, which was good. Still, the whole situation remained slightly awkward for her. Normally by the three-week mark of a job, she was comfortable in the house and had a set routine. She and Connor were doing great, but she'd barely seen Declan and they hadn't talked and she really had to tell him they should have a sit-down at some point. Maybe in the next couple of days.

The first weekend she'd been employed, Declan and Connor had gone to Sacramento to visit Declan's parents. Last weekend, Declan had been out of town at a conference and this weekend she had no idea what was going on.

"Do you and your dad have plans for tomorrow?" she asked.

"I don't know. He didn't tell me. If he's busy, what do you want to do?"

"I thought we'd go to the Star Eco Station."

Connor finished putting the flatware in place. "Do I have to hold the tarantula?"

"Not if you don't want to."

"Arachnids aren't ants," he said, his tone defensive.

She held up both hands. "You don't have to tell me. I'm perfectly fine with an ant farm but if you told me you wanted to start a spider colony, I'd run screaming into the night."

He grinned. "In your pajamas?"

"Very possibly."

His laughter was interrupted by the sound of the garage door opening.

"Dad's home! Dad's home!"

She watched him race across the kitchen and through the mudroom, then looked back at the table. Looked like there would be three for dinner and wouldn't that be fun.

Not that she was nervous. She wasn't. It was just she barely knew Declan. Which was fine—tonight they would have a conversation over lasagna roll-ups with ant-sized zucchini.

"…and Sunshine's going to help me with the ant farm. We're going to check online tomorrow and it's okay because I read three books and I've checked out two more from the library and I'll read them this weekend so I'm gonna know everything."

Based on the framed photographs she'd seen in Connor's room, Sunshine knew he took after his mother. He was small for his age, with a slight build and dark hair and eyes, so every time she saw Declan, it was something of a shock.

The man was big. Not heavy, but tall with broad shoulders and a lot of muscles. He had sandy-colored hair and green eyes, had to be at least six-two. With her only being five-four, that seemed a little extreme. He wore a suit and tie most days, which somehow made him even more impressive. He also had a presence about him—he was someone who was noticed wherever he went. She didn't know him well enough to have much of an opinion about him, but he seemed like a decent kind of guy. He loved his son and honestly that was all she cared about.

"Good evening, Mr. Dubois," she murmured as he set down his briefcase, then swept Connor up in his arms and turned the boy upside down.

As his son hung there, shrieking with happy laughter, Declan met her gaze. "We talked about this, Sunshine. Call me Declan, please."

"Okay, just checking."

"I want to keep things casual."

She liked casual. Now that she thought about it, casual was probably for the best considering she'd kicked off her shoes when she'd walked into the house and was currently standing barefoot, wearing jeans and an oversize T-shirt advertising a bar in Tahiti.

Declan turned Connor right side up, then glanced at the table. "That looks nice. What are we having?"

"Ant food!" Connor told him gleefully. "Zucchini ant sticks."

"Really?"

"Salad, lasagna roll-ups, garlic knots and zucchini fries," she corrected.

"The garlic knots are bread," Connor told his father. "I tied them all myself."

"Did you?" Declan ruffled his hair. "That's great. Give me five minutes to get changed and I'll be back to help." He picked up his briefcase and started for the hallway, his son at his heels. "Sunshine, do you drink wine?"

"Only on days ending in Y."

"Good. Why don't you pick us out a bottle of red from the wine cellar? You know where it is?"

"I do."

Except for Declan's bedroom, she'd explored the house that first weekend. She knew every place an eight-year-old boy could hide and had moved a bucket full of different bottles of cleaning solutions out to the garage. Yes, Connor was old enough to know not to play with stuff like that, but why tempt fate.

The house was typical for the neighborhood. Built in the 1920s with a strong Spanish influence, the structure was a U shape with a patio at the center. Just past the kitchen was the mudroom. Beyond that was a family room and then her en suite bedroom. Behind the attached garage was a large workout room she really had to start using.

Exiting the kitchen in the opposite direction led to a formal dining room, a formal living room, then the hallway curved. Declan had an office, then Connor's room was next, then the master.

The rooms were oversize, the beams in the ceiling original and the garden was something out of a fantasy. Sunshine didn't know much about plants, but she knew enough to keep her window open so she could smell the night-blooming jasmine just outside.

She walked toward the mudroom, stopping at the walk-in pantry. On the far wall was a wine cellar with glass doors. She figured it must hold at least four hundred bottles of wine, grouped together by type. She pulled out racks, searching for a relatively inexpensive red blend. Dinner was casual and the wine should be, too.

She found a foil cutter and bottle opener in one of the drawers in the pantry and carried the open bottle and two wineglasses back into the kitchen, then opened a bottle of sparkling nonalcoholic apple cider for Connor. If they were going to get fancy, it was nice to share.

While Declan got Connor settled, Sunshine dropped the hot rolls into a large bowl then tossed them with melted butter and garlic. The salad was already in place, as were the plates. She gave Connor and Declan each a roll before putting the extras on the table and taking her chair.

The kitchen table seated six. The three of them were clustered at one end, with her across from Connor. Without thinking, she put salad on his plate, only to realize that might be something his father wanted to do.

"Oh, um, sorry. Did you want to…"

"Go ahead," Declan said easily, pouring them wine.

She nodded, then waited for him to serve himself before taking the bowl from him and putting salad on her own plate. When she was done, she reached for her glass of wine just as Declan started to hand it to her. They bumped and the glass nearly spilled.

Sunshine felt herself flushing. Great. Just great. The awkward first days were supposed to be over by now. Living in someone's home, and being an almost-but-not-quite part of the family wasn't an easy transition.

Declan shook his head. "We have to work on our dinner skills," he said, his voice teasing.

"Apparently."

"The last few weeks have been hectic with my work schedule and we haven't had a chance to get to know each other. If you don't have plans, why don't you join me in my study after Connor goes to bed and we'll talk about how things are going so far."

"That would be nice," she said. "Thank you."

Connor held up his glass of cider. "I want to make a toast."

"Do you?" Declan raised his wineglass. "What is it?"

Sunshine picked up her glass and waited. She had a feeling this wasn't going to be the statesmanlike moment Declan seemed to expecting.

Connor grinned. "And jelly."

"Toast and jelly," Declan murmured, before taking a sip of his wine. "I couldn't be more proud."

Connor giggled. Sunshine winked at him.

"We went to The Huntington after school today," she said, picking up her fork. "To the Desert Garden."

"My favorite!" Connor announced.

"One day I'll get to see one of the other gardens. At least I hope so."

Connor raised his shoulders in an exaggerated sigh. "In two more times. I promise."

"Yay! And thank you."

"You're welcome." He turned to his father. "How's the hotel?"

"Good. The building approval has been finalized, so I can get to work on designing the gardens." He looked at Sunshine. "The decisions about the materials they're using will influence what I suggest."

"Sure. You wouldn't want the flowers to clash with the siding."

"Exactly. Connor, how was school?"

"Good. I got an A on my spelling test. We studied really hard."

"The lesson combined spelling words with different kinds of currency," Sunshine added. "Euro, yen, ruble, the word *currency*."

"That one's hard," Connor said as he finished his salad. "And *ruble* is like *rubble* but only one *b*."

"I'd heard that," Declan told him. "Good for you."

Sunshine had just stood to collect the salad plates when Connor piped up with, "Sunshine starts school on Monday and she's scared."

"Yes, well, no one's interested in that," she murmured, walking into the kitchen and pulling the lasagna roll-ups out of the oven.

"You're going back to college?" Declan asked.

"Back would be a misstatement, but yes." She slid the steaming pasta onto plates and carried them to the table. "I'm at Pasadena City College, taking a math class."

"Good for you."

"Thanks."

Once she was seated, she sipped her wine and told herself she didn't care what her boss thought of her lack of education. Just because he had an advanced degree and a fancy job and a house and a kid and his life was totally together didn't matter to her.

She sighed. It wasn't Declan, she reminded herself. He simply represented everything she didn't have. Roots. Direction. A plan. Her twenties had raced by in a series of relationships that left her with exactly nothing to show for the time except for a string of bad decisions and broken hearts. Some of those hearts had even been hers.

But that was all behind her now. She'd had a come-to-Jesus moment, she was focused and she had a life plan. And nothing and no one was going to cause her to veer off course. Of that she was sure.

Declan Dubois hadn't had sex in a year. Until a few weeks ago he honest to God hadn't cared, but recently he'd started to notice and now he cared a lot and it was becoming a problem.

The dry spell had started when he and Iris had been having trouble—if that was what it could be called. Not knowing if their marriage was going to survive or not, he'd taken to sleeping on the sofa in his study. Later, she'd been sick and sex had been the last thing on either of their minds. After her death he'd been in shock and dealing with the reality of having the woman he'd assumed he would spend the rest of his life with gone. There'd been Connor and helping him handle the loss of his mother. Sex hadn't been important.

But it sure as hell was now, although he had no idea what he was supposed to do about it. Dating seemed impossible and a few minutes in the shower only got a guy so far. At some point he wanted a woman in his bed, and not just a one-night stand, either. He'd never been that guy. He didn't need love to get it up but some kind of emotional interest was preferred. He hadn't been on a first date in ten years—how was he supposed to start now? Where would he meet women? Not through work—that never went well. Online?

He walked the short distance from Connor's room to his study and told himself he would deal with the problem later. Now that his son was asleep, his more pressing issue was to get to know the woman he'd hired to take care of his kid. Somehow three weeks had sped by. If he wasn't careful, he would turn around and Connor would be graduating from high school and he still wouldn't know anything about Sunshine.

He sat at his desk and opened the file the agency had given him when he'd first interviewed her. She'd been the fifth nanny he'd hired and he'd been desperate to find someone his son would like. Iris's death had been a shock. It had been less than a month from the time he'd found out about the cancer until she'd passed away. There'd been no time to prepare, to be braced, and he was an adult. Connor had a lot less skill to handle the impossibly heartbreaking situation. If Declan's parents hadn't come and stayed with them after the funeral, he wasn't sure either of them would have survived.

He scanned the file. Sunshine was thirty-one. She'd been a nanny on and off from the age of twenty. She had no formal training, no education past high school and a history of walking away from jobs before her contract was finished. He hadn't wanted to hire her, but he'd been desperate and the agency had insisted he at least talk to her. After blowing through four of their best nannies, he'd realized he couldn't refuse, so he'd reluctantly met her.

He didn't remember anything they'd discussed except to insist she and Connor spend a trial afternoon together, supervised by someone from the agency. Connor had come home and announced he liked her and Declan had hired her that evening.

The past three weeks had been a whirlwind of work and travel. He'd wanted to spend more time at home, getting to know her, watching her with Connor, but fate had conspired against him. Still, his son seemed happier than he had in a long time and he sure liked Sunshine.

A knock on his open door brought him back to the present. Sunshine stood in the doorway, her smile tentative.

"Is this a good time?"

He nodded and motioned to the chair on the other side of his desk. Sunshine sat down, then tucked her bare feet under her.

She was nothing like Iris. The thought was unexpected but once formed he couldn't ignore it. His late wife had been tall and willowy. Delicate, with small bones and long fingers. She'd been pale, with dark hair and dark eyes.

Sunshine was several inches shorter and a whole lot more curvy. Blonde with pale blue eyes. She had full cheeks, large breasts and an ass that… He silently told himself not to go there. Not only wasn't it appropriate, she wasn't his type. And again, not appropriate.

Iris favored tailored clothing in black or taupe. From the little he'd seen of Sunshine, she was a jeans and T-shirt kind of woman. She ate cereal out of the box, had no problem lying on the floor to play checkers with Connor and hadn't protested an ant farm in the house. Again—not Iris.

Not that he wanted anyone to be Iris. His wife had been his first real love and with her gone, he would never be the same. He wasn't thinking he couldn't care about someone again, he had no idea about that, he just knew he didn't want an Iris replacement.

"You and Connor get along well," he said.

She smiled. Two simple words that in no way captured the transformation from reasonably pretty to stunning. Declan hoped he didn't look as stupefied as he felt. After all, he'd seen her smile before. He should be used to it, and yet, he was not.

"He's adorable. How could you not totally fall for him? He's a serious kid, but also funny and kind. I know he misses his mom, but he's dealing. We talk about her whenever he wants to. I know he's going to therapy and I'm hoping it helps. Obviously the therapist doesn't say anything to me, but I would say he's coping well."

Her appreciation of his kid relaxed him. "Connor's special," he said, then looked at the open folder on the desk and decided to be blunt. "I wasn't sure if I should hire you."

Instead of getting defensive, she laughed. "I could say the same thing about you. I was hoping to go to work for a high-powered single mom, but the director at the agency talked me into meeting Connor and then I was a goner."

She pointed to the folder. "Is that about me?"

He nodded.

Her full mouth twisted. "Let me guess. The report says I'm terrific with kids. I like them and they like me. I show up on time, I cook, I help with homework, I'm a safe driver. When there's an emergency, I'm nearly always available. But…" She looked at him. "There's a very good chance one day I'll simply disappear with almost no warning. I'm gone and you're stuck." She shrugged. "Does that about sum it up?"

Her honesty surprised him. Was it a tactic or genuine? He had no idea.

She sighed. "It's true. All of it. I've walked away from at least a half dozen jobs. I would meet a guy and fall for him and he'd want me to go with him and I would. Just like that."

"Go with him?"

The smile returned, although with less gut-hitting power. "I tend to fall for men who have unusual occupations or who don't live wherever I am. A guy in a rock band, a travel photographer, a professional tennis player. One time the family I was working for took me with them to Napa. I met a guy who owned a restaurant and when the family went home, I stayed. On the bright side, he taught me how to cook."

She looked away. "I was young and reckless and I don't want to do that anymore." Her gaze returned to him. "I won't bore you with the details. Let's just say I woke up alone in a hotel room in London with no job, no boyfriend, no prospects. I flew home and moved in with my sister, then got a couple of jobs because hey, the nanny thing wasn't good for me or the kids."

He wasn't sure what he'd expected to hear, but it wasn't this. "So why are you back being a nanny now?"

"I'm good at it and I need the money. I want to do something with my life. Get an education, have a retirement account, be normal. Working as a nanny allows me to pay for school, have time to study and not have to worry about rent. I want to keep my head down and be smart. No more crazy, loser guys. I don't want to be that girl anymore."

The smile returned, leaving him just as speechless as before.

"More than you wanted to know," she said. "I'm being honest. You have no reason to believe any of this. You don't know me, which is kind of the point of the conversation, right? But I'm committed to Connor. I'm not going to walk away from him."

"Because you're not that girl anymore?"

"That's the reason."

It was too much information and he didn't know what to do with it all. She was right—he had no reason to believe her, and yet he did. Was that dumb on his part or intuition? He had no idea.

"Is that also why you wanted to work for a woman?"

She nodded. "I've had a couple of dads get handsy. It's awkward."

"I assure you I would never—"

She shook her head. "I know. You don't have to say anything."

She knew? How? And what did that mean? Had he become so incredibly asexual that…that… Dear God, he couldn't even formulate the question, let alone answer it.

She laughed. "You look confused. What I meant is you seem to be an honorable person. I appreciate that."

"Good," he said, not sure if it was good or not. Time to change the subject. "About your hours. Are they working for you?"

"They're perfect."

She was supposed to be available from 6:30 a.m. until 9:00 p.m. with the middle of the day off, five days a week. She also owed him every other Saturday and cooked dinner four nights a week.

"I'm sorry you had to work Sunday when I was on my business trip."

"Not a problem. You and Connor were gone the previous weekend, so I had that Saturday. Declan, I'm not keeping track of every single minute. If Connor gets up early or stays up late, that's okay. A lot of my job is being flexible."

"Thank you."

He confirmed she knew where all the local stores were, then pulled a credit card out of his desk drawer.

"I ordered this for you," he said. "It will be easier than giving me receipts and having me reimburse you." He smiled. "Don't go to Tahiti on it."

"Oh darn. And Connor and I were talking about taking a road trip just yesterday." She took the card. "He seems to be outgrowing some of his pants and his athletic shoes are looking really bad. Do you want me to take him shopping or is that something you prefer to do?"

"You can do it. For the next couple of weeks, I'm going to be knee-deep in the preconstruction planning for the hotel. Once that calms down, I'll have more time."

"Okay. Then I'll get what he needs right now and you can handle the rest. Anything else?"

His gaze moved from her mouth to her— He swore silently, telling himself being a jerk wasn't allowed. He had to get a grip or at the very least, get laid. Assuming he remembered how all that happened. He assumed it was like riding a bike—once he and the lady in question were naked, he would know what to do.

"Declan?"

He blinked. "Ah, that will be all."

She stood and slid the credit card into her back pocket. "Have a good night."

"You, too."

He wasn't sure how good it was going to be but there was a better than even chance he would be taking a shower in a bit. A long one. After he would lie alone in bed both cursing and missing the woman he'd been married to. The one who had betrayed him, then up and died before he could decide if he had forgiven her or not.

Need to know what happens next? Preorder your copy of
The Summer of Sunshine & Margot *today!*